9

"Can't you take a break?"

Tim put both hands on Sandra's shoulders, an intimate gesture that clearly confused her. Sandra sat still for a moment and then gently tapped on his fingers to release their hold. Tim, as if understanding her message, let go, and bending down, lightly caressed her cheek with his lips.

"My mother is very concerned about *you,*" Tim said gravely. "She thinks you overtax yourself. She would like you to rest more and leave all this alone." With an air of patrician distaste Tim indicated the electronic gadgetry.

"But I can't leave this alone." Sandra turned her eyes to the screens again. "I can't afford to take the time off. If I do the empire will collapse or . . ." she put a hand to her mouth as though to stop herself.

"Zac will seize control." Tim bent over her again. "Does it still matter?"

"Oh yes, it does. Very much."

Also by Nicola Thorne

Champagne

Published by HarperPaperbacks

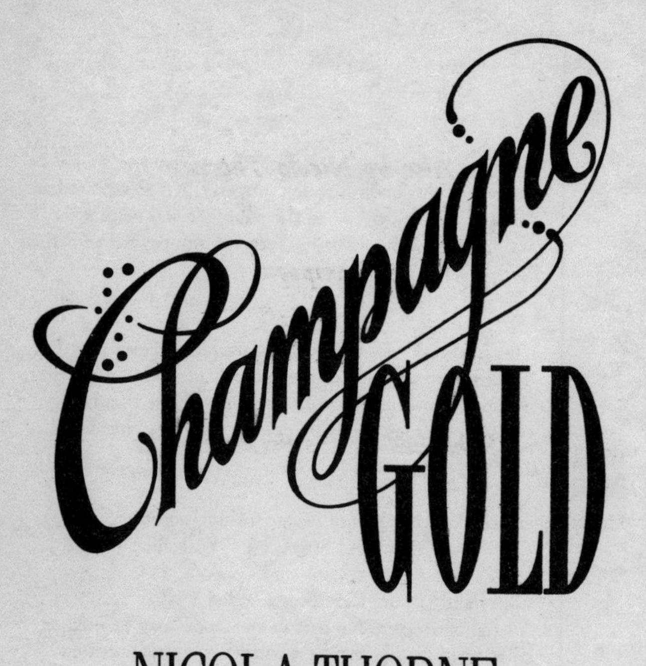

NICOLA THORNE

HarperPaperbacks
A Division of HarperCollins*Publishers*

This is a work of fiction. The characters, incidents, and dialogues are products of the author's imagination and are not to be construed as real. Any resemblance to actual events or persons, living or dead, is entirely coincidental.

HarperPaperbacks *A Division of* HarperCollins*Publishers*
10 East 53rd Street, New York, N.Y. 10022

This book was published in Great Britain in 1992 by HarperCollins*Publishers*, U.K.

Cover illustration by Herman Estevez

First HarperPaperbacks printing: August 1992

Printed in the United States of America

10 9 8 7 6 5 4 3 2 1

CONTENTS

Champagne Gold is the result of a happy working partnership between the author and François d'Aulan, president of a distinguished champagne house.

The Marquis d'Aulan conceived the original idea and, as a novelist, I was approached to write it. We worked together on an expanded synopsis and in the course of writing the book and afterward I received much helpful comment and advice from him. I am glad to say that he seems very happy with the result of our joint labors.

I am also grateful to Jean-Patrick Fiandé and Luiz Williams of Film Resources Ltd. and, finally, to Peter Janson-Smith of Bookers Books Ltd., who so effectively brought us all together.

Nicola Thorne

PROLOGUE

For mile after mile the Jeep bounced over the rough, uneven track that was at times scarcely discernible in the bush and scrubland of the Kora Game Reserve in northern Kenya. Occasionally it passed roaming herds of wild antelope, deer and gazelle. Small, fleeting animals continuously scurried for shelter, while brilliantly plumaged birds wheeled above or perched in the branches of the skeletal trees, craning their necks suspiciously toward it.

"Keep to the track," Peter Hartley had urged as he stood on the porch of his bungalow with his wife Christy to bid Michel and his servant Hassan a hurried farewell. For the letter had been sent on from Michel's home in Harare, delaying the news, the great news, by several days.

With mounting excitement Michel had read the letter and within an hour the Jeep was loaded, filled with petrol, and his brief holiday with the Hartleys was over.

Peter and Christy had remained for a long time on the porch, shielding their eyes against the late afternoon sun, watching the Jeep until it was obscured by the dust and out of sight. They were aware that Michel had made rather a late start and he would soon have to find shelter from the night.

"He'll never make Asako. I wish he'd stayed," Christy said

a little fretfully, "and left first thing in the morning. It's awfully late."

"Too much to ask that." With a fond smile Peter put his arm round her shoulders and led her into the long, low, cool lounge where the fans still whirled busily, counteracting the effects of the heat. "He's much too excited at the news."

"She must be quite some girl, that Sandra," Christy said, flopping into a chair. "Did you ever meet her?"

"Only once and she *is* some girl." Peter sat down opposite her. "I met her in Paris shortly after Michel met her. He was already in love with her and wanted to show her off to all his friends. It was only a brief introduction."

"I believe she's very beautiful," the newly married Christy said a little enviously. It was Peter's second marriage and her first, and she had the inevitable jealousy about her husband's past of wives in that situation.

The houseboy entered with the tea tray which was always served, English fashion, at four o'clock as the Hartleys, both ecologists, were English, on secondment to the Game Reserve.

Peter took his cup from the houseboy with a smile of thanks and sat back, stirring his tea thoughtfully.

"She *has* remarkable beauty and intelligence. An American living in California, she was an investment analyst when the bombshell burst."

"It's quite an extraordinary story," Christy said in between mouthfuls of tea. "Left a fortune by Georges Desmond, a man she never knew, the hostility of his family . . . and now . . ."

"Now," Peter said, his thoughts mentally following Michel through the bush, "she's having a baby. . . ."

As the darkness gathered about them, Michel reluctantly began to think about setting up camp for the night. He had hoped to reach Asako before dark but it was upon them sooner than he had expected. Maybe he should have stayed as the Hartleys wanted.

"There are bandits about," Peter had said. "Deserters from the

Somali Army have infiltrated the Reserve where they poach the cattle of the native herdsmen, steal from them, rape their women and, occasionally, kill them."

In the days of the British, he explained, the wild Somali tribesmen had been contained beyond the Kora boundary at the Tara river. But the Kenyans had taken a more relaxed attitude and the Shifta, as the Somalis were known, frequently crossed the river to make their raids on the elephants and rhinos, and cut down the precious trees for timber.

Michel looked at his watch, grunted at Hassan and then, braking, stopped the Jeep by a clump of trees.

"Pass me the torch, Hassan," he said, as he reached for the map and began spreading it out on his knees. "I'd like to get to Asako but it looks as though . . ."

Suddenly a shot rang out and the torch in Hassan's hand clattered to the floor. In the half-light Michel was aware of the staring eyes of his terrified manservant.

"Are you hurt?" he inquired urgently but Hassan, shaking his head, started to tremble.

"Bandits, Dr. Harcourt . . ." he stammered, "the terrible Shifta from across the border."

Michel doused the lights of the Jeep and turned off the engine.

"They're just hunting," he whispered. "If we stay here quietly . . ."

But the shots grew nearer and the voices more urgent and agitated.

"Poachers," Michel muttered. "If they see us they'll think we're game wardens who will betray them. I think we should drive on again as quickly as we can."

He reached for the key and switched on the ignition; a group of men carrying AK37 rifles emerged from the bush. One fired high, another aimed for the tires. There was a terrible hiss of escaping air as the Jeep slowly sank to one side.

Later that night the Laikipia Radio network which was the main link between the isolated pockets of inhabitants of the region—the farmers, gamekeepers, scientists, naturalists, teachers and tourists—began sending out an urgent message. "There has been shooting in the bush . . . police and medical attention urgently needed . . ."

ONE

The Secret Marriage

1

"Will you be requiring your car again tonight, Mademoiselle?" Jacques leaned deferentially toward his mistress as he helped her to alight from her Rolls-Royce onto the pavement of the Île Saint-Louis where she had her home.

"Not tonight, I have to study papers at home, thank you, Jacques," Sandra said with a smile, as he handed her her briefcase and a shopping bag from Hermès. "But at seven tomorrow, as usual."

"Bien, Mademoiselle." Jacques, immaculate in his navy-blue chauffeur's uniform, lifted his hat and saluted. *"Bonsoir, Mademoiselle."*

"Bonsoir, Jacques."

Jacques watched her as she approached the door of the house, inserted her key in the lock and turned to him to wave that all was well. There were so many kidnappings of powerful people these days that he combined his duties as a chauffeur with those of a bodyguard. He accompanied her on most of her visits: on inspections of the factories and various premises which were part of the Desmond industrial empire. Dressed in civilian clothes, he moved inconspicuously among the crowds, the raincoat he invariably carried over his arm concealing the bulk of his holster pistol.

As Sandra closed the door, Jacques got thoughtfully into the driver's seat. The woman he served with such devotion wasn't happy, her brow continually furrowed, her face a little lined, pale and drawn. She had been like that for some weeks now and the occasional visit to a clinic, outside which he waited a long time without ever receiving any explanation of the reason for the visit, worried him.

Sandra let herself into her private lift on the ground floor of the luxuriously converted *hôtel particulier* and closed her eyes as it rose swiftly to the top.

She was very, very tired.

Professor Pichon had told her she was overdoing it.

"Rest, rest and *more* rest, Madame," he had urged her. "Go down to the coast, take a week off, *enjoy* yourself."

Impossible. There was too much to do. Apart from the running of a huge business she had urgent personal problems on her mind: Michel so far away, her continuing war with the Desmonds.

In the living room Sandra dropped her briefcase on the sofa, reached for the remote control of the TV and turned on the set. Glancing at her watch she realized the news bulletin was coming to an end and she was about to zap off again when the newscaster assumed the voice and expression of one about to relay bad news.

"And, finally, the death has just been announced of Dr. Michel Harcourt, the world-renowned virologist who sacrificed a brilliant life in the forefront of medical research to work at a remote clinic in Africa to test his theories on the AIDS virus. His research on monkeys . . ."

But the rest was unheard by Sandra who had slumped to the floor. Fortunately the sofa broke her fall and there her maid found her only a few moments after the bulletin ended, leaning her head against it as if she had merely fallen asleep.

Professor Pichon felt that he knew his patient very well by now. He was a society doctor patronized by the powerful, the famous and the well-to-do, yet, apart from his little vanities, he was a clever, dedicated medical man who had known Michel

Harcourt despite their dissimilar personalities. The one sought glamor and fortune, the other avoided it. With the familiarity that he, alone, was permitted, he sat on the end of Sandra's bed in one of the private rooms of his clinic, formerly a huge mansion, overlooking the Bois de Boulogne. The noise of the traffic circulating the Bois was merely a distant hum and, as Sandra opened her eyes, she was aware of birdsong.

She gazed for a moment, uncomprehendingly, at Marc Pichon and then, rapidly blinking her eyes, looked round the room. Reassuringly he put out a hand.

"Relax, my dear Sandra, everything is all right . . ."

"But why am I here . . ." She put a hand to her forehead and, as she did so, her eyes fastened on the white name tag round her wrist.

"Professor . . ." She struggled to sit up but his hand moved to her shoulder and, with gentle pressure, he made her lie down again.

"There is no harm to the baby . . . you are perfectly all right."

Michel.

"Oh, my God!" Sandra put both hands to her face as her head sank back against the pillow. "Tell me it was a nightmare, Marc, not true."

She glanced at him pleadingly but, sorrowfully, he shook his head.

"It was shattering you should have learned it like that. Apparently they tried to reach your office from Nairobi, but, in the end, they had to send it over by Reuters' wire. It was flashed to all the news studios at once . . . my poor dear." He took her hand and, as the tears began to well in her eyes, he nodded approvingly.

"Weep, Sandra, weep all you can."

"I want to know," she said fiercely, "I want to *know* all about it. How . . . why . . ."

"He was staying with some friends in the Kora Game Reserve in Kenya. The Hartleys, well-known ecologists . . ."

"I've met them." She nodded impatiently.

"He received your letter." Pichon's grip on her arm tightened. "He was overjoyed at your news about the baby and set out immediately for Nairobi to fly to you . . ."

The tears began slowly to course once again down Sandra's cheeks and, for a while, Pichon let her weep, maintaining the gentle pressure of his arm for support.

"You must not blame yourself, Sandra . . ."

"But my letter sent him to his death."

"Nonsense."

Pichon removed his hand and moved from the bed to a chair, joining his hands in repose. He was a thickset, gray-haired man in his fifties with the comfortable contours and knowing expression of a wise farmer, which was indeed what his antecedents were, far from the patrician or well-to-do origins of his eminent colleagues. Yet women liked and trusted him; his warm presence was unthreatening, his skill reassuring. He was a father figure rather than an autocrat.

"Nonsense," he repeated. "Does not the Bible say we know not the day or the hour? It is a wise counsel, my dear Sandra, and you certainly did not send Michel to his death."

"I shall *always* feel guilty." Sandra violently shook her head. "I shall feel guilty until the day I die. You see"—as the tears began to flow freely again she clutched his proffered hand—"I was *not* a good wife to Michel. He wanted me to give up my work and live with him; but I couldn't."

"He knew that," Pichon said gently, "when he married you. You have told me that repeatedly."

"He had old-fashioned ideas about the roles of men and women," Sandra continued as if to herself. "He thought my place was by his side."

"Then he should never have asked you to marry him."

"He thought I would change. We were so much in love . . ." Sandra, her eyes dry now, gave a deep sigh. "And if I *had* stayed, again he would still be alive."

"You might have been with him," Pichon said gravely. "You might have been killed as well. You see, now, how stupid speculation is?" He rose from his chair and glanced at his watch. "Now, my dear, I must leave you. I have another patient in labor just along the corridor." He glanced at the closed door and then looked at her searchingly. "I believe you have a visitor. He has been waiting patiently downstairs for some time; but I don't know if you wish to see him, if you feel strong enough. You need not if you don't want to."

"Who is it?" Pichon's air of mystery intrigued Sandra.

"Zac Desmond."

"No, I certainly do *not* want to see him." Angrily her fist thumped the white counterpane of the bed.

"Don't you think it might be wise?" Pichon suggested, staring at her with his calm, gray eyes. "You will need now, my dear, all the friends you can get if the business you worked so hard at is not to collapse round your ears. I have spoken to Monsieur Desmond. He knows that you are unwell, and have sustained a great shock, and he genuinely wishes to help."

"But *how* does he know?" Sandra looked about her bewilderedly. "How does he know I'm here?"

"The whole world knows, Sandra," Pichon said with a rueful smile. "They know that you're here and why. You don't think the media wouldn't have sniffed that out in no time, do you?"

Zac Desmond entered the room. Behind him, his face almost hidden by a gigantic bouquet of flowers, stood his chauffeur. Zac stood to one side, a pleased smile on his face, and pointed toward the table by the side of Sandra's bed.

"There if you please, Maurice."

The chauffeur laid the bouquet carefully on the table, taking care not so much as to glance at the woman lying in the bed, then withdrew as obsequiously as he had entered, quietly closing the door behind him.

Sandra stared at the flowers and then at Zac, who joined his hands in front of him as if he were a supplicant.

"I am truly sorry, Sandra," he said. "I came to offer you the condolences of my family and myself as soon as I could. I want you to believe that we are one hundred percent with you in mourning the death of a fine man . . ." Zac's voice dropped to a whisper. "Even if we did not know he was your husband, we realized the extent of your infatuation with him."

Trust Zac to use a word like "infatuation" rather than love, Sandra thought, but the words as well as the expression in the eyes of Pichon as he uttered them haunted her: "You need all the friends you can get." If the Desmonds, from whom she was alienated, were willing to extend the olive branch, was she wise to refuse it?

Zac gingerly sat on the chair beside the table as if to admire the choice and most expensive blooms. He wore a dark, double-breasted suit and, as he rather nervously ran a hand across his hair, Sandra saw that it was thinning. But his dark jowls and piercing brown eyes were undoubtedly still powerful enough to hold a fascination for some women, but not her. They had been enemies almost from the day they met.

Zac saw the expression on her face and maybe guessed what she was thinking. However, for once in a long battle, he felt he had the upper hand. Finally Sandra was reduced to a role she would resent: that of a defenceless woman.

"Why *exactly* are you here, Zac?" Sandra wondered, as she settled back on the pillows, eyeing him in the cautious, almost hostile way he was accustomed to.

She, Sandra O'Neill, was not one to be deceived by appearances. To her the leopard could never change its spots.

"I feel it is time we called a truce, Sandra," Zac said after a pause, as if carefully choosing his words. "After all, we have *much* in common. We *both* have the interests of Desmond at heart and, as you are not in a condition to hold firmly on to the reins, as it were . . ."

"I can assure you I am *quite* fit enough to hold on to the reins," Sandra said firmly, pointing to a pile of files and documents, most of them marked *Private and confidential,* on the table beside her. "I am also having a terminal from our office computer installed here today."

"But your health . . . your baby . . ."

"Both are *fine,*" she insisted, then, her voice faltering, her gaze turned to the window and she sounded very far away as she spoke. "I learned of Michel's death by turning on the evening bulletin on the TV. You can guess it came as an enormous shock to me. I fainted and my maid phoned Dr. Pichon, who ordered me to his clinic for a checkup. After rest and treatment I shall be well enough to go home."

" 'Home', of course, being your apartment on the Île Saint-Louis." Zac's tone of voice changed slightly.

"I wonder why you should say that?" Sandra's eyes turned enquiringly to her old adversary.

"Well . . ." Zac paused with unaccustomed diffidence. "We have always thought of Tourville as home, Sandra. Even though we have avoided it since the court case, *you* know that Father wished we should *all* live there in peace and harmony. You, and us, that we should be just one happy family."

" 'Wished!' " Sandra's tone was sarcastic. "If wishes were horses . . ."

Zac looked puzzled and Sandra explained.

"It's an old saying, maybe one you don't have an equivalent for in French. 'If wishes were horses, beggars would ride."

"I see," Zac said politely, as if not quite understanding her meaning.

"The *point* is," Sandra continued, "that the thought of us all living together in peace and harmony is most unlikely, as likely as beggars being able to afford a horse or, in these days, a car."

"Oh, I *see.*" Zac's brow cleared and he attempted a smile. Then his air of gravity returned. "But I am seriously attempting to effect a reconciliation with you, Sandra. We would *like* to holiday at Tourville with you, to help you get better, to gather about you as a family should. You will have a little one to think of now, as well as yourself. A child without a father. If you could only bring yourself to accept us as family, to let bygones be bygones as I have often urged, you would be doing yourself and your unborn baby a favour. We want to help you. We really do."

It seemed *most* unlikely, Sandra thought as, with Jacques at the wheel, the silver-gray Rolls Royce purred along the straight road that led across the Montagne de Reims, through tall trees interspersed with clear patches of bright sunshine. On the slopes of the Montagne were the acres of vines, each belonging to different *négociants* who sold their crops to the big houses such as Desmond, Tellier, Piper Heidsieck, Delbeck and to smaller ones or cooperatives. For the art of making a great wine such as champagne was not in the grape itself so much as in the blending of the Chardonnay and the Pinot Noir, the exact composition of the formula which was the secret of all the great houses, as Sandra knew to her cost.

She shivered slightly under the rug that covered her knees and impulsively leaned forward, tapping the glass between herself and Jacques who slid back the panel.

"Oui, Mademoiselle?"

"Stop here a moment, Jacques," she commanded in her perfect French. "I wish to look at the view."

Obediently Jacques stopped, leapt out of his seat and opened the door of the car, putting out a hand to help Sandra descend. She was still a little unsteady on her feet, her face very pale, and she stumbled as she alighted. He looked at her anxiously.

"Mademoiselle, I think it is a *little* early . . ."

"Jacques, I am perfectly all right," she replied, tossing her fair, silky hair with its fashionable streaks, and giving him a grateful smile. "See, Tourville," she said a little breathlessly, pointing in front of her. "You know even now it brings a lump to my throat."

Jacques peered over her shoulder to look at the great house built a hundred years before by René-Zachariah Desmond, great-great-grandfather of the man whose own father had dispossessed him of his birthright and who had been striving ever since to reclaim it: Zac Desmond.

It was built in the style of a great English country house, being a rectangular building made of white Chilmark stone, two storeys high with four square towers, two at each end, and a colonnaded balcony which ran on either side of the house. In front was a large kidney-shaped lake on which was a stationary boat; it seemed at the moment to be patroled, as if for safekeeping, by two majestic swans. Behind the house were the stables where Tim Desmond had kept his string of polo ponies, now removed to the United States where he had decided to make his home. Three horses were kept for the use of members of the family and, in their absence, exercised daily by a groom.

A kilometer from the high, ornamental, wrought-iron gates of the château was the river Marne. Stretching away on either side were acres of perfectly maintained vineyards beyond the line of tall beech trees that sheltered the fishermen sitting on the bank, gazing hopefully into the still waters. On the far side was Épernay, second most important city in the Champagne region after Reims, and beyond that was the Côte des Blancs where the white Chardonnay grape was grown. To the right, in the far distance, was the Renaissance-style house once owned by the Widow Clicquot who had tried to outdo René-Zachariah Desmond by building a château even more magnificent than his own.

It was late afternoon and already the river was obscured by the rising mist hovering over the lower slopes of the town, lending a mysterious evanescent quality to the trees and giving an extra enchantment to the dying rays of the sun.

Jacques was amazed to see his mistress make a gesture with her hand as though she were wiping a tear from her eye and, as she turned toward him, he could see that her eyes were indeed unnaturally bright and her beautiful face was stricken with grief, a hopeless sense of longing.

"Mademoiselle," he said with concern, stepping forward, "are you all right?"

"I'm perfectly all right, Jacques," Sandra said, with a fleeting smile which, by its mystery, its fascination, reminded him of still photographs of the young Garbo. "I was just carried away for a moment by memories . . . memories of when I first set eyes on this château and, in my simplicity, imagined that it was the beginning of my happiness." She sighed and her large, limpid eyes, still filled with tragedy, stared at him.

"How wrong I was."

As the doors of the grand salon were thrown open and Sandra paused on the threshold she had a sense of *déjà vu* that, momentarily, seemed to paralyze her. She felt that again she was that rather fearful young woman—despite her air of confidence, almost an ingénue fresh from America—who had stood in exactly the same spot only a few years before. They were years in which she had risen from insignificance to power, an awesome power as chief executive of a worldwide organization embracing not only the famous Desmond champagne but aeronautics, machine tools, publishing companies and newspapers as well.

Yet, as she stood there in that moment, nothing seemed to have changed. The family now, as then, sat confronting her, the men standing, the women, backs ramrod straight, on the Louis XV chairs. Except for their dress they could all have been in the eighteenth century. Smiles were only half smiles, eyes carefully guarded.

As she advanced slowly into the room the tableau underwent a subtle change, a shift of emphasis; bodies relaxed, expressions became more friendly. It had been as though, for a moment, they had all been encapsulated in a time warp.

Zac's sister, Belle, broke the ice by leaving her seat as Sandra walked slowly toward her.

"Dearest sister," she said, throwing her arms round Sandra's neck. "What a *terrible,* trying time you have had. How grieved we are for you."

Sister? Dearest? Sandra tried hard to conceal her surprise, responding to Belle, as best she could, by a guarded peck on her cheek. Belle's pale, matt, perfectly made-up skin was cold and unresponsive to the touch like a sheet of glass. After the greeting the two women linked arms and went over to Lady Elizabeth who remained in her seat.

The face she presented to Sandra was one of composure, as if she were carefully and purposefully at pains to conceal her real thoughts and emotions from the woman who had brought such havoc to her family.

Sandra didn't attempt to kiss Zac and Belle's mother but held out her hand.

"How very nice to see you again, Lady Elizabeth."

"And *you,* Sandra." Holding on to her hand, Lady Elizabeth looked at her searchingly. "Gracious me, you *do* look pale, my dear. Here, sit next to me." She patted the seat vacated by Belle, and a hand as cold as her daughter's was placed on Sandra's.

At that moment Zac came over to her and, having seen her only a few days before, merely took her hand and kissed it. Then he turned to his brother-in-law Carl who, as if on cue, stepped forward and kissed Sandra on both cheeks. Sandra had always been fond of Carl, conscious of his tacit sympathy and support, maybe because he was married to a Desmond.

As he briefly held on to her, Sandra was overwhelmed by a feeling of belonging, that she was, indeed, in the bosom of her family: the real family that Georges Desmond had always wanted—and didn't all real families have sorrows as well as joys, good times as well as bad? And didn't she, Sandra—the Sandra of so many names, desperately in search of an identity—need the protective love of a family more than most?

Spontaneously she hugged Carl, holding him close to her for a moment and then, as he withdrew, she looked around her. The family was incomplete.

"Claire?" she inquired and immediately was aware of Lady Elizabeth beside her stiffening.

"We no longer receive Claire since she went to live with that . . . that painter. An illiterate street artist married to a Desmond!"

Observing them, Sandra saw the same expression of injured dignity on the faces of them all and the exultation she'd felt died immediately.

Nothing had changed with the Desmonds. They neither forgave nor forgot. How could she possibly have thought they would accept her?

And, as on that first time, they ate again in the family dining room known as the Italian room. Its walls were hung with red silk, its priceless furniture was the work of Italian masters and the black and white Venetian tiles surrounded the same still highly polished parquet floor. As on that first occasion Zac sat at one end of the table, Lady Elizabeth at the other.

But, apart from Claire and Zac's wife Tara—whose name no one mentioned at all, since she had left him the year before—two other important members of that original meeting were missing: Henri Piper who had guided her through so many of the machinations and schemes hatched by the Desmonds, and Timothy, Zac's younger brother.

"Is Uncle Henri well?" Sandra inquired of no one in particular halfway through the soup.

"Henri and Sophie are in America." Zac casually passed Sandra the basket of rolls. "And Tim has also established himself there, breeding polo ponies."

Sandra took care to avoid Zac's eyes and, clearly aware of her embarrassment, Zac coughed and cleared his throat loudly.

"I think I should say what is on all our minds, Sandra." Leaning forward, he gazed earnestly at her.

"And that is?"

"Why, your marriage, of course. Why was it necessary to keep it secret? We should all have been delighted to welcome the distinguished Dr. Harcourt as a brother-in-law."

Zac smiled at Belle who nodded approvingly, but Sandra's antennae detected an air of conspiracy, as if they had all set out with a specific intention to be nice. Gone, in a flash, was the sense of homecoming. Once more she was on her guard.

She looked slowly round the table, her gaze lingering on each of them in turn, and, choosing her words with care, said: "You must remember that after the court case which, in a sense, I won,

I was left in a state of severe shock." Her eyes alighted on the impassive features of Lady Elizabeth who seemed to be looking straight through her. "I discovered, in the most brutal way imaginable, that the woman I had believed to be my mother was not. I had my relationship with Tim, possibly a blood relation, called into question . . ."

"We said bygones would be bygones, Sandra," Zac intervened swiftly. "Please don't dredge up the past."

Sandra sighed. "Very well, to answer your question, Michel wanted me to give up the presidency of Desmond and remain in Harare. Of course, I had *no* intention of doing such a thing, betraying"—she allowed herself a brief smile—"the trust Georges Desmond had placed in me. Yet I loved Michel. I wished him to return to France and to work as head of the Desmond Foundation.

"He thought, however, that, as my husband, it would amount to nepotism. Despite the fact that he was a man of genius, people, who by nature are so petty, would be jealous. He wanted me to stay with him. I wanted him to return." She shrugged, aware of the tears stinging the backs of her eyes. "Impulsively we decided to get married, each hoping the other would change his or her mind. That, alas, was a year ago. When I returned to Paris, of course, I had a number of other matters needing my attention: the question of the sale of planes to the Gulf, the threat of insider trading and the SEC investigations . . . all . . ." She suddenly fixed Zac with her eyes as if to imply, "all brought on by you, Zac," but she did not say it.

"Michel and I continued to argue; but we loved each other. We met as frequently as we could, alas almost always for only a few days. Then two months ago I suspected I was pregnant. It was confirmed; but I hung on, undecided what to do. I felt Michel would use it as a weapon to *force* me to give up *my* work. I delayed telling him. Finally I felt I had to . . ."

Belle leaned back, but there was unmistakably a gleam of triumph in her eyes. "How *very* sad," she said, "because now you will have no alternative, will you, Sandra?"

"How do you mean?" Sandra looked puzzled.

"You will *have* to resign the presidency. Zac, I am sure, will gladly step in to take your place."

"Oh, there will be no need of that," Sandra said with a charming smile, realizing that her own duplicity was beginning to match that of the Desmonds. "Grateful as I shall be for his help in an *advisory* capacity, for the help of you all, I would never dream now of leaving Desmond. You've heard of working mothers, haven't you, Belle?" She flashed her a knowing smile. "After all, you're one yourself."

2

Forced inactivity during the remaining months of her pregnancy was alien to Sandra's mercurial temperament. She alternated between restlessness and frustration, necessitating frequent visits from Professor Pichon or a trusted member of his staff to ensure that she was obeying orders as she went back and forth between Paris and Reims.

She moved into a suite in the château that functioned as an office with word processors, fax and telex machines and various computers which, non-stop, blinked the prices of shares on all the stock exchanges around the world. Sandra spent much of her time sitting in a comfortable chair, her eyes on the various screens which beamed out up-to-the-minute information on the commodities or futures markets that was promptly transcribed by one of her three secretaries, headed by Antoinette Lagasse, who had been promoted from the Reims office as Sandra's chief secretary and personal assistant the year before.

Antoinette was a little older than Sandra, a woman born and bred in Reims, who had seldom stirred outside that city unless it was to visit relatives near Toulouse. But, although her life seemed very circumscribed, it was just this kind of background that suited Sandra after her experience with a previous secretary who had become an ally of Zac.

Divorced, but childless, there was a hint of tragedy in Antoinette's past; but her personal life never obtruded into her working life. Balanced and calm, incurious and discreet, Antoinette was an ideal choice and, especially in her present crisis, Sandra had developed a growing affection for her as her dependence on her deepened. She had brought herself up to date, acquiring all the skills that secretaries in a technological age now required. She was frequently dispatched on courses to improve her skills, together with the small brood of assistant secretaries employed in Sandra's office.

It was Antoinette who hovered by Sandra's side, scanning the screens, detaching the faxes, relaying work to be done to the two who were busy with their VDTs in the adjoining room.

She knew that Sandra should rest, but she also knew that work was vital for her. It was a stimulant that she needed, almost like a drug; but it was up to Antoinette to see that she did not overtax herself, that the decisions needing Sandra's personal attention were kept under control.

One morning after the routine business of the day had been attended to, Sandra looked up at her secretary, who had just brought in her morning coffee, the expression on her face that of someone who has just had a bright idea.

"Antoinette!" she exclaimed, leaning back in her chair. "Do you know I have never *really* had the time to examine this business with the thoroughness and care it deserves?"

"How do you mean, Madame?" Antoinette inquired respectfully, even though she could scarcely believe her ears, never in her life having worked for someone as thorough as Sandra. Having consumed her coffee in the room next door with her colleagues, she sat next to Sandra, pad and pencil in her hand.

"Ever since I came"—Sandra waved her hand vaguely in the air—"I have gone from crisis to crisis . . ."

"Nevertheless, Madame . . . no one *criticizes* what you have done." No one would dare, Antoinette thought to herself.

"Certain decisions were obvious." Sandra restlessly got up and, taking her coffee with her, walked across the room and stood gazing out of the window. "But there is a whole lot about the business that I don't know. It grew so much, you know, in Georges Desmond's lifetime." She finished her coffee and, walking back, replaced her cup on the table. "Antoinette, it's time anyway that we put all the back material relating to the group on computer."

"But, Madame," Antoinette protested, "it will take *years* . . ."

"Let it take years," Sandra said with the cheerfulness of one who didn't actually have to do the work. "But let us begin at the beginning."

Enthusiastically she rubbed her hands together, gazing with satisfaction at her trusted employee. "Although I believe you're right; we really might have a job for life."

In many ways it was a job for life, Sandra decided after a week or two during which files were brought from the head office for her scrutiny before they were sent to be transcribed onto disk by the staff, who had now been augmented to five.

Antoinette, busier than ever, bustled about making sure that each part of the business was methodically examined, transcribed and then filed away again, in case one day a virus should get into the computer and destroy all the valuable material from the past.

Sandra was in her element, sitting at her desk, or in a comfortable chair, her feet on a stool, making notes, or dictating to Antoinette or into a tape recorder. There were so many facets of the company which, as she had said, had grown from small beginnings to a huge conglomerate. Much dead wood had already been shed, businesses sold off which were neither relevant nor profitable, until a streamlined machine, which was the new Desmond Group, had existed. But there was a lot about the past that she didn't know.

Switzerland. Sandra frowned as she reached for the first from a pile of new files which had just arrived and lay before her.

In Switzerland there was the holding company which was a rather nebulous operation controlling the purely financial side of the business: the transfer of funds, sometimes legal matters. It was headed by a man called Hugo Dubuisson and she had only visited the office in Geneva once in the past four years.

Well, it seemed to run itself. She drew a file toward her and flicked over the documents which were largely balance sheets: calculations concerning the massive amounts of money that were moved around the world on behalf of Desmond. Her eyes strayed expertly over the figures as she turned the pages, and once or twice, for her own satisfaction, she drew her calculator toward her and checked the balances.

Everything seemed in order until she came to the balance sheet for the year she became president of Desmond. She checked the figures twice, the credits and debits, the overall financial position of the company, and then she checked a third time, but something still wasn't right.

"They've written twenty-five million dollars off as a loss," she said in an incredulous tone to Antoinette. "How can you write off twenty-five million dollars without explanation? It is in small print as well, just look."

Antoinette obediently followed the direction of her gaze. "It's a large sum of money, Madame," she murmured, and suddenly she turned and leafed through the file in her hand, saying with a note of excitement in her voice, "I think there *is* something here that may have a bearing on the matter."

"It's one hell of a lot of money casually to write off." Sandra took the sheet which Antoinette had detached from the file and laid before her, and studied it carefully. "Where did you find this, Antoinette?" she asked after a minute, her eyes still on the paper.

"It was tucked in the middle of the file, Madame, rather obscurely as though someone wished to hide it."

"I don't wonder," Sandra said grimly, and slowly she read aloud from a letter addressed to Georges Desmond, marked private and confidential and with the Swiss address on it:

"Dear Monsieur Desmond,

"Further to your inquiry, I have been unable to ascertain the

whereabouts of Monsieur Bernardo Romanetto, who left our employment without notification at the same time that the sum of twenty-five million US dollars was found to be missing. This money was due to be routed from this office via Zurich for the payment of machine parts to be delivered under the terms of our supply of Desmond 200 fighter aircraft to the Gulf. The money left this office but was never received by the bank at Zurich.

"You can rest assured, Monsieur Desmond, that this matter is being very carefully examined by our security department. As yet we have no definite link between the disappearance of Monsieur Romanetto and the money."

It was signed by Hugo Dubuisson, acting financial controller of the group.

"Well," Sandra said, sitting back. "What *do* you know about *that?"*

"All we know," Zac said testily later that day, "was that Bernardo Romanetto disappeared and was never seen again."

"But what about all that *money?"* Sandra looked at him incredulously as he paced up and down the floor of the salon where she had asked to see him before dinner.

"The money"—Zac threw out his hands as if the matter both exasperated and embarrassed him—"was never traced. Neither was Romanetto."

"But it wasn't right just to let the matter drop, surely?"

"You must understand, Sandra"—Zac turned to her appealingly—"that it was a *very* difficult time for us personally. As you can see, within a few days of that memorandum from the acting financial controller, whose appointment was subsequently confirmed, my father was tragically killed. Of course there was absolutely *no* connection between the two events, but the seriousness of the one helped to put the other, if not out of our minds then . . . we . . ." He shrugged and turned his eyes away, his voice dropping to a whisper. "You *know* what happened. Had I inherited the company as I expected the matter would have been pursued with the utmost seriousness, and Bernardo apprehended and brought to book." He stuck his chin in the air and the smile vanished from his face. "I wonder that you, who take care to be so well informed about everything, didn't find out about this yourself. By then it was your responsibility."

"Well, I didn't!" Sandra bit her lip. "I was never told, and it was never pointed out to me, and this is the first time I have heard about it."

"Four years later?" Zac's expression was skeptical. "For *you* who, a genius at figures, examine accounts with such care. I must say I find that most strange."

"Nevertheless, it is true. No one brought it to my attention and I didn't notice it."

"Then obviously you didn't go into everything well enough."

"Obviously."

"I must say I'm surprised, Sandra." By now his skepticism had been replaced by a smile of quiet satisfaction.

Sandra knew the reprimand was justified and she was angry with herself. She did not reply. Shortly after their conversation ended Lady Elizabeth came in and, pleading tiredness, Sandra begged to be excused from attending the evening meal, saying she preferred to dine alone in her room.

As she left, Lady Elizabeth raised an eyebrow and, when Sandra had shut the door behind her, turned to her son.

"Not as clever as she thinks," Zac said with a sly smile and, feeling suddenly rejuvenated, he quickly crossed to the side table containing a variety of bottles and decanters, from one of which he removed the stopper.

"Your usual aperitif before dinner, Maman?"

Sandra felt humiliated. Zac had scored again. Immediately after she left the salon she had all the Swiss files sent to her room and, pushing her dinner to one side, spent the rest of the evening going through them. But, apart from that one confidential memorandum, there was not another word about the missing Romanetto. It was as though all further reference to him ended. Yet the accounts the following year, made when she was nominally in charge, had clearly shown the loss.

Even though it had never been brought to her attention, she should have spotted it herself. She was a trained accountant and she prided herself on her diligence.

Too easy to blame herself now, but also easy to make excuses. She had, after all, been new at the time and the Swiss company, although a vital part of the group, was a subsidiary, by then run by a very competent man, Dubuisson.

Maybe if she went on digging she would find further anomalies; but the matter of Romanetto continued to annoy her and she resolved that she would follow it up as soon as she could.

She sighed and, putting the last file to one side, she stood up, removing her tray with the food almost untouched to a sideboard, and was about to return to her seat when there was a soft tap on the door.

"Who is it?" she asked.

"Marie, Madame," her maid replied.

"Come in, Marie," Sandra said warmly, going to open the door for someone she regarded as one of her few true friends. Marie had been with her since she had come to France to take up residence first at the Ritz and then at her apartment on the Île Saint-Louis. The faithful Marie came everywhere with her, packed and unpacked her bags, selected what clothes she was to wear for what occasion. She had even slept in the next room to her in the clinic, as though sensing her vulnerability, to be sure that her precious mistress had everything she needed.

Marie now entered with an anxious look on her face which grew even more grim as she saw the food untouched on the tray on the sideboard.

"Tsch, tsch, Madame," she clucked. "The good doctor said *you must eat.*" Each syllable was emphasized by a wag of her finger.

"The good doctor has not my worries, Marie." Sandra gazed at her sadly.

"Ah, pauvre Madame." Marie's face creased in sympathy. "I told you it was no good for you to come here. You should have remained in Paris where Dr. Pichon can keep an eye on you and see that you eat. I was not taken in by the family pretending to care for you."

Tears once again sprang unbidden to Sandra's eyes and she thought how different, how vulnerable the state of pregnancy made one, in all sorts of unexpected ways. It was known that complex hormonal changes took place which made even the most disciplined woman unable to control her emotions, those rapid changes of mood. At times she felt like a little girl in need of love and reassurance, rather than a world-class businesswoman, and she reached out for Marie's warm, brown, capable hand.

"See, Madame," Marie said brightly, putting a hand in the pocket of her overall, "there is a letter for you. I found it on the table in the hall."

She held it out to Sandra who took it in some bewilderment and stared at the writing: the large boyish scrawl that she recognized well.

"It's from Bob," she said excitedly, beginning to slit the flap of the envelope open, only to find that it was open already. *"Where* did you say you found it, Marie?"

"On the table in the hall."

"But my mail is brought to me directly from my office." Sandra slowly extracted the sheet of paper from the envelope which she put on one side. Then she began to read:

Dearest Sis,

I can still call you that, can't I? I know you feel for me as much as ever you did even though we now know that we are not related by blood. I know it was with my interests at heart that you sent me back to LA. But, Sis, I have not been able to settle. You know how much I loved Tara and I was sure that she returned my love, despite what she said. I am going to go to try and find Tara, Sis, and by the time you get this letter I shall be over there in Rome. I think that now, after a separation from Zac of over a year, she is ready to see me. Rome is a big place and she is lonely.

Well, I have been writing to Tara care of her brother Marco and she has answered all my letters. I am giving this to a friend and asking him to post it two weeks after I leave so that by the time you get it I shall have had a chance to try and woo Tara again and, despite the difference in our ages, tell her how much I love her and need her.

The letter went on but the writing blurred before Sandra's eyes and she put it on her lap while Marie, who had been watching her, went up to her, clucking again with concern.

"What is it, Madame? You are so pale. Not bad news from Monsieur Bob, I hope."

"Very bad news, Marie," Sandra whispered. "And I am afraid, what is more, that I am not the only one who knows it. Zac has undoubtedly intercepted this letter, read the contents and contemptibly left it open so that I can see he knows as much as I do: that my brother Bob is, in fact, making yet another attempt to steal his wife."

Zac left the side entrance of the Château de Tourville, so as to be unobserved, driving himself. His Porsche was soon lost in the trees that fringed the side of the narrow road which rose through the Montagne de Reims toward the city itself. Branching off, he followed a number of minor, unmarked roads that ran off the N51 like small capillaries until, between the villages of Rilly and Verzy, he came to a house. The *vendange* was in full swing and on either side the pickers were at work in the fields removing the clusters of black Pinot Noir grapes with their *épinettes* and placing them in small plastic baskets which were dotted across the vineyard.

The *porteurs* waited until the baskets were filled and then tipped them into the huge *mannequins,* oval-shaped baskets which could hold 176 pounds of grapes.

Zac slowed down for a moment and then stopped, his hands on the wheel, watching the work of the *vendangeurs* in the vineyards that stretched for mile after mile on all sides. These were not the Desmond vineyards, which surrounded the château, but the tasks and the object were the same: the manufacture of that priceless, golden liquid, the unique wine of the region: champagne.

Champagne was his birthright; in a sense it ran in his blood, and yet that birthright had been taken from him. The thought, yet again, made the veins bulge in his neck and, at the same time, his eyes stung with tears which, as soon as he was conscious of them, he angrily brushed away. Zac was a chauvinist: a manly man who would consider it a sign of weakness to show tears.

He restarted the car and resumed his journey, his face now dark with anger as his resentment gnawed at his soul.

He passed through the village of Rilly and on toward Verzy with its famous petrified forest, an arboreal curiosity, called Faux de Verzy. On the outskirts of this forest was a cluster of small houses, little more than a hamlet, with a farm and a sole *épicerie.* The largest house, a square, stuccoed building of some substance, with green shutters closed to keep out the sun, stood back from the road, protected by a high wall and a pair of wrought-iron gates which looked securely shut.

Zac stopped his car outside the gates and, after staring at them and the house thoughtfully for a moment, got out and peered through the bars, on one side of which there was a bell pull. Deciding by now that the owner was not at home, he nevertheless pulled it sharply and was surprised to see the door open and a woman of mature years gaze out at him, blinking her eyes rapidly in the strong sunshine.

"Monsieur Desmond," she cried and, hand to mouth, hurried down the path as if fearful of keeping the eminent visitor waiting too long.

"Is Monsieur Strega at home, Madame?" Zac hissed through the iron bars as the woman, producing a large iron key from the pocket of her apron, hastily unlocked the gate.

"Come in, come in," she called, nodding vigorously as Zac

pushed the heavy gate open. "Bring in your car, Monsieur, because I have instructions to lock the gate again."

Zac grimaced as he returned to the Porsche and manoeuvred it into the courtyard of the house.

As always, Strega was cautious.

Paul Strega, the son of Italian immigrants, had been involved in some way or another with Zac Desmond for half his lifetime. He had first met him when he acted as his batman during Zac's national service and after that Zac, who liked someone he could dominate, could control completely, had kept him in his employ.

Strega was a chameleon-like character, an apparently innocuous yet inwardly violent man who had been saved from a long prison sentence by Zac after his landlady in Épernay was found murdered. Zac provided him with an alibi; but there were only two people who knew the truth: Zac Desmond and Paul Strega. From then on Strega had to do as he was told.

There was no friendship, however, between the two men and, as Zac entered the sitting room where Strega was sprawled on the couch watching the television, he sprang to his feet in the manner of a subordinate, as though he were about to salute him.

"Monsieur," he said, pointing apologetically to his night attire, "had I known you were coming . . ."

"That's all right, Strega," Zac said offhandedly, waving his hand in the air. "You can wear your pajamas all day if you like. This, after all, is your own home."

Bought with my money, Zac thought, looking round. A place that bore a look of neglect despite the woman who came every morning to clean for him, a place that also lacked the element of having someone who cared for it, cared too, perhaps, for Strega.

Strega was always referred to by his surname by the Desmonds as though to use his Christian name would indicate a familiarity that they could not and did not feel. Strega was a functionary, a servant, and addressed like one. Strega, always Strega.

Zac looked him up and down carefully, a sneer on his face, but said, facetiously, "You look as though you'd just come out of jail, Strega. You have the pallor of someone who has been incarcerated too long indoors."

"I don't go out much when I'm here, Monsieur Zac," Strega mumbled. "If you don't mind I'll go and change while Madame Lamont brings you coffee."

Strega scuttled off before Zac had a chance to reply and he walked to the French windows, throwing them open to let in a little air.

"It is stifling in this place, Madame," he said reprovingly as the woman came in with two *café filtres* on a tray.

Madame Lamont shrugged and she gently placed the tray on a small, round table.

"It is Monsieur Strega, Monsieur Desmond. He doesn't like the light. He forbids me to open the shutters even on a rainy day. Anyone would think he had something to hide."

Zac looked at her sharply but she gave no indication of any ulterior meaning and, with a faded smile, withdrew, shutting the double doors carefully behind her.

Zac looked onto the neat garden which alone showed signs of care. Maybe there was a better, gentler side to Strega after all.

"Do you have a gardener, Strega?" he inquired, turning round as Strega, hastily stuffing his shirt into the top of his trousers, reentered the room. He had not, however, had time to shave and the day's growth of beard increased the impression of prison pallor.

"No, Monsieur Zac," he said, looking puzzled.

Zac waved a hand expansively in the direction of the French windows.

"So, you do all this yourself?"

"When I have the time," Strega said guardedly. "I am not, as you know, here very often."

He took the lid off his *café filtre* and carefully inspected the contents of the cup which he then raised to his lips. He took a gulp, then extracted a Gauloise which he lit before throwing the match into the fireplace. As he expelled clouds of smoke into the air around him he began to cough.

"You should take more care of yourself, Strega." Zac frowned. "There is no need to let yourself go just because you have not, at the moment, very much to do."

"I have *nothing* to do, Monsieur Zac," Strega protested vehemently.

"Exactly." Zac nodded. "That's why I am here. You are about to start on your travels again, Strega."

Zac finished his coffee and, the opposite of Strega in appearance as well as dress sense, sat down in a chair, fastidiously inspecting it beforehand to see that it was clean. "Do you remember Romanetto?"

"Romanetto?" Strega screwed up his eyes, which were almost lost in his puffy face.

"Bernardo Romanetto," Zac said impatiently.

"Ah, *Bernardo* Romanetto." Strega's look of bewilderment cleared. "Of the Geneva office?"

"He absconded with twenty-five million US dollars of Desmond money. He was never punished."

"It coincided I think, Monsieur Zac, with the death of your father." Strega assumed an insincere expression of sympathy.

"And the arrival of Mademoiselle." Zac knitted his expressive brows together wrathfully. "And it is *because* of Mademoiselle that I want you to resurrect Bernardo. She has suddenly found out about him—rather late in the day, you may think—and I think I can make good use of this weakness. A rather clever plan has come to my mind, Strega." Zac's eyes grew wide with enthusiasm. "It is quite breathtaking in its audacity and, should it work, it would make 'Madame' seem a criminal in the eyes of the world. Should it fail"—he gave a shrug of resignation—"no one will be any the wiser. Therefore, I want you to spare no effort, no expertise, to find Romanetto, and soon."

A look of anticipation came into Strega's eyes.

"You want me to kill him?" he said eagerly.

"Don't be such a *fool,"* Zac snapped. "What is the point of killing him before I have a chance to operate my plan? Have you no sense? I want you to *find* him. Find him and *use* him, Strega. If my little scheme is successful, finally I may get rid of the cursed Irish woman completely from our lives."

Strega's features contorted again in mock sympathy.

"I hear she lost her husband."

"She is at present in Tourville," Zac said with satisfaction. "She is now eight months pregnant and, hard though it is to think the bitch capable of it, still suffering from shock following the death of her husband. It doesn't prevent her sticking her nose into everything, past and present, however. I don't know where she gets the energy; but this time she may have taken a step too far. By snooping too closely into the past she may eventually find she has uncovered a hornet's nest. Believe me, my brain is working overtime with schemes to get rid of her."

Zac stood up and walked once again to the windows where, for several minutes, he stood looking out across the gentle, beautiful countryside of Champagne, yet his own violent thoughts were far from harmony with nature. Then he turned and gazed at Strega who was lighting another cigarette preparatory to a fresh onslaught of coughing.

"In the meantime I want you to find Romanetto, threaten him"—Zac held up a fist—"and then make him do what *I* tell you. That way we shall fix Sandra-the-pest for good."

3

Marco Falconetti bit anxiously at his lower lip, his response far from warm, nervous, even frightened, as he greeted his sister.

"You are *sure* no one saw you coming?"

Tara Desmond took a precarious perch on one of the armchairs of faded brocade that threatened imminent collapse even with the weight of someone as light as she. She was a dark-haired, imperious beauty and, despite being petite, in temperament far stronger than her brother.

Marco appeared to wilt under the sisterly gaze and turned away.

"What is it you're so afraid of?" she demanded, uncrossing her arms and tapping her very high heels upon the floor.

"You *know* what I'm afraid of." Marco turned round. "Or rather who."

"Zac."

"Precisely, and *you're* afraid of him too," Marco spat out venomously. "If you were not you would not be in hiding."

"Well, I'm not afraid of him anymore." Tara took a mirror out of her handbag and, gazing at her face with evident approval, applied a fresh layer of lipstick to her exquisitely pouting lips. "I have been hiding from him for eighteen months and I tell you, Marco, I'm tired of it. Besides, what is the point? *If* Zac really wanted to find me he could. Maybe he does not want me back. Maybe, after all, he is ready to give me a divorce."

"Then you will be penniless."

"I am penniless now," Tara protested. "I do not see my children. I am not a monster of a mother you know, Marco. I love and miss my children. I am ready to come out in the open and ask Zac for my freedom."

"He will never give it," Marco said, shaking his head. "He is too anxious for respectability. He will do anything to have you back. I know. I promise you he is a changed, chastened man. Every time he telephones he tells me." Marco sighed. "He also promises me that if you *do* return, he will ask no questions. He is also willing to restore this palazzo . . ."

"Tsch!" Tara exclaimed with a gesture of impatience. "How *many* times has he promised you *that!*" She began to count on her fingers with their beautiful, tapered, scarlet nails. During her enforced exile Tara had been careful not to let her standards slip. "One, two, three . . ."

"Oh, do shut up, Tara," Marco said irritably, producing a cigarette from a case and carefully fitting it into an amber holder. "You know my nerves are not what they were . . ."

"Your nerves, brother, were *never* your strong point," Tara observed sarcastically. "If they were you would not have let this place deteriorate the way it has."

She looked contemptuously round at the threadbare rugs and carpets, the moth-eaten tapestries on the walls; at the chandelier which seemed to hang dangerously by a thread. She inhaled the odor of damp and must . . .

"It is not my *nerves* that are responsible for this," Marco said peevishly. "It is my lack of fortune. Why should *I* be the one to inherit a palace when my father was almost bankrupt? You can't blame me for that."

"Don't *whine,* Marco," Tara said sharply, standing up and casually buttoning up the jacket of her elegant suit.

God alone knew, Marco thought, how Tara had managed to exist for eighteen months without the money she was used to, merely with a part-time job in a boutique. Unless she got it from elsewhere? A woman like her was never short of admirers. Tara was not the kind of woman to enjoy living frugally. Maybe she already had a rich protector whose name she would never dare divulge to her brother for fear—quite rightly—that he would pass the information on to Zac.

What, now, had made Tara so brave?

"Well." Marco nervously finished smoking his cigarette and then began agitatedly to stub it out. "Well . . . what do you want me to do?"

"Nothing," Tara said. "I simply want to live a public life, to come and see my brother when I feel like it and not skulk about the streets at night like a cat."

"I would still be very careful of Zac, if I were you," Marco said. "He is a man who, whatever he says, never forgives. If, if you like to tell me where you live . . ."

"I'm not silly enough for that!" Tara exclaimed with a sly smile. "If you want to get a message to me send it to the boutique." She took up her handbag and cast a despairing look round the funereal room. "I can't stay too long in this place. You know it really stinks . . ."

"Well?" Bob started anxiously from the chair in which he had been sitting by the window waiting for her to return.

"I told him I want to divorce Zac."

"You really *did?* You did!" Bob put an arm round her waist and hugged her so tight that she gasped.

"He is still afraid of Zac," Tara said a little tremulously.

"But you are not?" Bob looked gravely into her eyes.

She carefully avoided contact before she said in a voice scarcely more than a whisper: "No."

Bob's arms round her waist tightened. Sometimes, she thought, he forgot how small she was in comparison to him.

"Please, darling," she said, straining at his arms.

"Oh, my precious, I'm so *sorry.*" Bob released her at once and, instead, tenderly encircled her face with his big, strong hands. "I'm bulky, a beast . . ."

"No, you're not. You're very sweet actually." Teasingly she

took hold of his hand and led him to the sofa. "You don't know your own strength."

"I'm not letting you go now, Tara." Once Bob was sitting beside her his hand closed protectively over hers. "I'm here for good. I'm going to love you and support you and protect you."

"And our age difference?" For a woman of the world Tara tried, unconvincingly, to look like an ingénue. "Fourteen years is a long time."

"In other people's eyes but not ours. Look"—Bob jerked back his head—"if I were thirty-six and you were a twenty-two-year-old chick, no one would think anything of it."

"But that's not the way of the world," she said gently.

"It's the way of *my* world," he insisted. "It's the way it's going to be." Bob's jaw was firm, the light in his eyes determined, steely. For one so young he had, since she'd last seen him, developed a new air of decisiveness. His lonely sojourn in America had made him mature quickly. He did, indeed, look now like a strong man, a man years older than he was, no longer a boy. And in the short time they'd been together Tara felt a confidence she had not felt before, when he'd pursued her in Paris like an adolescent puppy.

Eighteen months had changed Bob as they had changed her. He got up and wandered to the window which overlooked a narrow Roman street in the Trastevere quarter where Tara had rented this small apartment whose address was known only to her and Bob.

Bob was a tall, bulky young man with the girth of an American football player. In other circumstances he would probably have had the mentality of one, but life in the past few years had been hard.

He had not had a normal childhood, had missed out on the love of a father and mother and, consequently, had been closely dependent on and, perhaps, over-protected by his sister Sandra.

When she had unexpectedly inherited Georges Desmond's billion-dollar empire, Bob could not avoid the limelight. He dropped out, experimented with drugs, finally followed Sandra to Europe where he met the woman of his life: raven-haired, ravishing Tara Desmond, an Italian noblewoman, an ex-model and the wife of Sandra's powerful adversary, Zac.

Tara had played with Bob, teased him, tormented him. Finally she had run away and out of his life.

Bob had returned to California, but he remained a man obsessed. He had only thought of Tara and, finally, he had found her. Marco had told him about the boutique in the Via Veneto, and there she was.

Tara had gone into the small kitchen and returned with drinks in her hand. One glass she passed to him, the other she kept for herself.

"Chin chin," she said, raising her glass.

"Cheers," he replied. "To us . . . forever."

Tara avoided his gaze.

"If it's a question of money," Bob said, with a note of desperation in his voice, "Sandra will give me everything I need."

"Are you *sure?*" Tara looked spiteful. "Her position is not so secure."

"What do you mean, it's not secure?" Bob, still in many ways the college freshman, looked puzzled.

"She is expecting a baby. Zac will close in for the kill while she is vulnerable."

"Sandra's tough. Don't you worry about that."

"Oh, but is she tough enough?" Tara's smile was tantalizing. "I believe the Desmonds have taken her to Tourville, ostensibly to protect her and surround her with love.

"Ha! Does *any* single member of that family know the meaning of love? It is more like the spider which entices the victim to its lair. I'm surprised Sandra is taken in by it if she is. She must be very desperate. Do *you* think your sister is safe with them?" She appeared abruptly to pull herself up and put a hand to her mouth. "Sorry, Bob. She's *not* your real sister, is she? I suppose you feel very bad about it. It must make a difference."

"I feel as though I had a limb cut off." Bob sank onto a chair and put his head between his hands. Tara impulsively went and kneeled beside him, taking his hand in hers.

"Sorry, I shouldn't have said that. It's just that you never mention it."

"For me it isn't real," Bob said, in a broken voice. "You've no idea the effect it had on me, hearing it like that on the TV newscasts, reading the account of the court case in the papers. It was as much of a shock for Sandra as it was for me and she wasn't even able to warn me because she learned it at the same time as the whole world. However, here's a strange thing." Bob drew his hands wearily over his face. "It has brought us closer together. It hasn't altered our love for each other; our truly fraternal love. She was always my sis and she still is, even though we know we're not related. She has promised me all the money and support I need . . ."

"Even with *me?"* Tara queried gently.

"Ah, that." Bob put a hand gently under her chin and drew her mouth toward him. *"That* I don't know."

However, instead of finishing their conversation in a passionate embrace, as he'd hoped, Tara slapped away his hand and jumped angrily to her feet. He slumped back into his chair and looked bewilderedly at her. Much as he loved her, her fiery unpredictable temper could be trying. One never quite knew how she would react to anything.

"But that is just the *point,* Bob." She provocatively encircled her tiny waist with her hands and, storming up and down the room, shook her dark tresses, the expression in her eyes furious. "You are such a *child* in so many ways. You assured me last night we would have enough money to live in the sort of comfort I'm used to. I can't do without it, Bob, not now. I'm sick of this sordid little flat and I miss the luxury of the life I led with Zac. To be frank with you, I do." She stared boldly at him as though defying him to contradict her.

"But you said you'd never go back to him." The hurt showed in Bob's eyes. "You *loathed* him and hated him, feared him. You told me only last night. Or was that pretense?"

"No, it was *not* pretense," she said sharply. "It was the truth. He is a horrible man, a man of violence. He raped his own wife, don't forget. He had my lover murdered . . ."

"You can't be sure of that."

"Oh, I'm sure," Tara said, nodding vigorously. "As far as I can be sure of anything I'm sure of that."

"Then why does he leave you here?"

"He's playing a game," Tara said, idly studying her nails. "Marco says he's changed, but I know Zac. Does a leopard change its spots?"

Bob, aware of a sudden stab of fear on his own behalf, looked instinctively behind him as if expecting the door suddenly to burst open.

"You have a son, Sandra," she heard a voice saying and, as the haze in front of her eyes cleared, they focused on the tiny form that the green-gowned professor held up to her, before placing it tenderly on her stomach.

As her newborn son uttered his first lusty cry, instinctively her arms encircled him and her eyes filled with tears.

"Is he OK?" she asked wonderingly.

"Perfectly OK. A nice healthy baby." The note of pride in the professor's voice made him sound as if he took some credit for the fact which, perhaps, in the circumstances, he did.

As the staff bustled around the delivery room, Sandra clutched her son, gazing into his eyes which, though unfocused, somehow uncannily seemed to stare back. From that instant the bond between mother and son was formed.

"Louis," she murmured, "Louis Harcourt," and the memory of the man who had given him to her but whom she would never see again, who would never see or be seen by his son, suddenly filled her heart with grief as well as joy.

A sympathetic nurse standing next to her noticed her distress and, sensing the reason for it, held out her arms.

"Shall I take the baby from you, Madame, until we make you a little more comfortable?"

"No!" Sandra's arm tightened round him. "No, I want to hold him for as long as I can."

"Sandra, he is *perfectly* all right." The professor gazed at her with professional concern. "He will not run away. We shall take good care of him."

"You don't understand, Marc." She looked gravely up at him. "He's all I have . . ."

"But I do, my dear, I do," the professor said, and Sandra, suddenly realizing how tired she was, allowed him gently to prize her fingers from the baby's arms and the nurse took him with a cooing, soothing sound as though to compensate him for the temporary loss of his mother.

"Louis!" Zac said with a sneer. "Probably after Louis XIV. The Sun King."

"No need to be nasty, Zac," Belle said, with a malicious smile. "Maybe it is after Louis XVI. We know what happened to *him.*"

Zac, breakfasting alone with his sister, looked as though he had not slept and threw down the paper announcing the birth, though, of course, he knew the details already.

"Louis," he murmured again as though the quite ordinary name given to thousands of Frenchmen held some kind of fascination for him. "Will he be Louis Desmond or Louis Harcourt or, maybe, Louis O'Neill." He glanced again malevolently at his sister. "After all, what do we call Sandra these days? No one seems to know.

"She will have to make a pronouncement on it," Zac said drily, spreading his toast, made in the English style, with a thin layer of butter. "Or maybe the cabal, the inner cabinet, will announce it, those trusted advisers like Dericourt and Legrand . . ."

"And Uncle Henri, don't forget," Belle added. Because of her care for her figure she only had half a grapefruit or a slice of melon for breakfast with black coffee and then she added two or three cigarettes to stifle the pangs of hunger.

Belle was a tall, slender woman of aristocratic appearance, a princess from head to toe, though she was only one by marriage. The color of her hair was basically chestnut, but the artifice of her talented hairdresser contributed a good deal to the final result: subtle tones and tints which varied with the season. She was an elegant, but undoubtedly sensuous woman, whose body sent out signals which were often misinterpreted by aspiring lovers. Belle's "come hither" look did not make her as available as she pretended, and few aspirants actually achieved the prize.

Not that Belle valued fidelity and she had long been out of love with her husband, a genial, bluff Austrian educated in England who liked nothing better than a day out with his hounds and his guns, shooting every fur-clad or feathered creature that moved.

Belle looked up from her coffee and saw Zac gazing at her.

"You think Henri Piper is *still* mesmerized by the Californian? You are mistaken, my dear. He is hurt and upset. She did not confide in him about her marriage; he only knew after we did that she was expecting a child. Besides, the jealousy of his wife has got him down, demoralized him. He knows now that Sandra used him, as she used and bamboozled us all.

"I tell you if it comes to the crunch Henri will vote not on the side of his erstwhile protégée, but with us."

"Are you so sure?" Belle glanced at her watch and made an exclamation as though it were later than she thought.

"Oh yes, I'm sure." Zac added a layer of English marmalade to his toast. "He has told me he feels she was not straight about the sale of planes to the Arabs; she used him to smear *me* with the SEC. He does not like being used." Zac's lips curled contemptuously. "He is a fool, our aunt's husband. Our father always considered him a fool, which is why he didn't trust him. Why do *you* think he didn't tell Henri what his intentions were in the event of his death?"

"He told nobody," Belle said bitterly.

"*That* is the strangest part of all." Zac bit on his piece of toast. "He told nobody except his lawyer. Haven't you ever thought it odd the role Laban played in all this?"

"Laban?" Belle screwed up her eyes. "I never thought about him."

"That's it," Zac said with an air of satisfaction. "No one did. One day I am going to find out more about that particular snake in the grass; but"—he wiped his lips with his napkin—"at the moment I have far more important things to see to."

Zac got up and helped himself to more coffee then, on his way back to the table and to her great surprise, pecked his sister's forehead. "Before this year is out, *mon cher coeur,* we shall have reinherited our patrimony. Believe me . . ."

He sat down and began stirring his coffee, a smile of pleasant anticipation on his lips. The pallor of the morning had gone and it looked as though his meager breakfast had restored his vigor and optimism.

"Is there something you're hiding from me, Zac?" Belle inquired, glancing cautiously over her shoulder. "If so there is no need. You know *I* am to be trusted."

"Oh, I know you are to be trusted, my dear," Zac replied, in the same low tone. "But I cannot tell you here. Walls have ears," and he looked meaningfully toward the door. "Just as we are waiting to receive the new mother and her baby I dare not risk telling a soul . . ."

"Zac, you must do nothing to harm the child," Belle said sharply. "That, as a mother, I could not tolerate . . ."

"My dear, am *I* not a father?" Zac looked offended. "Do *I* not care personally for my own two poor children while their mother frolics with her playboy lover in Rome? Of course I would not harm the child . . . oh no. We must make Sandra and her offspring feel welcome and secure at Tourville, the family home. We must lull her into a sense of false security, iron away her fears and worries, dull her suspicions. But, my dear"—he looked at the time and whistled—"I am leaving almost immediately for Rome. I will cut not only the puppy Bob down, but eventually his former 'sister' too. If I have my way I shall wipe them both off the face of the earth."

* * *

Jacques drove very slowly and carefully along the autoroute from Paris toward the city of Reims. But before they reached it they would branch off to follow a road that led south, through the vine-covered sides of the Montagne de Reims, through Passy-Grigny and Verneuil, until they reached the Marne and the road that wound along its bank as far as the Château de Tourville.

Sandra sat in the back of the car, and beside her was Mireille, a nurse she had engaged with the help of Professor Pichon, a young woman but one so capable that the professor did not hesitate to recommend her. Only the best was good enough for Louis Harcourt, and Mireille was one of these. She was twenty-five, a pleasant person with modest looks, but she had a friendly, outgoing personality. As soon as she saw her, Sandra felt instinctively that she trusted and liked her, and in the world of suspicion and intrigue in which she lived she desperately needed faithful and honest retainers.

Mireille was a girl who had seldom strayed outside her native Paris, unless it was to the homes of the well-to-do like Madame Harcourt, and she had little time to study the countryside when she did, or take advantage of its charms. But on this occasion so beautiful were the colors of autumn that her few gestures of appreciation were interpreted by Sandra as favorable and, as such, approved by her.

"Have you been to Champagne before?"

"No, Madame." Mireille shook her head, careful not to disturb the baby sleeping in her arms. "Last time with Monsieur and Madame Carduce I went as far as the Atlantic coast." She said this with some awe as though it were half a continent away instead of a few hundred kilometers.

In many ways she was an ingénue, but she was a fully qualified nursery nurse and anyone Pichon trusted Sandra trusted. Besides, she liked her and it was important to like someone with whom she was going to share a bond of such intimacy.

Louis was eight days old and had already gained weight. Because Pichon believed in the importance of cementing the bond to the mother, Sandra would herself undertake the task of feeding him for as long as she could. For that reason Pichon had demanded that the terminals from the Paris and Reims computers were switched off at Tourville, at least for the time being. Madame, he insisted, must take a complete holiday just to enjoy her baby, and the countryside, the beautiful countryside, of Champagne at its most fruitful time: the time of harvest.

Suddenly Sandra's heart was filled with a sense of joy: of love, peace and gratitude. Maybe after this time of horror things were going to change? Her baby was thriving, her breasts were full of the natural goodness of life, and the Desmond family seemed genuinely to want to embrace her *and* her child.

Maybe, after all, this was indeed a new beginning?

Mireille continued her murmurs of appreciation as they descended the winding road and the magnificent château came into view. She could scarcely contain her cries of amazement as the massive wrought-iron gates swung open and the stately Rolls was driven slowly up the long, tree-lined drive. As she stepped out of the car, Sandra had a special smile for Pierre, the Desmond butler who had greeted her on her first visit four years before. Was it *only* four years? It seemed like more.

He bowed as he helped her out of the car.

"Welcome home, Madame Harcourt, and welcome to the little one." Pierre's eyes smiled kindly as he turned to assist the nurse and, for a moment, he took the baby from her arms and held him in his own, his face wreathed with delight.

"He is *very* handsome, Madame," he said, carefully handing the baby back to his nurse.

"Oh, Pierre, it is much too early to tell!" Sandra smiled and then went up to each of the staff in turn and shook their hands as they greeted and congratulated her.

Then, as she came to the end of the line, the bobs, bows and curtsies, she looked up to see a familiar, formidable figure emerging from the doors, as if timing her appearance carefully, and, for a moment, she thought that the smile was slow to appear on Lady Elizabeth's face. But maybe it was her imagination.

"Welcome, Sandra," she said, greeting her with a kiss on each cheek. "Welcome to you and your lovely baby. The little prince. Louis . . ."

"This is Mireille, Lady Elizabeth, whom I have engaged to look after my son."

"How do you do, Mademoiselle?" Lady Elizabeth said and it was obvious at once that, though her command of French was perfect, it was not her native tongue. Georges Desmond had married the daughter of an English aristocrat, and his wife had always maintained an essential Englishness that manifested itself in tiny ways, not only in her and her children, but in the English bread that was served, toasted, for breakfast in addition to croissants or brioches, and the taking of afternoon tea precisely at four o'clock, usually in the main salon, whether she had company or whether she was alone.

Lady Elizabeth spent some time gazing at the infant and then nodded her approval.

"He is a dear little thing," she said, "but you must be tired, Sandra. Tea is ready . . . and then you and I must have a little chat."

"Of course, Lady Elizabeth."

Why did the feeling of joy go from her heart as though someone had cast a stone in its place? Why did a frisson steal over her? Maybe it was that the expression in those hooded eyes was enigmatic, unfathomable. Maybe there was a chill in the smile.

Lady Elizabeth Desmond was, after all, the mother of Zac and Belle and like them there was inevitably an air of mystery, sometimes a hint of menace, behind the kindly look in her eyes and the ostensibly friendly smile.

"I thought we would take tea in the conservatory," Lady Elizabeth said, as Sandra descended the broad staircase into the hall, where two of her Dalmatian dogs lay by the open door giving the whole ambience an air of graciousness and ease. Lady Elizabeth had changed from the afternoon dress in which she had received Sandra and her baby, and wore the old garden smock Sandra could recall from the first time she had met her, a long-sleeved, ankle-length garment not unlike a nun's habit, made of a coarse, gray material. On her head was the same hat, or one very similar, of yellow straw secured under the chin by a trailing chiffon scarf. Her beauty had hardly changed over the years, Sandra thought, taking her hand, aware once again of the old-fashioned perfume of violets when Lady Elizabeth offered her soft, powdery cheeks to be kissed.

"Do you feel rested now, dear?" Lady Elizabeth tucked an arm through Sandra's and the dogs bounded to their feet as the two women went to the front door, descending the five stone steps to the ground before they began their walk round the house to the conservatory.

In many ways it had an appearance now of neglect, as after the court case in England Lady Elizabeth had stayed behind as a guest of her brother Lord Broughton at his stately home of Farley Hall.

However, now, as on that first occasion, the atmosphere was tense even though Lady Elizabeth made an effort to ease it as she chatted about the shrubs or the trees that they passed in the garden, before entering the complex of greenhouses with their tropical plants: camellia, orchids and the white funnel-shaped polyanthus tuberose which were Lady Elizabeth's speciality.

"Pierre will serve us tea on the lawn as he did the first day we met, Sandra." Lady Elizabeth indicated a wrought-iron table and two comfortable chairs under the large, old oak tree. "It was four years ago, was it not, Sandra, that you first came to Tourville?"

Sandra nodded and took a chair just as Pierre appeared from the side of the house, followed by a footman and a maid bearing trays.

Yes indeed, little appeared to have changed.

"It was August," Sandra said.

"And what a lot has happened since." Lady Elizabeth took a seat beside her, nodding her thanks to Pierre as he directed the footman and the maid to lay out the exquisite porcelain cups, saucers and tea plates, the dainty cucumber and tomato sandwiches *à l'anglaise,* the fairy cakes topped with icing and glacé cherries, with green angelica to form the delicate branches.

"We will see to it ourselves, thank you, Pierre," Lady Elizabeth said graciously, nodding to Pierre, who seemed, however, to look at Sandra before giving the orders to withdraw. Sandra saw his expression and nodded too.

Because it was she, not Lady Elizabeth, who was in charge now.

Lady Elizabeth lifted the lid of the Queen Anne silver teapot, expertly inspected the contents and began to pour.

"I see Pierre wanted your permission, my dear," she observed in a low voice.

"I hoped you wouldn't have noticed."

"But it *is* your home. Georges left it to you. That was the painful part."

"I know."

She wanted to take Lady Elizabeth's hand and comfort her but she didn't dare. They had never had that kind of relationship.

"We are only here under sufferance."

"That's not true at all," Sandra protested, leaning back in her chair and gazing earnestly at Lady Elizabeth. "Zac said he wanted bygones to be bygones and so do I. I want us all to make a new beginning and work together. We have all had time to reflect, and we now know that nothing very good can come out of this continual fighting and discord."

"This is a time of reconciliation, not conflict, Sandra. I have returned here as you requested, and my children will come and go as freely as they please. I am sure that is what you wish." She paused, gazing interrogatively at Sandra who, however, deliberately did not reply.

Interpreting her silence to mean she agreed, Lady Elizabeth offered Sandra the plate of sandwiches; but Sandra was not hungry and shook her head.

"No, thank you, Lady Elizabeth."

"You must eat, dear. You have your baby to think of."

"Perhaps I'll have a cake, then," Sandra replied. "They look delicious. I remember these from the old days."

"Fairy cakes, my favorite from when I was a little girl," Lady Elizabeth sighed. "You see, Sandra, I have lived a very long and, in many ways, difficult life. Georges Desmond was not an easy man. He openly kept a mistress. He abruptly disinherited our eldest son without a word to me or anyone close to him. We then had to accept you, a complete stranger, in our midst. In the past year Zac and Tara have separated, perhaps they will divorce . . . Belle flits about doing this and that. Claire, well . . ." Lady Elizabeth pursed her lips. "We don't really approve of her husband, a street artist . . . Tim—" Here she paused and sighed. "I wish *he* would settle down. He is too restless. Perhaps one day he'll come home. I would like him to have married into the English aristocracy . . . he had *every* opportunity. Debutantes threw themselves at him. But then I suppose I am a snob."

"Where is Zac?" Sandra, intent on changing the subject, decided the cakes, after all, were so good she would have another.

"In Paris," Lady Elizabeth murmured after a pause. "It really *would* be nice, my dear, if he could be more active on the Board of Desmond again. I think you would find him a great help. He really is so anxious to be helpful." Sandra carefully avoided meeting Lady Elizabeth's eyes. "He really loves Tara and would like her to return to him. He is much changed since she left him. The events of recent years have, I think, made him a different person."

Different, Sandra thought, not nicer. But the circumstances of the occasion made her keep her thoughts to herself.

"Lady Elizabeth," she said abruptly, "I for my part will do all I can, from this day on, to normalize relations between the Desmonds and myself. I intend to keep the name 'Desmond' but, for the sake of Louis, it must be hyphenated to the name of Harcourt. For the sake of simplicity I shall be known as Madame Harcourt. I will do everything I can to make life easy and as pleasurable as possible for us all. However, as for Zac being more active on the Board"—she paused and pursed her lips—"I shall have to give the matter more thought." Yet even as she said the words she remembered Romanetto and the unsatisfactory, off-hand way Zac had dealt with her questions. Twenty-five million dollars indeed; as if the sum were a mere bagatelle.

"I do hope you can." Lady Elizabeth smiled confidently as she poured fresh tea. "Zac's so anxious to be a real brother to you. Believe me, dear, he really is."

And her smile was one of such trusting charm and ingenuousness that for a moment Sandra almost believed her.

After feeding Louis, Sandra sat for a long time in her low nursing chair holding the baby closely in her arms, enjoying this precious moment alone with him. In the nursery next door she could hear Mireille moving quietly about preparing his cot for the night. A great silence seemed to have descended on Tourville and she almost fancied she could hear the leaves sighing in the trees, the waters of the Marne gently flowing by; but, of course, she could not. It was a still night and nothing stirred; but a curious sense of peace filled her heart and she realized that the joy of her baby had to some extent replaced her grief at the loss of his father.

Pichon was right. It was good not to have the faxes stuttering out, the whirr of the computer machinery as it kept her up to date with the Desmond operations on which the sun never set. In each continent the group was engaged in some activity: machine tools, newspapers, aeronautics, the manufacture of computer software and, in the heart of Champagne, the wine itself.

She had often told herself that in her hectic, frenetic, jet-set life, she had lost touch with the core of the empire: champagne.

Maybe now that she had a few quiet weeks to herself while Antoine Dericourt, long-time ally and recently promoted to group assistant managing director, oversaw the business for her, it would be good to tour the vineyards with René Latour, trusted *chef de cave,* who had taught her all she knew about champagne, discerning even in those early days an excellent palate. A natural palate, he had told her. She would take a further look at the core business and go over the affairs of the whole group worldwide. It was while she relaxed from her hectic life-style that the really creative decisions could be made.

Sandra spent the next hour helping Mireille put Louis to bed. She enjoyed talking to the simple woman who had no cares, no apparent hangups, and great affection for her charge, whose pleasures in life were few but who, seemingly, enjoyed immersing herself in her job. Maybe that was why she and Sandra had so much in common.

There was five years' difference between herself and Mireille but they got on well, a relationship based on mutual liking and understanding as well as respect.

"And what did you think of Lady Elizabeth?" Sandra asked, as Mireille started folding the clothes and nappies that she had unpacked from the many suitcases that had followed on from Paris in another car.

Mireille's face remained discreetly blank and Sandra looked at her with surprise.

"Don't you find her charming?"

"Very much the '*grande dame*'," Mireille said offhandedly.

"Well," Sandra replied, "she *is* a *grande dame.* She is the daughter of an English earl and her husband was one of the richest men in France, if not the world."

"Ah!" But Mireille did not seem to think this sufficient to explain what she felt about Lady Elizabeth, and Sandra was curious to know more because she thought the woman she employed was a good judge of character.

"Come on . . . tell me, Mireille. It will go no further. She is no relation of mine and, until recently, we were not on speaking terms. You can say what you like, and it would interest me to know your real opinion of Lady Elizabeth. Honestly."

"Then, Madame, if you ask me . . ." Mireille knelt on the floor as she opened the bottom drawer of a chest and laid the fragrant, freshly folded towelling nappies inside. "If you *really* want to know what I think, and it is only my opinion, I would not trust her. If what you told me in the car about her family is true, that you superseded her son, then I think you can *never* trust her. She is very beautiful and agreeable and has all the charm in the world; but if you look at her carefully you will observe that it is only her mouth that smiles. The light in those English blue eyes is as cold as steel."

Sandra finished her toilette for dinner, clipped on a pair of ruby earrings that were a wedding present from Michel, letting her hands linger on them as she did so.

Had she loved him passionately enough? Had she been selfish? Had she *really* caused his death? There were so many mysteries, so many questions to which she did not know the answer.

Now Mireille, that shrewd observer of human nature, had put in her mind a whole new set of doubts about the sincerity of Lady Elizabeth, doubts in fact about the motives of all the Desmonds who were trying so hard, so obviously, to be nice to her.

Why?

She looked at herself in the mirror for a moment and saw a rather sad-eyed woman approaching thirty, with gold-blonde hair, aquamarine eyes of a colour that turned men's heads, a fine bone structure and an almost flawless complexion. Despite the birth of her son she knew her figure still looked good. She did not need to be vain to know she was beautiful. Only she hoped she was level-headed and sensible too.

For how long would she remain a widow? She did not know and she did not care because desire was dead and, as far as she was concerned, the only reason to enjoy life, to believe in it, was her baby.

She dabbed some perfume behind her ears and was about to go to the door when she heard the preliminary noise a telephone makes before it rings. Rapidly she picked up the receiver.

"Hello?"

There was a crackle of static over the phone.

"*Pronto.* This is a call from Roma, Italy. Is that Lady Elizabeth Desmond, please?"

"Who wishes to know?" Sandra asked in her own fluent Italian, her pulse racing.

There was a pause and then the voice said: "This is the Hotel Excelsior. Signor Zac Desmond wishes to speak to his mother. Who is speaking please?"

"Hello." Sandra heard the sound of Lady Elizabeth's voice as she answered on an extension.

"Is that Lady Elizabeth Desmond?"

"It is."

"I have your son on the phone for you, Madame. Wait, please. Signor Desmond . . ."

Quickly Sandra depressed the key, hoping that Lady Elizabeth would not hear it.

So Zac was in Italy, and his mother had said he was in Paris.

Why should she lie?

Slowly she made her way out of her room and along the corridor, halting at the head of the stairs so that she would not take Lady Elizabeth by surprise. Not let her know that she had been caught out in a lie.

Mireille was right and she, Sandra, had committed yet another act of folly.

With all that had gone before how could she ever think it possible to trust a Desmond?

4

Bob ran his hands down Tara's narrow waist as it broadened out to her rounded hips, her full buttocks which, viewed naked from behind, sent a frisson of ecstasy the length of his body.

As he raised his legs her rhythm increased, the cleavage between her buttocks widened and he gave a sudden gasp as the fluid drained from him.

Tara remained, still astride him, rocking gently to and fro. Then she bent herself, with the grace of a ballet dancer, backwards toward him so that their bodies were parallel and he could grasp her breasts and hold them. For several moments they remained like that, locked. Then gracefully, again in a movement reminiscent of the ballet, she rose and lay the other way, face down, her legs on either side of his face.

He kissed her feet, each toe, and she kissed his.

"I never guessed you were so sexy," she murmured.

"I knew you were," he said. "Everything about you is sexy, and I knew it the moment I saw you. Remember?"

"The night at Tourville," Tara said. "I think Zac deliberately left us together."

"But why should he?" Bob drew his mouth away from her ankle, looking puzzled.

"He liked to tease. He knew I liked younger men."

"You mean he *threw* us together?" Bob's eyebrows knitted

and he felt a diminution of desire. He gently eased her body away from his and, as she curled up beside him, his eyes fixed angrily on the ceiling.

"You're cross now," she said. "But you shouldn't be. You must realize, Bob, that everything Zac does is abnormal. He *liked* his wife to be admired by other men."

"You mean it was a 'turn-on'?" He looked at her savagely.

"You know he raped me," she said plaintively. "It was the thought of Livio and me making love in a garage. Some men are like that. If he knew we were here he'd feel the same. Oh, Bob." Protectively she threw her arms around him. "He must *never* know. You know what happened to Livio."

"But no one could prove Zac was behind that."

"*Everyone* knew Zac was behind it. It was an underworld killing that Zac initiated."

"Jeeze!" Bob wriggled uncomfortably. "Perhaps you should think twice about asking for a divorce."

"He doesn't know you're here." She reached for the packet by the side of her bed and drew out a cigarette. Bob didn't like her smoking and he wished she wouldn't. He was a clean-living, all-American boy and he thought it was a dirty habit. Her breath smelt and that was the only thing he disliked about making love to her: the taste of nicotine in her mouth.

Otherwise she was perfect.

She was thirty-six and he was twenty-two; he at his peak, she at hers. They were a terrific combination, sexually highly compatible.

How long could such perfection last?

"I wish you wouldn't smoke," he said as she put down her lighter and exhaled deeply.

"I'll give it up one day, I promise," she said. "When the strain is gone . . ."

"When we're married?"

"Oh, before then," she said lightly. "*That* won't be for ages."

Bob sat up and thumped the pillow on which he had rested his head.

"You always say that and yet I don't see why it should be. I've always said this was for keeps."

"Zac won't give in so easily."

"He's done nothing to try and find you."

"He's been to see Marco."

"How do you know?" Bob uneasily settled his head back on the pillow.

"Marco said I should keep a low profile."

"You didn't tell me that." His tone was petulant, like a small boy, and she was reminded again how young he was, how really undeveloped emotionally, as though there were a yawning chasm between his mature body and his college mind.

"I don't want to upset you, Bob. I don't want this to pass. Yet I'm scared that, one day, you'll leave me."

"You know that's impossible. I went to a lot of trouble to find you, didn't I?"

She threw back the sheet and sat on the side of the bed. He tried to clasp her once again, but she skipped lithely away from him over to the washbasin in the corner of the room. Beyond that there was a shower and toilet. No bathroom. It was a hole, no doubt, and he didn't know how a woman brought up as she had been, the daughter of one of the most illustrious Italian families, could stand such a place. But when he thought that, he remembered the Palazzo Falconetti and it explained her capacity for adapting from one life-style to another.

She might be used now to great wealth, but she had grown accustomed to great poverty too.

There was a mirror over the basin and, as she sluiced her body, he could see her breasts. The water trickled down her back and between her buttocks. He wished she would turn round so that he could see the pubic hair that sprang like a dark bush from her loins.

She turned round suddenly, flirtatiously, causing Bob to bound off the bed and seize her, trying to drag her back on it again; but she pretended to be reluctant and in the end he roughly picked her up while she kicked out her legs, and threw her on the bed again.

Suddenly Tara opened her eyes and, peering beyond him, the expression of joy, of teasing, changed in a second to horror. Seeing her expression, Bob leapt away from her just as his shoulder was seized and a punch in his back sent him reeling to the floor.

A small, squat, very ugly man, no taller than five feet, stood there, flexing and unflexing his hands, which were powerful and oversized in relation to the rest of his body. The door behind him was open but, his eyes fixed on Tara and her undignified posture on the bed, he unzipped his trousers, muttering under his breath: "Whore, whore," and, watched with speechless terror by Tara, he stepped out of his trousers and stood in his underpants. Crawling painfully across the floor, like a dog, Bob managed to sink his teeth into the stranger's leg and bite on it as hard as he could.

"Shit!" the stranger screamed, knocking Bob sideways on the head before he, too, fell to the floor, clasping his wounded leg from which blood was oozing.

Tara rose rapidly, winding the sheet round herself.

"Bob!" she cried, running over to him.

"I'll whip you for that, you puppy," the man cried. "I'll whip you until the skin comes away from your flesh."

Suddenly another man appeared at the door, his hands in his trouser pockets. No one was quite sure how long he had been there.

"You never do it right, do you, Niki?" he drawled. "You always get involved with the birds."

"With a broad who's asking for it." Niki gestured obscenely toward Tara who had run quickly into the bathroom.

"She is the wife of an important man," the stranger said. "You think he'd like to know she was screwed by you? You nearly made a great boo-boo there, Niki. Now . . ." The man gestured to Bob. "Get your clothes on."

"What do you want?" Bob, conscious of his nudity, had

reached for his jeans which he draped protectively over his intimate parts.

"I want you to get dressed and mind your own business," the man said in broken English. "Then shut your mouth and keep it shut and do exactly as you're told. That way no one gets hurt."

The man contemptuously stirred Niki with his foot.

"Put your trousers back on and *beg* me to say nothing about this, or you are as good as dead . . ."

"But I did *nothing,*" Niki whined, clearly in awe of his companion.

"It is what you were *going* to do," the man replied. But he didn't seem seriously annoyed, as though he operated on a low fuse. He was about the same age as Niki but tall. He looked like a business man, in a grey suit, his face neatly shaved, his thick hair parted at the side. He was a fleshy, sensuous man who at the same time looked very dangerous.

Tara came out of the bathroom fastening the belt of her jeans over a tight, figure-hugging sweater. She wore no brassiere and the outline of her breasts was as provocative as if she'd been naked.

"Who are you?" she snapped in Italian. "What do you want? If it's money I have none, but my husband . . ."

"Oh, no, it is not *money,* Signora," the stranger said politely. "And I apologize for the behavior of this animal here." He poked Niki with his foot again. "Get off the floor, you cretin, and you"—he pointed sharply to Bob—"go and get some clothes on, and quick about it."

Still holding his jeans over his genitals, Bob obeyed with alacrity while the man on the floor sat nursing the wound on his leg, clenching his teeth as though the pain were excruciating.

"He's probably poisoned me," he moaned. "I'm going to die."

Tara, with a bored air, went over to the bedside table and, taking a cigarette from the packet, lit it.

"If it's money—" she said again.

"I said it was *not* money," the man replied politely, also drawing a cigarette out of a flashy gold case from his breast pocket. "I'm afraid we have to take your boyfriend away for a while." He drew carefully on his cigarette. "It won't be for long . . ."

"Bob!" Tara sat down heavily on the bed again. "Bob has done *nothing* . . ." She stopped and looked at the man. "Are you from my husband?"

The man studied his cigarette.

"I can't say who sent us, Signora. Indeed, I do not know. I am given my orders and I carry them out. That is the truth . . ."

"Bob has no money . . ."

"I am simply under orders, Signora," he said calmly, continuing to stare disapprovingly at Niki who, clearly still feeling groggy, was trying to get into his trousers without covering them in the blood that soaked through his handkerchief.

"You're making a *meal* of this, Niki," he said angrily. "Hurry now."

"That creep bit me through to the bone," Niki continued to whine. "I could bleed to death."

The man in the suit raised his eyes to heaven and smiled at Tara as if in conspiracy. In fact, she rather liked him.

At that moment Bob came out of the shower room dressed in jeans and a T-shirt, running a comb through his hair.

The man in the suit then moved with surprising agility and, crossing the room, seized him by the arm.

"Bob," Tara said in a tearful voice. "It's you they want, not me."

"It's a kidnap?" Bob looked incredulous. "Oh Christ—why . . ."

The man in the suit drew a small pistol from his breast pocket and, sticking it hard in the small of Bob's back, motioned to the door.

"Get going," he said, with a pleasant smile at Tara.

"Ciao, Signora."

After him limped Niki, leaving behind him a trail of blood. As Bob turned to Tara, Niki hit him in the face with a good deal of satisfaction and Tara could then hear Bob half stumbling, half falling down the stairs until the door to the street closed with a heavy bang.

Just then Tara heard a car starting up outside; but she felt too weak to move.

Marco Falconetti, gnawing at a fingernail, looked at his sister as if she were an embarrassment. Crouched in the corner of one of his huge chairs she seemed like a small waif brought in from the storm. She hadn't stopped sobbing for an hour and, in another corner, Marco's friend Bruno gazed petulantly into his glass of wine and, from time to time, sighed deeply.

Tara had waited until dark before packing her bags and leaving the flat, taking a taxi to the Palazzo Falconetti where she found her brother and Bruno about to go out to dine.

The sight of Marco had released all the emotion she had held back and, flinging her arms round his neck, she had clung to him until he had been forced to return to the salon with its decayed tapestries, moth-eaten rugs and traces of former glory. Bruno, who was hungry, sulked and kept on darting venomous glances at Marco.

"I can't leave my sister," Marco said offhandedly. "Tara, do you want to eat with us? Bruno is hungry."

Tara shook her head and Bruno stood up.

"I'll be going then," he announced.

"No, I'll come with you."

"Oh, please . . . please don't go. Don't leave me, Marco." Tara looked up at him through her fingers.

"Well then, come with us. It's dark. No one will see you. Besides, what are you afraid of, Tara? They came for Bob, not you."

"Yes, but Zac was behind it," Tara spat viciously at him. "You *know* Zac was behind it."

"How can you be sure?" Marco, seeming completely unperturbed by the whole affair, reached for the tall Venetian goblet which still had a little wine in it and drained it. "Have you forgotten the connection between Bob and that other notorious 'member' of your family? Mademoiselle O'Neill, or whatever she now calls herself, is not without enemies. Whoever took your lover is far more likely to be connected with someone with a grudge against *her.* If you ask me, my dear sister, you're barking up the wrong tree."

Marco had little sympathy for his sister; a man wrapped up in himself and his succession of boyfriends, he had very little family feeling. His three brothers were successful professional men, his other sisters mostly married and safely out of the way. One had become a nun and languished in some strict order in the Tuscan hills, out of sight and largely out of mind.

Marco, the heir to a title with no assets, no money and only liabilities, had been hard put himself to make ends meet. He had little sympathy for a sister married to a very wealthy man who treated him as badly as Tara did Zac. Zac had frequently come to Marco's rescue financially and, indeed, owned half the Palazzo Falconetti. From time to time he had toyed with the idea of turning it into a hotel; but Marco, a master of procrastination, had so far resisted.

Bruno got up and joined his friend by the huge marble fireplace in front of which stood an urn of dried flowers, some years old if one were to judge by the thickness of the layer of dust covering them. This gloomy room, hedged in by narrow streets, was called the summer room although it seldom saw the sun. The winter room, scarcely more cheerful, had a fire in the winter and curtains that actually met in the middle to keep out the draft.

"*Are* you coming with us, Tara?" Marco reiterated, gazing at Bruno as Tara shook her head.

"Then we'll leave you. You'll be all right. If they'd wanted to take you they would have. They won't come looking for you now."

Marco bent down and gazed severely at his sister, shaking a finger in her face. "If you take my advice, my dear, you'll get on the telephone and you'll *beg* Zac to take you back. If you ask me you need protection, and he is the man to give it to you."

Sandra, her hands deep in the pockets of her coat, toured the underground cellars with Étienne Legrand, director general of the Éstablissements de Champagne Desmond, and Raymond Jourdan, the recently retired *chef de cave*. The wine from the new vintage had just been poured into large vats above ground where it would undergo the process of the first fermentation.

In the caves which stretched for miles under the imposing Desmond headquarters were millions of bottles, some lying on their sides, some in racks and others slowly turning on the mechanized *pupitres* which had replaced riddling by hand (a long and tedious process) in the days of the great Veuve Desmond, great-grandmother of Zac and his brothers and sisters.

"Nothing changes," Sandra said with a shudder of cold as she stood watching it. She turned to Legrand and gave him a smile whose radiance temporarily dispelled the chill. "It seems no time at all, does it, since you showed me round when I first joined the group?"

"No time at all, Madame." Legrand returned the smile. "And how much you have achieved . . ."

"And lost," Sandra murmured.

"Personally I am not in a position to speak, Madame." Raymond Jourdan stepped forward. "But, from the point of view of the fortunes of Desmond Champagne, your success has been remarkable. We now export twice the number of bottles we did before, especially to America, and that is despite the disaster of the vintage two years ago . . . which was not your fault," he added hastily.

"I was fortunate in the man we chose as our overseas marketing director," Sandra said. "Jonathan Dudley was, and is, first class in his job. We have not always been so lucky. Not long ago I learned that the man who was in charge of the group's activities in Geneva disappeared after embezzling a large amount of money just before I came."

"Bernardo Romanetto," Étienne Legrand murmured. "Yet he had been with the company since he was a young man. He was trusted by Monsieur Georges Desmond.

"Greed overcomes many people." Sandra nodded her head. "One day we will find Romanetto and ensure he returns the money; unfortunately so much time has passed and I have had so much on my plate."

"Understandable, Madame." Legrand's tone was sympathetic. "You have suffered grief, but also a great happiness. Madame . . ." He stopped as if he had not quite made up his mind either about what to say or how to put it.

"Yes?" Sandra looked at him encouragingly as they moved along, past the mechanized *pupitres,* the racked bottles, or those which were already standing upright ready to be transported aboveground for the *dégorgement.* The bottle was then topped up with cane sugar dissolved in wine (the *dosage*), recorked and sent on its way to the consumer.

"Maybe it is not my place to say it, Madame," Legrand continued after a pause, "but I have consulted with my colleagues here and it would give them the greatest pleasure if . . ."

"Oh, go on, Étienne, what is it?" Sandra's tone was teasing as she saw the bashful expression on his face.

"Last year was an exceptional year, Madame, a year for us to declare a great vintage. We wondered if you would permit a special blend to be made in honor of your son, as we did for the two-hundredth anniversary of the foundation of the firm, the Cuvée du Bicentenaire, and, perhaps, named after him: Louis d'Or. Would you permit that, Madame Harcourt?"

Sandra's hand flew to her mouth and now she was the one feeling embarrassed. "What a charming idea, Étienne. How *very* thoughtful and kind. How could I possibly refuse?"

"We would deem it an honor." Legrand grew more enthusiastic. "It is not done on the spur of the moment, Madame. We and our colleagues have all given it a great deal of thought and much discussion. We have appreciated what you have done for us, what difficulties you have faced, how you have tackled them." Legrand glanced at his companion who stared at the ground. "Something you may not be aware of, Madame, is that we all come from families who have worked in these caves for generations and we and our forebears were all devoted to Monsieur Georges Desmond and his father and grandfather before him. We of this generation were less than enchanted with his son, despite the undoubted grasp Monsieur Zac had of the business, the excellence of his palate. He and his sister, the Princess, interfered too much; they were too demanding, dictatorial, and did not let us get on with our work.

"We were, naturally though, shocked by the terms of Monsieur Georges's will. We are a traditional people disliking surprises. We were relieved when you proved yourself not only such an excellent businesswoman, with the ability to swiftly assimilate the finer points in the manufacture of our great wine, but also tactful, firm and unfailingly courteous in your dealings with us. In addition you showed that you, yourself, were the possessor of an excellent, natural palate.

"That what we all privately thought of Monsieur Zac was justified may be demonstrated by the fact that he let millions of liters of our superb wine go down the drain over the business of the *tirage.* For there is no doubt, Madame, as you know, that Monsieur Strega, his assistant, did not act by himself. He even rewarded Monsieur Strega with the purchase of a fine house in the forest of Verzy."

"Did he indeed?" Sandra said thoughtfully.

"Many of us commented on it. Little that goes on hereabouts escapes us, not that we see anything of Monsieur Strega. After the affair of the *tirage* he keeps well away from Reims. But he is known in Épernay," Legrand went on darkly, "and sometimes he says a little too much when he has too much to drink. He is indiscreet. He felt indignant over the matter of the *tirage* and resentful."

"In that case it's a wonder Monsieur Zac continues to employ him."

"Maybe he does not know; but Monsieur Strega has little love for his master. However . . ." Legrand seemed to think they had said too much and continued in a lighter tone, "We have a little lunch prepared upstairs, Madame. We do hope on this occasion you will consent to be our guest."

Upstairs the table in the boardroom had been laid to accommodate half a dozen people. Besides Legrand, Jourdan and herself there were Antoine Dericourt, now her number two, who had worked his way up in the group, and Jonathan Dudley, a Californian like herself who had worked in his own family vineyards in the Napa Valley before they were bought by Desmond a few years before.

Like her, Jonathan was bilingual and only French was spoken. The sixth member of the party was Gustave Havet, the son of an old friend of the Desmonds, Baron Havet, who had also lately joined the company to gain experience before taking over the running of his own firm.

Before the meal Legrand, who acted as host, made a short speech in which he offered Sandra condolences on the cruel death of her husband. "It was unimaginably sad," he said, "that at the height of his career, in the joy of his marriage to Madame and his prospect of becoming a father, he should be so cruelly taken. Our most heartfelt condolences to Madame, to her family and infant son.

"However . . ." Legrand raised his head and looked at the small, attentive group. "I am delighted to tell you that a short time ago I spoke to Madame Harcourt about our idea that we should make a special *cuvée* in honor of the infant heir Louis and she has graciously accepted. We shall choose some of our finest and oldest blends and the result should be ready for drinking in a year's time." He held up his glass. "To Louis d'Or."

"Louis d'Or," echoed the group and, raising their glasses, they turned to Sandra. She accepted the compliment but said nothing, smiling graciously as the speech was concluded.

It was, as usual, an excellent meal, superbly cooked by the chef who had provided boardroom meals for the Desmonds for twenty years.

Next to Sandra young Gustave was telling her about his own family plans for a celebration vintage. He was to be married and his bride was also a *champenoise,* her father a *négociant* at Épernay.

"I wish you every happiness," Sandra said. "You must bring your fiancée to dinner . . ." She paused and glanced round the table, then said, sotto voce, "I am thinking of buying a house in Reims, of spending more time here."

Next to her, Legrand, however, couldn't help overhearing. "But, Madame," he said, "Tourville is no distance at all."

"It is not really *mine,* Étienne," Sandra replied. "I have always regarded it as the home of the Desmonds and, much as I love it, I have found it difficult to feel at home there. Lady Elizabeth has returned from England and now Madame Tara Desmond, I hear, is to return from Italy."

The men made polite but incredulous noises at this piece of news which Sandra herself had only just heard. It had worried her because there had been no mention of Bob. Bob had also failed to collect the substantial check she had dispatched to the Banco di Roma, as he had said he wanted to buy an apartment. She didn't know where Bob was and her only address for him was care of the bank. Bob had been a trial as a teenager and even though he was one no longer he seemed unable or unwilling quite to grow up.

"I shall buy a house in the center of Reims and spend more time here." Sandra smiled. "My son will go to school here with the Jesuits. Oh yes, he will be baptized a Catholic like his father and I will bring him up according to the rites of the Church."

"Bravo, Madame." The elderly Jourdan, who was a daily communicant, clearly approved. "I cannot but commend what you said, and let us hope that, in due course, young Louis will follow you as head of the Desmond Group."

Suddenly Sandra felt as though the door had opened and a

cold breeze had blown through it. She looked round but it was closed.

"Please don't say that," she said. "It seems to be tempting fate."

"But it will happen, Madame, it will happen," Jourdan promised her, touching his heart. "I feel it here."

Sandra had been looking at the faces round the table. They were in their various ways loyal to her. Suddenly something struck her and she looked around the table again, counting heads. Someone was missing.

"Where is René?" she asked. "Was he not invited?"

"Ah!" Legrand seemed embarrassed and turned to Jourdan for support. "Well, Madame . . ."

"He did not wish to come, Madame Harcourt," Jourdan said. "He was invited but declined. Alas, I am afraid he has not forgotten the unfortunate business of the *tirage.* For a time, you will remember, he was under suspicion."

"Oh, but not by me," Sandra protested. "It was never for a moment in *my* mind that he was responsible."

"Nevertheless, he felt it very keenly," Jourdan said. "He was sure that, for a time, you did not trust him."

"But he is still *chef de cave,*" Sandra protested. "We have still to decide together on the *tirage* for this year."

"That will be *business,* Madame," Jourdan said tactfully. "The Tasting Committee is business. René would never neglect that. This luncheon is a social occasion in your honor." Jourdan shook his head. "Regretfully he did not wish to attend."

After lunch Sandra took Dericourt, Dudley and Gustave Havet to her office to discuss the plans for the year.

Antoine Dericourt was a staunch ally and friend; but he was a grey man, with little personality. As a number two, however, he was first class. Loyal, honorable, and very good at his job. Dudley had more style to him, but he would never settle in France, though he liked to visit as often as he could. The young Gustave Havet, though an excellent marketing manager, would inevitably return in time to his own family firm.

"Antoine." Sandra turned to Dericourt who had taken his place next to her. "This business with Romanetto is unsettling."

"Romanetto?" Dericourt appeared puzzled. "But that was four years ago, Sandra, just before you joined the group."

"That is why it worries me. I should have been told about it. I should have known."

"I think everyone thought then that it was past business, in the time of Monsieur Georges Desmond."

"Yes, but twenty-five million US dollars is a lot of money. It simply disappeared, and Romanetto with it."

"That's exactly what happened, Madame." Dericourt seemed nonplussed. "Of course, the whole group was thrown into confusion not only by Monsieur Desmond's sudden and tragic death, but by your appointment. For a time there was a sharp fall in the price of shares."

"I still can't understand why no one took it more seriously. For instance, where did Romanetto go?"

"There was a rumour it was the Far East."

"And no one followed *that* up?" Sandra looked incredulous.

Dericourt wriggled uncomfortably. "I think Zac wanted it hushed up. It reflected on him for not keeping tight enough control. It was his department and he was already out of favor with his father. He was particularly concerned that *you* should not find out because it would confirm the idea that you were rapidly reaching independently anyway: that he was incapable of running the company."

"It was never a cover-up?" Sandra demanded, tapping her fingers furiously on her desk.

"Not exactly . . ." Dericourt seemed unsure.

"But I should have been told that twenty-five million dollars had been embezzled. I suppose it had nothing to do with Zac"—she gave a wry smile—"in view of what we have since learned about his reputation for honesty."

"Oh, I *don't* think so." Dericourt looked more and more confused. "I mean why would he . . . embezzle money from his own company," he continued lamely.

"*I* can think of plenty of reasons. He has, after all, cost us many millions since. Now, Antoine, when you return to Paris I want you to find out all you can about Romanetto and how, if at all, Zac was implicated in it . . ."

"But why now, Sandra?" Antoine looked puzzled. "Why *now?* This happened a long time ago."

"Because it is important," she said sharply. "I was shocked when I found out about it and it bothers me still." She stabbed her finger on a piece of paper in front of her and held it out. "Romanetto, Antoine. I want all the facts, the amounts and what was done to find him and by whom, in detail. I want this information as soon as possible."

"Very well, Sandra." Antoine knew his boss and to argue with her was pointless. "I'll see what I can do." He turned to Dudley, with whom he disagreed about the merit of Californian wine, when there was a sharp tap at the door and everyone looked up.

"Come in," Sandra called and the smile on her face was replaced by one of concern at the expression on her secretary's face.

"Is anything the matter . . .?" she began.

"Madame," Antoinette said, interrupting her. Then she thrust a piece of paper into her hand and stood back while Sandra read it.

At first she was silent then, aware of the interest of the people round the table, cleared her throat and began to read in a steady voice: "Regret to inform you that Bob O'Neill has been kidnapped by unidentified men. A ransom of twenty million pounds sterling is demanded, or else he will be executed." It was signed by her agent in Rome: Arnold Parracini.

The room, at that moment, and the people in it resembled a tableau made of wax.

No one seemed to move, nothing stirred, as though caught in time and petrified.

5

"Madame Harcourt is getting too interested in Romanetto," Strega said, looking slyly at Zac.

"What? What?" Zac scowled but didn't take his eyes from the busy scene in the Avenue de l'Opéra as he stood by the window, turning over the change in his pocket as if his mind were preoccupied with other things.

In fact with good reason. There were plenty of things on his mind. He seemed to have a finger in this pie, a finger in that, all with one object: the ultimate removal of the woman he still thought of derisively as "The Irish woman". Once more he was being dragged, almost despite himself—or, perhaps in truth because he really enjoyed it—into the realms of the underworld. But there was no doubt that the illegal nature of his activities could fetch him a long prison sentence if he were ever caught.

Thank heaven he had people of the likes of Strega who were still prepared to take the brunt of his wrongdoing—and the possible penalties—in exchange for substantial sums of money.

"Romanetto," Strega said again and more loudly, trying to penetrate the long, almost uninterested silence, as if his master hadn't heard. Strega always had this notion of subservience in relation to Zac, a relationship they had had ever since he had served as his batman.

He didn't like him, but he was the boss.

"How could that whore possibly know anything about Romanetto, as we know nothing?" Zac inquired irritably.

"She is not getting interested in his *whereabouts,* Monsieur Zac," Strega said humbly, "but in his activity before he was discovered. Now, why should she do that?"

"No idea." Zac jangled the loose francs in his pocket again. "Unless you've been making a fool of yourself and messing things up again?"

He turned and glowered at Strega, who felt that familiar prickle of fear which the sight of Zac in a bad mood, or the malevolent stare of the Princess, always inspired. He knew he was a man who could, and would, kill; certainly not himself but by paying others. Monsieur Zac might be responsible for many things, but he would take care never to be caught.

"Monsieur Zac, I have kept my inquiries entirely private, as you insisted," Strega said with dignity. "Indeed there is *no* way Madame Harcourt could possibly know we are actively searching for Romanetto. In fact . . ." Strega drew himself up and a faint smile disturbed his normally impassive features. "I think I am on his trail."

"Oh, good." Zac turned and went back to his desk, a large affair with a tooled leather top, expensive like everything else in his room in the headquarters of the Banque Franco-Belges, of which he had managed to have himself elected president.

President, but it was not enough. He wanted his own company back, the organization that bore his name—Desmond—and he would stop at nothing to achieve this.

"Where *is* he?" Zac turned over some papers on his desk, as though even the whereabouts of Romanetto were of minor importance.

"I am not telling even *you,* sir."

"What do you mean, you're not telling *me?"* Zac looked at him indignantly. "You don't think *I'd* betray his whereabouts to the bastard?"

"Certainly not." Strega's glance strayed toward the door. "It is the people *around* one whom one cannot trust, Monsieur. It is through a source in the private office of Madame that I know she is interested in the activities of Romanetto before we discovered the facts of his embezzlement."

"Oh, indeed?" Zac felt his heart lift and a modicum of good humor return.

"You recall Paul Vincent, Monsieur, a devoted servant and friend of your father."

"Of course I do," Zac snapped.

"Well, Madame sacked him, as you know. He was not very discreet, alas." Beneath Zac's suspicious gaze Strega took a handkerchief from his pocket and removed a film of sweat from his brow. Zac could always turn the most innocent conversation into a form of interrogation. "Unknown to Madame his great-niece Marie-Claire Laurent has a position of some trust in the secretariat at the Étoile."

"But how did this come about?" Zac clasped his hands, his good humor nearly fully restored at this piece of news. "I thought she had every member vetted."

"She was not planted, sir," Strega went on. "The girl was simply looking for a humble job in a typing pool and was sent by an agency and subsequently employed in that capacity. It was not done deliberately, but when Vincent discovered what had happened he was able to poison the mind of his niece with the story of Madame Harcourt's behavior towards himself, an old and valued servant of the Desmonds. He thus encouraged her to let him know what was happening as a favor to him, a poor man, out of work. His niece is only nineteen and gullible. So far, very useful."

Zac, a man of unpredictable moods, suddenly felt peeved.

"And how come Vincent reports this to *you* and not to me?"

"Well, sir" — Strega carefully studied the tips of his shoes— "you were not very pleased with the way he bungled his attempts to insinuate himself with Mademoiselle, as she then was."

"He was a perfect fool," Zac said contemptuously.

"Exactly, sir, and, also, he received no pension for all the years he had been in your father's service, no thanks . . ."

"He did not deserve those either!"

"However, it is not *wise* to let ex-employees nurse grudges, sir, if I may say so," Strega said quietly. "I have taken the liberty of putting some work Monsieur Vincent's way, and he *is* grateful, to me at any rate."

"You did well, Strega," Zac said after a moment's thought. "Continue to use him and this stupid niece of his. Find out all you can and why, exactly why, that Irish tart has gone back three or four years just at this precise moment."

"I am given to understand that Madame Harcourt has been looking at every *aspect* of the business, past and present," Strega said, "and in the course of this thorough investigation—brought on by the time available to her on account of her confinement—the embezzlement of Romanetto, which had been hidden from her, came to light."

"It was not *hidden,*" Zac said sullenly. "She had only *just* joined the company. No one wanted her to get the wrong impression by letting her think it was full of embezzlers."

"Yet she felt she should have been told. You know Madame Harcourt, sir."

"Only too well."

Zac suddenly put down the documents he had in his hand and returned to the window, his chin sunk onto his chest, as he studied the traffic that plied up and down that busy thoroughfare from the Pont des Arts to Garnier's magnificent opera house.

"In fact it might rebound to our advantage," he said with another soft venomous hiss in his voice. "We may well be able to turn the bitch's sudden interest in a long-dead affair to her detriment." He rubbed his hands together and smiled. "Let us hope so, Strega? Hey?"

Tara opened the door of the house in the Rue de Varenne and slowly looked round. Silence everywhere. She pocketed the key and walked along the hall to the ebony table on which the butler left the mail, visiting cards, anything of interest that the master and mistress had not seen during the day.

The *hôtel particulier* stood back from the road from which it was separated by a high wall and a pair of stout doors. Only the little inner door had stood partly open and there had been no sign of the concierge who had, maybe, gone to the shops at the end of the road on some errand.

Tara put down her light case and glanced idly at the mail; mostly circulars of no interest. Then she crossed the hall into the ground-floor salon which was illuminated by a shaft of sunlight that shone on the polished parquet floor dotted here and there with exquisite Aubusson rugs.

She stood in the center of the room and raised her eyes to the ceiling whose intricate plasterwork had been executed in the late eighteenth century by one of the masters who had worked on Malmaison, the home of the Empress Josephine. It was a beautiful room and it was home. Tara gave a silent, mirthless laugh. Home.

Probably when he came back Zac would kill her. She had been away eighteen months; but now she was desperate. Now she was in need of protection and he was the only person she could turn to. At least it was a better alternative, and one she had weighed carefully, to being raped or murdered by a ruthless gang. She was, after all, the mother of his children.

Tara Desmond was a chastened woman when she came home after having left her husband who had had her constantly watched, escorted everywhere by a member of the underworld in his pay, after he had discovered her affair with a garage mechanic by the name of Livio.

Livio had been murdered and, briefly, Tara was arrested for the crime; but luckily for her the real criminal had been found. Or had he?

With Zac one never knew.

Tara, however, was one of the few people—the others being his elder sister and Sandra Harcourt—who were not afraid of Zac. Even his two children were afraid of him and in most people, certainly all his employees, he struck palpable terror.

Tara was wary of him, nervous when he was around, but not

afraid, because she knew exactly what he was like; she knew his strengths and weaknesses, his likes and dislikes.

Probably, above all, although he was incapable of fidelity—as was she—she knew that he was sexually besotted by her and her one hope now was that this had not changed, because it was the only way she could hope to hold him. She had nothing but her body to offer.

Tara sank into one of the Louis XV chairs and, after fumbling for her cigarette case in her handbag, lit a cigarette. She exhaled smoke, leaned back in the chair and closed her eyes.

Home.

She sat there for a moment and then she had the sensation that she was not alone in the room. She opened her eyes in sudden fright and saw not her husband but the butler, Gaston, looking at her with concern.

"Gaston!" she cried. "You startled me."

"I'm sorry, Madame," he said. "I thought you were an intruder so I moved quietly."

"And *would* you have been able to deal with an intruder, Gaston?" Tara smiled because the old family retainer was at least sixty.

"I would have known my duty, Madame Desmond," Gaston said stiffly. "I saw immediately from the hall that it was not a burglar and that I could enter without apprehension. May I take your coat, Madame?"

Tara shook her head. Although it was warm inside the house she felt cold.

"I'm going to go up to my room to lie down," she announced, stubbing out her cigarette. "Are my children at home?"

"They are staying with the Princess, Madame," Gaston replied.

"But what about their *school?"*

"I think there are arrangements for them either to attend school or have private tuition in Burg-Farnbach, Madame. They have not been living here for some time."

"But that is outrageous, preposterous." Tara's shrill, heavily accented voice seemed to reverberate through the hall, then, suddenly, she put her head in her hands. Had she not been a *bad* mother, the worst? She had not had any contact with them at all for eighteen months. Who was *she* to criticize their father?

"I think Monsieur Desmond thought it best for them, Madame," the butler said smoothly, "until he could make other arrangements." He paused and regarded her with some concern. Then he put his hand to his mouth and coughed. "Could you tell me, Madame, is Monsieur expecting you?"

"No." Tara got up and without looking at the servant walked toward the door. "And if he is dining at home tonight you had better lay the table for two, if you please."

Zac left his office at half past five, his usual time. He had been in a bad mood with Strega because his mind had not been on his work or Romanetto, but on the fact that his wife was on her way home. That much he had learned from Marco Falconetti. But then there was very little about Tara, or recent events concerning her, that he didn't know.

The problem was how much would she tell him, and how would she react to him?

She needed him, but he wanted her. Tara was his weakness. Perhaps his only one.

Tara Falconetti had been a world-famous model when Zac had met her, fallen in love with her and married her. The family had not really approved, suspecting that she had married him for his money rather than love.

But, whatever the reason, Zac had wanted Tara, and now he had her back.

And, hopefully, he would find her waiting for him in the Rue de Varenne. No wonder he had been bad-tempered with Strega.

For one of the few times in his life he had been nervous.

Six. That was when he was expected and the gates were wide open for him. He drove his car into the courtyard as the concierge came running out, her hand to her mouth, obviously bursting with excitement.

"I know, I know." Zac irritably waved her away as he got out from the car. "Don't make such a scene, Mathilde."

"Pardon, Monsieur," Mathilde said contritely, suddenly crestfallen. But even then she hurried on to explain: "Madame . . ."

"Tais toi, Mathilde," Zac commanded rudely and put a finger to his mouth.

He left the woman standing in the courtyard and hurried up the steps, to be met by Gaston at the door in a similar but more dignified state of excitement.

"Monsieur, Madame Desmond has returned," he intoned.

"Thank you, Gaston." Zac riffled through the letters lying on the table in the hall, betraying not by a look or gesture that he knew the news already, or even by the most subtle change of expression whether it was welcome or unwelcome. "Where is Madame?" His tone was offhand as if he had seen her merely the day before instead of eighteen months.

"She's upstairs resting, Monsieur; but she asked me if you would be dining at home and, if so, to lay two places for dinner."

"I am dining at home," Zac said. "Please inform Madame and say that when she is rested I would be glad to see her in the drawing room for the customary glass of champagne."

"Bien, Monsieur," Gaston said, in his turn betraying not a hint of surprise by the correct formality of his bow. "I shall inform Madame Desmond."

"A bottle of rosé, Gaston." Zac paused for a moment. "An old one, the 1979, for example. You should have time to chill it well."

"Of course, Monsieur." The servant bowed again and withdrew through the green baize door that marked the entrance to the kitchen quarters.

As soon as Gaston had gone, Zac's demeanor changed and, like a man who has unexpectedly recovered his youth, he ran lightly up the stairs, passing the bedroom he had formerly shared with his wife, to his study where, after closing the door and locking it, he got out a bottle of Scotch from his cabinet and helped himself to a good stiff drink.

Zac was reading the evening paper in the salon, one leg flung casually over the other, when the door opened, very quietly, and Tara crept in, almost humbly. She had gone to some trouble over her appearance and it was justified: she looked stunning. She had been one of the first patrons of Lacroix and she wore one of his models: a short dress with a décolletage and a bouffant skirt. With this she wore a matching diamond necklace and earrings which Zac had given her when their second child was born and, as she came slowly into the room, he looked at her, absorbing everything about her in an instant—her allure, her charm, her sexuality. He could remember the minute of the day he clasped it around her neck in the clinic, over the white hospital gown in which she had given birth.

How much he had loved her then.

He swallowed and, rising, put out his hands.

"Welcome home, Tara."

Tara didn't seem to know how to react to his welcome, but gazed at him with some bewilderment. This was not the Zac of old, the predator, the possessor; the man with an unbridled temper.

She clasped his hands as he drew her toward him and, inclining his head, kissed her chastely on the lips. After such a long absence she seemed to see him in a new light: a figure of power, almost awesome in his ability to control his emotions in what, for them both, was a time fraught with emotion. She leaned slightly toward him and he gently laid her head on his chest and began to stroke it.

For a woman who had expected a very different welcome—maybe even a beating from a man of violence—it was too much. She flung herself against him, put both arms tightly around his waist and gave in to uncontrolled sobbing.

Zac tightened his arms around her and rested his head against her hair, sighing deeply.

"There, there," he said, "there, there."

Savouring the experience, he let her weep and then, extracting a large clean white handkerchief from his breast pocket, and with a smile on his face, he tenderly dabbed at her eyes.

"Not like you to spoil your makeup, Tara. Incidentally you look ravishing tonight. Is it Jean Marvoine?"

She shook her head. "Lacroix. He should have come to us but we lost him. Belle thought he wasn't good enough; there would be difficulty with Maurice Raison."

Zac smiled and went on dabbing at her cheek.

"Belle never had very good judgment."

"Zac." Tara, having recovered, put her arms against him and gently pushed him away from her. "I can't understand this, you . . ." She looked up at him with tear-filled eyes and he knew he had never seen her so beautiful, or desired her so much.

"I knew you would come back to me," he murmured, taking her by the hand and leading her over to the table on which stood a bucket containing the champagne alongside two elegant flutes.

He let go of her hand and slowly began to undo the foil round the cork, then the wire, then, slowly, he prised the cork from the bottle with such care that there was never any question of spilling a drop. As a true *champenois* he was an expert and, after a satisfying "pop" as the cork came away, he carefully poured a little of the beautiful rosé liquid first into one glass and then the next, watching the *mousse* rise. When the bubbles had evaporated at the top he poured in some more until the glasses were three-quarters full.

Tara watched the ceremony with some disbelief, noting the tender expression on Zac's face, his calm unhurried action. It was like being confronted by a new man, someone she had not met before. What had happened to her husband since her departure? Had he undergone some conversion, consulted an analyst—a marriage counsellor, unlikely as it seemed.

This was not the man she had left behind, the faithless beast with rather disgusting sexual habits who had once raped her until she bled. Who was excited by the thought of her sleeping with other men.

Zac gave her her glass and then raised his, watching her intently over the rim.

"Welcome home, Tara, *ma belle.* Please never leave me again."

After they had drunk, their eyes on each other in a silent toast, he reached for her hand and drew her to the sofa, sitting alongside her as they each put their glasses on the tables on either side. He kept her hand in his, his touch cool and controlled.

"I am very sorry, Tara, for what happened. You have taught me a lesson and it is one I have learned well. I was a brute toward you, and I behaved badly. I treated you as a prisoner with that oaf Gomez following you everywhere. No wonder you ran away. *Please* forgive me?"

His expression was placatory, subdued, and she was reminded of their son Roberto when he was corrected for some misdeed.

"Where are the children?" she asked quietly.

"They are staying with Belle." He made a helpless gesture with his hands. "What could I do? I felt that I could not have them in this house without you. I do not understand them, much as I love them, and I cannot cope with them. Of course, I see them frequently and talk to them on the telephone daily so that they do not forget their papa. If you agree, this weekend we will go and visit them together and, perhaps, bring them back. That would make them very happy." He paused and looked meltingly at her again. "Would you like that, Tara? Are you going to stay with me? With us, *ma petite chérie?"*

Tara's eyes were already brimming. "Oh Zac . . . I never expected such a welcome, such understanding from *you* . . . you have no idea how awful it has been for me alone in Rome."

"I know, my darling, I know." He put an arm round her shoulder and squeezed it gently. "I can imagine; but when you went away it was a watershed in my life. As you hid from me I decided not to look for you. I felt that each of us, in our own particular way, was struggling toward finding the right thing to do. I did not want to use coercion or force with you again. I had to reform myself too."

For the first time Tara felt her old doubts and suspicions about her husband returning. Zac was being too nice. She had never seen this aspect of him except, perhaps, in the early days of their courtship. Could a man change so quickly, so soon? How much did he know? Dare she ask him?

Did he for instance know about Bob? If so, how had he learned? But Zac had an uncanny way of knowing everything. He had spies throughout the world, well paid to carry out his will, to report to him, as well as bring about the downfall of people he hated. She remembered Livio and shuddered.

Better not ask.

Later they faced each other across the candlelit table. The dinner, as usual, was perfectly cooked. They had champagne with their quenelles and a fine Château Lafite with the pheasant. Zac told her about the children and questioned her gently about what she had done in Rome.

She guessed that much of what she was telling him he already knew; but they had to pretend. It was a game.

"I worked at a boutique in the Via Veneto. I enjoyed it."

"Had they any idea who you were?" Zac's eyes as he looked at her were filled with admiration and she saw her spouse of fifteen years as a fine, even handsome figure. At one time she had eyed him with loathing; but now it was different.

"I used the name of our mother, Gamborini. She had so many brothers that Gamborini is not unknown in the upper ranks of society in Rome. 'Princess Gamborini', they felt, gave a little class to their shop and it was true. It was an elegant boutique and I enjoyed my work. It will give me lots of ideas for Jean Marvoine."

"Did you make friends?" For the first time Zac's tone changed subtly and Tara knew that by the innocuous term he meant "men."

She swallowed.

To confess to infidelity, which she had committed several times, would be foolish. It was time for the game again; to lie a little. Zac might assume but he could not really know about the succession of lorry drivers, mechanics, builders' laborers whom she picked up in the street for kicks, and who she would entertain in her bed for one or two nights, maybe a week, never more. Tara had always liked rough trade. It was the only thing that excited her sexually. A man hungry for sex, a bit of a smell, a little rough stuff. Zac had been a clumsy lover and had never satisfied or excited her . . . even when he had raped her. Then she had thought herself near death.

"Now that there is AIDS one has to be very careful," she replied, pursing her mouth primly.

"In that case, I'm surprised." Zac wiped his mouth with his napkin. "And delighted. After all these months of celibacy dare one hope that we could start a life together again? It is mutual, I assure you," he added quickly. "One can't be too careful in these times of sexual disease.

"Talking of AIDS, you heard, of course, of the death of Michel Harcourt?"

Tara nodded offhandedly. "It was all over the television, and that your 'friend' Sandra had married him in secret." Her teeth gleamed maliciously.

"Friend!" Zac felt a lump in his throat . . .

"I heard that you were together again as one big happy family in Tourville. I must say I was surprised."

"Well you might be," Zac said thickly, his expression changing immediately. "We simply tried to lull her into a false sense of security . . ."

"Ah . . ." Tara sat back with a knowing smile. "Then nothing has changed."

"Nothing has changed *at all.*" Zac's sangfroid left him and he began to show his irritability. "Except that our plan did not work. She exerted herself in her customary forthright and tactless manner, offending everyone. Oh no, 'Madame' the bitch is just the same. If anything she is worse."

"And you are *as* determined to be rid of her . . ."

"More so." Even the thought of his adversary seemed to have unbalanced Zac and seizing his glass he swallowed the contents.

At that moment the telephone rang in the hall and they could hear the quiet tones of Gaston answering it.

Both Tara and Zac instinctively listened until there was a tap at the door and the butler made his majestic entrance.

"There is a call for you, Monsieur Desmond. It is Madame Harcourt. She wishes you to come to the telephone immediately."

"Tell her I'm dining and will phone her back," Zac said, waving his hand in the air dismissively.

"She was most insistent."

"That is my message."

"Very well, sir." Silently Gaston withdrew and they could hear his voice growing louder, more and more irritated on the phone until at last the receiver was replaced and there was silence.

"I wonder what she wanted." Tara felt uncomfortable. Bob.

"Have you *any* idea?" Zac looked at her curiously, anxious to see if that faithless little hussy, the slut who was his wife, was capable of showing the truth on her face. But she was not. She was such an accomplished actress that her features only showed bewilderment.

"It must be something *really* important for her to call me at this time of night," Zac mused, glancing at his watch.

"Nearly ten."

"Maybe you should go and talk to her," Tara suggested. "Maybe your mother is unwell."

"In that case the Irish woman would not have telephoned me as she is keeping away from Tourville these days. I hear she is looking for a town house in Reims and is talking of paying more attention to the champagne business," Zac snorted. "She has the nerve to say it is where 'her roots' are. Did you ever hear such rubbish? Anyway"—he looked at his watch again—"if I am right, Madame Harcourt is in Paris and as I won't speak to her on the phone she will jump into a taxi and come round here at once. It will only take her five minutes."

"Here!" Tara looked extremely alarmed. "She will come here? Tonight?"

"If she is angry or perturbed enough to speak to me, and I will not speak to her, you need have no doubt she will be around." He looked steadily into her eyes for several seconds. "I don't see why *you* should be in the least alarmed, my love."

Tara sensed an air of enjoyment about Zac, and then she knew that he knew. But he would pretend, and so would she, that there had been no Bob in Rome, in the same way that there had been no Livio in Paris. Never any mention of either of them.

As Zac had predicted, not very long after they moved into the salon, there was the sound of a car in the courtyard, the bell rang violently and they could both hear urgent voices in the hall.

Zac smiled conspiratorially at his wife and then, rising, walked to the door and threw it open.

In the hall Sandra appeared to be in some argument with Gaston.

"Sandra!" Zac said, flinging his arms wide. "Do *forgive* me. I was about to telephone you; but, you see, I have been celebrating a very special occasion. Gaston, I hope you are not having the temerity to argue with Madame." He looked severely at the butler and then, with a hand lightly on Sandra's arm, pointed toward the salon. "You see, Tara, my dear dear wife, has returned home. We were having our first tête-à-tête dinner together."

Sandra, who was seldom caught off guard, appeared almost too astonished to move, but stood gazing through the open double doors.

As if quite unaware of her astonishment Zac, with a jaunty step, led the way into the salon where Tara, already on her feet, took one or two faltering steps toward Sandra.

The two women stared at each other—their eyes full of unspoken questions—and then they exchanged kisses.

"Sandra, a glass of champagne? This is a celebration."

"I can see that, Zac," Sandra said woodenly, "but I have come to see you on a matter of some urgency. I never guessed Tara would be here. You see"—she looked from Tara to Zac and back again—"Bob has been kidnapped."

She held out the piece of paper, feeling suddenly as though she herself had stepped right into some sinister trap.

Later that night Zac lay beside the nude body of his wife and found, to his surprise, that he was trembling. He felt like an inexpert lover who had just discovered what sex was about. He was almost too nervous to touch her and, remembering the past, almost frantically anxious to please.

For Tara it was the usual boredom, the routine of trying to respond, to please, that she knew so well. It was as though the eighteen months had not passed; that they had been together only yesterday.

Listening to his beating heart, suffering his attempts to stimulate her, she realized that by her return she had condemned herself to a lifetime of sexual boredom.

She would never dare attempt to run away again.

"What will you do about Bob?" she said, aware of his tension and nervousness—almost too frightened, now, to speak.

"What can *I* do about Bob?" Zac said in the darkness. "I never even knew he was in Rome. Did you?"

"No." Tara thought her voice sounded like the squeak of a mouse.

Suddenly Zac moved violently next to her, switched on the light by the side of the bed and then, leaning over her, put both his hands around her throat.

"Liar!" he shouted. "Liar, liar, liar. You lie to me or ever leave me again, Tara, and the next victim will be not Livio, not Bob or any of the other men you pick up like the common street tart you are. But *you.*" His grasp round her neck tightened—he banged her head several times upon the pillow until the teeth in her head seemed to rattle.

"Not Livio, not Bob, not this taxi driver or that sailor on leave—but you, my darling Tara. *You.* Do you hear, you little slut?" Once more he banged her head with a violence that shook the huge, canopied bed. *"You."*

6

Paul Strega enjoyed the feeling of importance that traveling the world on behalf of his master gave him. He was expected to travel economy class and his expenses were carefully vetted, but he could stay in reasonable accommodation and this allowed him some latitude in the matter of drink, entertainment, transport and so on.

It also meant that the better kind of call girls were available, and, in a city notorious for its licentiousness, its vice and its excesses like Bangkok, this was just as well.

Strega had spent part of the night in a brothel off the Patpong Road recommended to him by a man he met on the plane. There was a basic fee and extra for special services which Strega, in need of relief after a strenuous week, was glad to pay.

He now inspected his rather puffy face, with its dark stubble of beard, its greyish tinge, and decided there was no point in overdoing it. A vigorous young eighteen- or nineteen-year-old with all kinds of oriental tricks was perhaps too much of a challenge for a man well into his prime who, until recently, had been vegetating in a small village on the Montagne de Reims.

Better take it easy, he thought, as his hand holding his razor shook slightly. Tonight he would eat in the hotel at its celebrated restaurant, the Spice Market, and then take in a *kra-toey* (transvestite) show at the Calypso.

It was nearly noon. The elegant Regent Hotel on Rajdamri was, of course, air-conditioned, but outside Strega knew it would be hot, and noisy. Bangkok with its six million population was one of the most congested and noisy places in the world, its roads continually choked with traffic.

On the trail of the elusive Romanetto, Strega had been to Bangkok only a short time before, because all the leads had pointed to that beautiful and, above all, pleasure-loving country where vice of all kinds existed side by side with an ancient monarchy, a long history and some of the most majestic art in the world. Yet it was also the kind of country—in central Asia, almost surrounded by water and on the route through Burma, Malaysia and Singapore—for a man on the run, with something to hide, to get lost.

But then the trail had gone cold. Asia was a large place. Now, however, the latest information was that Romanetto was most definitely in Thailand, and either in the capital or not far from it.

During the day a member of the gang Strega had employed to find Romanetto would brief him on his whereabouts. Hopefully, Strega thought, it would not be necessary to move until the next day when he would have recovered from his night of lust.

He had just finished shaving and was dabbing his face with lotion when the shrill tones of the hotel telephone caused him almost to jump out of his skin. A pleasant Thai voice at the other end told him in perfect English that there was a visitor for him in the hotel lobby.

"Send him up," Strega said shortly, adjusting his towel round his waist. "I just got out of the shower."

Strega knew Dan Akhi well enough to receive him in a bathing towel. He was his main contact in the Far East, a Malay who worked out of a number of capitals. His organization was loosely on the fringes of the underworld, not too fussy about the methods it used to achieve results. It was he who, by following a number of leads, had finally put his finger on Romanetto.

Thailand, though Buddhist, was an affluent, civilized country that had never been conquered. Its monarchy was now a constitutional one and it was an easy, tolerant place in which to live. It was no wonder that an embezzler with twenty-five million dollars would have been attracted to a place where people lived and let live, where police were discreet and vice, as well as trade of all kinds, flourished.

Strega had his shirt and trousers on by the time Dan Akhi reached the fourth floor and the two men shook hands warmly.

"Help yourself to a drink," Strega said, pointing to a well-stocked sideboard, but the Malay shook his head, at the same time mopping his brow.

"It's hot outside," he said, then added with a broad smile, "but we're going to a really nice place, Mr. Strega, away from the heat. Cool, by the sea."

"You mean you've *found* him?" Strega flopped into an armchair, noticing that his hand was still shaking.

"He's not in Bangkok," Dan said, "that's for sure. But he *is* in Thailand."

Strega's normally phlegmatic face lit up with a brief smile of pleasurable anticipation. "Sure?"

"Positive," Dan nodded. "He's hidden himself in a place with no crime, therefore it has no police, with no cars or traffic because it has no roads."

"No roads!" Strega exclaimed. "How in the name of God do we get there?"

"First by airplane, then by boat. He is living in a bungalow on a beautiful tropical island called Phi Phi Don, off Arabi province." Dan kissed his fingers and blew imaginary kisses in the air. "Because no one expects any trouble it makes it easier for us to get Mr. Romanetto away. Incidentally, he doesn't call himself Romanetto."

"No, I wouldn't have expected him to."

"Mr. Rome. Bernard Rome."

"How very original." Strega's lip curled with contempt. "You'd never guess, would you?"

"It made it easier for us to find him," Dan chuckled. "Still not all *that* easy." He paused as if hoping for a compliment upon his remarkable detection. But he would never get that from Strega, who had learned from a hard taskmaster. Neither compliments, praise nor thanks.

"There is also a Mrs. Rome."

"Oh, really? I didn't know that." Strega picked his nose. "I thought he'd left her at home."

"Mrs. Rome is an Austrian lady whose real name is Eva Raus. We found out she was a high-class call girl with whom he'd become entangled. Probably why he stole."

"Well, well." Strega excitedly rubbed his hands together. "That *is* excellent news, Dan. When do we go?"

"I thought this afternoon if that's convenient to you, Mr. Strega," the Malay said politely. "We can spend the night in Phuket which is only an hour's flight from Bangkok and then I've hired a motor cruiser which will be manned by some of our men. We should be there by noon tomorrow."

"Damn!" Strega muttered under his breath. If only he hadn't had that night out. Now he needed *all* his wits about him.

Ao Don Sai was the only village on the beautiful island of Phi Phi Don which nestled in the Andaman Sea about twenty-six miles from the peninsula of Phuket. There was no airplane and, in good weather, the boat took about three hours.

Phi Phi Don was the larger of two islands, the smaller one being called Phi Phi. They were also known as the Pee Pee Islands and it could be imagined how ignorant tourists make a good deal of fun of this name.

Most people who visited Phi Phi Don considered it a paradise on earth with its lush vegetation, jungle-clad hills and glorious white-sand beaches. During the low season, though, storms were frequent and, sometimes for many days, the islands were cut off from Phuket.

At the center of Ao Don Sai there was a large banyan tree filled with bats; besides a few shops there were two simple restaurants. But there was no night life and the television from the mainland was often of poor quality.

When he had first found the island of Phi Phi Don, Bernardo Romanetto had, indeed, thought he had reached paradise on earth after all his wanderings, with no thought for the morrow. A bungalow was easy to rent, the villagers, used to tourists, relatively uncurious, the social life nil. On their journey through Europe and Asia, stopping off at many capitals on the way, he and Eva had disposed of sums of money that would cause little suspicion in a variety of names. He had lodged half a million dollars in Bangkok and every month they traveled to the city to draw funds, enjoy some meals and a little of the exotic night life.

It was while they were away on one of these jaunts that Dan Akhi, having followed clues all the way from Geneva via Delhi, Calcutta, Rangoon and Bangkok, had alighted on remote Phi Phi Don. The reason was a coincidence but, as life is made up largely of coincidences, it was not difficult to believe.

His cousin Sam Thi Akhi, who came from Kuala Lumpur, had been honeymooning on Phuket and, having gone for the day with his new bride to the Pee Pee Islands, had fallen in love with them as so many people had. They decided to extend their honeymoon by a week or two, staying in the village resort at Tong Cape. During the day they dived around the coral reefs in Run Tee Bay and at night, after a delicious Thai meal, they made love.

Not unnaturally they were reluctant to go home.

In this curious, coincidental way, Sam Thi Akhi and his bride made the acquaintance of a foreign lady, not old and not young, who had been shopping in one of the village stores that sold everything. She helped them out with their purchases, as she had some smattering of the language, and they invited her for a drink in a bar where she advised them to stick to fruit juice or the local beer. Thai whiskey was vile.

She told them nothing about her life in this tiny, remote island or why she was there, but she seemed incongruous, a misfit and, also, in some way, deeply unhappy. The encounter stuck in Sam's mind, so that when he and his new wife were telling his brother and sister-in-law several weeks later about their holiday, the subject of the foreign woman came up and Dan Akhi at once had a feeling about it, though it was probably a million-to-one chance, if not more.

But if Ao Don Sai was a paradise on earth to the honeymooners who would soon return to the civilized delights of Kuala Lumpur, it soon became a prison to the ill-matched couple who had sought refuge with twenty-five million dollars of Desmond money. Bernardo Romanetto, at forty-five, was a small, overweight man with a bald head and a paunch. Eva Raus was fifteen years his junior, tall, lissom, then a striking blonde whom he had met on a business trip to Zurich.

Meeting her seemed like a watershed to Bernardo who began to plan his embezzling operation with great care, patience and skill. Finally he told her he was going on a long trip abroad and invited her to be his companion. Eva was tired of hustling and although she did not love her curiously faithful client, she had grown quite fond of him, had even speculated about his home life. She thought a trip abroad might be amusing. She had not realized Bernardo intended it to be for life.

Phi Phi Don, when they reached it after many adventures, seemed to offer just the peace and security they needed.

But, for how long?

Eva gave a huge yawn as, from the balcony of the bungalow overlooking Run Tee Bay, she watched the long-tail boats that for about 150 baht could be hired for two hours' sightseeing. The wet season was just ending and the tourists would begin to flock in, when prices would rise by about fifty percent. Not that this made much difference to their life-style, which was about as good as they could get it.

However, it wasn't much use having so much money, Eva thought, turning over the pages of a *Paris-Match* that was at least six months old, if you couldn't spend it.

Or rather Bernardo could spend it; *how* he spent it, on drink. He had certainly never drunk as much as this in Zurich, where she had only ever seen him take the occasional beer as a regular drink, champagne for special occasions.

Bernardo came into the room smelling strongly of perspiration and scratching his armpits. She looked at him with disgust, tempered by humor. Sometimes she thought he was the nearest thing she had seen to an ape outside the zoo. Repellent in his personal habits, he had deteriorated considerably.

Bernardo wore a pair of Bermuda shorts over which his belly rolled like a large lump of blubber.

"You should take yourself in hand, Bernardo," Eva said sharply. "If you go on at this rate you won't live long."

English or American whiskey was hard to come by, and expensive. They brought it over in cratefuls every time they visited Bangkok. Eva had grown used to a tot or two and rather liked the stuff. By this time, of course, Eva knew all about the embezzlement and why they were where they were, but she had grown too fond of the life to change. She had even grown a little fonder of Bernardo.

When they were in the city, Bernardo seemed to sober up and dress smartly. He enjoyed the sights, eating in good restaurants and sleeping in comfortable air-conditioned rooms, in the Oriental, the Regent, the Hilton or the Royal Orchard Sheraton. He even began to go jogging in the mornings in Lumpini Park to try and regain his figure.

Only he never went jogging round the island. Sometimes he fished from a boat on the bay but, more often, he sat with a glass of whiskey in his hand, gazing out to sea or fiddling with the fuzzy picture on the TV screen.

Bernardo ignored Eva's remark and, half filling a glass with whiskey, moved into the kitchen to find ice. When he came back he walked straight past her onto the balcony and sat in a low, upholstered wicker chair. Putting his feet up, he began to sip his drink. He regularly had the shakes now and the first drink of the morning definitely helped.

Eva held up the field glasses with which she had been gazing at the bay and focused once more on the yacht which had anchored the evening before. She could see men moving about on deck and in the stern, under an awning, two others were sitting drinking. She didn't know why the yacht so intrigued her since many anchored at one time or another in the bay and this one was no different from the rest. It had probably been hired in Phuket for some deep-sea fishing, as water skis had frightened away the fish from the shallow waters.

"What a hole," Bernardo said suddenly. "What a *place* to end up in."

It was not the first time he had made this remark and one day she swore to herself she would stand up and scream. He talked most of the time in clichés, repeating himself over and over again.

"You *said* we were going to move on soon," she said, lowering her binoculars.

"Move on? Where?" Bernardo stared vaguely out to sea.

"Anywhere but here."

"But it's safe. It doesn't even have a cop. No one would ever find us here."

"I don't think they're *looking* any more." Eva once again raised her binoculars. "What's twenty-five million dollars to a Desmond? They've forgotten, if you ask me."

"Zac Desmond forgets nothing," Bernardo said.

"Then what is the *point* of stealing all that money if you're not happy?"

"Are you happy?" Bernardo, staring moodily at her, thought that, despite the life-style, she had retained her looks and her figure; she swam regularly, she was an attractive, reasonably intelligent woman. God knows why she had become a hooker. It was possible for a woman with looks and brains to make a good living without selling her body. Sandra O'Neill, who, from the picture on TV, was one of the sexiest, most beautiful women he had ever seen, had become an investment analyst, then the head of a large corporation. No, Eva still looked good. He was the one who had gone down. He regarded his pot belly protruding over his Bermuda shorts and tried to straighten up.

"I'm not very happy here, no," Eva said, as if she'd carefully considered the point. "I must say I thought life would be more interesting and exciting. But there's not enough to do here, dear." She smiled uncertainly at him. "And I am seriously worried that *you* will drink yourself to death. I think your fears are exaggerated. Why hide yourself away? I think they have all forgotten about you. I think we should seriously consider moving on. Besides we're conspicuous here. One day someone will tell someone and, then, you know . . ."

Suddenly he looked alarmed. "Where can we go?"

"Anywhere as long as it's a big place with something to do."

She observed from the corner of her eye that the boat was coming inshore to anchor at the jetty at Ao Don Sai, which was out of sight below her. It was a busy little port and the concrete path around the bay was about the only made-up road in the island.

"I'll give it a bit of thought," Bernardo said. "No use dying here with all that money. Might as well enjoy ourselves."

"Yes." She put down her glasses and began to feel better already. "Let's decide to do that. Let's stick to it next time we go to the mainland."

Sometimes they had lunch at the Mira Kum or Chao Koa—medium-priced restaurants which served good seafood and Thai beer. But today they were eating at home.

Eva, feeling in a better mood, went into the kitchen and was in the act of opening the fridge when the doorbell rang. She stiffened and immediately started to tremble.

The doorbell never rang. They had no friends or acquaintances on the island; they collected their mail, what there was of it—usually bank statements—in the village. She even did her own cleaning so as to keep out strangers. In her mind's eye she saw the yacht in the bay and felt as though she had had a premonition.

Bernardo appeared from the balcony, glass still in his hand. His face too looked anxious.

"Did you hear that?" he asked.

"It's the bell."

"Who can it be?"

"Go and see." She turned away so that he wouldn't see the fear on her face.

"I don't think we'll open the door. Maybe whoever it is will go away."

On most boats and yachts one usually saw men and women dressed for play with the object of enjoying themselves. On this boat, she realized, there had been only men. Men in suits. Men who did not look as though their prime purpose was enjoyment. That was what had puzzled her. Too late now.

Dan Akhi had decided to go to the bungalow alone. The previous night they had anchored after dark and gone ashore in a small dinghy to look at the lie of the land. The bungalow was at the top of a hill, set apart from others that looked just like it, and from it led a narrow ill-defined path to the beach which did not look as though it was much used.

But what they'd seen had satisfied them. Bernardo, like a fly, had flown into a trap; one that he had thought secure but, now, from which it would be very hard to escape.

Dan rang the doorbell again and decided that if they didn't answer he would return and get the men and they'd have to break into the house. There was nowhere that Romanetto and his woman could go, other than the jungle, and he doubted whether they would take to that.

He looked at his watch and was about to return down the path to the bay when the door opened and an attractive woman stood there smiling at him. She was deeply tanned and wore shorts and a T-shirt; dark glasses covered her eyes.

"Good morning," Dan said, politely removing his hat. "Mrs. Rome?"

"Yes."

"I'm from the tax authorities. I wondered if your husband was at home?"

"The *tax* authorities?" Eva said, aghast, at the same time looking behind her, thus completely giving the game away.

"You are resident here, aren't you, Mrs. Rome?"

"I thought my husband . . ."

"Maybe I could have a word with him."

Dan already had his foot in the door and Eva had no choice but to take him into the sitting room as Romanetto came out of the bedroom, hastily tucking his shirt into his trousers.

"Someone from the tax department," Eva said casually to him as he closed the door. "Just like home."

"The tax . . ." Bernard began.

"You should pay tax, Mr. Rome," Dan said, looking at him severely over a pair of freshly donned spectacles. "I can find no papers, no record of your residence here in Phuket."

"But we're . . ."

"Now you are immigrants coming from"—Dan pretended to look through several documents he had produced from a cheap briefcase—"Europe—Geneva, I think—and you have been resident here over two years."

"Just *under* two years," Bernardo insisted nervously. "I really don't see . . ."

Suddenly he turned at the sound of a footfall in the hall and then he stared at Eva who followed his gaze.

"Good morning, Bernardo," Strega said with a wide smile. "It's nice to see you again."

"None of the money is left," Bernardo repeated for about the tenth time. "At least not much. What there is you can have."

"And how much would that be?" Strega, who had taken the chief part in the interrogation, which had lasted all afternoon and most of the evening, was trying to keep his temper. In the kitchen Eva was making a meal, watched over by one of the men, while two others patrolled the grounds.

"Half a million."

"Half a million Swiss francs!"

"Baht," Bernardo said, at which Strega reached over the table and savagely hit him across the mouth. At the noise Eva rushed in from the kitchen but Dan, rising quickly, seized her arm.

"Don't intervene, or it might happen to *you,"* he said menacingly, pushing her back through the door. He was a man of apparent charm who, in no time at all, could show a different and surprisingly ugly side.

Strega stood up.

"Call in your men," he said. "I am tired of this charade. We've come halfway round the world to see you, Romanetto. It's taken a long time. We're not even going to kill you, not yet. You've wasted a lot of time, valuable time, and a great deal of money. Mr. Desmond, as you know, won't like that at all. Yet all he wants is your cooperation . . . and to get the money back that you stole."

"There *isn't* any money," Bernardo said stubbornly, and Strega struck him again.

This time one of the men shoved Eva in from the kitchen.

"This is a very nice broad you've got here," Strega said, eyeing Eva lasciviously. "A high-class tart I'd say. Expensive to keep up, was she, Bernardo?" Strega peered closely into his face. "I bet she pushed you to it." He thoughtfully eyed Eva for a moment or two. *"Mrs.* Rome. Now I hope you haven't gone and committed bigamy to compound your other crimes, Bernardo. Bigamy is a very serious offense, just as big an offense as embezzlement.

"If we turned you over we could see you get, let me see . . ." Strega closed his eyes and pretended to do a calculation.

"Just you shut your mouth . . ." Bernardo began, whereupon Strega opened his eyes again and pushed him squarely in the chest.

"Don't you be rude to *me,* Bernardo. Don't you *dare."* He looked at him calculatingly. "Did you ever see a woman *raped,* Bernardo?" His eyes roamed back to Eva, who stood there shaking. "Nastily, you know, so that it would *hurt.* Your tart will know all about rough sex but, my goodness, the five of us here could make it something she'd never forget . . . or you." Strega gave a dirty chuckle.

"She can't help you," Bernardo cried. "She knows nothing about it, so leave her alone."

"Get them *off!*" Strega jerked his head in the direction of Eva and one of the men standing behind her pushed her to the ground and attempted to tear off her shorts. She struggled but he succeeded, leaving her in a flimsy pair of briefs.

"Those off, *too,*" Strega commanded, but Eva, with all the strength she could muster, hung on to them, crying, "No, no, Bernardo, you *can't* let them do this to me."

"We'd *all* want our turn." Dan indicated the three other men who had come in from the garden and stood leaning against the wall, smiles on their faces. "Then we'd begin all over again. It could go on all night."

"When we've finished with her we'll cut out her tongue." Dan showed from the expression on his face how much he enjoyed the thought of cruelty. "But we will *still* get what we want . . ."

"Let me go and I'll tell you," Eva said, struggling to free herself. "Mr. Strega, I can see you're a gentleman. If *I* level with you I know you won't let them do these things to me. What have *I* done? I'm innocent. I didn't even know at first he *had* the money."

"It's true, she didn't," Bernardo muttered.

"When he told me at last how he could afford to live so well, I *told* him he was wrong, he should send it back."

One of the men had drawn back the top of her briefs and was looking with interest at what he saw inside.

"Leave her," Strega growled, and Dan looked menacingly at his henchman, raising a fist.

"Believe me, Mr. Strega." Eva realized she was gabbling but, impelled by fear, couldn't stop. "Bernardo has often repented of what he did. We have *not* enjoyed our life here.

It's a beautiful place but we're bored. We were just talking about leaving . . ."

"If you value your virginity, shut *up* and tell me where the money is," Strega said, showing her his fist, "and then I'll tell you pair of crawlers what I want you to do."

Antoine Dericourt was one of those gray, so-called "faceless" men, who proliferate in large organizations and inevitably, because of a combination of obsequiousness and undoubted skill, rise to the top.

He had been with the Desmond Group since he had graduated with a degree in engineering, and had gone straight into aeronautics just as Georges Desmond had taken over a small concern that was now one of the foremost manufacturers of fighter planes and small civilian aircraft in Europe.

When Sandra had assumed the presidency of the group his name figured prominently among those who were not only ambitious and capable, but loyal to her, rather than Zac. Dericourt had had little time for Zac, who was notorious for his favourites: "yes" men, who did everything they were told. Dericourt had not been among these and consequently was keen to excel in front of the new boss. It was largely thanks to Sandra's encouragement coupled with his loyalty and skill that the Desmond 200 was available in such large numbers when required.

Though managing director of the Aeronautics Group, Dericourt was also on the Board of Desmond and, as such, was Sandra's number two. Yet they were rarely in the same place at the same time, seldom met, and never socially, but communicated by telephone, fax or telex every day, sometimes several times a day.

When Dericourt got a summons to go at once to Reims from Clermont-Ferrand, where the main plant was, he lost no time in summoning the helicopter and within an hour was in the air and on his way.

The original news about Sandra and Michel, of her pregnancy, had made him wonder how long she could last, how long she would be able to outmanoeuvre Zac. Besides, although he admired Sandra, he was by nature chauvinistic, believing that a woman's place was in the home, her role caring for husband and children. He himself was only in his late thirties, happily married, with four young children of school age, a pretty wife five years his junior and a large house on the outskirts of the town.

To him women needed to be looked after and protected. One could certainly not put Sandra O'Neill in that category and yet, after all, she had behaved with a typical woman's weakness in her foolish obsession with Michel Harcourt.

As the helicopter hovered over Reims, Dericourt could see in the center of the old city the spires of the great cathedral, which was once the crowning place of the kings of France. They then made a swift descent toward the east where he could see the modern headquarters of the champagne business, with **DESMOND** clearly readable from several hundred feet up.

As he alighted from the helicopter, Sandra's secretary Antoinette emerged to greet him, followed by the porter to take his case. Dericourt turned and shook hands with the pilot and then, ducking under the blades, ran toward the building until he was out of range of the whirlwind.

"How *is* Madame?" he inquired urgently, turning to Antoinette as he smoothed his hair across his head.

Antoinette shrugged.

"She is not unwell?" he asked anxiously.

"You will see how she is." Antoinette smiled reassuringly. "She is waiting for you in her office."

Sandra was, in fact, standing at the window of her office as the helicopter came in to land on the lawn and, as Antoine looked up, she gave him a broad smile and waved.

She was already outside the lift as it rose to the second floor and, as the doors opened, she held out her hand.

"Very good of you to come so quickly, Antoine."

"I hope everything's all right, Sandra. Tell me, do you need the pilot? I said I'd let him know. How long do you want me to stay?"

"That depends." Sandra looked suddenly grave. "You might leave today or tomorrow. Or you might need the plane to take you further afield."

"Something *is* wrong." Antoine grimaced and preceded her into her office. This was a large, gracious panelled room with a desk that was of historical interest to the Desmond family, chairs, a long sofa and the best examples of modern art on the walls. Sandra spent as many of her few precious free moments as she could in galleries in London, Rome, Tokyo or Paris, or would even interrupt a business meeting to talk to a dealer who had something he, or she, thought she would like. She specialized in art painted since the war and was something of a connoisseur. On her office walls hung examples of the work of Julian Schnabel, David Hockney, John Hoyland and Nicola Hicks.

Like the paintings, the furniture, apart from the desk, was modern and luxurious: deep leather sofa and chair, one or two occasional tables, a drinks cabinet. In many ways it seemed to embody her personality. Like her there was an absence of clutter and confusion. The immediate impression was one of hard, concentrated work and calm.

Sandra led Dericourt to the sofa as Antoinette hovered.

"Coffee, Monsieur Dericourt?"

He nodded. "Coffee would be nice, Antoinette."

"I thought we'd lunch after our business." Sandra consulted her watch. "That should be in an hour to an hour and a half."

"Perfect!" Dericourt undid the bottom button of his jacket. He stretched out his feet and began to feel more relaxed. A personal call from Madame at six in the morning with orders to fly to Reims was not his usual, or preferred, way of beginning the day.

"Now," he said uneasily, "I suppose this is about Romanetto?" He threw out his arms in a gesture of despair. "Frankly the trail is cold. It is stone cold. I had no luck. None at all . . ."

He stopped as Sandra shook her head impatiently. "This time it is not about Romanetto—though I don't intend to let the matter drop."

She rose to her feet and, going to her desk, unlocked the top drawer. She extracted a very small sheaf of documents and carefully relocked the drawer again. Then she walked back and sat next to Antoine, who by this time had his strong, black coffee and was sipping it. As she walked, Antoine had the chance again to assess and admire her figure which he found was, despite motherhood, still perfect. She wore a beige suit by Jitrois and a scarlet shirt.

"How's the baby?" He looked up at her and, for a moment, her stern features, composed yet preoccupied, were transformed by the pride of maternal bliss.

"Perfect," she said. "I hope if you stay the night you'll see him. By the way, I'm buying a house in the center of Reims, not far from here," she added casually. "It's a beautiful old house, largely untouched by the wars, with a walled garden."

"Tourville too far?" He looked at her carefully.

"Tourville is too full of Desmonds," she said shortly. "Now to business."

"If it's not about Romanetto, then don't tell me Prince Abdullah has reneged on his order of additional planes . . ." Dericourt put down his *demitasse* on a nearby occasional table and donned a pair of horn-rimmed spectacles as Sandra passed a paper to him for his inspection. He took it with some surprise but before he had the chance even to glance at it she said:

"As you know, Bob O'Neill has been kidnapped. I have been trying to negotiate through Parracini, our Italian agent, but they wish only to deal with me. I *suspect* it is a trap and my life may be in danger."

"Mon dieu!" Dericourt exclaimed, and as quickly as he could read the first and subsequent papers she gave to him. They were mostly crude-looking letters compiled from newsprint but the message was clear: if she did not obey, Bob's life span would be very short.

He finished studying the material and handed it back to her. "He's not your brother. You know that now, and so should they."

"But I love him." Sandra looked at him appealingly. "Nothing has changed. We grew up together and I told Bob I would never desert him, let him down . . ."

"But what was he doing in Rome?" Dericourt took off his thick spectacles and leaned back against the soft leather. "I thought he was in LA?"

"He went to Rome to look for Tara Desmond. The trouble is I don't know whether or not he found her."

"Tara *Desmond?"* Dericourt looked incredulous and Sandra permitted herself a strained smile.

"Bob became besotted with her in Paris. I think it amused Zac for a time to have his wife desired by another, much younger man. However, after the Livio affair he had her watched all the time and, as you know, she left him. Bob seems to have decided to go and look for her." Sandra passed him the letter she had had from Bob. "That was a couple of months ago. I heard from him only once again"—she passed him another letter—"telling me his bank and asking for money to be paid into his account to buy an apartment. I mailed him five hundred thousand dollars but it was never drawn. I guess that was when he disappeared. When I received the ransom note I went at once to see Zac and, to my astonishment, Tara was there."

"Tara is in Paris *now?"* Antoine looked amazed.

"She was there in the house with him. They were having dinner. I simply welcomed her back and said nothing else. What could I say? She looked frightened but that might merely be because she was back with Zac. They volunteered no information and Zac was unable to help me."

"Did you consider that he might be behind Bob's kidnapping?"

"It had crossed my mind," Sandra replied guardedly. "But when I saw Tara I thought why would Zac kidnap Bob *now?"*

"Unless he'd done it some time before?"

That had *not* crossed her mind and Sandra appeared to consider it.

"You haven't heard from Bob for two months." Dericourt looked through the documents again. "There is a month between this letter and you seeing Zac, according to you; so why do you take so long to call me. Why?"

"I wanted to try and handle it myself or through Parracini. But I now don't think I can. I wondered, Antoine, you are a very skilled man . . ."

"You want me to go to Rome and deal with a gang," he gulped. "Sandra, I have four children under the age of fourteen. You know the reputation of these people."

"I thought it was too much to ask . . ."

"I'd do anything for you, Sandra, anything . . . but this . . ." Dericourt looked with dismay at the pile of documents. "This is *really* dangerous."

"Also outside your remit. I'm sorry." She attempted to smile at him. "It has nothing to do with business. Romanetto and the missing champagne gold—if we can call it that—was business . . ."

"I got nowhere with that," he said placatingly.

"Forget it." The flick of her wrist seemed an indication that the matter had somehow diminished in importance. Nevertheless, she looked deflated, as though he had let her down.

Anxiously Antoine rose. She was his boss, a woman he admired. An important woman who, like it or not, it was useful to please. He began to pace the carpet in front of Sandra. He stopped and held out both hands.

"You know I'd do anything for you; but the possibility of a gang like the Camorra . . ." He closed his eyes and a spasm seemed to pass through his body.

"I can't *pay* twenty million pounds. I have not the money personally and I can't raise it. At the most I am worth five million. I have offered them two and a half."

"And what did they say to that?"

"They offered to send me parts of Bob's body in sections. Beginning with his ear . . ."

"And you're *quite* sure Zac had nothing to do with it?" Antoine slumped by her side again.

"As sure as I can be." She paused and frowned. "I don't think even Zac is capable of something as despicable as this."

Suddenly Antoine got up and walked to the window.

"How do I get in touch with them?" he asked.

"Oh, but you just said . . ."

"And immediately despised myself for it." He turned to her and there was a new look of resolution on his face. "My wife and children would despise me too. After all, I am only going as a negotiator. We must play for time. Meanwhile . . ." He sat down beside her again. "See if you can up your offer a bit. Could you go to *five* million?"

"If I wanted to remain in debt for the rest of my life." Sandra looked at him with a wan smile. "Antoine, I can't thank you enough. I promise you will come to no harm. In Rome you might see Marco Falconetti, Tara's brother. If I suspected anyone of having dealings with the gang it would be him. Now . . ." Looking much happier, she glanced at her watch and got to her feet. "Antoinette, naturally, has lunch prepared for us next door."

TWO

The Lion's Den

7

The Desmond holding company's branch in Geneva was situated in the World Trade Center just outside the city and a short drive from the airport where Sandra's private jet had arrived a few hours before. She was flying from Geneva to Milan, Rome, Naples, on to Athens where she had a meeting with Olympic Airways, and finally to Barcelona where parts of the Desmond small civilian planes were assembled. With the cooling in world tension the outlook for the Desmond 200 fighter didn't seem so promising and, as sales dried up, she wanted to diversify into civil aviation. Her own plane was a prototype of the smaller executive type jet that was proving popular among the new breed of globe-trotting businessmen and women like herself.

Sandra sat across from the desk of Hugo Dubuisson, who had taken over from Bernardo Romanetto when he'd fled the country four years before. After discussing business matters with him, giving him an up-to-date account of all the various Desmond projects which would concern him, Sandra said: "Do you have the file on Mr. Romanetto?"

Dubuisson seemed rather taken aback by the inquiry.

"Your predecessor Romanetto?" Sandra tapped her feet impatiently.

"What sort of file, Madame?" Dubuisson appeared still puzzled by her question.

"There must be a file in personnel on Mr. Romanetto. I wish to know why someone who was capable of embezzling twenty-five million US dollars came to be employed in this organization; also how he found it so easy to do and, especially, why he got away."

"But it was a long time ago." Dubuisson, who did not know Sandra well, seemed both surprised and slightly unnerved by the question.

"Telephone personnel please, Mr. Dubuisson, and get me the file."

"But I do not know *why* you wish to see it, Madame." Dubuisson's hand was reaching reluctantly for the telephone.

"Mr. Dubuisson," Sandra said, beginning to show her displeasure, "please don't argue with me, but do as I ask. Now"—she held out a hand to Antoinette who accompanied her on business journeys and who sat behind her taking shorthand notes—"might I have the cash-flow charts for the Swiss part of our operation?"

As always, Antoinette had the documents ready.

"Romanetto!" Dubuisson was barking into the phone, his face by now rather red, his expression irritable. "Bernardo . . . yes. I'll wait."

He smiled confidently at Sandra, his hand over the mouthpiece. "They won't be a minute."

However, a minute passed and then two and three while Sandra spread the papers on the table and studied them, carefully trying to hide her irritation. It was strange that in a place like Switzerland, well-known for its efficiency, it took such a long time to find a simple file.

"Is it not on computer?" she asked, without raising her head.

Dubuisson was listening to someone talking at the other end of the telephone, his face gradually beginning to register its own irritation. Then he put down the telephone and shrugged.

"They seem temporarily to have mislaid it, Madame Harcourt. As soon as they find it they will bring it. All personnel files have, of course, been computerized, but we can make a print-out as soon as we trace it."

"It's taking a long time," Sandra said disapprovingly. "Anyway while we're waiting I want to point out the strengths and weaknesses of our operations in Switzerland. Now here . . ."

She began to issue a stream of figures, at which she was very good. The amount of information she retained, apparently effortlessly, astonished everyone. Occasionally she would look up to make sure Hugo Dubuisson was following her, but he kept on nodding and making intelligent comments while Antoinette took back the papers as they finished with them and issued new ones.

After half an hour Sandra seemed satisfied, looked at her watch and said: "We should break for lunch."

"It is all prepared in the boardroom, Madame."

"Meanwhile *where* is the Romanetto file?"

"Ah!" From the look on his face Sandra was sure he had not forgotten, and appeared as much mystified by the delay as she.

"I'll telephone again," he said and, as he lifted the receiver his hand shook perceptibly while he once again barked orders to the luckless individual in personnel on the other end of the line.

It appeared there had been no success.

"There is no record of Romanetto having worked here, Madame," Dubuisson said, sweating slightly. "It is a complete mystery."

"Then after lunch we'll go to personnel and look into it," Sandra said with equanimity. "There must be some explanation."

Sandra did not believe in large or long lunches, a fact with which her staff worldwide were familiar and, accordingly, this took under an hour. She knew Hugo Dubuisson less well than most of her managers because the operation was primarily a commercial one to do with the holding and dispersal of funds and ran itself. He was well qualified in financial matters, and had held senior posts in banking before joining the organization.

She could see, however, that he was nervous and ill at ease

during lunch and became more and more puzzled as to the reason as the meal progressed.

As soon as the meal was over and he was about to lead her from the boardroom straight back to his office, Sandra reminded him of the Romanetto file and he stopped, changed course, and led her along a corridor to a door marked **PERSONNEL.**

Inside there were several desks with both men and women working at them. On each desk was a VDT, some in operation and some not.

All the staff stood up as Sandra entered and she inclined her head in greeting and gave a friendly wave.

"How do you do everyone?" she said in French. "Please do sit down and get on with your work. Don't let me interrupt you. Now."

A small, dark woman got up from her desk at the end of the room, her VDT displaying a number of names.

"Bonjour, Madame," she said politely as Sandra extended her hand. However, her face, too, wore an expression of apprehension and she kept on looking at Dubuisson as if for support. "I am afraid we have been unable to find any reference to Monsieur Romanetto. His name is not stored in the computer nor is there a file in our filing system." She pointed to a steel filing cabinet behind her desk. "Some years ago we computerized all details of the personnel employed here; but we did retain basic references in case, for example, there was a computer virus introduced into the system." She led Sandra to the filing cabinet and pulled out the first drawers, flicking through the files which were listed alphabetically under "R". There were all the names under Ra, Re, Ri and Ro but after "Roland" there was "Ronaldi". No Rom at all; certainly no Romanetto.

"It is the same on the screen, Madame," she said, turning to the VDT where the same names with details were on display,

Roland, Henri
Ronaldi, Francisco

"You don't have any place where you file details of past staff?" Sandra's tone was gentle and courteous to try and allay the young woman's nervousness.

"These *are* past staff, Madame. These are all the files for the staff who have left." She pointed to the other desks in the room. "They deal with present staff, or vacancies that we have. When Mr. Romanetto, er, left, his name would automatically have been transferred to this section."

"Did you *ever* come across his name before?" Sandra stared at her searchingly.

"Yes, Madame." The woman lowered her gaze. "I knew Monsieur Romanetto as I have been here ten years."

"Then what happened to his file?"

"I honestly have no idea," and, as she looked as though she was about to burst into tears, Sandra turned to Dubuisson.

"Could we check with current names just in case there has been a mistake . . ."

"We have searched everywhere, Madame." The woman gestured toward her colleagues who were following every word of the conversation. "We all *know* he did but we appear now to have absolutely no record that Monsieur Romanetto ever worked here."

Sandra had not intended to stay over in Geneva but to fly straight on to Milan where her hotel had been booked. However, as soon as she left headquarters she directed her chauffeur into the center of the city.

"To the Sheraton, please," she said.

"Sheraton?" Antoinette looked at her with surprise. "Not the airport, Madame?"

"We have a mystery here, Antoinette." Sandra leaned back against the upholstered seat.

"Romanetto puzzles you. I can see that, Madame."

"Very much."

"Why, *why,* Madame? I can't quite understand."

Antoinette respected, even loved, her boss but she was often mystified by her. When the behavior of other people seemed governed by reason Sandra—an eminently rational being too—frequently appeared to act intuitively. Frequently, too, she was right.

As if in uncanny confirmation of her thoughts, Sandra said, "I can't understand either. Call it intuition. Romanetto's been on my mind and yet I have a thousand other things to think about. I can't tell you why." She looked at her and gave her the calm, serene smile that made even the heart of the practical Antoinette lurch. "But I want time to think about this before I leave Geneva. The first thing I want you to do when you get to the hotel is to find out if Madame Romanetto still lives here, and if she does, get her address."

Madame Romanetto was a small woman with dark hair streaked with gray who might well have put on weight in the years since her husband had deserted her. She had a weary, rather preoccupied air and had opened the door with some astonishment at finding Sandra on the other side of it.

"I know who you are," she said, standing back to admit her into a large, pleasantly furnished sitting room. "You are hardly ever off the news. I was so sorry about your husband . . ."

"Thank you, Madame Romanetto." Sandra gave her a smile of such friendliness and warmth that the woman's heart went out to her.

"But, why . . ." Madame Romanetto tried to appear calm but, clearly, was not. "Have you any news?"

"No." Sandra looked her straight in the eyes. "Have you?"

"None." Madame Romanetto led the way to a sofa and, sitting at one end, invited Sandra to occupy the other. The whole place had a rather transitory air, an air of impermanence, as though Madame Romanetto had only just arrived and would not be staying long. Maybe Madame Romanetto knew more than she implied.

"Have you lived here long, Madame Romanetto?" Sandra,

who prided herself on being a good judge of character, gazed searchingly at the woman.

"Oh no." Madame Romanetto folded her hands on her lap and gazed at them with a sad expression. "I had a beautiful house, Madame Harcourt, overlooking the Lake of Geneva. When my husband left I had to sell it. It was all I had. The only capital. My children are in boarding school and this is rented." She sighed deeply. "I don't suppose I shall be able to afford to stay here long."

"I'm really sorry."

"But why have you come to see me, Madame? Why are you interested in me?" Madame Romanetto looked perplexed.

"I'm disturbed about the mystery of your husband's disappearance."

"It was four years ago, Madame."

"I know and I have only recently come to learn the full details. Twenty-five million dollars is a lot of money, and yet no one seemed to go to any lengths to find him."

"I thought it strange myself." Madame Romanetto stared apathetically in front of her, her eyes vacant, as though she had suffered much and could do so no more.

"You see, Madame Romanetto"—Sandra paused as though anxious to find the right words—"I have come to see you because there is no trace, none at all, of your husband's details in the files of the Desmond Group. It is as though he had never been there."

"But he was there for twenty years!" Madame Romanetto exclaimed. "Monsieur Desmond, who appointed him, thought highly of him."

"I know, that's why it was such a surprise when he disappeared."

"It was a terrible surprise and shock." Madame Romanetto's face looked pinched as though she felt the cold and she pulled the jacket of her cardigan suit tightly across her maternal bosom.

"You never heard from him again?"

"Never. Not a word. That was the terrible part. He even

cleared every franc from his bank account and left me penniless. I had no money and, of course, couldn't ask the Desmond Group for any because of the circumstances under which he left. Although it was not my fault I couldn't help sharing in his guilt. Luckily the house was worth a bit." She looked at Sandra, her face lit, finally, by a wan smile. "I work in a confectioner's in the afternoons. It's not what I'm used to and it does not pay very well. But it's something and . . . it stops me thinking."

"Thinking what?" Sandra looked at her closely.

"Well, about what happened to Bernardo." Madame Romanetto's face was puzzled.

"Did you ever . . ." Sandra paused. "I hate to say this, Madame Romanetto, but did you ever think your husband might be dead? That someone, for instance, has done away with him? For a man such as you and others say he was, the circumstances are *most* peculiar."

"Dead?" Madame Romanetto said the word quietly, almost to herself; but Sandra felt quite certain she had had it on her mind before. Perhaps she knew something, after all, that Sandra did not know.

"There *was* a girl, another woman." Madame Romanetto seemed to have to steel herself to reply. "I always think she was the reason that Bernardo did what he did." She smiled pathetically at Sandra. "I believe they call it the male menopause, and we had been married for nearly twenty years."

Bernardo Romanetto, traveling under the name of Giorgio Leopoldi, sat nervously in his hotel bedroom watching the television screen. He gazed at it from early morning until late at night, sitting there picking his teeth and drinking quantities of whiskey, interspersed by late meals which were brought up to his room. He never went out but sat, his eyes on the screen, waiting for his mobile telephone to ring, which it did, several times a day.

If Sandra knew that every detail of her travel through Europe was being closely monitored at various checkpoints, like a rally driver, she might well have retraced her steps. On the other hand perhaps she wouldn't; being Sandra she would have tracked down those who were following her every movement, and wanted to know why.

Madame Harcourt had stayed overnight in Geneva. Why? Romanetto, who had been staked out in the hotel in Milan for over a week, felt very nervous. Geneva was a place that he had avoided at all costs. He still felt ashamed of his treatment of his wife. Paris too he had thought unsafe as the heart of the Desmond empire. Despite his name, he was a French-speaking Swiss and Eva was an Austrian who spoke many languages: French as well as Italian, German and English. Anyway, after nearly three years in Phi Phi Don Eva had been only too glad to arrive in London where, years ago, she had worked as an au pair to a banking family before finding her true métier as a purveyor of pleasure to men. Or, truthfully, it wasn't really her preferred way of life, but the pay was infinitely better than what she had earned looking after the spoilt children of rich people.

Traveling as a visitor, she booked into the Savoy, was given a suite overlooking the river and prepared to have a ball. Phi Phi Don seemed a long time ago, and very far away. She earnestly hoped she would never go back.

London was the one European capital where Desmond had no office. It imported its champagne through an agent in the City of London, but Sandra seldom had need to visit London so that, despite the vigilance of Scotland Yard, it had seemed a good place for Romanetto and Eva to stay for a while. They traveled as husband and wife, the Leopoldis, and, while she remained at the Savoy, Bernardo had been to stake out the European cities which Sandra was known to be visiting.

So far everything had gone according to plan. Strega remained behind at the base on the Montagne de Reims in contact with his source in Paris, the docile niece of Paul Vincent, the insignificant typist in the typing pool who had personally processed Madame's itinerary.

But why had she stayed a day longer in Geneva? Now it

appeared no one knew. The system was not foolproof, after all.

Suddenly the telephone shrilled and Romanetto, who sat with it constantly on his lap or by his side, was still sufficiently nervous to be startled by it every time. With a trembling hand he extracted the aerial and put it to his ear.

"Pronto?" he said.

"The bird has flown," Strega said in a prearranged code. "Destination on schedule."

"Good," Bernardo said and retracted the aerial. Then he realized he was sweating and his hands still shook violently. He was very, very frightened. He was not at all the right man for the job.

Sandra was to spend three days in Milan and, after checking in at the Principe di Savoia, drove straight to the office of the Desmond Group which had extensive links with the Italian wine industry, and large areas of land under cultivation in Umbria and Tuscany. There she was to confer with her financial advisers on the cost effectiveness of her investments in Tuscany. Beside her in the car sat Antoinette, going through various documents, lists of people she had to see.

"It may take up to a week, Madame," she said at last.

"We have the time." Sandra looked out on the bustling street of one of Italy's most important industrial cities. "I am even considering buying a villa in Tuscany."

"Do you think it *wise?"* Antoinette looked guarded.

"Do you think they'll kidnap me too?" Sandra was scheduled to meet Dericourt in Rome and see if he had made any progress in contacting Bob's kidnappers. "I'm thinking of Louis," she went on. "It would be lovely to take him there for the holidays, or maybe he'd prefer the seaside." Sandra sighed. It was so difficult to decide, such a big responsibility on one's own.

"You miss your baby, Madame, don't you?"

"Very much. I'm wondering if I'm doing the *right* thing by him as a mother . . . all this travel."

"He is very well looked after."

Sandra put a hand fleetingly on her bosom, thinking of those precious moments when she had felt the bonding with him was complete.

"But I had to abandon feeding him. Was that fair?" She gazed at Antoinette who, as a childless woman, looked nonplussed.

"I'm sure if the doctor thought . . ."

"The *doctor* would like me to have fed him for six months. Professor Pichon is all in favor of that kind of thing. I am too, but I simply couldn't do it. He made *me* feel guilty."

"There is no need, Madame," Antoinette said loyally. "I think you have been very brave."

Sandra phoned Mireille every day, sometimes twice. Louis was thriving; his new formula suited him and yes, of course, he missed his mother. Mireille, who filled in quite well as a substitute, was the soul of tact.

Sandra settled back in her seat and, putting on her spectacles, began to leaf through the documents the admirable and efficient Antoinette had prepared for her; but her mind was on something else and, removing her glasses, she leaned back, closing her eyes.

"Are you tired, Madame?" Antoinette removed the documents from her employer's lap.

"I'm thinking." Sandra opened her eyes. "The expression on Madame Romanetto's face when I asked if she thought her husband was dead was so odd. Quite unexpected. Not shock. Not grief . . . as if she knew something she wasn't telling me. She seemed to be totally unprepared for the remark, but not at all worried by it as if she knew that, in fact, he was well. Supposing"—Sandra turned to stare at her secretary—"just supposing she *knew* where he was and what he was doing. Do you remember the British spy Maclean who went to Russia and left his wife behind? Everyone thought she had no idea what had happened but, a few years afterwards, she joined him."

"You mean you think Madame Romanetto *knows* he is alive . . ."

"I feel pretty sure she knows he is alive. I thought it would distress her to mention death but it didn't. She looked very composed. Sad but composed. Maybe, like Melinda Maclean, she's waiting to join him when the time is ripe."

"But what about the girl, Madame? Madame Romanetto thought he had gone off with someone else . . ."

"That could just be an attempt to sidetrack me. I have only her word for it . . ."

Sandra sighed and, putting her spectacles on again, held out her hand.

"Let me read about our future Chianti. I'm going to take it back to Reims and let Latour have a look at it."

"Might not the Italians mind?"

"The Italians have been cooperating with him already. He is one of the best oenologists in the world. After this harvest we shall start to make the wine and Latour's expertise will be invaluable."

"And Cuvée Louis d'Or, how is that coming on?"

"I think it will be superb." Sandra smiled. "One of the finest champagnes in the world."

Sandra enjoyed her trip to Milan. It was a city she liked and her busy schedule helped to make her forget her many worries: the fate of Bob and the question of raising the money to ransom him; her duties toward her son; and, nagging away at the back of her mind with a persistence she could not explain, the mystery about Bernardo Romanetto.

She stayed in Milan for five days and then she flew on to Rome. It was a very strange feeling arriving in the city, where Antoine Dericourt was on the tarmac at the airport to greet her and take her personally to the group's Italian headquarters.

On the day before Sandra was scheduled to leave Milan a man stepped into the Banco d'Italia and asked to open an account. After a wait he was greeted by a functionary who invited him to sit down at a desk where, with ineffable politeness, he began to take details.

"In the name of Sandra Wingate?" he queried, after inspecting the particulars Romanetto had filled in.

"She's my boss visiting Milan," Romanetto said.

The clerk frowned and looked at the banker's draft made out in the name of Miss S. Wingate. It seemed perfectly in order though 200 million lire was a lot of money.

"We'll have to have her signature," he said. "If she wants to open an account here we need a signature. She should either make it in person or have it witnessed."

"But Signorina Wingate is a very well-known business-woman," Romanetto said, panic rising. "She hasn't the time for this sort of menial transaction."

"In that case I wonder she doesn't do it through her own bank."

The clerk, bored rather than suspicious, yawned and the palms of Romanetto's hands felt sticky. Inwardly he cursed. Strega was supposed to be an intelligent man and he could make a mistake as fundamental as this.

Come to think of it he should have foreseen something like this himself. As a financial manager used to transferring large sums of money he had forgotten that opening a personal account was different.

What a stupid, fundamental error! Maybe he had been too long away from his desk or, as Eva hinted, his mind was becoming sozzled with booze. He held out his hand for the banker's draft, hoping that the clerk didn't notice it was shaking.

"If you give that back to me I'll inform the signorina of the conditions. It's just that she's a very busy person . . ." The clerk smiled mechanically and handed over the draft together with the half-completed documents.

"If she's *that* busy she needn't come in personally. We just need her signature witnessed by a notary or a magistrate."

Romanetto grimaced with annoyance. "What a waste of my time, eh?"

The clerk politely saw him to the door of the bank and thought no more of it. For the time being.

* * *

Romanetto's hand shook even more as he clasped the telephone close to his mouth, shouting down it.

"You nearly blew the whole thing, you *idiot.* What a ridiculous mistake to make."

On the other end, in the safety of his house near the Faux de Verzy, Strega was trembling too. The thought of what Zac would say if he knew made him want to go urgently to the bathroom.

"You should have thought of it yourself, you cretin," he snarled. "You'll have to let me think this over. I'll call you back," and as quickly as he could he scuttled to the smallest room in the house.

There he put his head in his hands and sat for a long, long time. Supposing they'd already blown it, after so much preparation, so much money spent, by just one simple, elementary error?

Claire Borghi and Sandra had got on almost from the moment they first met. They both shared an antipathy toward the house of Desmond, of which Claire was a member, the younger sister of Zac. She was married to a painter, a street artist, and they now had three children. Claire, who had always been very thin, almost anorexic-looking, had now filled out into a rather plump Roman matron who fed her husband, children and herself on a staple diet of pasta. Sandra looked at her with approval.

Her visit had been unannounced and when Claire had seen her standing at the door of her flat she could scarcely believe her eyes. They fell into each other's arms.

Now the two women were sitting opposite each other, a pot of coffee on the table between them. The latest baby, Rocco, slept in his cot. The firstborn, Giuliano, and Francesca, the middle child, played quietly on a rug in the center of the room. They were clean, well-behaved and obviously happy. Being brought up away from the Desmond influence had done them no harm. On the contrary. Sandra had also admired baby Rocco, who was about the same age as Louis, and the old friends exchanged gossip and swapped news for some moments.

Claire was a Desmond by birth, but had never been one in spirit. She lacked the competitiveness, the drive and, it must be said, ruthlessness that seemed to be a mark of members of that family. After an unhappy first marriage to a French nobleman she had married, for love, a talented but unsuccessful painter, Piero Borghi, whom she had known many years before.

There was no doubt that she was happy. Sandra looked round the humble, cheaply furnished apartment and wished in many ways she could change places with Claire. How nice it would be to be married to an ordinary man, with three happy children and, no doubt, more to come.

Or would it? It might be fine for Claire, but how would it really be for her? Yet just as she threw back her head Claire thought how beautiful she was, how elegant, how cosmopolitan, and how much she envied *her.*

Life on a shoestring even with a man one loved and children one adored wasn't easy. After Tourville and the Château de St. Aignan, cheap furniture was hard to live with. However . . .

"In Rome for long?" she asked, pouring a fresh cup of coffee.

"A few days." Sandra's expression was serious. "I'm trying to get news of Bob."

"Bob?" Claire looked puzzled.

"You didn't know Bob had disappeared?"

"Bob was in Rome, and he disappeared?" Claire seemed nonplussed.

"Oh, then you don't know anything?" Sandra sat back and studied the wedding band on her finger which was the only jewelry she wore. Bob's kidnapping had not been notified to the police because the gang had insisted on it. That might have to change but, for the moment, she would cooperate.

"I know that Tara went back to Zac. She lived not far from here."

"Really?" Sandra sat forward. "Did you see much of her?"

"Practically nothing. Tara and I had very little in common. She always thought me very boring. When she first came here she was lonely and we did see a bit of each other. She even stayed here until she found a flat. Of course she used me." Claire gave an inconsequential shrug. "But then that was that."

"But what did she do all the time?" Sandra looked mystified.

"She worked at a boutique on the Via Veneto. Of course, she had family here and friends."

"And did she come to say good-bye before she went back to Zac?"

"Oh no!" Claire shook her head. "Haven't seen her now for months and I only know she went back to Zac because someone who knows that I'm related to him sent a cutting from *France-Soir.* I am happy and content here, Sandra. My family behaved abominably and I want nothing to do with the past."

"Once you were my ally," Sandra said sadly.

"I still am," Claire assured her. "But I don't know how I can help you."

Sandra then quickly filled in the details of Bob's disappearance, his letter to her from the States announcing his intention, his last letter from Rome.

"You never knew, then, if he and Tara met up?"

"No."

"Did you ask Tara?"

Sandra hesitated before replying.

"Not yet. It is difficult to get her alone. I don't want Zac to know what is up, obviously."

"Oh, I don't *think* Tara and Bob met up in Rome," Claire said doubtfully. "When she first came here after running away she told me that Bob was a mere child, and she'd run away from Paris as much to get rid of him as to get away from Zac. I don't *think* she'd have any interest in getting together again."

Giuliano had started to cry and Claire went over to him, trying to amuse him with the game he was playing. Sandra felt she had taken up enough of her time. Besides, she had a luncheon engagement. Around the corner, out of sight of the windows of the humble apartment, her car waited with her chauffeur and the ever-diligent Antoinette to take her to her next appointment.

She got up and straightened the jacket of her suit.

"I must go," she said, as Claire took the crying little boy into her arms to comfort him.

"Oh, don't go because of Giuliano."

"I must go anyway."

"Of course, you're busy." Claire's mind was still on the child.

"Do you miss the old life?" Sandra asked suddenly and Claire shook her head.

"I miss Mama, though. She cut me off completely. She never replied to my letters, has never seen her grandchildren." Her lips curled sarcastically. "Of course, if they found that Piero was a *count* or marquis, or if he suddenly made his name as a painter, she'd change her tune. The whole family would. They'd welcome me with open arms, but now I'm an outcast." She lifted her chin stubbornly. "I don't care though. I'm happy. I'm in love and I'm loved. What more could any woman want?"

Sandra smiled at her and, impulsively, leaned forward to kiss her cheek, murmuring in her ear as she did so: "You know, I envy you."

Claire returned her embrace and then she suddenly stepped back, her arms round the chubby legs of her toddler, as though a thought had come to her mind.

"Why don't you go and see Marco Falconetti, Tara's brother . . . now there's a man who might know something. He would know if Tara and Bob had seen each other. You can't trust him though. He's corruptible, he needs money and I know for sure that he was used by Zac, because Zac once sent money to him through me."

At her words it seemed to Sandra that bells started ringing in her head as though a vital clue, something which should have been obvious but was not, had slipped into place.

But, right then, she didn't know what it was.

The old woman looked with suspicion at the elegant pair standing on the threshold; the woman in a couture suit, the man in a double-breasted, blue business suit.

Such callers seldom appeared at the Palazzo Falconetti these days and the old woman was impressed. She stood back and invited them in and immediately the smell of must and damp assailed Sandra's nostrils and the uninviting chill of the place seemed to penetrate her bones.

"Wish I'd brought my coat," she murmured to Antoine Dericourt who stood behind her.

"The place could do with a refit," Dericourt replied laconically, turning to the concierge. "Is the marchese in?"

"Who shall I say it is?"

"Madame Harcourt and Monsieur Dericourt."

The woman shook her head, clearly unable and unwilling to memorize foreign names, and ambled off with a shuffling gait in the direction of a room at the end of the corridor, from which a dim light shone. There was a murmur, an exclamation of surprise, and then a man in his mid-forties, not very tall, and scarcely recognizable as the brother of the beautiful Tara, hurried along the corridor to greet them, roughly pushing the old woman out of the way.

"Madame *Harcourt,*" the Marchese Falconetti cried, making a deep bow. "If *only* you had let me know . . . of course, I recognized your face immediately."

"It's good of you to see us." Sandra gave him her hand. "May I introduce Monsieur Dericourt, the deputy managing director of the Desmond Group?"

"How do you do, sir?" Falconetti nervously rubbed his hands together and beckoned to them to follow him, keeping up a prattle as if to reassure them that, though the place might be damp and dark, it had a long and noble history.

"Built by Cardinal Umberto Falconetti, a patron of Brunelleschi," he said proudly, flinging open the door of the salon. Then he added deprecatingly, "Of course, it *is* in need of a little restoration."

Neither Sandra nor Dericourt spoke but they both looked with equal dismay at the sight of dereliction before them: faded brocade, chairs without seats, a three-legged table and a mound of ashes in a fireplace that looked as though they could have lain there since the time of the eminent patron of Brunelleschi. The one good armchair was occupied by a young man who stood up rather sulkily at a peremptory gesture from Falconetti.

"This is a friend of mine, Claudio Vengi. He was just about to leave . . ." Claudio's expression grew even sulkier but, at a wave from Marco, he slipped out by a side door, frowning bad-humoredly.

"People do drop in," Marco said irritably. "One would think I had nothing to do." He ostentatiously brushed one of the chairs with a flick of his wrist, dislodging an ancient cat who uttered a piercing shriek and fled, and bowed again deeply to Sandra. "Please do sit down, Madame Harcourt. I can't tell you how sorry I was to hear of the death . . ."

He prattled on, ensuring that Dericourt's seat was also as free of dust as he could make it, though many well-ensconced spiders doubtless lurked in its brocaded depths. Sandra would have preferred to stand, but politely perched on the edge of her seat.

"Yes, alas, we have never met, Madame, but I have heard about you from my Desmond relations."

"I dare say you have," Sandra said with a wry smile. "Nothing good, I expect?"

For a moment the marchese appeared not to get her meaning, and then gave a wide, knowing smile.

"Of course there was a little rivalry . . . quite understandable."

"I believe you used to carry out some tasks for Zac Desmond," Sandra said in a brutal attempt to cut through the persiflage.

"Oh?" A wary look came into Marco's eyes. "Of what nature?"

"That's what I'm asking you."

"Well, from time to time . . ." The marchese shrugged and rubbed his puffy fingers together. "Of course, he *is* my brother-in-law. Frankly, he lent me money. In exchange he has a share in this magnificent but decrepit palace." Vaguely a podgy hand gestured around the room. "It was his intention to turn it into a hotel. I don't know how."

"Oh!" Sandra felt surprised. She had imagined plots where, apparently, there were none. Marco was a fop, degenerate, a betrayer of his kind, his class. Very different from what she had heard of his clever brothers—the lawyer, the doctor, the businessman—and his beautiful sister Tara.

It was difficult to believe that he could be mixed up with bandits or that they would trust him.

"I came to see you, Marchese," she began diffidently, "because I thought you might be able to help me."

"Oh, if I only could, Madame." The marchese pushed his chair nearer her. "How may I have the pleasure?"

"Bob O'Neill has been kidnapped."

"Bob O'Neill?" the marchese echoed thoughtfully, a finger on his chin.

"Formerly thought to be my brother."

"Ah, yes, I remember." Marco tapped his head.

"He was particularly bewitched by your sister Tara."

"Ah!" The marchese smirked with pride. "Who is not? She was and is *still* an enchanting woman."

"Do you know if, by any chance, they saw each other in Rome?"

"You mean *here* in Rome? Recently?" He scratched his head before looking at her bewilderedly. "But why should *I* know such a thing, Madame? Do you think my sister would tell me, a business colleague, a confidant of her husband? Tara and I hardly saw each other while she was in Rome. We were never close. Besides," he added huffily, "she never even *told* me she was returning to Paris. I had to read about it in the papers."

Dericourt, who had remained silent, carefully watching the voluble nobleman, spoke for the first time.

"Marchese, is there any way, any way at all you could help Madame, do you think? She is very attached to a man she has helped to raise, whom she has always regarded as a true brother. To be truthful with you, the gang has threatened to kill him; they have demanded a huge ransom. Madame, even with her wealth, is unable to pay it, even if she wished. We lack a middleman, someone to negotiate with them. Is it possible that, with your background and connections, you . . ."

"How much were you thinking of?" the marchese replied, and the sums that came to his head in rapid succession were staggering, enough to free him forever from the stranglehold of Zac.

The well-dressed woman went into the entrance hall of the Banco di Roma in the Corso and asked for the head cashier.

"Who shall I say?" the doorman said.

"Signorina Wingate," the woman replied.

"Un momento, Signorina." The clerk disappeared and the smart-looking woman waited, tapping her feet, which was the only indication anyone could have had that she was apprehensive. However, although there were one or two appreciative glances, few people paid much attention to her and within a few moments she was shown into a small anteroom where the head cashier shook hands with her.

"Now, Signorina Wingate, how may I help you?" he asked.

"I wish to open an account and deposit a substantial sum of money with you," the woman said. "It is important, however, that this remains secret."

"But, of course, Signorina"—the clerk inclined his head—"the business of our clients is *always* confidential."

The woman took an envelope out of her handbag and placed it in front of the cashier. He opened it and looked at a banker's draft drawn on Barclays in Kuala Lumpur. Although he was too polite and well trained to register emotion the amount surprised him.

It was not every day, even in that sophisticated city, that a person came off the street to open an account with a bona fide banker's draft for one and a half million pounds sterling.

8

Zac stood up and, clearing his throat, looked first at the man sitting next to him and then around at the members of the Board of the Banque Franco-Belges which, having absorbed the Bank Pons-Desmond, was part of the giant Heurtey Corporation of Europe and America.

"I would like to introduce members of the Board to Mr. David Heurtey," he said in English, "who, following the death of his father two months ago, is making a tour of his European companies. It's the first time we've had the pleasure of meeting Mr. Heurtey. You're very welcome, sir."

"Thank you," David Heurtey replied and then stood up, fishing for some notes from his pocket. When they were in his hand he put on a pair of half-moon reading glasses and studied them for a few moments while the surprised members of the Board were able to assess him.

David Heurtey, the son of Ebenezer Heurtey II, who had died suddenly of a heart attack while fishing off the coast of Florida, was in his mid-forties, a tall, gray-haired, big-chested man with undoubted presence. He wore a well-cut sports jacket over gray flannels, a white shirt with a club tie, and he looked like someone who was on vacation rather than business.

David Heurtey in his youth had had a reputation as a playboy and he remained someone who liked to combine as much pleasure as possible with business. His main responsibility had been a string of gasoline stations and he liked to drive fast cars as well as play polo, a pastime he shared with Tim Desmond, whom he knew slightly. He never traveled without his golf clubs and had a handicap of ten.

Finally David Heurtey looked up and, with a frankly disarming smile, began by apologizing for his inability to speak in French.

"I hope to remedy that," he said, "because this is a country in which I intend to spend a lot of time. My brother Frank and I have divided our father's empire between us. I maintain gasoline throughout the world and European operations. Frank is in control of the parent holding company in the States. I may well make Paris my home." He suddenly looked down at Zac who, he observed, was scowling. "Don't worry, Monsieur Desmond." He put a hand jocularly on his shoulder. "I'll leave the banking to you. You won't catch me interfering in anything that's well run."

Was there a threat in this? Zac couldn't tell. In fact he knew next to nothing about David Heurtey and his sudden arrival had taken them all by surprise. Heurtey also owned Tellier Champagne and the Tellier brothers, Luc and Rudy, were hastily asked to the meeting and sat there looking as surprised and uncomfortable as Zac.

"America is very interested in the development of the European Community," Heurtey continued, glancing at his notes. "Heurtey will want to make its presence here much stronger, and we shall be forging links where we can with other compatible companies in preference to mergers or unwelcome takeovers, investing in some businesses while others invest in ours. With the abolition of trade barriers Heurtey expects to be there on an equal footing with our European partners . . ."

During Heurtey's speech Zac continued to stare at the desk scowling. David Heurtey might present himself as a regular guy, a fun-loving chap with his golf bags and his pretty secretary

Joanne; but Zac saw him as something different. He saw him as a threat.

After the informal board meeting there was lunch at which Heurtey was introduced personally to all the members and had a chance to chat for about five minutes each with those whose English was adequate. Zac hovered uncomfortably at his elbow, intent on catching every word, suspicious of a plot to remove some of his power, jealous of what he had.

David Heurtey was halfway round the room when he turned to Zac. "Is Miss O'Neill not here? Is she not on the Board of the bank?"

"Yes, she is," Zac snapped with more gracelessness than perhaps he intended. "However"—he swallowed in an effort to contain himself—"she has a finger in so many pies and, besides, she knows that I who, after all, *am* a Desmond, am perfectly capable of taking care of the group's interests in the bank's affairs."

"She is someone I'd very much like to meet," Heurtey said, not unaware of the ill-disguised undercurrent of hostility. "She . . ."

"Let me introduce you to Baron Martens," Zac went on swiftly. "Martens Bank became incorporated with us in . . ."

And so on and so forth.

Finally when Zac had completed his introductions Heurtey turned genially to him and said: "I have an appointment later this afternoon. Maybe we could have a few minutes together in your office over coffee?"

"Of course," Zac said. "Is there anything . . .?"

"Just a general chat, you know," Heurtey said casually. "Fill me in on a few matters. I'd like my assistant to sit in on this meeting. You met Ms. Pasarro?"

"Only briefly," Zac said frigidly. "I thought she was your *secretary* . . ."

"Secretary/PA." Heurtey seemed to be deliberately vague. "I believe she'll be waiting in the lobby now if you can call her up."

He then put an arm round Zac's shoulder and, as if he were the one in charge, led him into Zac's office overlooking the Avenue de l'Opéra while Zac's own secretary went down to collect Ms. Pasarro.

As she came through the door Zac decided she was something more than a secretary/PA. She was about thirty, a forceful-looking woman and not a natural blonde. She was attractive yet Zac found her repellent too. She was the sort of obviously capable woman, sexually sure of herself, whom he detested; a bit like Sandra. Yes, too much like Sandra: the same type, although even he had to admit that Sandra was beautiful while Joanne Pasarro was merely nice-looking in a handsome sort of way—a tall, arresting, well-dressed woman whom people would certainly glance at twice. She had a slim briefcase in her hand which she put on the floor beside his desk as she shook hands with Zac.

"I do hope you had something for lunch, Ms. Pasarro," Zac said. "Had I known . . ."

"Oh, I had an engagement, thanks, Mr. Desmond." Ms. Pasarro smiled broadly at Zac, as though to put his mind at ease, and then at her boss with whom she seemed on terms of easy familiarity.

Zac sat behind his desk and joined his hands together in an attitude of importance, also impatience.

"Now, Mr. Heurtey . . ."

"David," Heurtey said. "I do want us to get on, Zac."

"David," Zac corrected himself, "what is it you wish to discuss in particular?"

Heurtey slipped into a chair beside Ms. Pasarro, undid the button of his jacket, flung one long leg over another and gave him an engaging smile.

"I want to get the entire picture about the bank, Zac. I must tell you"—he spread his hands in the air as a blind person does who is trying to find his or her way forward—"there are some gray areas we are not too happy about."

"Oh? *Grey* areas?" Zac put his hands palms downward on his desk and knitted his brows together in his most fearsome manner.

"Yes; too much investment in too many pies, Zac. Not enough security. Not enough *profit.*"

"But the profits . . ."

"Are half of what they should be." Ms. Pasarro had suddenly produced a sheaf of documents. "We can't understand how you appear to do so much business and make so little money . . ."

"That was the problem before, I think, wasn't it, Zac?" Heurtey continued in the same pleasant tone of voice. "I mean with the Desmond Group when Miss O'Neill took over."

"She hadn't a clue what she was talking about." Zac seized a paper knife and began to wave it about as though he'd like to slit Sandra's throat. It was noticeable how every time he mentioned her name, his voice rose.

"Oh, but I think she *has,* Zac." Heurtey sat back in his chair. "She's a first-class businesswoman. I've never met her, but I hear nothing but good. It was strange, I thought, the way she edged you out of any control in the Desmond Group. She must have had a reason."

"She's a woman motivated by strong ambition." Zac's expression remained inscrutable. "Maybe she aimed too high." His face now carried the disdainful look of one aware of his own superior talent. "After all, Sandra Harcourt knew *nothing* about champagne, which is the core of the business. She knew nothing at all. She . . ." Once again he appeared on the verge of losing control of himself.

"She *quadrupled* Desmond's profits," Ms. Pasarro intervened, her tone just verging on the sarcastic. "She turned the aeronautics company round, making spectacular sales to some Gulf states . . ."

"The champagne business was a disaster . . ." Zac continued heatedly.

Heurtey nodded.

"The results were not good in the first year because of some error in the bottling procedure, but production picked up in the second and third. Globally, the Desmond Group's profits nearly rival Heurtey, which is a much bigger company. All in all we are very impressed with Desmond and will seek to increase our links with it. Surely that interests you too, Zac?" Heurtey re-crossed his long legs and, his head on one side, smiled. Zac thought it an odd, rather insinuating smile. He was beginning to think there was far more to Heurtey's sudden appearance, his ostensible bonhomie, than met the eye.

"Well, of course it interests me," Zac spluttered. "I'm a shareholder, after all. But you won't find Sandra all that easy to deal with, charming though she is." He joined his hands together and closed his eyes in an effort to contain himself. However, the tips of his fingers, tightly clenched, shook as though the struggle were too much for him. He opened his eyes. "She is both charming *and* beautiful, a most accomplished woman. However, having said that . . ." He paused to take a deep breath, like a fish coming up for air. "You will have to watch her *very* carefully. You may not know it but the SEC in the US were very interested in her dealings over the sale of the Desmond 200 aircraft, suspecting insider trading."

"Oh dear!" Heurtey teetered back on his chair and, from the vaguely mischievous expression on his face, Zac knew for certain that he was teasing him. "I thought they suspected *you.*"

Despite their initial encounter Niki turned out to be more friendly and forthcoming than Luigi, although he had a streak of sadism in him and when he had obviously been drinking could be nasty. Luigi seemed to suspect that Niki might be willing to do a deal with Bob, that he was not to be trusted, and initially he accompanied him on visits.

Bob's meals were brought by an old woman who could speak no English. Bob didn't know a word of Italian, but in his prison he set about learning it with the aid of a dog-eared phrase-book which Niki had brought him. In time Luigi's visits grew less frequent and Niki came alone.

Bob didn't know where he was except that it was somewhere in the city. From the noise of traffic, and the sound of bells, he thought he was still in Rome. In fact he was sure he was in Rome, but had no idea where.

They had tried to throw him off the scent by blindfolding him and driving for many miles, but they never left the city. He was sure of that; they just went round and round.

He had a room below ground, which he suspected was part of the cellars of a large house. It was a dim room, lit by a single bulb, and with only faint daylight coming through a narrow, frosted window high up in the wall which was protected by heavy iron bars. Bob had a camp bed, two chairs, a table and a portable gas stove for which he was grateful. If he stayed here much longer it would get very cold.

He also had a portable toilet, quite a modern affair with a lid, which Niki used to take out and empty every day. He washed from a bucket of water that the old girl brought him in the morning but he didn't shave. Besides he had no razor. He fancied that Niki and Luigi visited but that the old girl lived in the place, a concierge or something like that.

Neither Niki nor Luigi ever answered any questions about the reason for his capture or who his captors were. It was a strange timeless existence with only the phrase-book for company—although later there was a television—and yet time did pass. The little patch at the top of the opaque window grew dark and the light from the bulb stronger. Niki brought him an oil lamp for additional light at night and, Bob thought, comfort. For a man whose leg he had lacerated, Niki behaved quite well. Bob thought Niki felt sorry for him because, maybe, he knew he was going to die.

Bob didn't know how long he had been in his prison, maybe one week, maybe two, when Niki arrived one morning with breakfast and when Bob asked why he was told the old woman was ill. Niki seemed out of sorts, as though he had a hangover or had not had enough sleep, and he put down the tray with bread, jam and a pot of thick, black coffee and was about to take the portable lavatory away when Bob said:

"My sister is a very, very wealthy woman."

Niki got as far as the door and then stopped. "So?"

"She would pay a great deal to get me out of here."

Niki put down the container and, turning to Bob, made an unmistakable gesture with his finger across his throat.

"All the money in the world wouldn't save my life if you got out of here, *amico.* They would hunt me to the furthest corner of the earth."

"Who's 'they'?" Bob picked up the thick piece of bread and, realizing he was hungry, spread it thickly with jam.

"They," Niki said, pointing with a stubby finger at Bob, "want you here, and that is all I can tell you. Who did you say your sister was?" He was about to unlock the door which he was always very careful to lock behind him, keeping an eye on Bob. Thickset and dim-looking he might be, but, in a funny way, Bob respected him. This Italian was streetwise; he was no fool.

"I didn't," Bob replied. "I never mentioned her name."

"Oh, I thought you didn't," Niki said with a smile, but there was something about his manner that suggested to Bob that Niki might, after all, be bribable. If he worked on him slowly, gaining his friendship, there may be a way of getting out of the lion's den.

Sandra sat listening to the conversation between the representative of Olympic Airways and Antoine Dericourt, who had joined her for this stage of the negotiations. Although it was nearly Christmas the heat in the room was almost overpowering and her eyes felt heavy with sleep.

The night before there had been a party, and one the night before that. At the weekend she'd flown back to France to spend two nights with Louis, and then she'd come straight on to Athens. The plan now was to go on to Madrid, Barcelona, and then back to Paris.

Antoinette sat next to her taking notes; in front of her was a pile of freshly opened mail. The meeting took place in the Athens headquarters of Desmond, within sight of the Acropolis.

The Olympic representatives were excited, or seemed to be,

about what Dericourt and his colleagues, who had flown down from Clermont-Ferrand, were saying about the leasing of short-range executive jets. If they could have an exclusive contract with Desmond, maybe they could capture a world market?

"Why not fly on with Madame," Dericourt suggested, "to Barcelona where some of the parts for the plane are being assembled?"

"Why not?" Sandra murmured.

If it was Thursday it must be Barcelona.

Sometimes she felt almost too tired to speak, but her febrile brain never missed a thing. This weariness, which was new, she recognized as a symptom of the conflict between her desire to be a successful businesswoman and her wish to be simply a mother at home with Louis.

After the Greeks had gone Dericourt paced up and down in front of Sandra's desk, exaggeratedly rubbing his hands with glee.

"I think we've got them. If we give them an exclusive license . . ."

"Wait a minute," Sandra said rapidly, running her eyes over a fax that Antoinette had just handed to her. "This might change the situation." She handed the paper to Dericourt who quickly scanned it too.

"David Heurtey? Why should that make a difference?"

"Because," she said, settling back in her seat and gently turning round, "he is the new joint head of the Heurtey Corporation, in place of his father who died several months ago, and Heurtey, as you know, have a very big interest in aeronautics. For this type of aircraft they're our chief rivals in the world."

"There's plenty of room for us both." Antoine shrugged.

"That's what you think." Sandra rapidly began to draft a return fax to her Paris office. "He wants a meeting with me as soon as I get back to Paris." She looked up. "Antoine, we should get on to Barcelona and get that deal fixed with Olympic as soon as we can."

* * *

"You're sure this is the final call?" Romanetto said into the portable telephone.

"Final. Sure," the voice replied from the other end.

"Barcelona wasn't on my schedule."

"Well, it should have been. That or you've made yet another mistake." His tone sounded ominous.

"I haven't any money left," Romanetto whined.

"Just enough, I think."

"If I deposit what I've got I haven't a sou left for myself."

"What a pity," came the sarcastic voice at the end of the line. "Maybe you could just squeeze a little more from your sources in the Far East. Otherwise my principal here might be very angry."

"Shit!" Romanetto said and put down the phone.

In the looking glass above the dressing table of their hotel room Eva was carefully putting on her mascara, pausing every now and then to stare approvingly at herself.

"Do you know," she said, fluttering her lashes carefully to dry them, "I think I get to look more like Madame Harcourt every day." Then she slipped into a favorite couture suit of Sandra's which had been spirited away from the selection of clothes she kept in her office, by Vincent's niece.

"This time we'll have a photo," Romanetto said with a sigh. "You going into the bank, you coming out of it. Then we quit."

"Be careful not to get too close," Eva warned him.

"*Then* we're finished, washed up, kaput." His voice sounded very strained and tired.

"Why do we do it then?" she said, looking at him with surprise.

Romanetto sighed again.

"Because we have no choice. That man is a killer; but only let him wait. One day I'll get my revenge."

Zac looked with satisfaction at the photograph on his desk.

"Excellent," he said, beaming at Strega who stood anxiously

on the other side of the desk. "No one could tell it was not Sandra."

"A *very* careful examination of the grain by an expert *might* tell it," Strega replied, sharing with his master a habit of biting his nails.

"And it is her suit?" Zac looked at him sharply.

"Oh yes. It is couture by Thierry Mugler, a favorite of Madame's."

"And it is now, I hope, back in her office."

"Of course." Strega smiled smugly.

Zac leaned back and tapped the top of his desk approvingly.

"You're very efficient, Strega. I congratulate you on this one."

"Romanetto wants his dough," Strega said offhandedly, taking a chair and studying the photographs again.

"What dough?" Zac looked up in surprise.

"Well, expenses, you know. He's blown every franc he had. He has to have *something* to live on."

"I don't see why." Zac looked affronted. "He was simply paying back what he stole. He is lucky he wasn't sent to prison. Let him find a job; others do."

Strega tried to put on a reasonable face to someone who, he knew, was an unreasonable man.

"But Barcelona *was* extra."

"I thought it would be a nice touch, Barcelona." Zac looked at the ceiling.

"I had to advance him money for Barcelona."

"Then you were a fool, Strega." Zac rose abruptly. "You let that ruffian hoodwink you."

"I knew he hadn't the money." Strega's voice was whinnying.

"And I tell you he *had."* Zac thumped the table.

"Do you think I'd have given him money if I thought he didn't need it?" Strega made a choking sound as he imagined the chances of a profit draining away; not only a loss of profit, but a loss, period. If Zac didn't pay up he would actually be *out* of pocket in this very intricate and costly operation which, he thought, he'd stage-managed superbly.

"Look, Strega." Zac gestured toward the door. "I'm a very busy man. You handled this well and I'm pleased with you." Suddenly his voice changed and his tone became malicious. "But if you think I'm going to feather your nest and that of the crook you're dealing with you're mistaken. Romanetto stole twenty-five million dollars. He has been lying low, not living luxuriously since that time." He leaned forward and glared at Strega. "What about all the *interest* on twenty-five million bucks? It amounts to a few million. Plenty to take care of the deposits and keep a little to live on."

"I tell you he hasn't got a fucking sou." Strega unintentionally raised his voice as his frustration increased.

"Then do your sums again, Strega." Zac sat back in his chair. "And buzz off. There's a good man." He flapped his hand toward the door as though he were brushing off some unpleasant small insect which had crept onto his clothes.

As Strega left, the door on the far side of Zac's office opened and his sister Belle came out. She had a frown on her face and, as she sat down, the frown deepened.

"Do you think that was wise?"

"I think it was just." Zac managed to look smug. "Strega is a double-crosser, Belle, *you* know that. He never does anything that he doesn't gain by. He and Romanetto have probably hatched a nice little deal between them. Don't you worry, there's plenty of money there. Must be. I tell you, I am not at all worried on that score. Forget it."

"I've never liked Strega," Belle went on, as if she weren't listening. "I think he could be dangerous."

"I've never liked him either," Zac replied. "He's pigheaded and he's also a worm, to mix my metaphors. But I don't think he's dangerous, to me, that is. At a word from me the authorities could arrest him for the murder of the old lady in Épernay which, incidentally, he did commit."

"That happened a long time ago." Belle studied her long

carmine nails. "He knows a lot about all the illegal tricks *you* have been up to since."

Zac leaned forward and tapped his forehead.

"Look, that man is *not* a thinker. The gray matter is very dense. He is afraid of the police, he is afraid of me. In the end he will do what I say. Tell you what, I'll have a word with him later and toss him an anchor. When we get rid of the Irish woman, as we will very soon now, I'll promise him a really important job in the new revamped Desmond Group of which I shall be head."

The Princess von Burg-Farnbach was, if anything, more devious than her brother. She was a malicious, evil-minded woman who also had more brains than Zac, but not his power. In the France of her father—and despite his strange will—equal rights and the liberation of women did not figure.

Since Sandra had sacked Zac from Desmond he had built up a very strong position in the Banque Franco-Belges; he had a number of deals he was arranging, most of them just on the right side of legality. Zac, however, had a faith in his own powers, his own blinkered vision, that few people could shake.

"David Heurtey struck me as a very shrewd man," Belle, who had met Heurtey at dinner the night before, continued.

"Shrewd?" Zac gave a bellow of laughter. "He's a middle-aged playboy. He thinks of nothing but golf, horses and water sports."

"I don't agree with you and I wonder why he's here at this time, and who that woman is with him."

"His personal assistant."

"You think so? You think he would have invited a mere PA to an important dinner?"

"Americans are like that." Zac shrugged his shoulders. "You know they are. Democracy gone mad. Maybe she's his mistress. Some people might like her looks—not me. Too hard. She could be a lesbian."

Belle ignored his attempts at frivolity.

"Did you see how her eyes roamed over everyone at the dinner table, how she listened to everything, but said very little? Probably knew her place."

"Zac!" Belle tapped his desk. "Be serious. You are too chauvinistic. If you ask me, that woman doesn't miss a thing. She makes me uncomfortable. So, why is she here?"

"Oh, Belle, *ma soeur adorée!*" Zac said in a wheedling tone, rising and walking round the desk toward her. "Why must you worry your beautiful head about things that have no importance? Why torment yourself *imagining* things?" He sat next to her and took her hand in his. "But one thing *does* worry me a lot, my dear . . ."

"And that is?" But she knew already and her eyes avoided his.

"A certain diplomat with whom you spend too much time. It is the talk of the town, or shortly will be if you are not more discreet."

"He's a very attractive man." Belle had a telltale light in her eyes.

"Yes, but a *Romanian* . . . is it wise? Ceausescu is the greatest rogue in Europe . . ."

"Oh, Radu knows what he's like," Belle said with a laugh. "Anyway he's only with the *trade* delegation. Scarcely a proper diplomat."

"That's what I mean . . . trade *is* very important as far as we're concerned. More than one indiscreet woman has gone to prison or lost her job through sleeping with a foreign diplomat. Not like you to let your heart rule your head."

"Well, I'm not betraying any state secrets and Radu is not after any. It is purely"—Belle flashed him a smile—"what you call a physical affair. We spend too much time making love to discuss trade secrets, *not* that I know any. He is a very hot number that one, I promise you, and trade—except of a certain kind—is the last thing on our minds."

Zac got up and began pacing the room.

"What worries me, Belle, is that it's not *like* you. You have always been so careful, so cautious, so discreet. What has come over you now?"

"Radu's family were old Romanian aristocrats. He is not a peasant and he detests Ceausescu. He thinks his power will not last and that plots to kill him abound. If that happens Radu will seek asylum in the West . . ."

"Good God!" Zac cried in alarm. "I hope he is not in any plot to kill Ceausescu. Think of what the effect on you might be, of the scandal if your affair were revealed."

"Oh, *I'm* not involved." Belle gave him one of her brilliant smiles. "I'm just the one he spends the money on. He seems to have plenty of it and I say 'thank you' nicely."

"But, Belle, you're *not* short of money."

"I am, if you want to know." Belle was suddenly serious. "Carl is living on the last of his family money, and since the Irish whore stole *our* patrimony—yes, I could do with a bit more."

"Then *work* for it." Zac, rapidly losing patience, began to shout at her. "Work for it. That fashion house is scarcely functioning. Once you were an intelligent, clever businesswoman. What happened to you?"

"Our father died, *mon cher,*" Belle replied bitterly, "that's what happened, and a certain woman we both loathe decided to introduce her detestable self in our lives. She took over the company, she took over our lives, drove us from our home . . ."

"Yes, but Jean Marvoine . . . *your* fashion business. It was doing very well."

"Well, I'll tell you something." Belle's tone was contemptuous. "You have to thank *your* wife for running *that* down. I worked as hard as I could but I hadn't the flair she had nor, frankly, the interest. Now you can sell it for all I care." She got to her feet and reached for her handbag that lay on the floor at her feet. Then she got out her makeup bag and began to touch up her face. Before she shut the mirror she looked into it for a long time, liking what she saw: dark, almost black eyes; full, sensual lips on which the color of carmine against tanned skin looked strikingly good. Her deep chestnut hair had a streak of blonde; the color undoubtedly artificial but skillfully done. She was thirty-three and she just about looked it. But she might go on looking that age for a number of years: a good-looking, well-preserved woman at her peak.

She snapped her compact shut and, rising to her feet, leaned over to kiss her brother lightly on the top of his head.

"Take care, *mon vieux.* Don't plot too hard. I have to hurry now because I have a date."

She gave him a wicked, mirthless smile and, before he could speak, had left the room, clicking the door shut behind her.

The El Cid Hotel in a back street of Barcelona was not quite what Bernardo had grown accustomed to in the past few years. When he had first embezzled the money and gone on a wild spree with Eva it had always been the best suite in a series of the best hotels, all the way from Geneva to Bangkok and beyond.

But Bernardo was, if not clever, at least financially astute, and knew all about money, about investing it as well as how to spend it. In fact he didn't like spending it much, which was why he and Eva had ended up in Phi Phi Don instead of Bangkok, or even Kuala Lumpur or Singapore where rents and prices were too high. He had put his ill-gotten gains on long- and short-term deposits, low and high rates; he knew when to leave it where it was and when to remove it, so that the four years since he had been in hiding had seen his investments grow handsomely. That is until Strega caught up with him.

From then on it had been downhill all the way.

Bernardo Romanetto was a modest man from modest circumstances whose father had never risen above the position of clerk in a Swiss bank. He had, however, had his sons well educated, and although Bernardo had started in a humble capacity in the Desmond offices, by dint of hard work he had worked his way up. He not only worked hard, he was ambitious and had just the right amount of imagination to get to the top.

In many ways his imagination was his undoing. Although he was the financial manager of the Desmond Group's holding company he had ample opportunity to see how others lived, especially the Desmond family with its houses and yachts, its private jets, its strings of polo ponies, its art collection, its access not only to the good life but to the respect and esteem which wealth brought.

In time Bernardo grew jealous and greedy. He wanted more.

Bernardo had married, at twenty-five, a woman from the same background as himself: a clerk in the bank where his father had still worked, and would until the day he dropped dead in the street from a heart attack—an uneventful life somewhat dramatically and eventfully ended. Lisa Baldini was from the same family background, Swiss-Italian and, at twenty, she had been a bright, pretty girl with childbearing hips and big breasts.

It is doubtful whether Bernardo would ever have looked elsewhere had it not been for his greed. His desire to be bigger and better, more successful than he was, inspired him to seek physical and sexual gratification outside his home despite the comfortable house that his wife kept, the excellent food she served, the three happy, prosperous and clever children who were all doing well at school on the way to university.

As his scheme for acquiring more money than he was entitled to grew, Bernardo began to act out the sort of life he fantasized about. He began to drink, patronize bars and, eventually, he ended up with Eva who charged him nearly as much for one night as he earned in a week. Despite this he began to see the fascinating, beautiful woman who made him feel so important—virile as well as rich—behaving all the time as though he were the important, wealthy man he aspired to be.

When he met Eva, Bernardo had been staying at the best hotel in Zurich on Desmond business and, thereafter, he made many excuses to go to the same place—the financial heart of Europe—stay in the same hotel and, always, he called Eva's agency in advance to make sure she was free. For him—champagne and roses man that he became—she always was.

He lied to Eva, telling her that he was a venture capitalist who traveled all over the world; that he was so rich he was about to retire and take a well-earned holiday although he was only forty-five.

It wasn't until they came to Bangkok that he told her the truth.

He never knew why Eva hadn't gone straight back to Vienna where she came from, except that she probably thought she had burned her boats. Maybe she even loved him a little or thought she owed him something for the good times he had given her. Or, maybe, as he'd escaped for so long, she thought at last they were safe, until the dreadful day that Strega arrived and Bernardo's game was up.

For a time, as they traveled Europe in the footsteps of Sandra, she thought the good times had returned again. She even enjoyed the little games of deception, the dressing up as Madame, perhaps, even, the danger involved. She thought once they were out of Strega's clutches they would be free. Bernardo had told her that he had enough money for them to escape to, say, Australia or South America and begin all over again.

But then the screw started to turn. Barcelona was tacked onto the itinerary and Barcelona was three million dollars too much. Barcelona represented the money he still had left, and when that was gone there was nothing.

Not a dollar, a franc, a peseta or a sou.

Bernardo hung around in the El Cid drinking, while Eva went out to look for work. But she was long out of practice and she no longer liked what she used to do. When a man accosted her in the street and she brought him back to the El Cid Bernardo angrily threw him out, accusing her of turning him into a pimp.

"Get something *respectable,*" he'd bawled at her, "work in a shop."

Bernardo drank and brooded; above all he hated and then, one day, he got in touch with Strega and told him he wanted to see him. He made it sound just menacing and dangerous enough to know that Strega would make the journey.

The day he was due, Eva—who hated him even more than Bernardo did—decided to go and visit a friend who told her that an art gallery wanted a saleswoman. For some reason she thought Eva would be just right, even though she knew nothing about art.

Bernardo saw her to the door, then shut it carefully, locked it and, kneeling under the bed, drew out his suitcase in which, under spare pairs of pajamas, there was a 4.5 revolver. He took it out, sat on the bed, emptied it, cleaned it with his facecloth and refilled it again. Then he tucked it inside his waistband and waited for the telephone to ring.

That morning he had shaved carefully, collected a suit from the dry cleaners, put on a fresh shirt and new tie.

He didn't want to greet Strega like a man who had nothing left.

All afternoon Bernardo waited in his room smoking, drinking in moderation, just to keep topped up which, as a near-alcoholic, was something he needed. Otherwise his hands shook and he became nervy. He wanted Strega to think he was still in control.

The afternoon drew to a close, the traffic in the street outside grew more dense as people made for home, and in no time at all Eva would be back. Bernardo didn't want her there for the interview and he was beginning to get edgy, fidgety and nervous again when the telephone sounded and he was told there was someone for him in the lobby.

"Send him up." Romanetto found it hard to keep the excitement out of his voice. Then he replaced the receiver with a hand that shook, glanced at himself in the mirror, put a few drops of peppermint in his mouth to disguise the smell of booze, straightened his tie and went to the door.

Outside it stood not one man but two: Strega and, a pace behind him, a man with the most menacing eyes Bernardo had ever seen, worse than the hoods he had brought with him to Phi Phi Don.

"Now look here . . ." he began, stepping back.

"Get out of the way, Romanetto," Strega said as he pushed past him into the room. "Where's the girl?"

"Miss Raus," Bernardo said with dignity, "is out."

"Good!" Strega turned round and beckoned to his companion who, with very soft steps like a burglar, had come into the room. "This is an associate of mine, Señor Gomez."

Bernardo nodded briefly, but Gomez ignored him and began to prowl the room like a cat looking for a place to do its business.

"Who the hell is *he?*" Bernardo demanded.

"An associate, I said. He is here to see that there is fair play."

"Fair play!" Bernardo laughed. "You call what has happened to *me,* fair?"

"You call what you did to the Desmonds *fair?*"

"They could afford it."

"It was still stealing, Bernardo." Strega leaned toward him, his voice very soft, almost as though he didn't wish his companion to hear. "Stealing is a crime." He wagged a finger back and forth across Bernardo's face. "Very naughty."

"I did what was asked of me, and more," Bernardo protested. "I have paid back not only every penny I took, but the interest I had accumulated for my old age. Hardly fair, is it, to expect someone like me to start again . . ."

"So that's why you want to see me?" Strega threw his hat onto a table and slumped in a chair. In the corner Ignacio Gomez stood watchfully, saying nothing.

"Well, I have no money. I am destitute. I did what you told me to the letter. Eva cooperated, you know she did."

"She did." Strega nodded. "Her impersonation of 'Madame' was excellent. Yes, we are pleased with what you did." He turned toward the sweating man and gave a broad smile. "You have repaid your debt, Bernardo. Monsieur Desmond is satisfied. He will bring no charges, and you are free to go."

"Free to *go!*" Bernardo roared. "To where may I ask? I haven't enough money to pay this fucking hotel bill."

"Then you will have to send your girl out to work again." Strega gave him a broad wink. "I wouldn't mind being her first customer myself."

Bernardo crossed the room, his fist raised in the direction of his tormentor, when Gomez caught it in a steely clasp.

"Careful," he growled, "or I break your arm in six places."

Strega got up and made the gesture of one washing his hands.

"You really disgust me, Bernardo. You are not at all grateful. If Monsieur Desmond were to tell the cops what *we* know, you would be sent to prison for twenty-five years. We would put bigamy and drugs in for extras."

"And what if *I* tell what *I* know?" Bernardo stuck out his chin. "What if *I* told them about the 'sting' you have in mind for Madame Harcourt, a greatly respected businesswoman? I think a lot of people would pay a great deal of money to know that."

Strega hunched his shoulders.

"You wouldn't be such a fool."

"What have I lose?" Gathering strength as his courage flowed back, Bernardo pointed a shaking finger at him. "I tell you, Monsieur Strega, unless the equivalent of five million Swiss francs is made available to me by noon tomorrow, in mixed currency, I shall go to Madame Harcourt and tell her everything I know. Everything. Then you will see who will get a sentence for twenty-five years. I can promise you it won't be me."

That night Bernardo took Eva to the best restaurant in Barcelona and ordered champagne.

"I see the talks went well." Eva smiled with pleasure at the suggestion that the good life appeared to have returned again.

"Very well."

"Strega actually *agreed* to pay you?"

"Oh yes!" Bernardo pretended to look surprised. "That was the agreement. He knows I have to disappear and I must have something to live on. Three million francs was the interest," he chuckled, "with some more on top of that."

Eva gave a low whistle. It felt good to have a champagne glass between her fingers once again.

Yet only that afternoon she had planned to leave Bernardo, to quit while the going was good. But in a way she couldn't altogether understand she felt they belonged together, as though they were really married. Who knew, with money in the kitty maybe one day they would be.

"Where do we go to start our new life?" she asked, leaning across the table so that Bernardo could see her cleavage, her full breasts close together.

"Where you like, my love." He dipped his finger in his champagne and then, leaning across the table, inserted it suggestively between her breasts.

"I always liked the idea of Brazil," Eva murmured.

"Brazil it will be." Bernardo looked up to order more champagne. "I'll get the tickets tomorrow."

"But do you have the money?" She looked surprised.

"By tomorrow, yes."

"You're sure that Strega will keep his word?"

"Oh sure, sure. He has too much to lose. Desmond has too much to lose."

Eva's expression changed.

"You actually threatened him, a dangerous, evil man like that?"

"Oh no." Romanetto was anxious not to worry her. "But, I mean, if he reneges on the deal he has a lot to lose, hasn't he?"

"I suppose so," Eva said. But she looked doubtful.

The next day Eva was packing while Romanetto paced the room, smoking, drinking, restless, until he got on Eva's nerves.

"For God's sake go and get the tickets," she said. "Go for a walk; do anything."

"I have to stay here to get the money."

"He's bringing it *here?"*

"I wish you'd shut up," Romanetto snapped at her, "and trust me."

Eva suddenly sat down on the bed, her hands on either side of her; she began to sniff the air as though there was a smell she didn't like.

"There's something wrong," she said. "I don't like it. Strega's taking you for a ride. You never trusted him before, why should you now?"

"Look!" Bernardo stared fixedly at her. "I have something against Strega that will make *him* keep his promise, Desmond too. Remember how much I know. All right, I did threaten him, but only a little. I told him that if anything went wrong I would go straight to Madame Harcourt. Don't you see they're framing her, setting her up? Why, I could probably get *millions* if I told her what I knew . . . come to think," he said after a pause, "when we're out of the way and the money's in the bank I might still do that. A pension for life," he added as an afterthought.

Just then the telephone rang.

The collection point was to be an even smaller, crummier hotel on the other side of town, in a mass of dark alleys near the cathedral. The entrance smelled of urine and the lobby was so dark that at first Bernardo couldn't see anyone, let alone the person he was looking for.

"All in used notes, different currencies," he had specified to Strega.

"All present and correct," Strega had told him later on the phone. "Monsieur Zac *quite* understood."

"Oh, that's good."

It all sounded a bit unreal, but Bernardo believed him. When Eva had suggested that she found the transaction incredible in view of what they knew about Strega, that she should go with him, or the money should be delivered to their hotel, he had dismissed her fears.

"They like to play it this way," he told her, "cloak and dagger. I'll be back by five. They want to be finished with the whole business."

"Another night in this stinking hotel," she had sighed.

"And the day after that, Rio," he had said. "Leave it to me, my darling." Then he'd kissed her.

There was a clerk at the desk looking through a ledger and Bernardo was about to approach him when a shadow seemed to rise from a chair and went up to him.

"Mr. Romanetto," the shadow said. "Señor Gomez." He held up a case he was carrying in his hand, his expression solemn and unsmiling.

"It's all there?" Even Bernardo, half sharing Eva's fears, stared at it in disbelief.

"It's all there."

"I shall have to check."

"Of course." Gomez gestured around him, put down the case and lit a cigarette. "Take your time."

"I can't count it *here.*"

"Wait, I think there's a small room off the hall," Gomez said. "You'll have privacy there."

"Personally, I'd rather go back to my own hotel . . ." Bernardo began. "And you with me."

"Mr. Romanetto," Gomez said, with the air of a man trying hard to keep his patience, "if you think I have enough time . . ."

"Oh, very well," Bernardo said irritably. Then he lifted the case, found that it was quite heavy, and followed Gomez to an open door while, at the desk, the clerk was engaged in talking to a woman who undoubtedly worked there.

"You've brought me to a brothel," Bernardo mumbled.

"Yes," Gomez said with a half smile, "it's a hotel with services. *You* should know the sort of thing."

Bernardo ignored the suggestion as Gomez opened the door which led into a small, impersonal lounge with a television set in the corner. Bernardo swept the case onto a table in the center and began to count the notes in various denominations that lay stacked on top of one another in thick piles.

Gomez turned on the television, lit another cigarette and sat with his back to him. Bernardo gave a sigh of relief. After all it was not a trap; so far, so good.

"That's it," he said after twenty minutes had passed, "as near as I can make it. No forgeries, I trust."

Gomez didn't reply but switched off the television set and picked up his hat from the chair next to him.

With a sarcastic smile he opened the door and stood back for Bernardo to pass him, bowing slightly as he did.

Together the two men walked to the door of the hotel and Bernardo paused, offering him his hand.

"I guess this is where we part," he said.

"As a matter of fact I'm coming your way," Gomez replied conversationally. "Maybe we could share a taxi? That case is heavy."

"No, thanks . . ." Bernardo began, and yet the case was very heavy. "Well, maybe to the airport," he said.

"You're leaving without the girl?" Gomez looked surprised.

"She's meeting me there," Bernardo said. "Passports, tickets, everything to fly out."

"I should buy you a drink," Gomez murmured as they turned into the dank narrow street with two dogs sniffing at each other in the middle. "You're a very lucky man."

"You work for Strega?" Bernardo asked and then paused to give one of the dogs a sharp, unnecessary kick in the ribs.

Gomez stopped and looked at him.

"Now that I don't like," he said. "Why kick that poor animal when it's only trying to enjoy itself? You're a mean-minded bastard, Mr. Romanetto."

As he leaned forward and grabbed Romanetto by the collar the last thing the Swiss saw were those malevolent, brown slits that were Gomez's eyes.

As he sagged to the floor, the blade of the sharp stiletto that had impaled him protruding from the base of his spine, Gomez frisked him. He removed everything from his pockets, including his comb, tore any labels from his suit and removed his shoes. He did everything so quickly that before the dogs, who were the only witnesses to the bizarre scene, had time to resume their amorous activities, he had gone, leaving his inert victim lying staring up at the sky with vacant eyes.

Two days later, a black scarf over her head so that she already looked like a widow, Eva Raus stood for a long time gazing at the corpse the morgue attendant had wheeled out. All she could see were his face and, incongruously, a bare toe to which a ticket had been tied, stating the place of death and approximate time.

"Every means of identification had been removed from him, Madame," the morgue attendant explained in poor French. "Even his shoes."

Bernardo's eyes were still open as though what had happened had surprised him. She even thought he seemed to know her, and hastily turned her face away so that he wouldn't see the lack of recognition on her face.

She shook her head and, pulling her scarf even further over her face, went to the door. "How terrible," she murmured, pausing as she reached it. "Poor man."

"You do not know him, Madame?" The attendant looked surprised. "You are sure?"

"Quite sure. That person is certainly not my husband. I never saw him before in my life."

Sandra, wearing a white coat like the rest of her companions, gazed with some excitement at the bottles set out in a straight line in front of her. Each one contained a different blend of wines; so many from the Côte des Blancs, so many from the other *petits vins* from the Marne valley.

With her in the room were Étienne Legrand, Marcel Dupois, the head cellarman, a technician, Charles Morot, and René Latour, the *chef de cave* who, for weeks since the *vendange,* had kept his eyes on the fermenting wines in large *celliers,* or stores aboveground, which were maintained at very strict temperatures of around twenty to twenty-five degrees centigrade.

For weeks René and his colleagues had been sampling the wine lying in the vats in order to decide how much should be used for the vintage *cuvée,* how much for the non-vintage *cuvée* and how much should be stored for the future.

It was from a proportion of this new wine and old that the new *cuvée* Louis d'Or had been blended and was now waiting to be tasted. Sandra had a sense of mounting excitement as Étienne carefully poured a little of the wine from the first bottle into a glass.

"Of course, this is more than an assembly of *vins clairs,*" he explained carefully. "The *prise de mousse* will develop the taste, but basically this blend will be excellent."

Sandra sipped the pale, limpid liquid in her glass, allowing herself to swallow a little, and then spat the rest into a spittoon. "It looks and tastes very fine," she said at last.

"Wait until you taste the rest." Legrand glanced at René Latour who stood a little apart from the group thoughtfully eyeing the liquid in his glass. "What do you think of it, René?"

René rolled the liquor round in his mouth and then spat it into a leather spittoon on the floor.

"Pas mal," he said offhandedly and, as Étienne reached for another bottle, he drew out a large white handkerchief and wiped his lips, suddenly catching the eyes of Sandra who was gazing curiously at him. For a moment he stared at her and then, lowering his eyes, he turned away as Legrand poured the wine into a second glass.

"René," Sandra said, taking the new glass from Legrand, "is there anything the matter?"

"Nothing at all, Madame," René replied stiffly, putting the glass to his lips.

"Have you been sufficiently consulted in this procedure?"

"Of course, Madame." Yet he still avoided her eyes and concentrated on sampling the liquid in his mouth.

"René is *responsible* for it all," Legrand said in some surprise. "It is he, as cellar master, who decides on the blends for the tasting committee, and he who has selected the blends for the Louis d'Or *tête de cuvée* which, we hope, we shall market in a year or so's time."

"Oh, not for his birthday?" Sandra sounded disappointed.

"And that is, Madame?"

"September," Sandra replied.

"Alas, it would be better to wait a little longer, Madame. The longer the aging the better the aroma. We should not rush."

"Of course," Sandra said. "In that case let us make it a celebration for Christmas. We can announce it well in advance . . . the publicity people are getting very keen . . ."

"Christmas should *just* be all right," Étienne said, but he sounded rather doubtful.

Sandra, however, knew he was cautious: an older man nervous of newer techniques, who wished to leave things exactly as they were.

Finally the selection was made and the new prestige *cuvée* Louis d'Or pronounced a well-balanced blend of new and old wines. Sandra had removed her white overall and gone up with her colleagues to the boardroom where lunch had been laid.

She saw, however, that there were places for only four of them and, as Charles and Marcel waited respectfully for her to take her place, she said, "Is René not to join us?"

"He sent his apologies, Madame." Charles looked apologetic. "I think his wife is not well."

"I see." Sandra unfolded her napkin and tucked it into the top of her jacket then, crumbling the roll on the plate beside her, said in a controlled, even voice, "Does René dislike me so much because of what happened three years ago?"

"Madame, he does not *dislike* you," Étienne replied. "It is not his place to like or dislike. He has been with us since he was a boy, and his father before him. He . . ."

"Remains loyal to the Desmonds . . . he does blame me for what happened to the disastrous *tirage.*"

"I do not think he blames you, Madame." Marcel, who was the youngest present and now head cellarman, a position previously held by Latour, looked up as the waiter hovered with a bottle of champagne in his hand, waiting to pour. He nodded and, as the *mousse* rose in the glass, Étienne continued:

"I think you will find *this* vintage *cuvée,* Madame, approximates to the one we have chosen this morning. No, don't distress yourself about René. He is an employee, loyal to the firm for which he works and the person who pays his wages." Étienne's eyes twinkled in a smile. "*You,* in effect, Madame Harcourt," and he lifted his glass. "Health to you and your baby son."

"Thank you," Sandra replied and, when they had toasted her, she raised her glass to them. "Thank you all for your devotion and loyalty."

"How is your house coming on, Madame?" Charles inquired, tackling the salmon mousse which was the first course.

"Very well. I'm delighted with it. It is quite close to the Cathedral, and has a pretty walled garden. We are in now and settling down well."

"And you will live there permanently, Madame?" Étienne seemed genuinely interested. "Here, in the very heart of Reims?"

"Close to its heart," she replied with a smile, "and close to my heart." She leaned back in her chair, fingering the stem of her glass. "The past years have not been altogether happy ones as you all know and I think the main reason, apart from personal ones, is that I have got too far from the heart of the business. Champagne is like a tree from which too many branches have sprung; we have lost sight of the core of the business. I have many good lieutenants. Aeronautics has now grown to a giant and in Antoine Dericourt I have the best manager you could imagine: an engineer who knows the business inside out. The newspapers I have under the management of Émile Marché who, again, is a first-class newspaperman. In the years I have been in control I have rationalized and we are now only concerned with those enterprises at which we excel. I have got rid of supermarkets and estate agencies, and the numerous peripheral businesses which were not making money.

"I myself intend now to concentrate on champagne, Georges Desmond's great love, in order to make the Desmond *marque* the equal of any of its rivals and, of course, the foundation of which my late husband . . ." She paused and the men, observing her with sympathy, saw the muscles of her neck tighten as she made an effort to control herself. ". . . of which Michel was so proud, will become one of my chief interests to perpetuate his memory, his achievements in the field of virology. No, you will see a lot more of me in Reims in future and'—she allowed herself a brief smile—"a little experimentation, perhaps, with mechanical methods."

"Ah, Madame." Étienne pretended to groan and wring his

hands. "I thought you had abandoned those ideas you were so fond of when you first joined us?"

"Perhaps I have learned a little," Sandra answered. "In fact I have learned a lot: 'make haste slowly'," she said in English. "But I do think there are certain things we can learn from the manufacturers of Burgundy and Bordeaux. I have not altogether abandoned the idea of mechanizing the *vendange* . . ."

There was a discreet tap at the door and Antoinette put her head round.

"Yes, Antoinette?" Sandra beckoned to her.

"Madame, I am very sorry to interrupt you; but you have an unexpected visitor. He sends his apologies and doesn't wish for a moment to disturb you. He has already lunched and I have given him coffee and asked him to wait in your office, Madame."

"And who is this caller?" Sandra said peremptorily. "My engagement book, as you know, is full for two weeks."

"Madame, I dared not refuse to let him in," Antoinette said with an apologetic smile. "It is Monsieur David Heurtey of the Heurtey Corporation."

As Sandra went into her office David Heurtey got languidly to his feet and, with an engaging smile, put out his hand.

"Madame Harcourt, please *do* forgive me . . ."

Sandra stared at him for some moments before shaking his hand and inviting him to sit down. She then sat opposite him, crossing one leg over the other.

She wore a pale-lemon suit by Lacroix with a slightly bouffant skirt, no blouse and pearls at her throat. Her stockings were so fine that it was almost possible to think her legs were bare, and she wore a pair of plain court shoes which matched her suit.

Her beautiful blonde hair was just above her shoulder line, and a thick swathe swept back from her forehead.

Sandra never wore much makeup except around her eyes where the blusher and skillfully applied mascara enhanced their aquamarine unfathomable depths, almost like the deepest sea.

Heurtey thought that reports of her were not exaggerated and that she was the most beautiful woman he had ever seen. He sat down slowly, still looking at her.

"Your photographs do not do you justice, Madame Harcourt."

"Thank you," Sandra said with that air of frank courtesy that was equally engaging. "Are you here on business, Mr. Heurtey? It would have been nice to have known you were coming. We have just had a pleasant lunch at which you would have been most welcome. So, I take it that there is some reason for you wishing to surprise me?"

"Good heavens, no, Madame, not at all." Heurtey genuinely looked shocked but Sandra was not taken in by him. She suspected he was a good actor with the manner of a poker player. She was in fact very annoyed at this unscheduled arrival but to have refused to see him was unthinkable.

Heurtey went on: "I should explain my abrupt arrival by saying that I am partly on vacation. But I am taking time off to look into the European affairs of our corporation of which I am joint managing director. I am in Reims to look at the operations of Tellier, and as I drove along and saw the great name of Desmond I could not resist popping in. Do forgive me. This is a purely social call and when I return to Paris I will ask my assistant, Ms. Pasarro, to set up an official meeting with you. I could not, however, resist the temptation to see the great House of Desmond, or the redoubtable lady who runs it."

"Mr. Heurtey," Sandra said, "I am delighted you came, popped in as you said, but I have meetings all afternoon." She went to her desk and turned over pages of her diary. "However, as you are here presumably for a few days I would be delighted if you would be my guest for dinner. Are you free, for instance, tomorrow evening?"

"I'm sure I am," Heurtey said, without looking at his diary. "If I am not I will make myself free. I would like nothing better than to become better acquainted with you, Madame. I think we have a lot in common. Dinner tomorrow? May I know where?"

"My secretary will call you at Tellier." Sandra led the way to the door. "Would you like to have the brothers join us?"

"Why don't we spend the evening by ourselves?" Heurtey suggested. "As the heads of rival corporations who have done battle in the past, but who have much to gain by cooperation, we have a great deal to discuss."

"Tomorrow then at eight, at my house, I think." Sandra opened the door of her office and pointed to Antoinette in the outer room who, with headphones on, was typing onto the word processor in front of her. As soon as she was aware of the door opening she removed them and stood up.

"Antoinette will give you the address." She put out a hand and gave him a dazzling smile. "I very much look forward to seeing you then, Mr. Heurtey."

Heurtey bowed as she waved and then reentered her own office. He nearly whistled, but just stopped himself in time. After all the legendary Sandra O'Neill deserved her reputation.

Antoinette, watching him, saw on his face the expression she had seen many times before.

One would be a little jealous if one did not admire Madame so much as well. She handed him a card.

"Madame's personal address," she said matter-of-factly. "Will you be requiring a car, Monsieur Heurtey?"

"This is not the image I had of you, Madame," David Heurtey said with a smile on his face as Sandra sat with baby Louis on her knee, having just presented him to her guest. She wore white silk trousers with a colorful shirt from Ungaro, and he felt that she looked the very quintessence of the picture of a Madonna and child brought up to date by the twentieth century: the slim, beautiful Madonna, the chubby, red-cheeked infant.

Sandra, her hands tightly clenching those of the baby, smiled. "Even a businesswoman has her weaknesses."

"I'm glad to hear and to see it." David Heurtey sat back clasping his knees, his eyes still on Sandra as if he were spellbound.

"Was the reputation so very terrible?" She threw back her head as little Louis decided that the man opposite him was someone he liked and gave him a big, toothless smile.

"Not at all," David Heurtey said hurriedly. "One of great respect and admiration for a woman who, in a few short years, turned a business on the brink of bankruptcy into one of the most successful corporations in the world, despite many set-backs."

He paused and turned his attention to an inspection of the iridescent lights of the chandelier which, like everything else he had seen in the house, was in the best of taste.

It was an old house in the style of the *hôtel particulier*—so typically French—with a tiny, paved courtyard, a flight of steps leading to double doors and a staircase leading to the salon on the first floor, where it was much lighter. He had no idea what the back aspect was as night had fallen, but as this was the center of Reims he imagined it to be an enchanting walled garden, perhaps looking onto the back of a similar house. The brocade curtains were drawn and the imposing room had warmth and charm, the peculiar cosiness of a place lived in, and loved. He guessed Sandra now spent a great deal of her time in this part of old Reims.

There was not a lot of furniture, but what there was was good. Despite the atmosphere already engendered, the house bore signs of recent occupancy; there were even a few packing cases still in the hall.

Sandra mentally noted his observations as he studied the room as if seeking clues to the personality of its owner. He too had an air of repose which she liked and, to her surprise, she had discovered an almost immediate affinity with him, unlike her relationship with his father, the redoubtable Ebenezer. With him she had almost literally crossed swords when the smaller House of Desmond had dared to try and take over the much larger Heurtey Corporation, a bid which was doomed to failure. She imagined that this was why David Heurtey had been anxious to inspect her, wondering whether he would find friend or adversary.

He was a big, powerful man with considerable charm, perhaps too much. She wondered what really went on behind those intelligent but rather pale eyes. Just then there was a tap on the door and the nursemaid entered.

"May I take Louis for his bath, Madame?" she said, extending her arms.

"This is Mireille, my right hand." Sandra introduced them. Heurtey, who was the soul of New England courtesy, got up and politely shook her hand.

Mireille held Louis out for another kiss from his mother who then, with a rather wistful expression, watched him being taken from the room.

"I think it's something you would like to do yourself," Heurtey said with a sympathetic smile.

"It's something I usually do myself," she corrected him. "That's why I like to be in Reims. We finish at five or five-thirty and I go straight home. It is not so hectic as Paris. I entertain here very little."

She indicated the champagne standing in a silver bucket. David rose immediately and, drawing the cork with ease, slowly poured a little, first in one flute then the other, critically watching the *mousse* rise.

"I hope you like pink champagne," she said. "Some people consider it a woman's drink. I happen to love it."

"So do I." Heurtey held the glass toward her. "To the health of your baby, Madame Harcourt."

"To dearest Louis," she said, indicating to Heurtey that he should sit next to her. "My staff in Reims have suggested that they should create a special *cuvée* in honor of my son, to be called Louis d'Or."

"What a splendid idea." Heurtey carefully sat down beside her.

"Of course I was very honored; but the thing has mushroomed. We are not true Desmonds and I would never have dreamed of suggesting it myself. My publicity team have seized on the idea. They love it." She looked at him and laughed. "I shouldn't be telling you all this, the head of our great rivals Tellier."

"Oh, but Tellier knows it already, Madame." Heurtey sipped the wine in his glass. "They are green with envy. If only they had had the idea. If only they had something to celebrate. I lunched with Luc and Rudy today and they told me all about it."

"Really?" Sandra seemed surprised. "I didn't realize it would be so well known. It *was* intended to be a secret."

"I should imagine there is very little in Reims that remains hidden for long." Heurtey got to his feet and reached for her glass. "May I offer you some more of your own excellent vintage?"

She watched him as he crossed the room, took the champagne from the bucket and began to refill the glasses. It was a curiously intimate gesture, as though he felt at home, even lived here. She felt extraordinarily at ease with him on such a slender acquaintanceship.

He was, she decided, quite unexpected, not in the least like his father, who had been a rather stuffy cantankerous gentleman with a patrician face, but the business mannerisms of a Brooklyn gangster. She hadn't imagined that his son, who must be in his early forties, could be quite so obviously civilized, though he resembled his father physically with his high, disdainful brow and long, aquiline nose. Maybe, when crossed, the façade would drop but, somehow, she didn't think so.

"It's odd that we didn't meet before." She took her glass as he sat down next to her again. "I wasn't very popular with your father."

"When you launched your takeover bid?" Heurtey threw back his head and laughed. "I'll say you weren't. I don't think I ever saw him in quite such a rage, though I saw him in a good few. The things he had to say about you, Madame, were not said in the language of a gentleman. Of course, I know better!"

"Oh!" Sandra put her head on one side. "How?"

"I'm not such a ruthless man of business as my father. He lived it twenty-four hours a day. I like to enjoy myself. Also, I'd seen your picture. I was anxious to meet you."

Sandra ran her finger gently round the rim of her glass.

"You *are* a flatterer, Mr. Heurtey."

"No, I'm being truthful. At the time you attempted the takeover I was also married; but even a married man can admire a beautiful woman."

"And married no longer?" she inquired, taking care not to sound too interested. Clearly Heurtey was putting his cards on the table, establishing, in advance, the rules of the game. She thought the contest might be an exciting one.

David Heurtey shook his head.

"Alas, no. My wife and I were married twenty-two years. I am now forty-three and she forty-two. We were very young. Eventually she fell in love with another man because she complained I spent too much time away from home." He gave a rueful nod. "I'm afraid it was true. Not because of my work, not because of other women, but because I like to play golf. I like to play on all the best courses in Europe and the States and indeed at one time I thought I'd make the Ryder Cup team. Not any longer."

"Your poor wife was a golfing widow?" Sandra's look of sympathy seemed to be for the wife.

"Exactly. I thought that, although she detested the game, in her way she was happy; she had friends, family, we have recently become grandparents. But she had also fallen in love with one of our oldest friends, whose wife had died of cancer. They saw a good deal of each other. I knew about it of course . . . anyway"—he shrugged his shoulders, looking as though he didn't very much mind—"our children are grown-up, very sophisticated about the whole thing, and everyone's happy."

"Even you?"

"Oh, yes. There has been no acrimony at all. I am happy, I realized at last, not to feel guilty, though I must confess to you,

Madame Harcourt"—the end of Heurtey's nose twitched—"I no longer like playing golf *quite* so much. Maybe I needed to get away from my wife."

At that moment Sandra's butler entered to announce dinner and, finishing their champagne, they followed him into the dining room which was on the same floor.

This room too was simply furnished with a round, highly polished mahogany table with cabriole legs and chairs obviously by the same maker. The walls were covered in gray silk and there were some valuable eighteenth-century paintings on the wall.

"The absence of much furniture or many pictures here," Sandra said, as her butler held out her chair for her, "is because I have only just moved in. In fact"—she turned to Heurtey who was also sitting down—"you are one of the few people I've entertained since this dining room was finished. The table by René Jacob, who also made the chairs, was only delivered from the sale room yesterday."

"I'm deeply honored." Heurtey inclined his head.

"I chose the table because in Reims I prefer to have small dinner parties. In Tourville I can have a banquet for fifty or even a hundred. Here I can only have eight."

"In that case I feel most privileged, Madame."

"I think you could call me Sandra," she said, turning to him. "I shall call you David."

"Delighted," David said, then, appraising the broccoli soufflé he had before him on the plate, he tasted it. Finally he nodded approvingly. "This soufflé is excellent. You have a marvellous chef."

"He is the chef we use at our main office in Reims. Then if I am entertaining in the evening he works for me."

"And you think you'll settle in Reims?"

"Yes, I do." Sandra, having tasted the food and found it to her satisfaction, sat back and sipped her champagne. "I don't want to quarrel with the Desmond family. I never did and when . . ." she paused briefly for a moment, as if experiencing pain, and then continued quickly, ". . . I lost my husband they were very good to me. It seemed for a while that we might all live as Georges Desmond wished, in harmony as a family . . . but it was not to be. They feel, and always will feel, a deep sense of antagonism toward me, of outrage that a husband and father made that extraordinary will . . ."

"And it *was* an extraordinary will." Heurtey leaned casually on his elbow. "Didn't you think so at the time?"

"Oh yes, I did . . ."

"So extraordinary," Heurtey went on, "that one can hardly believe he made it."

"How do you mean?" Sandra rang the bell and then sat back.

"Well, did it ever occur to you it might be a forgery . . ."

"A forgery . . ." Sandra fell silent as her butler entered and removed the plates before serving the main course, which was a simple filet de boeuf, with fresh young Fleurie, full of flavor, to drink.

They were well into their meal when Sandra added, "A forgery I should have thought was out of the question."

"No one knew of his bequest. Not his wife, not his eldest son, not, if we are to believe it, even his lawyer."

"His lawyer was the only one who *did* know about it," Sandra said thoughtfully, realizing that her appetite had suddenly gone. "He drew it up."

"So he was the only person who knew?"

"As far as we know. His name was Maître Laban."

"A doubt seems to have entered your mind. Excellent wine." Heurtey drained his glass and, in the familiar manner he had adopted, helped himself to more, the bottle having been left on the table when the butler, at Sandra's request, withdrew.

"Yes," she replied, "for the first time a doubt *has* entered my mind. Why did it never enter anyone else's—Zac's, for example?" She looked curiously at Heurtey. "He seemed to accept it. He hated it, but he accepted it."

"Because it was written into the will that if anyone opposed it they would be disinherited. Zac hoped, in his own Machiavellian way, to disinherit you. He couldn't take the risk of going to court, could he, Sandra? No wonder he plotted against you."

"You seem remarkably well informed and interested in this matter." Sandra suddenly rang the bell.

"Oh, I am." Heurtey gazed thoughtfully at the table, drumming his fingers on it. "I am. Very."

The butler reentered and, until the end of dinner, hovered in the room, serving the cheese, the sweet. There was little chance to resume the intimacy of their conversation until they returned to the salon for coffee and the doors were shut.

David Heurtey, lighting a cigar, clearly at ease, said, "It is *very* good to be here, Sandra." He stretched out his legs before him and smiled at her.

She leaned an arm on her chair and looked at him, but without smiling.

"Now that we are alone again, David Heurtey, will you tell me why you came to see me?"

"Ah!" David pretended to carefully inspect the tip of his cigar. "I already told you. Who has not heard of Madame Harcourt, and yet I am one of the few people of any note who has not met you. Also, as my company owns the Banque Franco-Belges, and we have a champagne house that nearly rivals yours—you note," he added with a smile, "I say 'nearly'—we have a lot in common. But for a trick of fate you might have been my boss, as you once tried to take over our company."

"That was a very long shot," Sandra said with a laugh. "It was a bit naughty. I think I was drunk on power at the time."

"Well, you could have succeeded. It certainly made my father *very* angry." Heurtey smiled. "And I enjoyed seeing my father angry."

"Did you not love your father?" Sandra wondered.

"Oh, very much." David held up a hand. "Don't misunderstand me. But we were just the two boys and he kept us down, giving us relatively menial jobs in his organization, which is why I became addicted to golf. He did to us what Georges Desmond did to his sons. Fathers can be very jealous. Now that I am in control, at least of one half, I am very interested. I want to learn all I can, and every time I read anything about the European operations something seems to come up about Zac Desmond, not always in a very complimentary light." David sighed and relit his cigar which had gone out. "That man takes so many risks he is very lucky to survive in business."

"He is," Sandra agreed, pursing her mouth grimly.

"His achieving presidency of the bank," Heurtey went on, "was a piece of barefaced skulduggery. He never gave sufficient notice of the meeting. My father was on his way over, but he held it before he arrived. Technically he could have disqualified Zac but it would have put the bank in bad odor, undermined investors' confidence. So Father supported him. Zac is a very cute operator."

"Cute's the word," Sandra said. "But sometimes not quite cute enough. He always gets found out. Sooner or later someone discovers what he's up to. He bought wildly into all sorts of unrelated businesses which I had to sell off. Even though he remains nominally on the Board, I consult him as seldom as I can. To tell the truth it is unwise completely to trust him. To give you an example: just before I arrived, the financial manager of the holding company embezzled twenty-five million US dollars and was allowed to get off scot-free."

"You mean he was never prosecuted?" Heurtey looked amazed.

"He was never *found,"* Sandra replied indignantly, "and no one even seemed to take the trouble to look for him. This and all sorts of other more minor scandals I was able to discover in the few weeks before and after my baby was born, because I could take the time I needed to look into all the group affairs in depth."

"Other women would have been reading books on raising children," Heurtey said gently.

"Oh, I did that too," Sandra replied casually. "Naturally I went into all that *very* thoroughly as well."

She paused and studied Heurtey's face for a moment or two as though weighing him up. "Incidentally, David, to change the subject completely, I hear you are accompanied on your travels by a beautiful assistant. Should I have asked her tonight?"

"Not at all." David shifted in his chair. "She's not really my assistant."

"Oh!" There was a roguish look in Sandra's eyes. "Something else, perhaps?"

"She's on secondment to me from an American firm of corporate accountants. I realized I knew far too little about our European operations. They're too diversified: electronics, banking, sports equipment, champagne. She's looking into everything for me. I want to be sure that every aspect of the business is right on the ball. Her name is Joanne Pasarro. She's quite a girl."

"Well, well!" Sandra said with a note of amusement in her voice. "I look forward to meeting her."

René Latour stood respectfully a few paces away from Zac, watching with some interest, but also a degree of unease, the display of temper from a man he had known all his life; after all they were the same age and had attended the college of oenology together. The only difference was that one was superior to the other, who was never allowed to forget it.

"A new *cuvée* did you say?" Zac exploded again. "In honor of that little . . ."

"In honor of Madame's son, Monsieur Zac," René said again. "I thought you should know,"

"You thought *right!*" Zac brought his fist down on the Boudin bureau which was one of the most priceless antiques of the many in the Château de Tourville. "A special *cuvée* is only made for something *really* special like" — wildly Zac gestured around—"like the wedding of the Princess Elizabeth of England before she was Queen, the millennium of the Persian Empire by special request of the Shah of Iran, the launching of the first astronaut Neil Armstrong on the moon . . . do you mean to say that the Irish tart considers the birth of her bastard an event that compares with any of these?"

René winced but said nothing. In the corner, carefully listening to all that was said, sat Belle. When she realized that Zac's firework displays might antagonize someone whose services were possibly valuable to them, she rose and said soothingly to her brother, *"Mon cher frère,* why should it offend you so much?"

"Because I do not want the name 'Desmond' besmirched by that little . . . little . . ." This time the *mot juste* finally failed him. "What a *nerve* that woman has, what impudence."

"I believe it was suggested to Madame by Étienne Legrand," René said. "In fact the whole staff was consulted." René paused and the tone of his voice changed. "But not I."

"And why were you left out, René?" Belle's tone was deceptively gentle and encouraging. "Surely *you* as *chef de cave . . ."*

"I was left out," Latour said bitterly, "because they knew I would not approve. Madame and I have not been close since she suspected *me* of being involved in the affair of the *tirage,* Monsieur Zac. As you know I was not."

"Oh, that is all forgotten, that nonsense." Zac flapped his hand with irritation in the manner that one swats a fly.

"But not by me, Monsieur Zac," Latour insisted. "She thought I was conniving with . . . with whoever . . ."

"We *all* know who was responsible for it." Zac thumped the priceless bureau again. "We have no doubt about *that.* That rogue Pagés was *entirely* responsible for it . . ."

"But he was just a very humble man, Monsieur Zac." René screwed up his features in bewilderment. "In charge of the computer room. What on earth . . ."

"Maybe Strega also was too foolish, ambitious. I don't know." Zac was obviously anxious to drop the subject. "Anyway, René, forget it; it all happened a long time ago."

"But Madame has not forgotten it, Monsieur Zac, and neither have I . . . that is why I am here."

For a moment Zac looked unnerved and Belle rushed forward to rescue him.

"What do you mean, René?" Her low, beautifully modulated voice was calm and encouraging. The Princess was always regarded with some fear by the Desmond employees, but also with respect. No one had missed her when she ceased to take an active part in the champagne house's affairs. She had, however, an acknowledged palate and, above all, she was in the direct line of Desmonds.

They were in the library at Tourville and she invited René to be seated and sat down next to him, peering into his eyes. "*Do* tell us what you mean," she said again.

"I thought it presumptuous of me, Madame," he said nervously, as Zac's expression too changed, and he stepped forward with, at the same time, a cautious glance at the door.

"Speak softly," he said. "The Irish bitch has her spies everywhere."

Latour's eyes rounded with horror and beads of perspiration stood out on his face.

"It's all right; she's not *here* and all the staff are off duty. You can confide in us with confidence. You have a plan, have you not?"

"Well, I thought . . ." Latour looked sheepish. "Maybe *if,* somehow, the *cuvée* was spoilt Madame would look foolish. But you see we cannot do anything like the *affaire* of the *tirage* though I was innocent then—because I shall be blamed again. I confess the matter has left me a little resentful. I have not had the promotion in the firm I hoped . . ."

"But you have a very important job, René," Belle said with her brilliant smile. "You were made *chef de cave* in place of Jourdan."

"Monsieur Legrand should have retired years ago . . ."

"Ah, you wish to be *director* of the Établissements Desmond. Well, you will, you will." Zac sat on the other side of the nervous *chef de cave* and patted his arm. "When we return to take up direction of the group's affairs which, with your help and that of others, cannot be very long now. Now, dear René, tell me, what simple method could we use to destroy the upstart's plans for the little prince, and make her once more the laughingstock of the world?"

10

Sandra rose from her desk and reached the door just as it was thrown open with a flourish and her visitor appeared, his saturnine features, for once, wreathed in smiles.

She always anticipated a visit from Zac with some apprehension and his air of bonhomie surprised her. He embraced her warmly and then followed her into the office—his father's office, the one that should have been his—exclaiming: "My dear Sandra, let me congratulate you. What an excellent idea. A *cuvée* in honor of the baby Louis? Couldn't be better. And as this year is a good year we shall blend it with some of our great reserve wines. Mind you"—for a moment he frowned—"we do not have very much of this, say enough for two hundred thousand bottles? Still, such a reserve *cuvée* will fetch a high price. We have to beat our competitors, Dom Pérignon, Delbeck, Roederer and Krug. It will be the most expensive champagne of the year. And *le plus snob.* Everyone will want to buy it."

Recovering from her surprise, Sandra relaxed and pointed to a chair.

"Why, thank you, Zac. Do sit down. However, I must tell you it was not *my* idea but that of our staff. Legrand put it to me and asked me if I'd mind. Of course I said I didn't."

"Then that is even more of a tribute." Zac felt in his breast pocket. "It shows how thoroughly you have integrated yourself with them, how much they, quite rightly, respect you. Now, my dear." With the paper taken from his pocket in his hand, Zac leaned forward as if in confidence. "For a prestige *cuvée* you must have a special bottle and I have taken the liberty of making a few sketches which, with a new and distinctive label such as we designed in the fifties for Marilyn Monroe, will be a collector's item; one that people will, perhaps, keep in their cellars for years before opening it."

Sandra, surprised, pleased, but still a little suspicious, took the paper on which were drawn a number of well-executed sketches with bottles of various designs, all of them showing a long, narrow neck of extreme elegance. Even the labels had been designed with, on all of them, the distinctive name "Louis d'Or: *tête de cuvée*".

"I see you even know the name," she said and in her heart she recognized that familiar sensation, a dark feeling of mistrust which she always associated with any proposal from Zac.

She studied the designs for a few moments, aware that he was watching her eagerly, and then she put them on her lap and gazed at him.

"Zac, just why are you doing this?"

"I beg your pardon?" A look of surprise, even hurt, came into his eyes.

"I don't see why you are going to all this trouble."

Zac got up and walked round the desk that had belonged to his great-great-grandfather, rubbing a finger lovingly along its sheen. Then, with one hand still on the desk, he gazed sadly at her.

"My dear Sandra, can you not accept the olive branch that I and my family have so generously extended to you? Can you not bring yourself to *believe* in our protestations of friendship—pure, genuine and sincere, our wish finally to bury the hatchet, to forget the unhappy past?"

He trailed off as Sandra appeared unmoved, a sardonic twist to her lips. Then she rose, put the sketches on the desk and went round to the other side.

"I do find it very hard, I must confess, Zac, to understand such a complete change in your character. You see, in the past you have tried to seduce me by words such as this and I have believed you because I wanted to. Of course I realized what a shock your father's will was and your resentment of me was understandable. But you fought, opposed and tricked me. It is hard now to accept that you really want to be friends."

"I am a realist," Zac said, running a hand over his head to smooth his hair. "It's as simple as that. I've said it before and I'll say it again: let bygones be bygones. With Louis d'Or we can start again. I do assure you, Sandra, that I want to do everything I can to convince you of my good faith, and that of my family. So I have designed this bottle for you." He gave her a deprecating shrug that was rather touching. "It took me many hours . . . and yet you don't appear to appreciate it."

"Oh, I do, but I question your motive. Why should Louis's birth be such a joyful event for you?"

"I am sorry you mistrust me, Sandra," Zac said, ignoring her question. "I shall not beg, I promise you; but I think I may be able to help you over one thing. I think I can help you to recover Bob. There, will *that* be a sign of my good will?"

"Oh, *Zac!*" Abandoning her reserve, Sandra flew impulsively toward him. "How can you do *that?*"

"I have made that idiot of a brother-in-law of mine do a little work," he replied contemptuously. "He is up to his eyeballs in drugs; in the debt of the underworld. I have asked him to try and find who is holding Bob and how, and I am using all the influence I possess through him and Tara's family to restore to you a man you love very much. I can't be more sincere than that, can I?"

Sandra put a hand on his shoulder, a gesture that caught him unawares, and seemed for a moment to alarm him.

"What can I say? If you restored Bob to me it would seal our friendship for life."

"Good." Zac seemed pleased with the interview and, taking her hand from his shoulder, kissed it.

"I shall fly to Rome personally this weekend to check on how the investigation is going." His expression changed. "I hear by the way that you have bought a house in Reims, Sandra? I hope that doesn't mean you are to give up visiting Tourville altogether? My mother has a soft spot for you."

"Oh no, I shall be there most weekends," Sandra said breezily. "It's just the settling-in process. You and Tara must come to dine . . ."

"As soon as I return from Rome, and if I have any news I will telephone you at once." Zac seemed genuinely delighted. He picked up the papers with his designs on them and let them drop again. "Sandra, why don't you have Latour glance over these? He is the best possible man in the business.

Sandra stood thoughtfully at the window of the office looking out into the courtyard where Zac's Mercedes waited, his chauffeur still in the driving seat. It had been a quarter of an hour since he had left her office and she had stood there, intending, as a friendly gesture, to wave him good-bye. Why hadn't he appeared?

At that moment he came to the door, accompanied by Étienne Legrand, and they stood chatting in a friendly way before shaking hands. The older man then stood back while Zac got into his car and leaned forward to give instructions to his driver. He then looked up, saw Sandra and waved. She waved back and, when the car was out of sight, walked slowly to her desk and stood going through the designs. They were certainly most attractive.

There was surely nothing at all wrong with designing a new bottle? What harm could there possibly be? It was not like an addition to the precious composition of the *cuvée,* such as the very important *liqueur de tirage.* Yet knowing Zac as she did it was so difficult to trust him, to bury the hatchet. How could she know whether or not this time he was sincere? Why should she doubt that he had changed, and that this was a genuine gesture of friendship, and what sort of life would she lead henceforward if she let it continually be dominated by suspicions? If Zac were trying to be friendly, if he could really help her, above all, if he could restore Bob. . . . As for suggesting René Latour, that was a good idea. She would draw her *chef de cave* into her confidence and, at the same time, try and find out the reason for his lack of warmth toward her.

One thing she knew for sure was that there was an honest man, a citizen of Reims who had worked for the company all his life: a man whom she could trust.

Later that afternoon she sent for Latour, whom she saw often but usually in his laboratory and in the company of others. He was always very polite, punctilious and correct; but he didn't have the warmth toward her that the other members of the staff had. He seemed to hold back. She guessed that he was a diffident, reserved man, who was probably like this in private life, who kept himself to himself.

Latour slid quietly into her office at about half past four. She liked the English habit of taking tea in the afternoon and, as she was just finishing, she offered him a cup. Politely he refused and she invited him to sit down. For a moment she thought he would say he preferred to stand, but then he sat in an armchair as far away from her desk as possible and, hands joined, stared owlishly at her through an oversized pair of spectacles.

She called her director, Étienne Legrand, by his Christian name as she did all the other employees; but not Latour. For some reason he had always been "Monsieur" and she so addressed him now.

"Thank you for looking in to see me, Monsieur Latour," she said and, taking the clutch of designs from her desk, pulled up a chair to sit next to him. Hastily he tried to help her, they almost collided and then they both sat down rather awkwardly together.

"Is everything all right in the laboratory, Monsieur Latour?" she inquired, casually sifting through the papers. "The fermentation is going according to plan?"

"It will be a great vintage year for all our wines. As for the special *cuvée* Louis d'Or, that will be one of the great bottles of the century."

"That's excellent news." Sandra looked gratified. "When shall we be able to drink it?"

Latour thoughtfully screwed up his eyes.

"Certainly this time next year, but better left for a few years."

"By his twenty-first birthday will it still be drinkable?"

"Oh, certainly." Latour's expression remained inscrutable. "Above all in magnum."

"But maybe we will have another one for that occasion?" Sandra suggested pleasantly.

"If Madame wishes." Latour bent his head, but without smiling. He wore his white coat and his manner was one of restlessness, like that of a busy man wishing to be back among his blending and testing equipment, the tools of his trade.

"I shan't detain you for more than a few moments," Sandra said, "as I imagine you're busy." She spread out the sketches Zac had left her on the table between them. "Now, Monsieur Desmond has very kindly suggested a new design for the bottle for Louis d'Or, also a label. But the bottle"—she looked at him quizzically—"is an odd shape, don't you think?"

Latour, still expressionless, adjusted his spectacles and looked carefully through the sketches, nodding as he did so.

"Unusual, but exquisite, Madame." He sounded quite enthusiastic and, selecting one of the designs, put it in front of Sandra. "Were I asked my opinion I would suggest *that.* Aesthetically and technically it seems to me the best."

She studied the design in question, where the bottle had a particularly long, fragile neck. Aesthetically it was undoubtedly beautiful, but was it also practical?

"You don't think it's too delicate?" she inquired.

Latour blinked. "Delicate? In what way, Madame?"

"Would it not be difficult to rack? Might there not be a risk of breaking?"

Latour shrugged.

"Certainly one would have to be most careful. But our

cavistes are experienced. I would suggest the *remuage* by hand and not in the mechanized *pupitres.* But as there are only two hundred thousand bottles . . . yes. I don't see why not."

"You already know the number of bottles?" Sandra was struck by the fact that Zac had said the same thing. Then she remembered how long it had taken for him to reach the main door from her office.

"I would say *about* two hundred thousand, Madame," Latour replied and, as if he could read her mind, added, "Monsieur Zac popped into the laboratory today after his visit to you. He was very excited by the new *cuvée* and we talked about the final blending, which Monsieur Zac clearly approved. His enthusiasm for a new *cuvée* and a specially designed bottle was most pronounced." Latour paused and when he spoke his voice was unusually emotional. "Monsieur Zac has a *great* knowledge of our business, Madame." Latour got suddenly to his feet as if he had done what he had been asked for. "There is one thing, Madame," he added. "I suggest you keep the design of the bottle secret."

"Why?"

"It is so unique that you would not wish to have others imitating it. It is unique, but would be easy for unscrupulous people to copy."

"That's a good point," Sandra said, "one I hadn't thought of. I'm grateful to you."

"*And* I could suggest an expert firm of glassmakers to make the mold. They are unsurpassable for quality. As for the label" — he shrugged as if this did not interest him too much—"I would suggest that our advertising agency has a look at it. I think perhaps Monsieur Zac's design could be bettered. It is a little ornate."

"Well, thank you *very* much for your advice, Monsieur Latour." Sandra rose with her *chef de cave* and accompanied him to the door where she put out her hand. "I am so pleased to have your cooperation on this project."

"You are *most* welcome, Madame." Latour took her hand

with a limp clasp of his own. "I am always entirely at your service."

Claude Maison, the head of the art department of the advertising agency employed by Desmond, seemed scarcely able to contain his excitement as, from his portfolio, he produced his sketches and laid them on the table in front of Zac, Sandra and Monsieur Fournier, the head of the famous glassmaking company which had made Desmond bottles for over a century.

"We were tremendously fired by Monsieur Desmond's designs," Maison said, with an obsequious bow in Zac's direction, "and I think, I hope you will agree, that our art department has produced some of its finest work."

Sketches of various shapes and sizes of bottles were followed by a profusion of gorgeous labels, each new presentation rivalling the previous one in typography, style and layout. Prominent were the words *Louis d'Or Champagne Desmond* which made Zac's gorge rise, though he was careful not to show it.

Sandra had seen the sketches at the presentation in Paris by the firm, and she had adhered to the slim, elegant bottle with an elongated neck which was graceful and aesthetic, as pleasing to the eye as its contents would be to the palate.

But when she announced her choice to Monsieur Fournier he grimaced and glanced at Zac.

"What do you think of this, Monsieur Desmond?" he asked the man whom he had known and whose judgment he had respected for years. "Too thin, eh?"

"Mmm!" Zac's brows drew together and, leaning over, he made a pretence of carefully studying the sketches. "It is certainly *very* pleasing. I admire Madame's taste. It is mine, too, as a matter of fact."

"But the width, Monsieur Zac," Fournier protested, making a calculation on a piece of paper in front of him. "It will be such a delicate bottle, the calibration will have to be carefully calculated. This will make it extremely expensive."

"Oh, expense is of no importance at all." Zac looked at

Sandra for confirmation. "This bottle will not retail for less than 350 francs. I think I am right in that, am I not, Madame?"

"At least," Sandra said with a smile. "We make a special *cuvée de prestige* and charge accordingly."

"Well, if expense is no object . . ." Monsieur Fournier shrugged thoughtfully and lit a cigarette. Then he scratched the side of his cheek with a tobacco-stained finger. "I am not at all happy about that neck."

"What makes you *so* unhappy?" Sandra looked searchingly at him. "Do you think it not a good idea of Monsieur Desmond?"

"Madame." Monsieur Fournier bowed formally in her direction. "It is a very elegant, beautiful bottle, and we have had the privilege of making bottles not only for Champagne Desmond but for other equally distinguished houses for over a century. In olden days, Madame, champagne bottles were made exclusively by glass blowing and it was not until the end of the century that special molds were devised to cure the unevenness of hand-made bottles. In fact, Madame, automatic machinery for the production of champagne bottles was not invented until the Second World War and it is largely this type of machinery that we use today.

"You see, Madame"—Monsieur Fournier, warming to his subject, concentrated his gaze on her as though instructing a novice—"because of the carbonic gas present in the production of champagne, because of the processes of second fermentation, of *remuage* and *dégorgement,* stresses which normal wine bottles are not subjected to, the champagne bottle has to be extra strong. In fact it is the heaviest in existence, weighing just over two pounds. The neck of the champagne bottle facilitates the fall of sediment and extraction of the cork; so the narrower it is. . . ." His expressive mouth turned downward again. "Though very elegant it is *not* very practical."

Zac expressed his obvious irritation at what was being said by shuffling the papers on the table before him while Claude Maison's expression was one of gloom, of hopes dashed.

"Well, if what Monsieur Fournier says is correct . . . we shall have to redesign . . ."

"Nonsense!" Zac raised his voice as if to stifle any protest. "For such a special event as the birthday of the heir (he choked over the word), we wish to produce an exceptional *cuvée* in an exceptional bottle. The design has been chosen by Madame Harcourt and myself. Thus it is important to put the mold into production and deliver the bottle to us very quickly. *If* you don't feel capable of making the bottles, please say so."

Monsieur Fournier gave a Gallic shrug and scratched behind his ear again.

"*Anything* can be done, Monsieur Zac, as you know. The neck can be specially strengthened by using . . ."

"But it must not be too *thick.*" Zac looked as though he was beginning to lose his temper. "Really, Gérard, if you find the whole thing *so* difficult we can easily go elsewhere." He made as if to rise, and Monsieur Fournier jumped to his feet.

"Please, Monsieur Zac, I beg you not to take this attitude. You know that we are capable of producing the best glass in France, and, as you have said you are willing to pay, we will carry out your instructions."

"To the letter." Zac thumped the paper with the approved design. "To the merest fraction of a millimetre."

"To the merest fraction of a millimetre as specified, Monsieur Zac." With an air of relief, Fournier reached for the design and rolled it up as if, by this swift action, he had secured the contract.

"Perhaps you'd let us have a sample when you begin the manufacture." Sandra once again was full of foreboding. Had Zac, in his enthusiasm to please her with the most beautiful bottle, overlooked sensible precautions? "I would like one or two of your experts in Reims to be sure . . ."

"Sandra!" Zac turned eyes of exasperation to the ceiling, looking to Claude Maison for confirmation. "Don't forget that we can't be permanently protected against infringement of copyright and its subsequent commercialization. Our competitors will be free to copy it and we shall be defenseless."

"But, Zac"—Sandra tried to sound reasonable—"we must trust our staff. After all, the formula for the *cuvée* is known only to them."

"Then trust no one but Latour," Zac snapped. "He is the *only* man whose judgment I trust about *anything.*"

Fournier seemed to decide that this concluded the matter and gestured toward the door.

"And, now, to celebrate the occasion we have prepared a little lunch, Madame, Monsieur . . . if you would step this way."

Inwardly Sandra sighed, but her expression remained pleasant. When was there *not* a little lunch attached to any occasion, however big or small, in this nation of gastronomes?

On the way back to Reims Sandra and Zac sat in the back seat of the car, Claude Maison on a seat facing them. In his hands he clutched his precious plans but his face, despite the excellence of the lunch, the truffles specially brought from Périgord the day before, looked anxious.

Zac was smiling happily, smoking a cigar, gesticulating, obviously full of enthusiasm for the plans.

"We shall try and invite the President of France to the celebration dinner . . . it will be a birthday dinner, naturally, Sandra?"

"It will be a little *after* the birthday. The champagne cannot be ready before this time next year . . ."

"Let's make it a second birthday." Claude Maison appeared to brighten.

"Don't be *absurd.*" Zac looked at him with disgust. "This is to celebrate the *birth* of Madame's son. What significance has a *second* birthday?"

Stinging from the reprimand, feeling like a schoolboy in short pants, the artistic head of the large advertising agency bit his lip and looked anxiously out of the car window, as Zac went on.

"Unfortunately one cannot hurry up the process of making an exceptional *cuvée,* although we are doing all we can."

Sandra took careful note of the "we" but said nothing.

Once again beset by doubts, she looked carefully at the profile of the man next to her but his expression remained enigmatic. Why should he wish to celebrate the birth of someone who might one day succeed her? Her son would come before his, or any Desmonds.

Had they really turned the corner? Was he really now her friend?

"As for *your* interference, Maison," Zac said coldly to the publicist, "if you are not careful we shall be removing our account from you . . ."

"But Monsieur Desmond," the poor man spluttered, "what did I do? I merely suggested that in view of Monsieur Fournier's objection we would have to take another look at our campaign. I . . ."

With an expletive Zac interrupted him. "You undoubtedly think yourself an excellent advertising man, and I'm told you're the best, but you know *nothing* about the making of glass bottles for champagne. *I,* on the other hand, know almost all there is to know, and when I say something in public, be good enough not to disagree with me. Is that clear, Maison?" Zac pointed his cigar at him as though it were a weapon. "Quite clear? You do as you are told. *No* interference . . ."

"I assure you, Monsieur Desmond, I did *not* mean to offend you. I was *not* interfering."

"You did what you thought best, Claude." Sandra nodded consolingly at him. "It's true we may have to change promotional material if, for any reason, the neck is too narrow or the glass too thin. It might burst, might it not, Zac?"

"Certainly not, if carefully handled," Zac replied. "And a lot will also depend on the temporary cork, the *bouchon de tirage,* but I shall see to that myself and ensure that it is the best Catalan cork, made only of one piece. It will be specially fitted to the shape of the neck and you will have no trouble at all."

"In that case," Sandra said with a grateful smile, "I leave it all to you who, after all, are the expert."

"Thank you, Madame." Zac's self-satisfaction was evident, but Sandra turned rather sadly away.

In the years since she had come to France she had gained much information, she had been told she was an exceptional pupil, but nevertheless she still felt she had a lot to learn.

Whereas with Zac—champagne was in his blood.

"Of course, you trust him completely now?" David Heurtey, listening to the story of the new special *cuvée* and the visit to the glassmakers, cast an anxious glance at Sandra.

They were meeting at his apartment in the Ritz which renewed for her old memories of her first year in Paris when she had lived there herself. Also there for the first time she had met Joanne Pasarro who turned out to be not so much beautiful as interesting; a tall, elegant woman, a blonde like Sandra but not, one guessed, naturally. She had dark, rather strange eyes and a thin, determined mouth. Attractive, but not beautiful.

Joanne looked as though she had seen a lot of life. She had that rather weary air of the worldly wise.

"Trust Zac?" Sandra looked at him askance. "In matters like this, yes. Wouldn't you?"

David Heurtey rose and refilled his whiskey glass, a beverage he seemed to prefer to champagne, which was the only thing about him, so far, of which Sandra didn't quite approve. He would drink champagne, but if asked to state a preference would choose bourbon, with no water or soda and heavily laced with ice.

However, for herself and Joanne there was an ice bucket with a bottle of the 1979 vintage and two glasses.

Sandra had the feeling that Joanne might possibly have preferred bourbon as well, but she didn't say so and gladly accepted her champagne, though she tossed it back like vodka or whiskey and not a fine, delicate wine.

Joanne wore a grey suit and a black shirt, her blonde hair tied back in a ponytail. She could have been thirty-six to forty and had deep lines on either side of her mouth. She certainly wasn't beautiful, but she had allure, a certain *je ne sais quoi.*

Somehow Sandra didn't think she was David Heurtey's mistress and somehow also, though she didn't know why, she was glad.

She watched David tinkering with the whiskey, the ice in his glass, his attitude one of a man who was playing for time.

"I should tell her," Joanne said at last. "She must know a lot of what we know."

"Good heavens," Sandra exclaimed, "why all this mystery?"

"Because Zac is a mysterious fellow." David Heurtey sank deep in his comfortable chair. Once more he wore flannels and a well-cut sports jacket in preference to a business suit, as if he had spent a day at Deauville playing golf. Maybe he had. He was a rather odd, enigmatic man, an atypical American businessman, and Sandra knew she was beginning to feel drawn to him despite such a short acquaintance.

"Sandra, we know about as much about Zac Desmond as you know." David took a mouthful of whiskey. "And that is plenty. We know he was disinherited by his father in favor of you and that he has spent most of the last four years trying to inch you out."

"Understandably," Sandra said laconically. "He was the natural heir."

"All right, quite understandable." Heurtey nodded while Joanne was gazing out of the window, apparently across the gardens at the heart of the Ritz. "But he didn't always try and inch you out honorably. He pretended to cooperate but he was working against you. Right?"

"Right!" Sandra looked puzzled. "Why, how do you know all this?"

"Because he is the head of a very important part of my group, a group in which I have begun to take a keen interest since my father's death. While my brother looks after the States, I am to be in charge of Europe. Therefore I did a lot of homework before coming over here."

"Joanne too?" Sandra acknowledged the other woman with a smile.

"Joanne was not in the picture then." Heurtey shook his head. "In fact she has only joined me quite recently."

"Oh?" Sandra didn't wish to appear too interested.

"Joanne is actually a corporate investigator," Heurtey went on. "From the well-known firm of Iliffe Corporate Investigators. She is a trained accountant, has also been a detective, a member of the fraud squad."

"Sounds sinister."

"Seriously, Sandra"—David looked reprovingly at her—"I want to know all about the European companies in my group—the bank, the champagne, the electronics, the gas station complex. Who is honest, who isn't. Whether we're making sufficient profit. Joanne goes through all the books and reports to me." He touched the tip of his nose. "She can smell them out."

"Sure can," Joanne said with disarming confidence.

"Zac Desmond, for instance." Heurtey looked at the ceiling. "Desmond worries me. Is he really fit to be the head of a large investment banking concern? We find, for instance, that Franco-Belges is losing quite a lot of money instead of making it; unwise investments, dollars and francs frittered away. He seems to cling to the coattails of the German Federal banks, but do they have the deutsch mark at heart rather than the franc?"

"I thought with the European Exchange Mechanism they were on the same side?" Sandra's smile was noncommittal in an effort to hide her concern as to what Heurtey was saying about Zac.

"Not necessarily. In business, as in politics, one side is always trying to outmanoeuvre the other. It seemed to Joanne, looking at the books, that the Germans passed to Zac the unwise investments and kept the safe ones for themselves, but, as they advised so and so, Zac, respecting them to the point of idolatry, does what they suggest."

"But Zac is meant to be a venture capitalist," Sandra interrupted him. "He takes risks."

"Too *many,*" Heurtey sounded severe. "Too little security from assets; sometimes, no assets at *all.*

"I am, frankly, anticipating a takeover within the terms of the European Community in the next few months and that is another reason I am here: to safeguard our interests, as well as to keep an eye on the likes of Zac Desmond. Now, in all your dealings with Zac, tell me your experience. Can you say you *really* trust him?"

Sandra paused for a long while before answering him. She had a feeling of disloyalty even though she had no blood ties with Zac. To betray him was like letting the side down.

"I have never actually known him to have done anything dishonest," she said at last. "To be frank I have never been able to prove anything other than that he is sometimes a careless man of business, as you already seem to know, and that where deals are concerned he lets his emotions overrule his head."

"But what about the purchase of shares which preceded the huge deal with the Arabs to buy the Desmond 200?" Joanne asked. "The suggestion of insider trading. Didn't you think he was up to his eyeballs in that?"

"I thought, but I had no proof."

"*And* the destruction of the bulk of your wine shortly after you joined the company." Joanne seemed to have done her homework on the Desmond Group too.

"Oh, you know about that? Well, no one could blame Zac for that, although many people tried. . ."

"All linked to Monsieur Strega." Joanne thoughtfully lit a long American cigarette.

"You know about Strega?"

"Yes, we know about Strega." Joanne smiled mysteriously. "And, tell me, did you ever hear of anyone called Romanetto?"

For the next half-hour Sandra sat listening to a story which at times seemed to take her into the realms of fantasy. Yet it all came back to a man called Paul Strega whose origins were obscure, whose father was a steelworker in Longwy, a heavily polluted industrial town on the border of France and Belgium.

His father died when Paul Strega was seventeen and, with a family to help keep, he joined the French army because it offered security and a chance to travel.

It was there that he met Zac Desmond, served as his batman and had continued in his service ever since.

Why?

"Strega's name kept on appearing in all these underhand deals," Joanne continued in a monotone, apparently still using the almost infinite resources of her memory as if she were an actress who had complete mastery of her lines, "but they were connected with Desmond and, ultimately, with Zac Desmond.

"In the affair of the *tirage,* shortly after you joined the firm, why would a man, an underling like Strega, plot with so lowly a creature as Raoul Pagés, head of the computer department at Desmond, to ruin the wine? You didn't believe it *really,* did you, Madame Harcourt?"

Joanne had been watching Sandra carefully and their eyes met. Sandra didn't reply to what she assumed was a rhetorical question. Joanne continued: "Over the years you have diminished as much as you could Zac Desmond's authority, obviously with good reason: to protect yourself. Yet he has tried to cling to power, which he not only covets more than anything else, but which he thinks is his by right. Isn't that so?"

"It is so," Sandra acknowledged. "You do seem to know everything." She wondered if they knew about Bob.

"How does Romanetto come into this story?" she continued. "I'm curious to know."

"Romanetto comes into it again through Strega. Romanetto disappeared four years ago with twenty-five million US dollars."

"Yes, I know. Without going into details I investigated it quite recently. I even went to see Madame Romanetto and something about her made me wonder if she knew her husband was alive."

"Indeed!" Joanne nodded her head firmly. "Romanetto is

very much alive. We know that Strega tailed him to Thailand and that he has reappeared again in Milan."

"And how do you know that?" Sandra looked with astonishment at Joanne.

"I make it my business to know these things." Joanne continued to look mysterious as, at that moment, the telephone rang and Joanne answered it in fluent French.

She listened, nodded and then spoke to Sandra.

"Monsieur Dericourt is here, our dinner guest."

"Don't let's keep him waiting then." Heurtey leapt up and, disappearing in the direction of his bedroom, called over his shoulder, "I'll change in two seconds and join you in the lobby."

David Heurtey had not yet been introduced to Antoine Dericourt and the object of the evening was to fill in any details which might be of interest to both organizations. Sandra thought it politic for the head of Heurtey to meet her deputy.

It was obvious from the beginning that Dericourt was impressed not only by Heurtey's charm but by his business acumen which, in a way, surprised Sandra too.

For much of the meal she remained silent, listening, observing. The elegance of the great restaurant and the quality of its food provided an atmosphere that was conducive to relaxation, and she realized just how tired she had been.

If Heurtey impressed Antoine it was obvious that the American was impressed by her deputy, whose expertise in the field of aeronautical engineering was second to none. In his enthusiasm to explain every aspect of their work Sandra wondered if Antoine were telling him too much, and she also speculated about Joanne, the woman with a mind like a camera.

The Heurtey and Desmond organizations were bound by nothing more than a common shareholding in the Banque Franco-Belges, although compared to Heurtey's share the Desmond one was small.

Antoine was in full flight about the development of the Desmond executive jet when Sandra coughed discreetly. Antoine stopped and looked at her, his face flushed a little, perhaps with excitement, perhaps too much wine.

"If you're not careful, Antoine," Sandra's tone was jocular, "Heurtey will be moving in for a takeover. He'll know more than we do."

"Oh, I would never do that, Sandra." David looked distinctly shocked.

"Why not?" she smiled. "All's fair in love and business. After all, I once tried to take over American Heurtey."

"Yes, that was a bit misguided." David laughed.

"Oh, but it has been done before. Smaller companies taking over larger ones."

"Say though, Sandra"—David Heurtey leaned languidly across the table and joined his hands—"I think that we can do a lot of business together, maybe buy into each other's companies."

"First, I will have to see what you have on offer"—Sandra glanced meaningfully at her watch—"besides a not very successful bank. Now, if anyone wants to come back to my apartment for a drink let's go now because I have a very early start in the morning."

"Where to this time?" Heurtey signaled for the bill.

"Rio de Janeiro," Sandra replied.

"Do you have interests there too?"

"Interests, of a kind."

As he reached for his credit card she stood up as though to curtail the conversation.

Helping her, Antoine wondered what she had to do in Rio as it was one of the few South American capitals where they had, in fact, no business interests. She hadn't told him.

Heurtey paid the bill and Joanne went to the powder room while Sandra and Antoine stood at the door of the restaurant waiting for the car which had been called.

"What business do you have in Rio?" Antoine asked, casually reaching for a cigarette.

"It's personal business, Antoine."

"I see . . ."

"To do with Bob." She kept her voice very low. "I'm trying to get the money for his ransom on better terms than I can get here."

"It really *is* a magnificent view," Heurtey said an hour later as the four stood in front of Sandra's wide panoramic windows watching the sweep of the lights of the *bateaux mouches* as they plied up and down the river. Sometimes they turned at the Île de la Cité, sometimes they continued further upriver. To their right the great shadow of Notre Dame brooded over the city as it had for so many centuries past.

Before Christ, the Parisii tribes, composed of fishermen and boatmen, had set up a township on the largest island in the Seine which had been called Lutetia. It was later conquered by the Romans and in the fourth century its name changed to that of the tribe which had discovered it, Paris.

Sandra wasn't sure how much of its history was known to her guests assembled by the window but, certainly, they were as struck by its beauty as, day after day, was she—whether while grabbing a coffee first thing in the morning, returning at sunset after a long day in the office, or late at night after a trip abroad when her staff served her a late supper which she ate by the window.

"I wonder you want to live anywhere else but here." Joanne, tough lady that she was, still appeared deeply moved by the beauty of the scenery.

"I don't *want* to live anywhere else but here," Sandra replied, "but I have to. I have to have a house in Reims to be near the champagne business, which is the heart of our group, especially now that the special reserve *cuvée* is being made and marketed: Louis d'Or, in honor of my son. Besides," she added, as an afterthought, "Reims is better for Louis than Paris with its pollution. I have to think of him."

There was a lull in the conversation. It was late. Heurtey looked at his watch. "Well, I think we'd better be going," he said, stifling a yawn. "How long will you be in Rio, Sandra?"

"As long as it takes." She led the way to the door but before she got there it opened and her butler, Hubert, stood there with a package on a silver tray.

Sandra looked at it in some surprise.

"This was just delivered for you, Madame." Hubert proffered the tray. "I was told it was urgent."

Sandra stared at the package, wrapped in brown paper and secured with Sellotape. Her name was rather crudely written on the outside, and also incorrectly spelt: **HARCORT.**

"Don't you think you should be careful?" Joanne said. "It could be an explosive."

Hubert's hand holding the tray trembled and Heurtey took it up and put it to his ear.

"I think you should call the police," he said.

"Can you hear anything?" Sandra looked anxious.

"No, but I don't like it."

"Let me open it *very* carefully," Joanne said and then, half joking, "Everyone stand well back."

Carefully, methodically, she undid it. The brown paper and Sellotape came off to reveal a small, narrow box. They all looked at the box and Joanne took a deep breath; gently she took off the lid. Nothing happened. There was no explosion.

Inside on a bed of tissue paper was a severed human ear.

11

When Sandra came to, the light streamed through the curtains into her room and she blinked her eyes rapidly several times, wondering why her head felt so heavy, she herself so tired. She gazed at the clock by the side of her bed and, to her horror, saw that it was eleven o'clock. Her plane had been meant to leave at seven.

Frantically she rang her bell but when she tried to jump out of bed she slumped back again feeling weak, giddy, ill. She sat on the bed, her head in her hands, and then the hideous memory returned.

"Oh, my God," she murmured and the dread came flooding back again.

The door opened slowly and in came her maid carrying a tray on which there was her accustomed breakfast: freshly baked bread, apricot jam and a pot of English tea.

"Marie," Sandra cried, "why on *earth* . . . what has happened?"

"Mademoiselle Pasarro is waiting for you in the salon, Madame. She spent the night here and she wondered . . ."

Sandra then observed Joanne standing behind Marie at the door. She wore slacks and a jacket over a silk blouse.

"Hi!" she said with a little wave. "Is it OK if I come in?"

"Of course." Sandra thankfully got back into her bed.

"You have to take it easy you know, Madame." Marie wagged her finger severely at her mistress. "The doctor said . . ."

"The doctor was here?" Sandra looked aghast.

"He gave you a shot," Joanne said. "You kind of went distraught when you saw the ear, then you fainted. We were worried. Thought you'd had a heart attack. David sent immediately for the doctor and also an ambulance; but when the doctor saw you you were beginning to come to. He gave you a shot and Marie put you to bed." Joanne held up two small phials. "Here's your medicine. One of each, three times a day, with water."

Joanne had a jocular note in her voice rather as though she were trying to take the drama out of the situation.

"Now, Madame." Marie finished fussing, pouring her tea, buttering her bread . . .

"I can't face anything to eat, thanks, Marie." Sandra propped herself up on one arm. "But I would like a cup of tea. Never got over the habit," she observed to Joanne. "Tea in the morning. Always."

"I like tea too," Joanne replied, "but no one seems able to make it outside of England. Too much coffee gives me the shakes." She looked behind her at a chair. "Would you mind if I sat down, or do you prefer me not to see you in your deshabille? Anyway, the doctor says you should spend the day in bed. He's going to look in again about noon."

"I have to go to the bathroom," Sandra said, pushing back the duvet. Marie passed her her robe and put out her hand.

"Let me help you, Madame."

Sandra, with the aid of her maid, tottered rather unsteadily to the en suite bathroom, and when she returned Joanne was reading *Le Figaro.* Sandra sat on the side of the bed and reached for her cup while Marie looked on anxiously.

"I can't understand myself fainting," Sandra said, with an air of self-derision. "I only fainted once before when I saw about Michel on the TV."

"That's understandable." Joanne, with a sympathetic smile, put aside the paper. "The doctor said you had low blood pressure and when you get a shock, you black out. Seeing that ear unnerved us all, I can tell you."

Sandra didn't reply but gulped her tea and when she had finished Marie poured another cup.

"There, Madame," she said, with the tone of a mother soothing a small child. "Already the color is returning to your face." She passed her a chunk of bread spread with thick apricot jam. "Now, try and eat a little. The doctor says you should."

"She's mothering me." Sandra smiled for the first time that morning.

"I wish she would mother *me,*" Joanne replied. "I lost mine years ago and you can't replace them."

"That's true." Sandra stared in front of her, thinking of the woman thousands of miles away in California who was her real mother: a woman who had never, she was sure, nursed her at her breast and, most certainly, never either wanted or loved her.

Certainly the omniscient Joanne knew about Virginia Wingate. All the world did. They had learned it from the court case in London when she had sued a newspaper for libel and all her past had been revealed to a curious, prurient world.

"I expect you know about my mother?" She raised her head and looked at Joanne, who smiled at her, again sympathetically.

"Mine wasn't much better," she said quietly. "One day remind me to tell you the story of my life and you'll think you were lucky."

It was at that moment that Sandra decided she really liked this curious woman with her thick accent from the Bronx: her curious, quirky, direct style, her knowing ways. She put her feet up on the bed without getting under her duvet and realized she already felt better.

She was a woman who recently had lacked close friends of any kind; no real intimates, male or female. Her husband was dead and Henri Piper, who had been such a stalwart until she married Michel, had gone to live permanently in California.

Consequently the loneliness of people in high places had come to one who formerly enjoyed the company of friends.

"I'd better have those pills before the doctor comes." Sandra put out her hand.

"Sure." Joanne gave her the phials and Marie hovered with a glass of water. Sandra popped them into her mouth and swallowed them.

"I hope they're not tranquilizers," she said, suddenly suspicious.

"I'm sure they will do you good whatever they are." Joanne sounded practical. "Anyway he seemed like a nice guy and knew you."

"Dr. Rameau?" Sandra looked at Marie inquiringly.

"Bien sûr, Madame," Marie nodded. "He came at once."

"Rameau wouldn't give me anything that knocked me out," Sandra said. "He knows I hate that kind of thing." She paused and stared at Joanne in the cool, direct way so many people slightly feared. "We are avoiding something, aren't we, Joanne?"

"The ear?" Joanne nodded. "Antoine told us all about your brother."

"And *you* didn't know?"

Joanne said with an air of resignation, "Our surveillance freaked out there. Heads will roll—not mine, I hope."

Joanne rose and went to stand at the window which had the same wonderful panoramic view as the salon. But, on a grey day like this one, the magic was gone and Paris had that slightly worn, polluted look of any other city without sun and a haze in the sky. Joanne turned round and, crossing her arms, looked at Sandra.

"Sandra—I may call you that, mayn't I? You can trust us. Frankly I wouldn't be at all surprised if Desmond didn't have something to do with Bob. After all, Bob was in Rome and so was Zac's wife."

"I'm not sure they were there at the same time."

"Well, that's what I intend to find out." Joanne stretched her arms above her head. "You are to go back to Reims and rest, enjoy your son for a few days, look after your champagne business and I"—Joanne stuck a finger in her chest—"I'm off to Rome . . . where I have connections."

"What sort of connections?" Sandra asked enviously.

"Well . . ." Joanne spread her hands in front of her. "My father, who died when I was small, was a mobster. He was gunned down by a rival gang. My mother eventually ran off with another guy and put me in an orphanage." She smiled at the expression on Sandra's face. "I told you that when you heard about me you'd consider yourself lucky. I never starved but it was tough. I ran away from the home at fifteen and decided I wanted to make something of my life."

"And you did," Sandra said admiringly.

"Yes." Joanne tilted her head. "I did. I went to law school—joined the police. The one mistake I made was in marrying a guy called Pasarro."

"I thought that might be your father's name."

"No. My father's name is notorious. I would never have kept it. Jack Pasarro was also a lawyer; but he wanted babies and for me to stay at home. I told him it wasn't my scene and we split, quite amicably. The police force were broad-minded about my parentage. In fact they thought it might be useful."

"And was it?"

"Useful, a little dangerous. I went back to the law and decided to combine legal work with detection. Now David Heurtey has no objection to my going to Rome to see if I can get a lead on Bob. Some members of my father's family are in quite respectable positions . . . you understand, are legit; the others . . . well, doesn't do to ask too many questions."

Joanne thoughtfully rubbed the side of her nose. "Know what I mean?"

As a result of his long incarceration Bob was discovering a patience, a forbearance, of which he hadn't previously known he was capable. He read a lot; he was allowed to watch TV, and he spent at least two hours every day exercising on the hard stone floor.

His main companion was Niki, who appeared at least once a day and would sometimes stop and watch TV with him or play cards. They also spoke Italian, as learning the language was one of Bob's other tasks in prison. Altogether, except for the deprivation of the company of Tara, it wasn't a bad place to be. There were no responsibilities, no decisions, above all, no feeling of futility. His imprisonment had given him a sense of purpose: to survive, and the odd thing was that after his initial captivity he never again felt frightened.

Bob was convinced that Sandra would bail him out and that, one day, he would be free.

At first he thought he would be able to bribe Niki, but he soon realized this would not be the case. Niki was very frightened of someone; maybe it was Luigi, who appeared every now and then, or maybe it was someone else. Bob soon gave up trying to bribe him and, instead, welcomed his visits as they provided him with, if not friendship, at least companionship.

Niki was an awkward, bulky man and one day as they sat together watching TV, like some odd couple, Niki suddenly slid sideways off his chair as a shaky wooden leg collapsed under him. The chair, made of wicker, had been very old and taken from a kitchen or some domestic environment.

"Hell!" Niki said, getting up and rubbing his bruised behind, at the same time giving the chair a sharp kick. "All *that's* any use for now is firewood."

Bob rose and tried to put it together, but he knew it was no use.

"You'll have to get another," he said with a cajoling smile. "Try and get something more comfortable, there's a nice boy. This gives me backache." Then, with the patience he had learned in his prison, he bent down and very carefully stacked the broken pieces of chair by the wall, watched, with some bewilderment, by Niki, who went and sat on the bed where he lit a cigarette.

"You know," Niki said, as he threw the match on the floor, "there's something I can't understand about you."

"What's that?" Bob now sat gingerly on the remaining good chair.

"I can't understand how a guy like you, used to women, the easy life, can tolerate it in a place like this. Yet instead of becoming more restless you seem to be more content. It beats me."

Bob put his hands around his knees and gazed at the floor. "You have to be philosophical, Niki. I'm either going to be killed or I'm going to be freed and I think the longer I stay alive the greater the chances of being freed. How long have I been here now? A month?"

Niki shrugged.

"About a month," Bob went on. "I'm being held for ransom and Sandra is going to get that money together. There's no other way, is there?"

Niki scratched his head again, stubbed out the cigarette on the floor and went to the door.

"Better get you that chair," he said, "while I remember."

"Get something really comfortable," Bob called after him, and then he watched with a look of resignation on his face as Niki nodded and then carefully locked the door after him.

He never forgot.

Bob thought he'd see Niki later in the day but, to his surprise, he was back very soon. He could hear him grunting as he came along the corridor, and a heavy thud outside the door. Then there was the scratch of the key again and, panting, he staggered into the room with a huge armchair, a very different affair from the one he had broken.

"Jeeze," Bob exclaimed, "this is a *beauty,* an antique. Where did you find that, Niki?"

Niki growled and began to dust down the heavy brocade before he put it in its place in front of the TV.

"Better not say anything," he said with a sly glance. "Maybe some family heirloom."

And, although he didn't realize it then, that was the first inkling that Bob had about where he was.

Antoinette admitted David Heurtey, and Sandra rose immediately to greet him. Behind her desk was the Arc de Triomphe and, beyond that, the spectacular stretch of the Champs Élysées.

David Heurtey whistled. "This is a very fine view, Sandra. You've got some of the best locations in France."

"I feel privileged," Sandra replied, pointing to a chair. "Can I get you coffee?"

"No, thanks." David shook his head. "I drink too much of the stuff in the morning. Forgive the informality, Sandra"—he indicated his open-necked shirt and blazer—"but I'm off to Deauville. There's a match play championship there today."

Sandra crossed her arms, shook her head and leaned back in her chair, the expression on her face ambivalent.

"I *know* you don't approve, Sandra," David went on. "You think I should be hard at work." He smiled disarmingly. "I'm the last to change the habits of a lifetime."

As Sandra still didn't reply, but the expression on her face told him she was not disarmed, he went on: "I guess I know what you're thinking, but you must face it: I'll never become as dedicated as you. For instance"—he pointed sternly at her—"you have no right, no right at all, to be where you are now. You should be resting in the country with Louis, like the doctor told you."

"I'm going there this weekend," Sandra said, suddenly running her hands over her face, which David thought looked tired and worried. If anything the weariness made her seem more beautiful, even more desirable, the touch of melancholy enhancing those fine features, adding hidden depth to her deep, aquamarine eyes. David Heurtey's heart lurched and, although it felt like love, he knew it was also partly apprehension that a woman of such charm, character, determination and yet withal ethereal beauty and essential femininity might break his heart.

David put his hand in the breast pocket of his blazer and,

drawing out a paper, carefully unfolded it before laying it in front of Sandra.

"And this is?" She took it up and stared at a list of incomprehensible figures that resembled a medical formula. The address at the top was that of a well-known laboratory in Paris.

"The ear did not belong to Bob," Heurtey said quietly. "Someone was playing a very cruel trick on you."

"Oh, my God!" Sandra clutched the paper and the little color in her face drained, leaving it unnaturally pale.

"Your doctor gave us the name of the hospital in LA where Bob went after his swimming accident. Well, we checked with the blood group, and his and that of the person whose ear you received were different. Bob is O, the ear is A. The ear is at least six months old and, according to that report, if you turn the page over, it came from a cadaver. It has all the appearances of having been preserved for some weeks, maybe in formaldehyde or the ice box of a morgue. Very nasty, very vicious thing to do."

Heurtey stood up and went over to the window, gazing for a moment out at Chalgrin's massive triumphal arch commissioned by Napoleon but not completed until after his death. From the circle the twelve avenues leading off it resembled the points of a star. Haussmann's reconstruction of the square had been inspirational.

"Don't you think this has a *personal* element, Sandra?" David asked at last.

"In what way?" She turned to him, puzzled.

"Designed to hurt *you* personally, though Joanne says that this form of mutilation is common with gangsters. However, in that case it would come from the person himself. You remember when Getty's grandson was kidnapped his ear was mutilated?"

Sandra shivered.

"This has been sent primarily to scare you, to warn you. They must have known you would find it didn't belong to Bob."

"I think they're putting the squeeze on," Sandra murmured. "If I don't get that money, next time it *will* be Bob's ear. If he's still alive, that is."

"Look!" Heurtey crossed the room and perched on her desk as though, in a relaxed way, he felt at home and comfortable with her. "I can let you have some of that money, save you crossing the Atlantic to go to the bank. I can but I don't want to. I've a lot of faith in Joanne. She's a tough cookie." Heurtey stood up and glanced at his watch. "I've got to be going."

"I must be going too." Sandra also checked the time. "I'm lunching with Tara."

"Oh?" David looked up, interested.

"Ostensibly it's to discuss her fashion house which is in the doldrums. We part own it, and we're either going to sell it or put some more money into it. Obviously I also want to talk to her."

"Obviously," David said, extending a hand. "Well, good luck."

"And good luck with your golf," she said, realizing at the same time that he was holding on to her hand rather longer than it took for a mere handshake.

"Say, could we have dinner next week?" Heurtey looked into her eyes. "Just the two of us?"

"I'll have to think that one over." Sandra turned her back on him sharply, rather too sharply, in order to collect her things from her desk.

When she turned round, instead of seeing him waiting for her reply, she saw that he had gone, exited silently through the door, his long, loping figure going casually across the outer office, waving to Antoinette and the other staff who worked there. Slightly panic-stricken, she watched him for a few moments before she began to follow him.

By playing hard to get she had almost lost Michel. Only, when she did get him had it been really worth the game? She was a much wiser woman now than before.

She closed the outer door of her office and, smiling at Antoinette, gave her a few instructions which the dutiful secretary noted down. Antoinette then watched her boss walk slowly in the wake of David Heurtey, taking care not to catch up with him.

Tara was fifteen minutes late. Sandra, who liked punctuality, felt irritated and sipped her iced Perrier, her eyes on the door of the restaurant which was near the point where the Champs Élysées joined Avenue Montaigne, the headquarters of the House of Jean Marvoine.

When Tara arrived, leaping from her car, which had sped up to the curb with a squeal of brakes, she dashed through the door looking wildly about her. It was the act of a habitual late arriver and Sandra watched it with some amusement while the maître d'hôtel approached Tara, whom he knew well, and then showed her to the table by the window where Sandra was sitting.

"Oh, darling, I'm *terribly* sorry . . ."

Things seemed to drop in all directions from Tara's arms: a handbag, small parcels, a folded newspaper which she could easily have left in her car. One of the packages seemed to be for Sandra and, retrieving it from the floor, Tara handed it to her with a smile.

"Peace offering?"

Seeing it, Sandra froze, and hesitated before accepting it. It was the same size as the package which had contained the ear.

"Do open it, darling." Tara thrust it nearer to her. "I thought they were just you."

Unlike the sinister missive, however, this was beautifully wrapped and tied with a blue ribbon and when Sandra opened it she saw a pair of earrings made of lapis lazuli which would, in fact, go well with the colors she usually liked to wear. Earrings, though misjudged, were not the present of a woman who felt in any way guilty and Sandra raised her eyes and said simply: "Thank you—they're lovely." Tara bent to receive a kiss on the cheek, still managing to scatter small objects about her as she sat down.

She was, in fact, performing, making her presence not only known to everyone in the restaurant, but not forgotten. She had once been a celebrated fashion model and she still liked to star.

"What will you have to drink?" Sandra asked once she had settled. "I'm afraid I've only got until three."

"Oh, a glass of white wine will do." Tara was wearing a dress by Maurice Raison, chief designer for the House of Jean Marvoine, made of soft black wool nipped in to her very narrow waist by a gold belt. It had a roll neckline like a sweater and, although it was nice, it didn't look couture. Sandra recognized the Raison style, although, as she lowered her eyes to the menu, she thought that, lacking expert direction, the standards in the House were slipping. There was too obvious a skimping of material, a lack of real style.

Maurice Raison, once such a big catch, was *vieux jeu.*

After they had ordered Tara rapidly finished her drink and asked for another.

"Would you like a bottle?" Sandra inquired, beckoning the wine waiter.

"Let's have a bottle, then," Tara agreed brightly.

"I don't drink at lunchtime, but if *you* would like a bottle . . ."

"Oh, not a whole bottle for me!" Tara protested. "Won't you have just a teeny weeny glass?"

"Maybe a teeny weeny one then," Sandra smilingly agreed, and promptly gave the order to the waiter.

Then she sat back, looking at her guest, whom she hadn't seen since the day of her return to Paris.

"You've been terribly hard to get," she said at last.

"I've been *terribly* busy." Tara moved the cutlery around the table nervously. "This and that, being away for so long . . . Zac has become frightfully possessive . . . you know."

Although Sandra nodded understandingly, there was something about Tara that wasn't quite right. Tara was an impetuous, vain woman who liked to imagine that she was twenty-two rather than thirty-six; but there was another dimension to her on this occasion which, at first, Sandra couldn't quite fathom.

When she had stopped fiddling with the cutlery and adjusting her beads and her brooch and bangles, looked at the time at least twice, she raised her eyes to meet those of Sandra, who then realized what was the matter.

Tara was afraid. Obviously afraid. Her lips were smiling but her eyes were black with fear. She was unhappy and she was afraid and she wasn't eating. The apathetic way in which she ordered her food demonstrated this and when it came she toyed with it, drinking a lot.

First of all she asked about Louis, and the new house, as if she wanted to dominate the conversation. Sandra replied in a measured way, trying to calm whatever unspecified fears her guest had. Were they, by any chance, to do with Bob?

"I'd simply *love* to see him," Tara said. "Do you keep him in Reims all the time?"

"Most of the time."

"Lady Elizabeth says she *never* sees you at Tourville."

"I've been busy getting the house straight."

"But you do want to go to Tourville, don't you?" Tara pushed a very thin slice of smoked salmon round her plate and looked apprehensively across the table.

"Of course."

"Because things between you and the Desmonds are all right now, aren't they?"

Sandra's pause before answering spoke volumes.

"I don't know," she said finally in a voice so quiet that Tara scarcely heard it. "Tara, I wanted to ask you . . ." she began, but Tara, as if anticipating the question, hurried on.

"Really they *very* much want to make up for what happened in London. Lady Elizabeth and Zac and Belle. Tim, I suppose also, but Tim's not there. Claire . . ."

"Did you see much of Claire in Rome?" Sandra said suddenly.

"Oh, very *little,*" Tara replied without thinking. "We've scarcely a thing in common, you know. I'm afraid Claire always had something of the peasant mentality in her, and she's married a peasant. She has grown absolutely enormous." Tara thrust out her own trim stomach and mimed a football with her hands. "And has become a complete Italian peasant woman."

"Oh!" Sandra gazed at her plate, thinking of the decrepit Falconetti palazzo. It was surely better, in Tara's opinion, to live in a decayed palace than marry a man you loved. But Tara was a snob, and, to her, position and money meant a lot.

Was that, after all, why she had returned to Zac?

"I know what you're thinking," Tara said defensively, as if reading her mind. "You're wondering why I came back to Zac. Well . . ." She tapped her fingers on the table and when the waiter came to remove her plate, which was half full, and hesitated, she told him to take it. "Well, I missed him. My eighteen months away gave me time to think and I realized not only that I missed him, but that I loved him." Tara twisted her lips and smiled, as if knowing Sandra would find it hard to believe her. "Oh, I like the life-style too . . ."

"Did you negotiate with Zac to come back?" Sandra asked quietly.

"How do you mean 'negotiate'?" Tara looked alarmed.

"You know, make a deal . . ."

"Oh no. No deal. I just returned."

"And he accepted you? Just like that?" Sandra didn't attempt to conceal her amazement.

"I found him a changed man. He had missed me and he wanted me. I missed the kids. Yes, Zac *is* a changed man, a disappointed man, but he seems, now, to be trying to make amends all round."

Tara looked carefully at her wrist to make sure that her dress, with its long sleeves, covered the scar that Zac had made with a cigarette he'd stubbed out on her arm.

As she lied her heart was beating so violently she thought she would faint. She was amazed she could even pretend to keep some sort of control. But then she was an actress, someone used to showing herself off to best advantage and, in order to deceive this knowing, clever woman opposite her, she had had to act her head off.

Partially she was successful. Sandra couldn't see the scar or hear the heartbeat, but she knew a nervous woman when she saw one and she recognized fear; she could even smell it. She was not deceived.

"About Marvoine." Sandra leaned her arms on the table as Tara helped herself to another glass of wine, maybe her third or fourth. "The figures are disappointing."

"Look!" Maybe emboldened by the wine or what, Sandra didn't know, but Tara also leaned her arms firmly on the table and stared at her. "I don't care a shit about Marvoine. I never really did. Zac thought it would give me something to do and, in a sense, I did enjoy it. But I can't run a fashion house myself and, frankly, Belle is not interested."

"Belle is not interested?" Sandra raised her voice in surprise. "I thought it was Belle's baby."

"It *was* Belle's baby," Tara said slyly, "but she now has another one."

"Another interest?" Sandra raised her eyebrows, thinking, quite naturally, because of Belle's background, of champagne.

"Oh yes, another interest." Tara's voice was light and mischievous and the nuance unmistakable.

"A man?" Sandra suggested.

"Not just 'a man,' " Tara teased. "Being Belle it couldn't be just *anybody.*"

"Prince Charles," Sandra suggested with a smile.

Tara rolled her eyes.

"The very *opposite.*" Leaning right across the table she hissed, "A *communist.*"

"A *what?*" Sandra hissed back.

"A Romanian diplomat. Actually he is not a communist at heart, his family was a very good one under the old regime. But he is a diplomat serving a communist government, so one must suppose he is one. He is very charming, but then these Latins mostly are."

"She's having a full-blown affair with him?" Sandra couldn't disguise her interest.

"Oh, *very* full-blown, my dear." Tara's tone was sarcastic. "She, who was always the first to criticize *me,* is never out of bed. She told me they once made love for twelve hours without stopping."

"My goodness." Sandra smiled. "The mind boggles."

"Twelve hours. She had multiple orgasms and he came twelve times."

"She really was joking." Sandra felt she wanted to burst into laughter but kept her face straight.

"No, well . . ." Tara looked doubtfully at her. "That's what she said."

"My dear Tara"—Sandra leaned back—"these Desmonds can invent anything."

"Why should she invent it?" Tara looked puzzled.

"I don't know." Sandra was beginning to feel that, if she didn't get round to the real purpose for the lunch, she would be too late. "Maybe to make you jealous, who knows? Listen, Tara"—her voice changed to an urgent whisper—"did you happen to see Bob in Rome?"

"Bob?" Tara's voice emerged almost as a squeak. "Bob was in *Rome?"*

"He went looking for you."

"When was that?"

"Well, that's what I'm not sure about." Sandra sat back, drumming her fingers impatiently on the table. "It may have been before you returned, or just after. I'm not sure because I lost contact with him."

"You mean *you* haven't seen him?" As far as Sandra could tell Tara's question was genuine.

"I haven't seen *or* heard from him. I've . . . I've had a demand for a huge ransom allegedly from an Italian gang."

"Bandits!" Tara sounded genuinely horrified. "They kidnapped him, you think, and took him to the hills?"

"I don't know. I really don't know. They . . . sent me an ear."

"Oh, my *God!"* Tara put her hands over her face. "Oh, Bob, poor *Bob."* She seemed overwrought and genuinely so. She pulled out a handkerchief and dabbed at her eyes. "Sandra, you know Bob was crazy in love with me. But he was a kid, a boy. I am fourteen years older than him . . ."

"But did he *ever* contact you in Rome?"

"No," Tara protested with a shudder, her hand still half concealing her face, "no, never, never, never. You must believe me, Sandra, I *never* saw him."

And, somehow, Sandra believed her.

A little while later they walked onto the Champs Élysées where both their chauffeured cars were now waiting. Sandra felt more dejected than she had expected, as though she had relied too much on the lunch providing a clue, any clue, as to Bob's whereabouts.

"Believe me, I'm *very* sorry." Tara's eyes were still wet. "I wish I could help. He was a nice boy, a good boy . . ."

The tears now rolled down her cheeks and Sandra was touched by this evidence of her feeling for Bob. She put an arm round Tara and strolled with her to her car as the chauffeur jumped out to open the door. Sandra stood looking at the chauffeur in his neat, navy-blue uniform and peaked cap as if he reminded her of something or someone.

"Tell me, Tara," she said as she saw her into her car, "didn't you once have a bodyguard?"

"Oh, don't mention *that* to me." Tara avoided eye contact with Sandra as her chauffeur leaned forward to make sure she was comfortable in her seat. "That *horrible* time."

"What was his name?"

"Name?" Tara put a finger to her mouth as if thinking.

"The name of the man who guarded you?"

"Gomez," Tara said with another shudder. "And don't think I'll ever forget that."

And don't think I will either, Sandra thought to herself as, stepping back from the curb, she waved as the Jaguar sped along the Champs Élysées toward the Place de la Concorde.

* * *

There was little love lost between Zac Desmond and the Tellier brothers, Luc and Rudy, although their backgrounds were similar. They both came from champagne families and a cordial relationship, superficially at least, had existed between them for nearly a century.

Over the years Desmond had rather disdained the image of Tellier in the wine world with its popular image of bubbly for the masses. Desmond, with its rigorous standards perfected over many years, insisted on quality, made fewer bottles and was drunk in the best hotels and restaurants in the world. However, there had been mutual, if friendly, rivalry in the past and talks of mergers until finally, in a surprise move, Tellier was bought by the Heurtey Corporation and discussions with Desmond promptly ended.

Well, almost ended. Since the advent of Sandra, Zac had, from time to time, not been averse to a little plotting with his erstwhile rivals, mostly with the intention of discrediting them, making them feel foolish or appear foolish in the eyes of their parent organization. To succeed in his ambition to be president of the bank he quite unashamedly used them, and discarded them again.

Ebenezer Heurtey, the father of Frank and David, had been on his way over to investigate the situation with Tellier and the Banque Franco-Belges when Zac seized the presidency. At the same time, but coincidentally, Ebenezer suffered the first of the three heart attacks that were to incapacitate him during the last years of his life.

The brothers Luc and Rudy disliked the Heurtey umbrella as much as Zac had hated being under the control of Sandra, and when David Heurtey appeared in person and started rooting about—asking questions and getting gimlet-eyed Joanne Pasarro to examine the books—it made them nervous. They had nothing exactly to hide, but they didn't wish to reveal too much either.

Thus, in conditions of great secrecy, Luc and Rudy had sought a meeting with Zac and, as Tara and Sandra were lunching in another part of the town, they were eating smoked salmon with a bottle of chilled white Burgundy in the boardroom of the Banque Franco-Belges with its magnificent view of the opera house.

This working lunch had been decided upon in preference to eating in a public place where they might be known, their movements noted and motives speculated upon by rival business acquaintances and *négociants.*

The three agreed that they disliked David Heurtey, but when the Telliers showed Zac their plans, behind carefully locked doors, he liked them even less than he liked the new president of the European operations of the group.

The idea was for Tellier to buy into a much larger drinks concern with a worldwide reputation which would then make a reverse bid and swallow up Heurtey.

"This is crazy," Zac said, throwing the papers back on his table once he had examined them. "I don't think you've thought this through. A company of your size can't possibly *buy* into Cassini Drinks; they could swallow you hook, line and sinker."

"They could also swallow Heurtey," Rudy said with a gleam in his eye.

"That's true." But Zac continued to look truculent. "How did you propose to finance it?"

"With your help." Luc threw a quick glance at his brother.

"My help?"

"The bank's help."

"But if my fellow directors saw a crazy scheme like that they'd throw it out immediately. We haven't the funds at Franco-Belges."

"You could have alliances with other banks, such as Sandra Harcourt had to finance her enormous airplane deal."

"That was a huge project." Zac dismissively waved it away. "God knows how she did it. I think she must have slept with the presidents of all the main banks in Germany and Switzerland . . ."

"Oh, come, Zac!" Luc, who was a family man of impeccable morality, looked abashed. "We all know that Sandra Harcourt . . ."

"You know nothing at *all* about her," Zac said aggressively.

"I do think we should avoid discussing *moral* questions," Luc interrupted, pursing his mouth prudishly, "or making unsavoury innuendos. After all let those who are without sin cast the first stone."

His eyes swiveled meaningfully toward Zac, who was about to move on to a further discussion of the business in hand, when there was a hammering at the door on the other side of which he could hear the shrill tones of his wife.

"Zac, are you there? Let me in," Tara demanded. There was further banging and, as Zac jumped up, the Tellier brothers exchanged anxious glances.

"Maybe we'd better go . . ." Rudy made as if to get up.

"Oh, she's probably forgotten her checkbook," Zac said uneasily as he made his way to the door and cautiously unlocked it. He was met by a human dynamo who, regardless of the company, threw herself at him and began banging her fists against his chest.

"How *dare* you," she said, "how dare you? Murderer, mutilator . . ."

"Tara." Zac gripped hold of her hands and shook her. "Control yourself. The Telliers are here. What on earth are you on about . . ."

"We really should go . . . I can see this is a domestic matter of some urgency." Luc and Rudy, abandoning their lunch, had both made their way to the door. "Give us a call, Zac, when you've thought about our proposal."

They looked nervously at Tara and edged through the door where an even more nervous-looking secretary stood in the outer office and mechanically handed them their coats.

Zac rushed after them and, in a low voice, said: "My wife is very distraught."

"I can see that," Luc replied.

"She's suffering from a nervous breakdown. She's not well. Please keep this incident to yourselves."

"Oh, you can rely on us, Zac." Rudy smiled his thanks to the secretary. *"We* know how to keep a secret."

Leaving his secretary to see them out and telling her then to go to lunch, Zac hurried back into the boardroom and again locked the door before turning on Tara, who was sitting at the head of the table, in his chair, glaring at him. Once Zac had closed the door she jumped up again, disregarding his tense face, his pursed lips. Once more she hurled herself at him and started pummeling his chest but this time, because he had no audience, he shook her so violently that she was lifted, literally, several inches from the floor and then he flung her into a corner of the room where she fell in a heap on the carpet.

Whimpering, she got to her knees and began to crawl along the floor like a baby attempting its first steps.

"Get up," Zac thundered, "and tell me what the *devil* is going on." His hand trembling, he pointed toward the door. "Do you know what those men will do? They will hardly wait to get home or to their offices before picking up the telephone: 'Guess what happened today in Zac's office?' " His cruel mimicry of Rudy's rather high voice was quite convincing. " 'Tara came *rushing* in and started to beat the living daylights out of him. He said she's having a nervous breakdown . . .' "

"You what?" Tara demanded.

"How else could I explain the words 'murderer' and 'mutilator'? Begin by telling me exactly what you *do* mean."

Tara levered herself up by gripping the side of the table. She had been a victim of her husband's violence before, but now she didn't think it mattered. She didn't really care if he killed her now because, one day, he surely would.

"You kidnapped Bob." Her voice between sobs was hysterical. "You . . ."

Zac hit her across the mouth and pointed to the door.

"Do you want my secretary to hear your lies, you slut? Keep your voice down."

He hit her again and, as she started to whimper, he went to the door and surreptitiously opened it. The outer office was deserted. Thank heaven his secretary had done what he told her and gone to lunch. He locked the door again and crossed the room where Tara was now sitting on the floor, her legs spread out in front of her, her skirt up over her knees.

He imagined how many men had seen her like this, had desired her and violated her. His heart hammered in his chest and he thought his veins would burst as he warred against the twin emotions of desire and hatred, wanting her and rejecting her at the same time.

"*You* kidnapped Bob," she cried. "You never denied it. You know you did . . . and *now* you've nearly killed him cutting off his ear. What a terrible, hideous thing to do, even for you, Zac. What a loathsome monster you are . . . will you *never* stop at anything in your desire to get rid of Sandra Harcourt?"

Zac sat in a chair, trying to control himself, breathing as evenly as he could. After all he didn't want to follow the example of Ebenezer Heurtey and die before he had accomplished his task.

He looked at the woman on the floor in front of him and suddenly his rage left him. She was pathetic; she had no money and no talents, and few assets except her looks which would soon desert her. Seen in the nude she was a little thick round the waist and those once magnificent breasts were beginning to sag. There were tiny crows' feet at the corners of her eyes. He reached out a hand and, seeing his change of expression, she gave him hers.

"What are you going to do?" she asked as he pulled her up.

He then, quite roughly, pulled down her dress, tearing the neck and exposing her brassiere, which he again tore roughly away. He took her breasts and squeezed them between his palms, then he wrenched her dress right down to her hips—her lace panties, the frivolous little suspender belt which kept up her sheer black nylon stockings.

She feared she was going to be raped again but, instead,

releasing her breasts, he let his hand run down her waist, over her stomach, inside her panties to her groin, saying as he did:

"You're getting old, Tara. Your breasts sag, your waist is getting thicker, your stomach fatter. Your hips are beginning to spread. The pores on your face are enlarging and you'll change. No matter what you do it's inevitable. But I love you and I want you but one day, if you go on like this—hysterical madness, bursting in on me when I'm in conference—I'll have you put away. You will become an object of pity and no man will want you—not even me."

He pulled her to him and put his arms round her, his mouth very close to hers.

"You belong to me, Tara. I can do what I like with you. Forget about Bob or any of the men who've fucked you in the past." His voice grew mellifluous and his hot breath warmed her cheeks. "I never killed any man in my life, or any woman but, my darling, you came very near today to making it a first for me."

He then kissed her with such violence that her tongue began to bleed and as she wrenched herself away from him he saw the blood oozing out of her mouth. He drew his handkerchief from his top pocket and, approaching her again, gently dabbed it while she gazed at him with horror and revulsion.

"Did you tell Sandra that you thought I'd kidnapped Bob?" he asked.

"No."

"Are you sure?"

"Quite sure."

"Or that you thought I had anything to do with it?"

"No, I swear." She put her hand to her mouth and when she withdrew it stared at the blood on the tips of her fingers. "We had lunch . . . about Jean Marvoine . . . she told me . . . about Bob's ear. She asked me if I'd seen him in Rome. I said I never had . . . but I felt I hated you, Zac, for what you've done to Bob."

"My dear," Zac said, dabbing at her face again, the rage on

his face replaced now by an odd expression of tenderness, "when you see Bob again, if you ever do, he will have both ears in place."

He gave a chuckle that in its fiendish glee convinced Tara, if she had any doubt, that her husband was indeed mad.

"It was just a little game," he went on, "but remember that any game played with me by anyone who is not completely honest with me is a dangerous one. Now get your clothes straight as best as you can and come home with me."

Then, with an air of contempt, he turned away and began straightening his papers.

THREE

The Fatal Flaw

12

Sandra sat tapping her fingers impatiently on the desk while, in front of her, his stance subdued and respectful, stood René Latour in his white coat. Before them on the table were three green bottles of a most unusual shape, rather like the old Armagnac bottles but not so squat and with a long, tapering neck. Nervously hovering also was Claude Maison who had arrived from Paris with a sheaf of rough designs for new labels and suggestions for the nationwide promotion of Louis d'Or.

Knowing that her irritation was irrational, Sandra had gone swiftly through these, criticizing each one and rejecting them all as too tasteless, too glossy; too, in short, over the top. Claude Maison had been told to go back to the drawing board and try again.

The reason for Madame's annoyance was now apparent to the two men who waited with her in the room, to her secretarial staff who hovered anxiously over the telephones and fax machines in the outer office.

Monsieur Zac Desmond was late, so late it seemed that he might not arrive at all. Yet he had left his office ostensibly en route to Reims. An hour had passed, two. Zac should have had plenty of time to arrive.

Coffee had been drunk, they'd gone through the roughs for the advertising campaign, looked at the bottles again, discussed the shape, the thickness, the color, whether it was the right shade of green—always used for champagne which was sensitive to light.

It was now nearly lunchtime.

"Well," Sandra said, "I'm afraid we shall have to postpone this for the time being as I have to fly to Tokyo this afternoon and can't possibly put it off."

"But, Madame Harcourt, do we *need* Monsieur Zac's approval?" René Latour appeared uncustomarily agitated. "He has, after all, seen the design and approved it."

"But not the finished bottle, the chosen design," Sandra said. "It's such an unusual shape that I want to be certain *he,* the originator, is quite happy with it. In other words," she murmured sotto voce, "I want him to take some responsibility in case something goes wrong."

"But what *could* go wrong, Madame Harcourt?" Claude Maison was also decidedly ill at ease. If he lost the Desmond account it would be disastrous for his firm and Madame had shown her displeasure at their efforts, which he and his colleagues had thought rather good.

"My dear Claude . . ." Sandra sat back and continued drumming her fingers on the desk. *"Anything* can go wrong when Monsieur Zac Desmond is concerned."

And, suddenly, she wondered why she had gone against her better judgment and allowed him to interfere, yet again.

It was her fatal flaw.

Or had her fears, her imagination, again got the better of her? Zac had been helpful, conciliatory, friendly. Even David Heurtey was beginning to think he had been mistaken in his judgment of the man. Now she and David were to fly to Tokyo together to look at a plant they were thinking of buying as the first Heurtey/Desmond joint venture: a fully automated airplane assembly system using robots. Perhaps she was nervous about going away with David, too.

René Latour coughed discreetly and, putting a hand on one of the bottles, held it up to the light.

"It is perfect, Madame. The color is exactly the right shade of green—not too light, not too dark. I can't see how Monsieur Zac could do anything but give it his full approval. If the decision is not taken immediately the glassmaker will be unable to start manufacture and precious time will be wasted. I will not be able to guarantee the quality of the wine unless we have a minimum of fifteen months aging in bottles, even though forty percent of the Cuvée Louis d'Or originates from previous *vendanges.*"

Sandra lowered her head, joined her hands and studied her nails, painted a soft pink, which she thought David would like, together with the mauve mohair suit Lagerfeld had created for her. Yes, she had gone to some trouble over this journey. Five days alone in Japan together. A lot could happen. Ostensibly it was meant to be strictly business, but she was aware of that certain frisson she felt when she first met Michel . . . and she had been right about that.

"Very well," she said at last. "I wish Legrand were here to give it his blessing in the absence of Zac, but . . ." She nodded her head vigorously in the decisive manner her staff were used to. "Yes, go ahead, begin the bottling."

"Taking the *greatest* care with the cork," Claude added anxiously.

"Thank *you,* Monsieur Maison." Latour, who was not a tall man, drew himself up. "I think I do *not* need to be told my business. The *bouchon de tirage* has been specially made from the finest Catalan cork and each one will be inserted not by machine, as is customary, but by hand to avoid fracturing the delicate glass."

"Forgive me." The PR man looked a little abashed, a little frayed. "I did not mean to offend."

Sandra seemed relieved that she had made up her mind and a shadow cleared from her face. "That done, you must excuse me. I am going to have lunch at home to say good-bye to my baby and I have to be at the airport at three." She held her hand out firmly to Latour.

"I hope all goes well, Monsieur Latour. Thank you for your cooperation."

"There is just *one* further thing, Madame," René murmured, producing a sheaf of papers in triplicate from the pocket of his coat. "I must have an order for your approval of the design of the bottle so that production can begin straightaway."

Carefully, respectfully, he placed the papers before her, indicating with a stubby forefinger the place where she should sign.

"There, if you please, Madame."

Sandra picked up her pen, leaned over the paper and frowned.

"Is this really necessary? I have never signed a piece of paper for the manufacture of a *bottle!"*

"But because of the fact that these are very special bottles, Madame, of a design unusual in champagne"—René seemed to lay particular emphasis on the word "unusual"—"I felt I should take the extra precaution, especially as Monsieur Zac is not here. I alone cannot take the responsibility."

"Oh, very well." Sandra signed with her customary flourish and then handed the papers back to him with a smile.

"Please keep the bottom copy for yourself, Madame," René said, detaching one copy and carefully folding the others. "Just as a record."

With that René Latour turned and walked slowly out of the room watched by Sandra, who was aware of a familiar feeling of foreboding creeping up on her. With the absence of Zac, the signing in all innocence of a piece of paper presented to her by Latour, her mind naturally flew back to that time when she had made a mistake about the *tirage* which nearly crippled her career.

"Strange chap," Maison said, as Latour gently closed the door. "I don't really think I understand him."

"Nor," Sandra said, her hands busily gathering material together on her desk, "frankly, do I."

"I've been looking forward to this," David Heurtey said as the steward in Sandra's private jet uncorked a bottle of champagne and began pouring it into two tall flutes.

Sandra undid the jacket of her suit and sat back, crossing her legs and giving a deep sigh. "I know it's business, but it seems like a holiday—even a few hours of relaxation in the air."

As usual David looked as though he were on holiday already in dark gray trousers and a cashmere jacket of a heather mixture.

"Busy time at the office?" He picked up his drink and gazed at her across the table between them.

"Difficult and . . ." She looked at the steward who, interpreting her expression, withdrew into his galley after asking her what time she would like dinner.

"Well, it's Zac again," Sandra said as the plane banked steeply, leaving French airspace. She could hear from the crackle of conversation in the cockpit that they were over Switzerland. There would be two refuelling stops before they reached Japan. Time to unwind.

"Zac?" David looked puzzled.

"It's a silly thing, but I had it on my mind all the way to the airport. It's simply that I don't trust him." And rapidly she sketched for him the affair of the bottles and Zac's unexplained absence. "I only wish Étienne Legrand had been here, the director of Desmond Champagne. He is *so* dependable. But he is spending some months in California investigating our vineyards there."

"Well, I don't see what could go wrong with a bottle," David said reasonably.

"It's a special bottle with a long, thin neck, very elegant. Zac designed it."

"But if there *is* something wrong with it he takes responsibility." David helped himself to a nut. "I think you're too worried, my dear. Even Joanne seems to think that our doubts about Zac may be ill founded; that he is not so much a villain as a poor businessman, lacking in judgment."

"That's what *I* always thought." Sandra nodded her agreement. "The trouble is, though, one never really knows. I have yet to *prove* that he is connected with a single act of villainy. It's just that one can't help being suspicious of anything he *suggests,* and yet if I turn down all his suggestions it would be unreasonable. He is, after all, still a member of the Desmond Board. He stands to lose as much as anyone if there is something wrong with the new prestige *cuvée.*"

"But why should there be anything wrong with this *cuvée?* Hasn't it been tasted?"

"Oh, yes! It's fine. In fact everyone who knows considers it's potentially glorious."

"My dear, then you have nothing to worry about."

Heurtey leaned over and patted her hand, allowing his to linger for a moment before removing it. "He didn't *make* the bottles, did he?"

"No. They were made by a first-class glassmaker."

"Well." David threw out his arms as if that settled the matter. "Forget it." Then he delved into the briefcase on the table between them and produced a sheaf of documents. "Believe me you have your work cut out to digest all this before we arrive in Tokyo. My staff worked overnight to get all the details complete."

"Talking of staff"—Sandra produced her spectacles from her case and looked at him with a curious light in her eyes—"where is the invaluable factotum Joanne?"

"Joanne is in Italy, my dear," David said gravely, "on my orders, but going about *your* business."

Antoine Dericourt stood in the lobby of the Excelsior in Rome and glanced yet again at the clock. Joanne was half an hour late. He wandered out into the Via Veneto as if looking for a sign of her in the busy crowds that thronged that fashionable thoroughfare.

He didn't know Joanne very well, or whether she was likely to be punctual or not. But he guessed her business made her prone, perhaps, to unpunctuality so he tried to calm his nerves by going back into the hotel lobby and taking a seat. There he attempted to concentrate on *The Times* of London which, even in these times of swift communications, was a day old.

Antoine Dericourt felt out of his depth in the labyrinthine ways of kidnapping and intrigue. The previous time he had been in Rome on behalf of Sandra he was unable to discover a thing; he had not known where to start, or how. He was an engineer, a family man, uxorious and devoted to his children. He was the kind of man who left his office at five thirty sharp in order to get home in time to help them with their homework, before a pre-dinner drink with his wife, a chat while they ate after the children went to bed. There would be an hour in front of the television and an early night.

Dericourt rose early in the morning, helped to get the children off to school, drove the two youngest there himself and was always at his desk by eight thirty. It was a life-style that suited him although he was an ambitious man, aware that Sandra Harcourt had helped him make the most of his ambitions. He was grateful to her and that was the only reason he was in Rome, despite a feeling of uselessness. Absolute uselessness. He leaned back and sighed.

If only he could go home.

Suddenly a voice said: "I'm glad you read an English paper. Does Madame insist on it?"

Joanne, looking tired, flopped into the chair next to him and immediately produced a pack of Camel cigarettes. Popping one into her mouth she lit it with an elegant silver lighter and then put cigarettes and lighter back into her bag.

"No." Dericourt put down his paper and grinned. "Madame doesn't *make* me do anything I don't want to do."

"That surprises me." Joanne smiled. "She is a *very* formidable lady."

"I owe where I am to Sandra," Antoine said quietly. "Please don't think that I have any ideas about her other than admiration, respect and gratitude."

"Oh dear!" Joanne pulled a face. "I see I've offended you. I didn't mean to. You took me too seriously, Antoine. I like her too." She paused for a moment and then said, in a different tone of voice, "My boss likes her lots."

"I gathered that."

"He's even scrambled together some deal to get her to go to Tokyo alone with him. He had the staff working at it without sleep for fifty-six hours."

"But it is important. It is an assembly line of robots for our airplanes and could do wonders to the price."

"Oh, I see you're *extremely* loyal." Joanne gave one of her loud laughs. Antoine found her rather outrageous, fascinating and different from any woman he had ever known. She was certainly very different from Fleur Dericourt to whom he had been happily married for ten years. "So why don't we grab a drink?" Joanne looked round. "I guess we're off duty for the rest of the day."

"That's good." Antoine stood up. "You want to drink and eat here, or go out?"

"Why don't we drink here and then go out? Let's find a little 'trat' that is not known to any good food guide. I'll change and we'll wander through the streets of Rome at night, tra . . . la . . ."

Antoine was nonplussed, unable to tell whether she was making a pass at him or not. He decided to err on the side of caution.

"Sounds like a very good idea," he said cautiously, "except that it's late and I'm tired. I would very much like to hear what you have to say, though, and suggest we eat in the hotel."

"OK." Joanne looked at him and smiled. "I get the message. No fun. Happily married, huh? We'll eat here and we'll take an *early* night."

"It isn't *that.*" Antoine felt foolish as she led the way through the lobby to the bar. "It's . . ."

"Look, Antoine." Joanne stopped and stared at him. *"I'm* not trying to seduce you. You're not even my type. I just had a hard day, lots of hard days. This is dangerous business. All *I* suggested was a meal, not a fuck . . ."

"In that case"—Antoine hurriedly ran his finger round the collar of his shirt—"let's find a trattoria . . ."

"No, we'll eat here," Joanne said firmly. "I'm quite happy. As a matter of fact I'm hungry too." She perched on a bar stool and ordered a highball. Antoine ordered Scotch and water.

"All I can tell you," Joanne said an hour later as, a little more relaxed, they sat in the restaurant of the Excelsior eating a meal of gourmet standards, "is that Bob is *not* held by any known organizations like the Camorra, Mafia or the Ndrangheta. One of my uncles is right at the top of a powerful group which shares in the spoils of organized crime. He has assured me of this."

"You sound quite proud of him," Antoine said.

"Yeah, I am. *I* am proud of him because he is a police informer, and if he is discovered he will die the most terrible death. But he is against the power of the mobs and, for the moment, he plays a double game."

"Where does he hang out?" Antoine asked.

"Right here in Rome." Joanne looked surprised. "Where did you think? A mountain cave?"

He could see that he'd upset her by his behavior before dinner. She was defensive, a little brittle. He thought, perhaps, that he bored her. After all he was just an engineer.

"He's in the travel business," Joanne said offhandedly. "It's useful."

Antoine leaned toward her across the table. "But how does he *know?*"

"They *know.* He would know if the brother of Sandra O'Neill was being held by the mob, but especially *his* mob. He is absolutely certain that Bob has not been taken by any of the big ones, which is what I always thought."

She put a piece of escallope of veal into her mouth and chewed it thoughtfully; then she washed it down with a gulp from her glass of Verdicchio. In many ways she was rather mannish in her behavior, as if she wanted to project herself as a tough woman. Her voice and her laugh were loud, her manner brusque. To him she was not conventionally pretty, nor remotely attractive. But she still intrigued him: a person one neither liked nor disliked but somehow wanted to know more about. Well, she *was* an ex-cop, a detective with an uncle who was a mobster. Those were two interesting things for a start.

"The big boys would definitely have sent the ear of the real victim," Joanne said almost conversationally. "They wouldn't mess about with phony corpses."

"Then who does your uncle think has Bob?"

Joanne dabbed her lips with her napkin and broke off a piece of bread. "He thinks that he must be held by someone with a vendetta. Would that mean anything to you?"

"Not a thing." Antoine lowered his eyes.

"Not even Zac Desmond?" A tantalizing smile played about her lips and she bent her head toward her plate, concentrating on her food.

"You see," she said later, "it makes sense. He hates Sandra. He wanted his wife back."

"Zac would *never* do something like that." Antoine vigorously shook his head. "Never. He would never stoop to kidnap. After all, he *is* a Desmond. His father was one of the most powerful men in France; his mother an English aristocrat."

"I've known some very well-connected people do horrible things," Joanne drawled.

They were back in the bar again, Joanne seeming to have an insatiable capacity for alcohol without showing the effects. Antoine was drinking black coffee, Joanne malt whiskey.

"What I *know* of Zac Desmond doesn't discourage me from thinking him capable of such a thing."

"But what can he do with Bob?"

"He will release him in his own good time." Joanne's gaze was speculative. "When and how I don't know, but look"—she gazed at him intently for a moment—"this is strictly between you and me. It is mere supposition and I could fall on my ass if I was wrong. My boss would kick me all the way back to the States." She tapped her head. "This is mere supposition, call it instinct. All I have to do now is try and find out if I'm right."

She glanced at the clock on the wall and then at her companion. "Bedtime, baby," she said. "If you don't get enough shut-eye Madame will be *very* cross with you."

Strega looked nervously behind him toward the door of the bar in Montparnasse, as if any minute he expected someone to come in he didn't want to see. There was some justification for this reaction. He spent much of his life in fear of the consequences of his criminal or semi-criminal behavior.

"It's *idiotic* of you to have exposed yourself in this way," he hissed to the woman hunched up on the bar stool next to him.

"You're lucky I didn't ask you to meet me in the Ritz!" she hissed back.

In fact Strega had suggested some venue in the country but, in view of the body she'd seen in the morgue in Barcelona, Eva Raus insisted on meeting him in a public place.

"Well, what is it you want?" Strega's fingers drummed impatiently on the bar counter. Eva thought his face greyish-looking, unhealthy, as though he drank too much or took drugs. She also thought he looked frightened, though that didn't surprise her. Eva Raus was very frightened herself.

Eva put her mouth close to his ear and whispered: "Bernardo's *dead.*"

Strega made as if to fall off the bar stool with shock and Eva, watching him carefully, thought his reaction was genuine. His fingers, clutching the edge of the bar, appeared strangely white against the stained brown wood. She noticed how well kept his hands were, nails beautifully pared with distinct, crescent-shaped cuticles as though he had them manicured. She realized that Strega liked the soft life and would do a lot to keep it.

"Dead?" he whispered. "How do you mean 'dead'?"

"Dead, dead," she repeated, almost with relish. "Murdered in Barcelona, Mr. Strega, and the money you sent him was stolen."

"I can't believe it."

'Well, you'd better. I saw the corpse. He'd been stabbed several times in the chest." Eva paused for a moment, her eyes brimming over with tears. "I'll confess," she went on, "I had a soft spot for the bastard. You wouldn't call it 'love', but I got fond of him over the years we were together."

"Of course," Strega muttered, nodding his head. "How appalling."

"And *you* knew *nothing* about it, Mr. Strega?" Her eyes searched his face carefully for signs of deceit.

"Absolutely nothing," he averred vehemently. "That fucking Gomez has got away again with my money *and* my reputation."

"Oh, Mr. Gomez," Eva said thoughtfully. "He was your intermediary?"

"Gomez told me he left Bernardo in a hotel in Barcelona with a suitcase full of money. Gomez swore it to me, on his mother's grave."

Eva, to whom Gomez was simply a name, didn't know how much or how little that sacred venue would mean to him. Her face remained impassive.

Tentatively Strega put one of his soft, manicured hands over Eva's on the bar. "Honestly, Eva, if I knew who the villain . . ."

"He took all the money, Mr. Strega; nearly five million Swiss francs. I had to hitchhike back to France."

Strega licked his dry lips.

"Did you tell . . . er . . . the police you recognized Bernardo?"

"Of course not," she snapped. "I said I didn't recognize him."

"Quite right." Strega breathed with relief again.

"I asked myself what was the point?" she went on, producing a cigarette and flicking it into her mouth. "We weren't married. I had nothing to gain by it. Only, maybe, have to pay for his funeral which I couldn't afford."

"Quite."

Eva gave a long drawn-out sigh, expelling smoke with some force.

"But I do know where he is, and how he died . . . if necessary. You know what I mean, Mr. Strega?" There was a dangerous glint in the eyes that swiveled in his direction.

"Look, Eva." Strega turned wrathfully to her. "I know *noth-*

ing about Bernardo's death, or why it happened. Greed, I guess, either on the part of Gomez or somebody else. I sent that money to Bernardo and I sent it in good faith. I knew he felt badly done by Zac Desmond and he was. I found that money myself because I didn't want to lose a friend."

Eva's mind boggled at the word "friend." It made her instantly suspicious of Strega's veracity—or the lack of it.

"I thought I might be able to use Bernardo again," Strega went on, "and I wanted to keep him sweet. Now, Eva"—he clutched the bar again—"it will have to be just you."

"Me?" Eva looked at him and then threw back her head and laughed.

"Shut up," Strega hissed, "you don't want everyone looking at you."

"I'm sorry, Mr. Strega." Eva lowered her head but she was still smiling. "If you think I'm going to *work* for you again you can reconsider. I've had enough of you and your tricks, your lies and broken promises. I am not even convinced, I'll tell you frankly, that you were *not* behind the murder of Bernardo. The whole story sounds unconvincing to me. All I want from you is some money and then I'm going to disappear from your life and maybe, who knows, resume what I did before?" She paused a while and shrugged. "There may be the risk of AIDS but, in many ways, perhaps it's safer."

"Look, Eva." Strega put a hand on her arm. "You will never have to work again. I need you and Mr. Desmond needs you. We have to pick up that money in the same way it was deposited. That is vital and this time it's to be in cash. Seeing Bernardo is not here I'll be waiting outside every time to 'escort' you. You'll be perfectly safe."

He thought she was very naïve to have done what she did without question. She seemed to have done whatever Bernardo told her; yet she didn't give the impression of being a stupid woman.

"Say, what *is* this?" Eva snarled at him. "A sting?"

"It's a *kind* of sting," Strega replied mysteriously. "It's very important and a lot of big, important people are involved. What you have deposited you have now to pick up, only in smaller amounts and over a longer period until you have all the twenty-five million dollars again."

"I don't understand it."

The barman came up and Eva ordered another vodka Martini.

"You're not meant to understand it and, believe me, that's your protection. Look, Eva"—Strega leaned forward and his facial pallor had been replaced by a flush of excitement—"you told me you liked the good life. You don't want to go back to whoring again, really, do you?"

"Not if I don't have to." Eva gave him a tantalizing smile. "But I do want to be rich, Mr. Strega, and I don't mind how I go about it. That's why I went in with Bernardo. I could tell he was a crook."

"Then listen to me, Eva." Strega's grip on her arm tightened. "And do just as I say."

David Heurtey was already at the breakfast table when Sandra entered the dining room. Even by Japanese standards, they were early and he was dressed for riding. The dining room was empty and the waiters bleary eyed. Sandra, looking as fresh as if she'd had eight hours' sleep instead of only four, looked at him, perplexed.

"David, you can't go *riding* today. I mean, that is, unless you're going to be ready by nine."

"My dear, I'm going riding all day." He shook out the *New York Herald Tribune,* folded it and placed it on the table between them, then removed his spectacles. "There are some very fine stables, I'm told, about an hour's drive from Tokyo, and Mr. Shimuri is picking me up in"—he glanced at his watch—"a half-hour."

Sandra shook out her napkin and, as the waiter hovered, ordered orange juice, tea and Melba toast. It was important to hide her irritation because, although she didn't know David very well, she knew him well enough to have realized already that he was his own man, with a deep resentment of interference by anybody in his affairs.

David tucked his reading glasses in his breast pocket. "Sandra, you know you can cope very well without me. Yesterday you were splendid. You know exactly what to do and how to do it. You're a much more skilled negotiator than I am. Yesterday, and the day before, we ironed out all the practicalities of licensing and so on before adopting the system. We both like it and agree it will work for us. Today is detailed work and, frankly, it's something I intensely dislike."

"But essential to the running of a good business." There was an acid note in Sandra's voice.

"Oh, I agree." David looked surprised. "But I am not that kind of person. I have people to do that sort of thing for me. I make the decisions; they see they are implemented and"—he leaned across the table toward her—"if you take *my* advice, my dear, you will do that too. You work much, much too hard. Take a break. Come riding with me today."

"I wouldn't dream of it," she said, avoiding his eyes. "Besides I like hard work."

"You should take *more* time off."

"I don't see why?" She tilted her face at him and he looked lovingly at it.

"Because," he said gently, "you are a *very* beautiful woman but one day that lovely face will show the strain of too much work, too many late nights. Already you wear spectacles."

"Only for work."

"Most people with normal eyesight don't need to wear spectacles until they're middle-aged, for that kind of thing."

"I find your remark sexist," she said. "Save that kind of talk for the Geisha."

"Oh, *Sandra . . .*" He stretched out his hand but she refused to be mollified.

"Seriously, I do. I am a beautiful woman and so I must not work too hard. That's a sexist attitude. In the nineteenth century some people actually believed women's brains were different from men's and they were incapable of strenuous thought."

"I wouldn't think that about you," David protested.

"Thank heaven for that."

"Health's nothing to do with sexism." He smiled, flexing his muscles as though he were playacting. "I'm all in favor of it. I exercise a lot. I'm in my mid-forties and I am fit and well because I exercise a lot, play a lot of sport, and I intend to go on doing so. Now, my dear"—he looked at his watch and rose from the table—"can I leave all the business to you?"

"I suppose so," she said, thanking the waiter who had brought her tea.

"You don't look pleased." He gazed down at her.

"Frankly, I'm not. I thought this was a joint venture, David."

"It is. It is." He leaned over the table, as if to reassure her. "We have agreed on it. We ship the plant; we build a new factory. We are partners, Sandra."

"There is still an *awful* lot to be done."

"We have three more days. Today I'm riding and one day I must play golf. But that leaves a day for work. Anything, you say what."

"Oh, really, *David.*" Sandra's temper snapped and she threw her napkin on the table.

"My dear, I always combine work with pleasure," he said, straightening up. "And, please, don't forget it."

Then he put his lips to the palm of his hand and blew a kiss toward her.

Sandra sat back, watching him stride out of the room, tall and elegant in jodhpurs and hacking jacket, flashing a smile to the waiters. He was a gentleman, a charmer. People loved him. She knew that she was beginning to love him herself. But . . . oh, *why?* Why even *think* of committing herself again to a man with whom she was not a hundred percent compatible?

Both Michel and David were powerful, strong-willed men, attractive to a woman like herself. Yet there was too much chance of conflict: each of them unwilling to be led. In a position like this it seemed to be the woman who, inevitably, lost.

Radu Lupescu had the skin of a boy, soft to the touch. In many ways it was an almost feminine body, with little hair, slim-waisted, slim-hipped, not very tall. The hair on his head was straight, black and heavily greased, which Belle didn't like. But there was nothing physically repulsive about him as there was about Carl, who was covered with hair, like the animals he was so fond of shooting. It seemed to sprout from every part of his body, like grass. Carl lacked finesse, tenderness, and Radu seemed to have a plenitude of both.

Because his face, like his skin, was so pale, his hair so black, he always had a facial shadow despite the fact he shaved so closely. His intensely blue eyes were hooded beneath straight black brows. In many ways he reminded Belle of the pictures one saw in old books of a gigolo of the twenties or thirties, or a waiter in some old German or Parisian café.

Had all the arts of a gigolo too.

Belle, Princess von Burg-Farnbach, was a bitter, rather lonely woman, who possessed the same streak of malevolence and ill temper as her brother Zac. She had been devoted to her father, neglected as a child by her mother who believed, like most of the British aristocracy, that children should be seen but not heard, and that boys were preferable to girls. Consequently Zac and Tim had received the full complement of motherly love, or such as Lady Elizabeth felt she had the time or inclination for, whereas the girls, Belle and Claire, had practically none. Belle in particular had suffered for it all her life.

Both mother and father had been frequently away and the children were flung together, left to their own devices, yet with a multitude of servants. Inevitably Belle and Zac, being most alike in temperament and closest in age, paired off. Tim liked the company of friends, riding horses and playing vigorous games, and Claire became almost reclusive. At one time she had wanted to be a nun.

It was not surprising, though maybe unfortunate, that this curious upbringing had produced Belle, an ambitious, restless and unfulfilled woman, mother of one son, Constantine, who was brought up pretty much as she had been in the splendor of a Bavarian castle and surrounded by servants. And, as was the case with his mother, his parents were frequently away, with the added disadvantage that he had no siblings and was consequently left more to his own devices.

Belle did her duty at the Castle of Burg-Farnbach in the Austrian Alps, at the villa in Costa-Smeralda and the chalet in Gstaad, acting as hostess to friends, mostly Carl's, whose main joy in life was the killing of anything that moved through the forests or across the fields, be it fur-covered or feathered.

Belle was an excellent horsewoman but any other form of sport except, perhaps, skiing bored her and as she had once broken her ankle on the ski slopes she had given up the sport for fear of going lame.

Belle and Carl lived life very much apart. She adored Paris and she felt happiest in the family home on the banks of the Marne. She had never really become an Austrian princess, being, by inclination, a Frenchwoman, a Parisian, a lover of parties, dances and late late nights.

This was how she had met Radu Lupescu, at a diplomatic party given by the British ambassador to Paris. She was the only one of her family to be there and she was just beginning to get bored and to think of going when she saw Radu eyeing her, and a little later her cousin the Honorable Edgar Fitz-Caldwell, who was on the embassy staff, brought him over to introduce him to Belle.

"I'm sure you'll have an awful lot in common," Eddie had said. "Radu is just about as bored with everything as you."

"Is it true?" Radu had inquired with a smile which had interested her, and that was the beginning of the affair.

Belle liked everything about it: the excitement; the danger; above all, Zac's disapproval of Radu being a communist diplomat. She was a perverse woman and this was a perverse situation; she thrived on the unusual, the bizarre or the sinister.

Radu, however, was a communist only in name. He hated the dictator who had confiscated his family home and fortune and who ruled Romania with a tyranny which was equal to that of any of the medieval despots.

But, in common with everyone else, Radu was afraid of disloyalty to a master who through his sinister secret police seemed to know everything.

He was doubly afraid of them learning about the Princess von Burg-Farnbach, yet this too, for him, added the same touch of spice to the affair that Belle enjoyed. They were indeed soul-mates.

Radu lived in a large, dark apartment in a block on the Boulevard de Courcelles near the Parc Monceau. It had no view of the park but looked onto the other side. Belle used to drive there, leave her car in a nearby street and walk the short distance to the block, always using the rear entrance. Sometimes she swore that the place was watched; that there was a man with dark glasses and a trilby hat who took up his stance by a bus stop where he could keep an eye on the main entrance. If this was so, she didn't care, but the subterfuge gave her even more of a thrill.

Radu told her she had too much imagination.

Their social life, however, was restricted. Belle was too well-known to risk either her reputation, or his job, by being seen too frequently in his company, so they ate at small bistros on the Left Bank, or even in the neighborhood of the Boulevard de Courcelles, in which metroland they would be unlikely to meet either his friends or hers. Occasionally they met at diplomatic parties in the company of Eddie Fitz-Caldwell and his wife.

But actually they preferred his apartment because there they could revert to the animal instincts which were really their reason for being together. Belle knew richer, better-looking, more cultured men who would be her escort in Carl's absence;

but no one had quite the satyr-like quality of Radu, his zest for tough, rough sex.

Radu was a skilled and consummate lover, an ardent, passionate man, and Belle felt transformed into a woman enslaved by her senses when she was with him. She never knew she had so many orifices capable of giving so much pleasure, something that the sybaritic Russian Empress, Catherine the Great, was alleged to have discovered too.

When they were not performing some carnal act, or sleeping after it with exhaustion, Radu would cook them an omelette made with cheese, tomatoes and plenty of herbs in his tiny kitchen which, with bread and a good bottle of wine, rivalled many of the more extravagant feasts Belle had enjoyed at starred restaurants in her lifetime. They would sit huddled nude or in gowns on either side of his ancient gas fire and frequently after the joys of eating and drinking, the act of copulation, of sensual gratification in its many forms, would begin all over again.

Belle used to return to the Rue de Varenne, to the family apartment on the top floor, almost sick with exhaustion, satiated with the novelty of the sexual frenzy she and Radu shared with each other. Then she would lock her door and take another bath and think about him, and think, and think.

Was it love?

Love in the afternoon suited Belle: *cing à sept.* It didn't always suit the Romanian Embassy and Radu had to be careful. Sometimes he wondered if the man across the street with dark glasses, a trilby and reading a paper was just a figment of Belle's imagination or whether he might indeed exist. He would lift the lace curtain and look out of his window, but all he saw were people standing at the bus stop and, sometimes, merely shadows.

He opened an eye and saw Belle looking at him. She had the most beautiful breasts he had ever seen: full, yet taut, voluptuous. To take one in his mouth was to have the primeval satisfaction akin to suckling from the maternal breast. He even imagined, sometimes, that he could taste milk.

Belle put a hand on his penis, but he gently removed it. It

reacted swiftly to her touch, oblivious of his desire to control it, like the tail of a cat.

"No time, my darling." He raised his head to look at the clock. "There is an evening reception and I have one hour to bathe, dress and be there."

"Just a quickie," Belle wheedled with an enticing smile.

"Not even a 'quickie'." Yet his hands strayed over her breasts, her stomach, and, perversely, he inserted a finger between her legs, penetrated her deeply and, withdrawing it, discovered it was deliciously moist. He licked it and gave it to her to do likewise.

Belle shuddered and tried to ride him but, with the nimbleness of a gymnast, he leapt away off the bed and ran into the bathroom where soon she could hear the sounds of the shower and Radu singing.

She lay on the crumpled bed with her legs wide apart, hoping he would find the sight irresistible. That swift finger penetration had brought her to the edge of climax, but not quite. She felt, consequently, restless and dissatisfied, but when he returned he had on his underpants and was fastening his socks with their ridiculous old-fashioned suspenders below his knees, as though one had never heard of elastic tops. Maybe in Romania they hadn't. Then, not even glancing in her direction, he fastened his clean shirt with the tails that flapped idiotically back and front.

His face was newly shaved, his hair sleeked back and his long side whiskers emphasized the gigolo aspect rather than the scion of an old and distinguished Romanian family.

"Oh, *darling,*" he said, with a regretful air when at last he looked at her, "you can be so *very* provocative, Belle. Cover yourself or I shall be tempted."

"Be tempted," Belle urged him.

"You are a randy little witch, or do I mean bitch?" Radu said, sitting on the bed by her side.

"Just finish me off," she implored him and, lowering his head, his tongue darting in and out quickly, she achieved the most tremendous climax, so much so that it hurt and, as he wished, perversely, to continue, she pushed his head roughly away.

"Get off," she said, turning on her side.

Radu, his mouth wet, raised his head and gave her a beatific smile.

"Bitch," he said, but in a fond, not contemptuous, tone of voice. "You want it like a dog."

Then he rose, turned his back on her and continued to dress just as though there had been no interlude between the time when he emerged from the bathroom and now as, detaching his trousers from the hanger, he climbed into them, tucking his shirt in. He then selected a dark-blue tie from a rack, and took from the floor a pair of highly polished black shoes.

"What are we going to do, Belle?" he said prosaically after a moment. "I might shortly be posted home or to another place."

Belle turned again on her back and, drawing the sheet right up to her neck, peered at him, her eyes startled.

"You're not serious, Radu?"

"My dear, I am." He looked at her in the mirror into which he was gazing as he tied his tie. "I have been here three years. I want promotion. Anyway, I have no choice."

"Then where you go I'll go," Belle said, "as Naomi, though in very different circumstances, once said to Ruth."

"I *beg* your pardon?" He turned round with a polite smile.

"Of course, I don't suppose you were brought up to be familiar with the Bible."

"Alas, I was not." He returned to his tie.

" 'Whither thou goest, I will go.' It is a quotation from the Bible."

Radu brought his shoes over to the bed and, bending down, began to put them on. Then, without commenting on the biblical quotation, he said, matter-of-factly: "If I go to Bucharest you don't want to go there, do you? There is nothing in the shops, nowhere to eat and you're followed everywhere. You would *die.*"

"But supposing you went to Venice or Rome?"

"Seriously, Belle, you *would* come with me?" Fully dressed and obviously pleased with his appearance, he sat on the bed, his expression one of interest. "But how could you? What about your family, your husband, your job . . . your child? You're joking."

"I'm not." Belle's expression surprised him. He thought she enjoyed the fun of their affair and was not the least bit serious. "Except perhaps my son, little Constantine. You would *love* him, Radu. *I* love him . . . but his father never likes him even to come to Paris."

"Why not?"

"I think he thinks I'd never go back to Burg-Farnbach if he did. Perhaps he's right. Oh, Radu." Restlessly she tossed about on the bed. "What am I to do? I'm an unhappy, discontented woman except when I'm with you. If you went back to Bucharest I think I would die."

"No, you wouldn't do that, my dear." Radu glanced at his watch again, his expression anxious. "I shall have to take a taxi. Good-bye, my love." He bent and swiftly kissed her. Then he took a hat from the chest of drawers near the door and, with it in his hand, waved. "Don't forget to lock up *carefully* before you go."

"When shall I see you?" she called, but he was already out of the door.

After he'd gone, Belle lay for sometime in the bath. She was used to a maid so she never tidied up or made the bed. When he came home Radu would find it as she'd left it: crumpled sheets, a duvet on the floor . . . maybe he'd put his nose to the bed and smell her. Maybe he wouldn't.

It was a dingy, rather depressing flat with cheap rented furniture, holes in the carpet. Not at all the kind of thing she was used to. Yet its very sordidness had a strange kind of appeal: the off-cream walls that had not seen a paintbrush for many years; the faded brocade curtains at the windows; the cornices and motifs on the ceiling which had probably been there a hundred years ago when it had been the town house of some rising, bourgeois family. Everything was second rate, make do; but she liked it. It seemed to have the same fin-de-siècle charm as Radu had, as though it, like he, belonged to another time, another world.

But was it love? She got out of the huge, old-fashioned bath with its brass taps and dried herself with care.

No, it was *not* love; it was lust. It was a fantasy. She would never forsake the life she lived to follow him. It would not last but, while it did, it was very, very nice.

13

Christine Palmer thrust out her long legs encased in jodhpurs and riding boots and, raising her arms, stretched them luxuriously over her head. She ran her fingers lightly through her blonde, curly hair and looked at the man sitting opposite her, who was similarly dressed except that he wore a hacking jacket instead of a cashmere polo-necked sweater.

The castle of Burg-Farnbach was an ancient fortress which occupied a commanding and very beautiful position high up in the Bavarian Alps. It had for centuries been the home of the noble Burg-Farnbach family who traced their origins back to Charlemagne. The castle was set amid mountains which were ideal for skiing, and forests which provided fodder, fur and feathered, for the hungry guns of the huntsmen, particularly its head, Prince Carl, who had been taught how to use a gun almost before he was out of rompers.

It was largely because of their opposition to Hitler that the fortunes of the princely family had declined. Carl's father, Prince Otto, had escaped into exile in Switzerland with his young family and when they returned after the war it was to find that the castle had been used by high-ranking Nazis who also enjoyed sport, and all its priceless antiques and treasures had been looted and pillaged.

The task of restoring the castle to its former glory cost Prince

Otto the remainder of his fortune and, ultimately, his life. Fortunately, before he died his eldest son Carl had married the wealthy daughter of the millionaire Georges Desmond. Belle had liked Carl well enough—they had known each other since childhood—but she had never really loved him. However, the title of "Princess" was coveted by her father as well as herself and there were other advantages. As a married woman she would be free to live the sort of jet-set life she enjoyed, at the same time as being a nominally dutiful wife to Carl. She bore him an heir but after two miscarriages refused to have further children. Carl accepted this, and also his life-style with Belle. Sometimes they were together, but more often they were not. No questions asked.

In its way it was a good life until the death of Georges Desmond had thrown the whole family into disarray. Belle who, up to then, had been considered a fairly normal woman, although moody and prone to vindictiveness, became almost psychotic in her detestation of Sandra, her determination, with her brother, to get rid of her. All the bad instincts of Belle came to the fore: the malevolence and cruelty which, in their childhood, had made her and her brother the despair of their many governesses and nursemaids.

Sometimes Carl felt she had become a woman he no longer recognized and, in a way, he came to fear her too.

The Palmers and the Burg-Farnbachs had also known one another for years. They used to go on holiday together and visit one another's homes. Lady Palmer had a perfect bloodlust; the more inert, bleeding—sometimes only maimed—bodies she saw littering the grounds or the woods after her efforts, the better she felt. Her flat in London and country house in Hampshire were crammed with trophies of the chase: the larder and the deep freeze groaned with the plucked or dismembered corpses of pheasant, grouse, woodcock, stag, and even the humble rabbit did not escape.

The Palmer tradition had naturally extended to her husband Sir Wenham Palmer, who was accidentally killed during a shoot in East Africa. Were they capable of such emotion his prey might have enjoyed the sight of their persecutor carried unceremoniously on a litter, bleeding, as had so many of their fellow creatures.

However, the body of Sir Wenham was not stuffed and hung in the ancestral hall but given a decent Christian burial in the family parish church.

It was after Sir Wenham's death that his widow and Carl grew closer together, largely out of loneliness. Belle was practically always globe-trotting and Carl, who loved the comforts of home, stayed in Burg-Farnbach with Constantine, waiting for each hunt to follow the other, and in the winter he skied.

Christine and Carl sat now on either side of the great log fire, somnolent over their whiskies after a morning's riding. This time it was just for fun as it was not the killing season. They had ridden hard, however, and enjoyed an aperitif before lunch. Then they usually went to bed, rose again and enjoyed an enormous meal in the handsome dining hall of the castle.

"Well . . ." Carl looked at his watch. "Just another one before lunch, dear?"

Christine held out her empty glass which Carl took with a fond glance.

"You know," she said, as she watched him remove the stopper from the decanter, "you really should ask Belle to be more discreet. People are beginning to talk about her in Paris and that . . . 'Romanian' diplomat."

"People are beginning to talk about *us,*" Carl said, pouring two good measures of whiskey.

"Oh, I don't think so, Carl, are they?" Christine looked surprised. "I thought we were being awfully discreet."

"So does Belle."

"But Belle doesn't know about us, surely?" Christine looked aghast.

"Belle knows everything." Carl handed her her glass. "She and Zac have a network of spies and information that rivals the FBI."

"Oh, Carl!" Christine took a large gulp of whiskey. "You do shock me."

"Why? She leaves us alone, we leave her alone." Carl perched on the arm of her chair and dropped a kiss on her head. Christine was thirty-six. He felt comfortable with her. She was no beauty, the product of an English upper-class upbringing, was inclined to fat but had a good sense of humor and a lot of money. This was terribly important. Carl could never have managed without. He was not yet poor, but he had little to spare and Belle always looked after her own financial affairs to the point of meanness. Christine was generous and affordable, and Carl was very fond of her.

"I never dreamt . . . are you *sure?"* Christine looked anxiously up at him. "Has she said anything?"

"Oh, no. Belle and I have an unspoken agreement not to interfere in each other's business. But she knows . . . you can be sure she knows."

"Well, I'm damned!" Christine said, striking her thigh, and then she felt rather pleased. If Belle went too far with the Romanian diplomat, began to make herself ridiculous, who knew but that Carl, to save the family name, might well wish to divorce her?

Everyone could tell that Madame Harcourt was unhappy and displeased about something, and that it had to do with her visit to Tokyo. It couldn't have been anything in connection with business because that had been successful. There was only one assumption: David Heurtey.

She had gone with him, but they had come back separately. Sandra was anxious to return to work, but David found that the Japanese had golfing skills that he hardly knew about. His hosts had invited him to a friendly game and he decided to extend his visit. Disgusted, Sandra flew back, leaving David to return by scheduled airline.

Antoine Dericourt seemed to bear the brunt of her bad humor and he thought it unlike her.

"Is anything the matter, Sandra?" he inquired a few days after her return.

"What could be the matter?" she snapped, without looking at him.

"You're not yourself."

"I am perfectly myself, thank you, Antoine," she replied, with a withering look. "I would be grateful if you could keep your mind on the business in hand, and not my personal affairs."

Ah, so it *was* something personal?

This bad temper was uncharacteristic, but he was too shrewd and practical a man to question her further. They resumed their examination of the plans for the new plant, then discussed where it would be built and how long it would take.

Gradually, in her enthusiasm for the project, Sandra's bad mood seemed to disappear and, over lunch, she apologized to him.

"That's perfectly OK, Sandra," he said, breaking open a bread roll. "We all have our off days."

"I've never known you anything but calm-tempered," she replied contritely.

"And I've seldom known *you* rattled," he answered. "So forget it. I guess you've got a lot on your plate. The worry about Bob . . ."

"The worry about Bob *is* quite something," Sandra admitted, "and especially Joanne's news. If Bob is *not* held by any of the big gangs, who is holding him?"

"We have to negotiate as though it were one of the 'biggies'," Antoine said, "and if you are going to make a payment you will have to make it soon. Personally, I think we should tell the police. Especially if it's *not* a well-known gang. You will then have no gangland vendettas to fear. Someone is going to get pretty desperate, pretty soon . . ."

"I can't go any better than my offer of two and a half million," Sandra said firmly.

"That will show them *you* know it's not the Camorra. You wouldn't dare risk offending them by offering so little."

Sandra put her head between her hands and, after staring for a few minutes at the table, suddenly raised her head.

"I think you're right," she said. "We're floundering. Let's defy them and call the cops."

"So, why did you not inform us before, Madame?" Commissioner Renard looked disapprovingly at Sandra across her desk in the Étoile.

"Because they instructed us not to. Naturally I was afraid on Bob's account."

"But you are now *not* afraid?"

Sandra corrected him. "I am *more* afraid than ever for my brother. I believe the police can handle this kind of thing discreetly. I'm sorry I didn't call you before."

"If you had told us at once, when it *did* happen, we would have had more chance of finding Mr. O'Neill, Madame. Now the trail will be cold."

The Commissioner had been given the letters, told of the telephone orders and shown the severed ear which had been pickled and now floated somewhat incongruously in a jar in front of him. These he examined with an ill-concealed expression of irritation, discussing them in a low tone, which Sandra was unable to hear, with his companion, Divisional Inspector Stoessel of the Paris Prefecture of Police.

In order to deal with a matter of such gravity with people of such importance a very senior policeman indeed had been selected to interview Madame Harcourt. Baptistin Renard was Chief Commissioner of the Serious Crime Squad and had been involved in a number of notorious affairs in which he had acquitted himself with distinction.

Finally he turned to Sandra and, his tone of voice severe like a headmaster admonishing a recalcitrant child, said, "A crime has been committed, Madame, a very serious crime by a person or persons as yet unknown."

"The pathologist thought it might be the ear of a corpse, someone already dead, say, taken from a morgue." Sandra, though remaining polite, appeared unimpressed by his attitude.

"It is a very *nasty* joke in that case, isn't it?" The Commissioner gently revolved the jar round and round on the desk in front of him. Then he sharply raised his head and looked at Sandra.

"Could it be someone you know?"

Sandra shook her head.

"I have no idea."

"You look nervous, Madame."

"I *am* nervous," she said. "And I'm afraid."

"Have you many enemies?" The Commissioner consulted his notebook while, by his side, Inspector Stoessel made notes. "I notice the name of the Desmonds figures prominently in the background notes I was given about you because you are, of course, Madame"—he made a polite bow—"so very well-known."

"The Desmonds and I have had disagreements."

"Very major ones I hear."

"They were settled in court." Sandra wished she'd had her lawyer present, instead of Antoine who remained well out of the way, standing looking out of the window as though the events had nothing to do with him. "Since then the family and I have made a determined effort to get on and I think we have been successful."

"Mmm!" The Commissioner seemed unconvinced. She thought he looked like a stockbroker.

Yet Renard was more like his namesake, a fox, than a financier. He was a university graduate, a highly placed police officer, and applied to the ordinary work of detection a keen, analytical and astute brain.

After a few more formal questions the two policemen took leave, promising to be in touch and to see her again very soon.

As soon as they left the room Sandra wearily shook her head.

"You were wrong, Antoine. You were wrong. We should not have called them in. He was so hostile. The way he looked at me one would think *I'd* done it."

"Oh, I think you did the right thing," Antoine said, but he too was uneasy and when later he saw Joanne Pasarro she made no secret of her feelings.

"At least you could have consulted me," she said angrily. "Hell, I've done all this rooting around. You know the police hate private detectives. Did anyone give them my name?"

"No." Antoine felt sheepish. "It was my advice."

"Then you were *stupid!"*

He looked at her across the table but knew that he deserved the reprimand.

"I'm terribly sorry." He reached across and put a hand on her arm. "I should have consulted you. I still think it does no harm."

"It should have been a matter of negotiation, of us getting together . . ." Seeing his face, Joanne relented and put a hand on his shoulder in a comradely gesture of sympathy and, in a moment of gratitude, he leaned over and kissed her hand.

In a corner of the same restaurant but out of sight Zac watched them with a pleased smile on his face.

"Well, I don't know," he said.

"What is it?" Belle had her back to the room and didn't turn round.

"I have just seen something remarkably interesting." Zac bent his head intimately toward her. "Do not turn round but, in a corner behind you, Antoine Dericourt is having dinner with the assistant of Mr. Heurtey, the *soi-disant* assistant, and he has just kissed her hand."

"I don't *believe* you." Belle was itching to look but, instead, sat gazing at Zac's excited face.

"Nevertheless, it *is* true. What a good idea it was of yours, my dear, to eat at this insignificant bistro where no one knows us and where, they think, no one knows them!" Zac seemed to be enjoying the joke.

Belle ate here with Radu, a fact she didn't mention to Zac. Belle liked her food and she liked style and, though this restaurant was listed in none of the guides, she felt it would not be long before it was.

Everywhere else she went in Paris she and Zac were known, and if they talked in the Rue de Varenne Tara listened. There was always someone behind closed doors. Yet here . . .

"Do you think they have spotted us?" Belle hissed.

"They are too busy with each other," Zac said suggestively.

"Really? I thought Dericourt *adored* his wife."

"I tell you they have eyes only for each other. I've been watching them. He held her hand. She put her hand on his shoulder. He then bent to kiss her hand. They have the intimacy of lovers. Oh dear, I wonder if the Irish tart knows about this: that her faithful lieutenant may be conspiring against her."

"But why should they conspire against *her?"*

"Because 'Madame' returned from Tokyo in a bad temper. Rumor has it that she wanted Heurtey for a lover and something went wrong. He is too keen on the golf course, so she came back without him. What a snub for the whore!"

Zac ducked again as though he thought he might be observed.

"I *think* we're just out of sight," he murmured. "I can see them, but they can't see me. Dericourt has his back to me and I have only met the secretary, whose name I can't recall, once."

"But she knows you?"

"Oh, she knows me. Kept on snooping around in the office. Let's hope she doesn't see me. I think they are ready to go anyway."

"Then they *must* have seen us." Belle looked alarmed.

"No, no, calm yourself." Momentarily his hand rested on hers. "The restaurant was very busy when we came in. It is only because it is less crowded now that I've spotted them. Anyway they seem too engrossed with each other." Zac still watched them with the intensity of a voyeur. "Yes, he is paying the bill. They are going . . . Right." He gazed after them as they walked to the door. *"Voilà!* They have gone. That is *really* something now with which I can blackmail Dericourt."

"Why should you want to blackmail Dericourt?"

"I have my reasons, *ma petite soeur chérie."* He gave her one of his most inscrutable smiles. "All will be revealed at the best possible time."

"Oh, *Zac,* you make me tired," Belle snapped at him impatiently, holding out her glass for more wine. "You think you are so clever, so astute. I am not at all sure you are wise to bring the Tellier brothers into the Cassini deal."

"They brought *me* in, *ma belle soeur.*" Zac raised his thick eyebrows in surprise. "They came to *me* for the money."

"Heurtey is bound to hear about it sooner or later."

"I think later, when the deal is done. He is too busy playing golf and courting the tart, much good may it do him. I tell you I had very little opinion of him when I met him. I have even *less* now. He lets Sandra call the tune and trails after her like a poodle. He is, if you ask me, even more of a weed than Harcourt. I also have it on good authority he is a bad paper man. Unlike Sandra, he never bothers with trifles, but lets subordinates do all the work. If I had to borrow a hundred million he probably wouldn't bat an eyelid until the deal was through. He is half asleep, that one. Goodness knows what Sandra sees in him unless he has a big cock."

"Sometimes you can be *too* crude," Belle said with mock disapproval. "You can't leave too much to chance, someone may find out." Belle glared at him. "And, anyway, you are paying too much for the money by going to banks in the Middle East! Turkey does not have the kind of money you need and the interest rates are exorbitant . . . fifty percent, I'm told."

"Belle, it is only short term," Zac said tetchily. "I wish I hadn't told you so much now. Look, if I finance Tellier to buy the Cassini group we can buy *our* independence from Heurtey."

"But they have to oversee everything."

"Well, they've been very lazy about it, especially since he arrived. Let's hope we can get this one through without them spotting it."

"I still mistrust the Telliers."

"Me too; but I think this deal is a good one. It will make me a multimillionaire. They need me and I need them because, eventually, it is my intention to swallow *them* as well." And Zac, with a flick of his wrist, beckoned good-humoredly to the waiter and ordered another bottle of champagne.

"I don't know what you think you're celebrating," Belle said irritably. "I hate paying three times the price of what our *own* champagne is worth in a restaurant."

"But, my dear, you are not paying."

"It's the principle."

"I wish *you* would stick to principles, Belle," Zac said, his expression rapidly changing from raillery and becoming accusatory.

"And what do *you* mean?"

"Get rid of the red diplomat. People are talking."

"Let them talk."

"But it does *us* no good, my dear. We have our fingers in too many pies. When I bring off my 'coup' against the Irish woman *you* must be seen to be above reproach."

"When you bring off your coup against Sandra," Belle said derisively. *"When!"*

"Oh, it won't be long now," Zac said mysteriously, "and, meanwhile, I understand from Latour little Louis is beginning to piss in the underground caves beneath Desmond."

"Really?" Belle's face lit up. "So *soon?"*

"Little by little," Zac said with heavy sarcasm. "The naughty boy hasn't been trained on the potty. Just a fraction, a trace but, by the winter, it will be a deluge, and the *cuvée* will be ruined. *Then* I intend to complete my destruction of 'Madame'. I do not speed. I am not in too much hurry but when it happens—zonk!" And Zac hit the palm of one hand with the fist of another.

"You mean you have to wait until winter to release Bob?" Belle stared at him. "All that time?"

"My dear, don't panic. My plan is working slowly, but well. Soon the money will start to be withdrawn in small amounts. I know what I am doing. I take care. I can tell you, by Christmas the face of the tart will be plastered on all the front pages of the papers again . . . *she* will be the one in the dock."

* * *

Abruptly Belle bade goodnight to Zac outside the Rue de Varenne and, instructing the chauffeur to drive on, left him standing perplexed and annoyed on the pavement. She was so obtuse . . . perverse. Whatever he said it would make no difference. Off she went to spend the night with the randy diplomat.

Zac shrugged his shoulders and went into the house where Tara awaited him, hopefully in black stockings, a suspender belt and nothing else. He would make her kneel on the bed begging for mercy as he beat her little bottom until it was bright red. He forgot all about his sister in the anticipation of things to come and hurried up the steps.

Meanwhile near the Boulevard de Courcelles Belle tapped on Paul the chauffeur's shoulder and told him to stop and wait for her.

"How long, Madame?" he inquired, his face inscrutable.

"Maybe until dawn," she said, with the arrogance her staff were used to. Nevertheless, they were well paid for what they did. Paul always brought a few pornographic magazines to while away the hours of waiting, enjoying in picture and print the crude images of what he imagined, or hoped, the princess might be doing in practice. He would relish the chance of screwing her himself. She was a really sexy lady.

He sighed and, his hands on the wheel, watched her as she almost ran along the pavement until she turned the corner and was out of sight.

Belle ran up the back stairs, her high heels tap-tapping on the stone steps. She always had a feeling of excitement, even frenzy, at the thought of seeing her lover which, when she got to the fourth floor, made her quite out of breath. She always paused outside the door to get her wind before inserting the key, and her heart continued to race when she peered round the door to see whether or not he was there, usually sprawled in front of the television with a cigarette in his mouth.

But tonight everywhere was in darkness and, as she groped for the light, there was a strange eeriness about the apartment that rather frightened her, as though the whole place spoke to her in some mysterious fashion.

"Radu?" she whispered, before turning the switch and flooding the room with light.

In fact everything was the same except that the curtains were still drawn back and she could see that familiar red haze in the sky which was caused by the glare of the lights of the city at night. As her eyes grew accustomed to the light she realized what was the matter, the reason for the apprehension.

The apartment was empty; empty, that is, of all signs of a human presence or even that one had ever been there. There were no books, papers, bottles or glasses, no half-full ashtrays, no TV set and, as she went into the bedroom, she found the bed had been stripped down to the mattress.

She looked in the cupboards and they were empty, so were the top of the dressing table, the drawers, the wardrobe, the chest by the side of the bed.

The inference was obvious: Radu had gone. He had gone without warning, without saying good-bye. She looked for a note, on the mantelpiece, by the bed, but there was no sign of one. Had he tried to warn her and she had ignored the warning? When he'd told her he might have to go she said she'd follow him. Perhaps, not really knowing her, he'd taken her seriously. Perhaps he'd been afraid she'd be after him.

Belle, Princess von Burg-Farnbach, dressed in her fashionable outfit by Yves St. Laurent, with her fashionable heels, her leather handbag and soft kid gloves, sat down on the bed and, for a few minutes, gazed at the floor.

Then she threw herself full length on the mattress and howled.

When she let herself out of the flat it was morning. She had fallen asleep and woken up cold, hungry and bewildered until the reality of the situation hit her.

She went to the bathroom, but that too was stripped and she didn't linger.

She let herself out of the apartment and went down in the lift, something she used to avoid when Radu had lived there. It was all in the past now.

As she stepped out of the old-fashioned cage lift the concierge was washing the tiled floor and, for a moment, leaned on the mop watching her.

"Bonjour, Madame," she said slightly cheekily, as though she knew.

"Bonjour," Belle replied coldly. "Monsieur Lupescu is no longer there?"

"He has left, Madame." The cheekiness was replaced by a mocking stare.

"When?"

"Two days ago, Madame. A van came and took all his things."

"Merci, au revoir."

"Au revoir, Madame."

Belle hurried down the outside steps of the block, anxious to be as far away from it as she could. She stood for a minute or two looking for a taxi and then she remembered the car which she had left round the corner.

Paul, accustomed to her nocturnal habits, was probably comfortably asleep in the back. She hurried past the block, stopping only momentarily to stare at a recently erected notice: *Apartment à louer.*

They had wasted no time. Radu must have known for weeks that he was going.

Such is love, she thought, trying to dismiss it from her mind but, inwardly, she knew she felt humiliated; very badly humiliated, and also betrayed.

Étienne Legrand stood in front of Sandra's desk, white-coated, a bottle in his hand, his expression dour.

Sandra looked up from her writing and gazed at him.

"Yes, Étienne?"

The director shook his head, his expression became even more forlorn, and he put the bottle down on the table as if to distance himself from it.

"There is something *wrong,* Étienne?"

Sandra put down her pen and gazed at the bottle. "You don't like the design? I thought as much." She crossed her arms and assumed a stubborn expression with which Étienne was quite familiar. "We wanted to ask your advice but you were not here."

"Whose idea was this design, Madame?" Étienne's tone was so polite that Sandra was convinced he knew the answer.

"Monsieur Zac suggested it."

Étienne pursed his lips and nodded. "He should have known better."

He then pointed to a sign of moisture between the cork and the rim of the bottle. In fact it could be seen that one or two drops had, at some stage, made their way down the neck of the bottle, held carefully upright in Legrand's hand.

"It is the *'couleuse,'* Madame. It is weeping."

Sandra felt a spasm of alarm and, pulling the bottle toward her, examined it intently.

"What exactly do you mean, Étienne?"

"The cork is too humid. The wine is escaping from the bottle."

"Which is abnormal?"

"You *know* it's abnormal, Madame." Étienne's tone was impatient because he had been her wine master and she had been such a good pupil.

"Of course I do; but why?"

Legrand shrugged his shoulders impassively and kept them hunched, his arms folded across his chest, his expression lugubrious.

"You often have a little weeping. In the old days it was quite a problem, but it had to do with the design of the bottle as well as the cork. Now it's not uncommon in some bottles; but I am more anxious here than normally because of the special design of this bottle. The neck is too long, too thin; the thickness of the cork is not adapted to the calibre of the bottle neck. This is the *real* reason for all this weeping. Personally, had I been consulted, I would have strongly advised against such a bottle, Madame. I'm surprised at Monsieur Zac. Did Latour know about this?" He gazed sharply at Sandra.

"Of course he did."

"Did *he* approve it?"

"Yes."

"Well . . ."

A sense of real panic began to rise in Sandra's breast. "Surely *all* the bottles won't be affected?"

"Oh no, not at all." He seemed loath to reassure her. "At least, I hope not. This is a bottle I happened to pick at random. I noticed it before I inserted the aphrometer to check the pressure of the second fermentation just as a matter of course. Before I removed it I thought I should show it to you. Seepage was not uncommon in the old days, but has largely been obliterated thanks to modern methods. Perhaps Monsieur Zac, in his enthusiasm for his design, overlooked this."

"Perhaps he did," Sandra muttered under her breath.

"I beg your pardon?" Étienne, who was a little deaf, cupped his hand to his ear.

"Nothing." Sandra shook her head. "I think we should go to the cellar and inspect *all* the bottles."

"It is pointless, Madame." Étienne shook his head. "You cannot inspect two hundred thousand bottles, which I understand is the number racked in our caves. On the other hand there is nothing we can do to alter the situation. If there *is* massive seepage much of the wine will be ruined. We shall just have to wait and see how it turns out."

Sandra turned to her desk and, lifting her telephone, spoke rapidly down it. "Please find René Latour and ask him to come up, would you, Antoinette?"

The reply was inaudible and Étienne continued to gaze at the bottle with its telltale dried globules of wine.

Latour, who must have been in the building, took no more

than two or three minutes to appear in Sandra's office. She watched him with great care as he came through the door, but he did not appear in the least ill at ease.

"Madame?" He smiled politely at her and also at Legrand.

"Étienne has been showing me this bottle, Monsieur Latour." She pointed to the one which stood before them on the desk.

"Yes, Madame?" Latour clasped his hands in admiration of the shape. "It *is* exquisite. The glassmaker has made a masterpiece."

"Are you quite happy with the design?"

"Of course!" Latour's cautious features showed sudden surprise. "Why not?"

"Étienne has found some seepage."

Latour shrugged his shoulders, a philosophical expression taking the place of his look of surprise.

"That occurs in *any* bottle. Are you worried, Étienne?" He looked at his colleague with apparent concern.

"I would never have chosen this shape for the bottle," Étienne replied stiffly. "The neck is too thin, too long. The corkage is the real problem: either the cork is too tight and it will be impossible to uncork the bottle, or it is too loose and we shall risk the weeping."

"I wondered if we should inspect all the bottles." Sandra looked dubiously at Latour, who echoed Legrand's opinion.

"Madame, there is nothing we can do. The wine is made, the yeasts are fermenting. We shall have to hope that only a few bottles are affected. I'm sure you will find that's the case. In any event I'll keep a careful eye on the situation, with frequent inspections."

"Bon." Legrand removed the bottle from the desk and looked at his watch. "If you will excuse me, Madame, my wife is expecting me for lunch."

"Goodness, I didn't realize it was so late!" Sandra exclaimed. "Of course, off you go. Please, though, leave the bottle behind."

With some hesitation Legrand replaced it on the desk and, as Latour was about to follow the older man, Sandra called out:

"Monsieur Latour, would you stay behind for a moment? I'd like a word with you."

Latour seemed unaffected by this announcement and merely nodded his acquiescence and, as his colleague shut the door, he turned to Sandra, who invited him to sit down.

"Yes, Madame?" he asked politely.

"Monsieur Latour." Sandra, sitting opposite him, elegantly crossed her legs and folded her hands in her lap. "This is a little disquieting, is it not?"

"I don't understand, Madame Harcourt." René too folded his hands and his gaze was both questioning and confident.

"Are you not worried about the possibility of the wine weeping?"

"No, I am not."

"Did you *ever* consider it?"

"No. It is a problem I thought we had conquered years ago."

"But not with a special bottle."

"I have no experience of these specially made bottles. I must accept the opinion of the experts. I would have thought the glassmaker knew what he was doing. The specifications were exact."

"Drawn up by Monsieur Desmond," Sandra said.

Latour nodded. "Drawn up by him and approved by you, Madame." Latour smiled in her direction.

"But I know nothing about bottles. I relied on advisers who, I thought, knew what they were doing."

"But it is your final responsibility, Madame," Latour said. "And you did sign the order."

Sandra rose from her chair and, to conceal her agitation, walked to the window where for a few moments she stood gazing into the courtyard: that pretty quadrangle festooned with vines, an old fountain playing in the middle, one or two workers going about their business, a car arriving and one departing. All very routine and normal. There was something, she thought, very familiar too about this situation: she had got into the same kind of trap as she had before. She had, acting on advice, signed the order for the *tirage* about which she then knew nothing; but in that case fraud was subsequently proved to have been involved. Could it possibly be the same this time? Did lightning strike twice?

And why, why had she *ever* attempted to trust Zac Desmond? She turned to Latour.

"I would like to go to the cellars now and have a look, regardless of what Étienne says. A huge publicity campaign has already been launched for the world's most exclusive champagne, the new *cuvée* Desmond. If there is widespread weeping then it would enable me, at the very least, to stop the advertising campaign and making, once again, a fool of myself."

"Why not invite Monsieur Zac, Madame?" Latour suggested blandly. "After all *he* has some of the responsibility for this too."

Every weekend Zac and Tara drove to Tourville to spend it with his mother, occasionally his sister, sometimes Sandra. Ostensibly there were still good relations between Sandra and the Desmonds, but it was, at best, a tepid affair. Sandra chose to spend fewer weekends in the bosom of her so-called family, preferring to be alone with Louis. Often David Heurtey drove down from Paris and stayed at Les Crayères in Reims.

Their relationship since Tokyo had not developed. She liked him and was attracted to him, and she was sure the feeling was mutual; but between them there was an air of hesitation as though each was sending out signals of caution to the other.

However, there was no doubt that she enjoyed David's visits. He would arrive on a Saturday and take her out to dinner. He would return for Sunday lunch, after which he enjoyed playing with Louis. Sometimes they all went for a walk with Sandra pushing the pram, and her new little poodle Pim trotting along on a leash. It looked just like an informal family outing except for the private detectives, one for her and one for David, who followed discreetly behind.

During the week she and David would speak on the telephone, mostly about business, which he still seemed happy to conduct mainly from his suite at the Ritz.

The Heurtey offices near the Odéon were competently managed and run by a staff of about twenty; but David seldom visited them. He relied on telephone, fax and intuition. He also liked to work for only half a day so that he could either go riding in the Bois de Boulogne or play golf.

Sandra didn't wholly approve of a man who was partly a playboy. This aspect of his life reminded her of Tim. Yet Michel never took time off, never played at all—and Tim played all the time. Maybe David was somewhere in between. Certainly she was excited by him physically. One day, she was pretty certain, they would be lovers.

The day Étienne brought her news of the weeping was a Friday and David was expected down on the Saturday. In the course of the afternoon after Latour had gone she decided to change the plan and called David who, for once, she was able to get at his suite in the Ritz.

"David, it's Sandra."

"Hi!" he said with genuine pleasure in his voice. "I'm looking forward to tomorrow."

"David . . ." She paused because she'd wanted him to come, but then she continued: "Something's cropped up. I'm afraid I'll have to call off this weekend."

She could sense the disappointment in David's voice as he replied.

"Is it anything serious, Sandra?"

"Well, it could be, otherwise I wouldn't have canceled. It's to do with business."

"Of course," he said in a tone that was slightly sarcastic.

"David, it is *serious."*

"My dear, *any* business with you is serious."

"I wish you wouldn't talk like that, David. It upsets me."

"And it upsets me, Sandra, that you seem to eat, sleep and drink business. You put it before anything else, any personal relationship, any chance we have . . ." He stopped abruptly as though he felt he was going too far. "I find it most unfeminine."

"Thank you for that sexist remark, which I'll ignore," she said coolly. "Something has come up today and it involves Zac." Sandra hesitated, wondering how much she should tell him. In the end she told him what had happened, concluding:

"You see he designed the bottle for the *cuvée* for Louis. He suggested its unique shape."

"You never learn, do you?"

"For heck's sake, a *bottle,"* Sandra said angrily. "What on earth do you think could go wrong with that?"

"Probably has a hole in the bottom." David chuckled and his superior attitude irritated Sandra.

"There's a family gathering at Tourville." Sandra found her sense of irritation growing. "I do hope you understand."

"I do," he said rather formally. "But I'm disappointed."

"So am I," she said, her lips close to the mouthpiece. "Truly."

14

It was a long time since they had all gathered together around the table in the huge dining room used for formal occasions at Tourville. Belle had motored from Paris with Zac and Tara and their children, Gaida, Roberto and Constantine. There was no sign of Carl.

Sandra thought that Belle looked unwell, her face drawn and pale, with large shadows around her eyes. She was heavily made-up but the effect was theatrical, half real.

By contrast Zac seemed in a particularly good mood, pleased with himself and attentive to Tara, constantly by her side. But there was no doubt that Tara had changed. Her flamboyance had vanished, she seemed apathetic and spoke rarely or only when spoken to. It was possible to imagine she was on some kind of sedative. Even her beautiful black hair looked lackluster, and her fine dark eyes no longer had the sparkle that had once marked her out as a top international model.

Zac, in fact, was very satisfied with life. He had a docile wife, whom he'd frightened into submission, and all his plans for the defeat of his detested enemy were working out. Now all he had to do was hoodwink Sandra by attempting to use the weekend in front of them to convince her, by his charm and sincerity, that he was on the side of the angels. Unlikely, but he could only try . . .

In this charged atmosphere it was not easy for Sandra to feel relaxed at dinner, despite the elegant surroundings, the gourmet dishes, wines of unsurpassed excellence. There was no doubt that Lady Elizabeth had subtly slipped into the role of being its chatelaine again. Once more Sandra was made to feel that she was a guest.

"Where is Carl?" Sandra asked, when the servants had withdrawn after serving the hors d'oeuvres: a selection of *fruits de mer* and local crudités served in an excellent sauce, with which they drank a pink champagne, the celebrated Desmond '79.

"Killing something, I suppose," Belle said offhandedly.

This brought a smile to Zac's face. "But you like a little killing too, don't you, *ma petite soeur chérie?* Birds, stags, that kind of thing, as much as he does?"

"I enjoy the hunt." Belle glared at her brother. "But not as much as Carl, unless there is some other attraction . . ."

Sandra felt lost in a conversation that, she felt, was full of double entendres.

"You might as well know," Belle said at last, seeing the expression on her face, "Carl has a mistress, an English woman called Lady Palmer, who is even more keen on blood sports than he is. There was even a rumor she shot her own husband in Kenya . . ."

"Oh, my dear, that is ridiculous!" Lady Elizabeth intervened. "I mean . . ."

"How much do *you* know of it, Mother?" Belle asked her. "Did you make inquiries?"

"I know, naturally, about the death of Sir Wenham because the Palmers are friends of ours in England. It was most definitely an accident."

"But quite convenient if you want to get rid of your husband, nevertheless."

"I find this an astonishing conversation," Sandra said suddenly. "I feel as though I'm an intruder."

"But so *like* the Desmonds," Tara added.

"What do you mean by that, my angel?" Zac inquired in the silkiest of tones.

"Always accusing people, without proof, of some wicked deed."

"We are not accusing anybody," Belle protested. "But at the time Christine Palmer was definitely under suspicion. She was arrested by the Kenya police and freed because of lack of evidence."

"Well, let's hope Carl takes care," Lady Elizabeth said. "We are all terribly fond of Carl. Even Belle remains fond of Carl, don't you, my dear?"

"Of course I'm fond of him." Belle popped a succulent oyster in her mouth and, after disposing of the shell, wiped her fingers carefully on her napkin. "Carl and I have long since gone our separate ways and everyone knows it. But we like, and respect, each other, and *that* is what matters."

"I think Carl has chosen more wisely than you," Zac said, frowning.

"Zac, would you *please* leave my own private affairs out of this?" Belle shouted at him.

"But, my dear"—Zac looked round the table—"we're being terribly frank. Isn't that what families are for? Carl has chosen an English gentlewoman for his companion, while you have chosen a communist diplomat, a highly questionable choice, which reflects on us all."

Belle rose and, still glaring at her brother, dashed her napkin onto the table.

"Will you shut up?" she cried. "Just shut up, that's all, and mind your own bloody business." She pointed one of her scarlet nails at him. "There's many a tale *I* could tell about you, Zac Desmond, if I once began . . ."

"Oh, be *quiet,* you two." Lady Elizabeth put her hands to her ears. "We are meant to be having a happy family reunion with Tara and Sandra present for the first time for ages and you two go at it hammer and tongs, hurling unjust and dangerous accusations all over the place. Now, Belle, *please* sit down and resume your meal."

"Only if Zac apologizes." Belle remained standing, glaring at her brother.

"Apologize?" Zac seemed to find the idea amusing. "About what, pray?"

"You have done nothing but attack me since I sat down for dinner . . ."

"That is *utterly* false, I . . . I deprecate Radu Lupescu, that's all. He . . ."

Belle put a hand to her mouth as if to prevent herself from screaming and, in an obviously highly charged state, ran out of the room, almost colliding with Pierre the butler, who was just coming through the door.

"Pardon, Madame," he said, stepping hurriedly to one side.

He then entered and recommenced his duties, directing the footmen, who followed him, in clearing the plates from the first course and serving the consommé. For a moment he stood by Belle's plate and looked questioningly at Lady Elizabeth.

"Will the princess be returning for her meal, my lady?"

"I think not, Pierre," Lady Elizabeth replied. "She is not terribly well tonight, not herself, and if she requires anything later you may take it to her room."

"Very well, my lady." Pierre bowed and one of the footman, hovering by his side, removed the dish and Belle's place, which seemed to leave an awkward gap at the table.

Pierre remained in the dining room while they ate their bouillon and it was not until the main course was served and the Burgundy had been poured that Lady Elizabeth asked him to leave the family alone.

"I'll ring when I need you, Pierre."

"Very well, my lady." And that perfectly trained butler, who had been engaged as a houseboy when Lady Elizabeth had come to Tourville as a bride and was nearly as old as she was, withdrew, closing the door solemnly behind him.

"I don't know what has got into Belle tonight," Zac said. "What a performance . . ."

"You might not know, in that case, that the diplomat has mysteriously disappeared," Lady Elizabeth said sotto voce. "She told me so in great distress a day or two ago."

"Disappeared!" Zac looked at her sharply.

"She had an arrangement to see him the other night and when she went to his flat there was no sign of him. It had been cleared out completely."

"My God, did something happen to him?"

"Belle has no idea. She had no warning. He rented the furnished apartment by the month. A short time before he had mentioned to her that he might be sent to another posting."

"Well, I, frankly, am jolly glad of *that.*" Zac raised his glass to his lips. "I'll drink to his departure and welcome it. Belle was getting herself talked about, Mama. She was becoming increasingly indiscreet in Paris, going to diplomatic receptions and openly carrying on with him."

Lady Elizabeth inclined her head as if to say she retained a mother's impartiality. "Before the war his family were well-known nobility, close to the king."

"Then they should have left the country with him."

"I believe they were all shot."

"Mmm!" Zac gazed at his plate. "Well, in any case, I'm glad he's gone."

"You simply can't think of anyone being happy, can you, Zac?" The bitterness in Tara's voice surprised Sandra, who found herself staring at her.

"My darling, that is a *very* unfortunate remark coming from *you'*—Zac leaned toward his wife who sat opposite him—"as I do everything in my power to make you happy, and I like to think that, at last, I have succeeded."

It was then that Sandra observed an ugly mark on Tara's bare arm she had not noticed before. It looked like a burn that had not quite healed. It was on the underside of her arm and would normally not be exposed but, from where Sandra sat, she could see it quite clearly. She suddenly had a vision of someone stubbing a cigarette out on it and recalled vividly that jerky, impatient way that Tara disposed of her stubs, often leaving them still half alight in the ash-tray. Involuntarily she closed her eyes and decided that this happy family weekend was gradually turning, as she might have known it would, into a bad dream.

Coffee and liqueurs were taken in the drawing room. Belle did not reappear and Tara and Lady Elizabeth went into the television room to watch a favorite series while Sandra and Zac found themselves alone.

It was a warm spring evening and the doors leading onto the terrace were wide open.

"Do you think it's warm enough to sit outside?" Zac suggested pleasantly.

"Why not try?" Sandra took her coffee and preceded him through the French doors where, as night fell, the shadows of the tall trees, outlined by a full moon, appeared quite magical. The swans, which should have been asleep, glided on the lake, causing tiny ripples on the still surface, while, from the woods behind the house, the night birds had started to call.

"It is so lovely here," Sandra said, taking a deep breath as she sat down.

"Sure you're not too cold, Sandra?" Zac looked solicitously at her. "May I say," he said, glancing at her, "how particularly beautiful and elegant you look tonight; but then you always do." Sitting beside her he inclined his head so that it was practically touching hers.

"Sandra, I value this chance to have a talk to you. We don't talk enough and I would like you to think you can come more often to Tourville, to this house which, after all, is yours. We miss you. We really do."

Sandra felt immediately on her guard as she stirred her coffee. "That's very kind of you, Zac; but I have so much on my plate at the moment and . . ."

"Sandra"—Zac's head leaned nearer still—"there was a *little* matter I wanted to talk to you about, seek your help and cooperation."

"And what's that?" It was hard to keep the suspicion from her voice.

"I have an interesting business venture that I think will be very profitable. I cannot divulge all the details as yet, but I think it would reward you well without risk. I know that you're looking for money to obtain Bob's release, and this may well fit the bill. The check, of course, could be made personally payable to you. There are ways of dealing with this."

"I should have to know a little more about what you're talking about," Sandra said cautiously, sensing a trap.

"All I can say," Zac said mysteriously, "is trust me. But I would like the price of Heurtey shares to go up. They are now a little low."

"They're restructuring, you should know that." Sandra looked surprised.

"I know that, but they could be higher. If you could bring yourself to buy on behalf of Desmond, say, twenty-five million francs' worth I . . ."

"But I must know *why*. What you're suggesting is bordering on the illegal."

Zac pretended to look shocked.

"Share support is not illegal . . . and if I offer you a sweetener, who is to know?"

"That *is* illegal," Sandra said flatly.

"Who would know? A few millions, personally, to you . . ."

"I could never think of it." Sandra found the turn the conversation was taking more and more surprising. "Have you not read about the Guinness affair in England? That is exactly what you're suggesting. Share rigging to jack up the price."

"Oh no, it's nothing like that, I can assure you," Zac said loftily. "But give it some thought and please"—in the moonlight Sandra was aware that the air of bonhomie had left Zac's face, which looked pale and tense—"for the sake of the family, not a word to David Heurtey." Suddenly he stood up as if the matter were now closed. "I think if we join Mama and Tara we'll just be in time to see the latest news."

Sandra slept badly that night, tossing and turning despite the silence and tranquility around her. It was the vibrations in the house that were bad: that sense of evil that seemed almost inescapable on a visit to Tourville.

Why should Zac tell her about some peculiar pecuniary deal, that he might know she couldn't possibly agree to? He must also know, as he made it his business to know most things, that she and David Heurtey were friendly and she would hardly keep an item of news like this to herself.

What was Zac plotting now?

Louis was sleeping in a cot in the room next door which was linked to hers by an intercommunicating door and twice she got up to look at him and reassure herself that he was all right and slept undisturbed. Once she thought she heard a cry as if someone were in pain, and she recalled that ugly mark on Tara's arm and the peculiar change in their relationship. Previously Tara had treated him almost with contempt. Now she seemed craven. What had he done to her since she'd returned from Italy? Had he beaten a confession out of her?

The cry came again but this time she remembered the abundance of bird life in the trees outside and thought it was probably some luckless creature of the night which had fallen victim to a bird of prey.

Despite her restlessness Sandra knew she must have had some sleep because the morning, and the beauty of the day, the sun streaming through the wide windows of her large room, took her by surprise. She looked at the clock by her bed and saw that it was eight. She rang the bell for her morning tea and then slipped out of bed and ran lightly across the thick carpet to Louis's room.

The cot was empty.

Her first feeling was one of alarm—the fear of kidnap never

far away—until she heard the sounds of running water and Mireille entered with Louis, naked, and wrapped in a towel.

"Bonjour, Madame," she said, with her bright smile. "Did you sleep well?"

Sandra sank down on the nearest chair. "I don't know, I had nightmares about Louis . . ."

"Oh, Madame, did you think something had happened to the little one?" Mireille noticed the look of panic on her mistress's face. "Madame has too much on her mind, too many concerns. There is no need to be afraid, especially here in this lovely place. Besides, Madame, who would wish to do you harm by stealing your lovely son?"

"Anyone." Sandra looked distractedly at her. "Anyone, Mireille. That's the trouble. They steal a harmless child and blackmail the parents. You must have read about the Lindbergh baby. There have been others."

"In that case, Madame," Mireille said, hugging Louis, "although the gates are locked and there are bodyguards in the house, in order to set your mind at rest I myself will sleep with Louis and will have my bed placed in his room. Madame can then rest easily, knowing that her precious darling will come to no harm."

"Oh, Mireille, *thank* you." Sandra's eyes were full of gratitude. "That would be absolutely wonderful."

"Then Madame will be sure of the rest she needs." Mireille looked at her critically. "Today you do not look yourself."

Sandra ran her hands over her face and gave a wan smile. "I know that, Mireille; but there are many reasons for it."

Hearing the sound of her maid moving about next door, she rose and went to kiss Louis, who put his hands out to grip her finger. Reluctantly she let him go and, pausing at the door, said: "I will go and have my morning tea and that will restore me."

Mireille smiled but when the door closed behind her employer her eyes were troubled.

One seldom saw Madame so out of sorts.

* * *

By the time Sandra had bathed and dressed and descended for breakfast she found that Zac and Belle had eaten and were out riding. Lady Elizabeth always breakfasted in bed and the only one still at the table was Tara, who greeted her in an unusually friendly manner. She wore well-tailored trousers and a long-sleeved, pleated shirt which now concealed the wound on her arm.

"Hi, Sandra," she said brightly, "come to keep me company?"

"I almost overslept." Sandra helped herself to scrambled eggs from the selection of dishes on the sideboard as one of the footmen appeared to ask her what she would have to drink.

"Coffee, please," she said, "and English toast." Sandra sat opposite Tara and, taking her napkin from its silver ring, smiled. "You look very well this morning, Tara. I thought you were very subdued last night."

"I had a headache," Tara said in an offhand manner. "The time of the month, you know how it is."

"I'm sorry. Yes, I know how it is."

"You look as though *you* didn't sleep well, Sandra." Tara regarded her critically. "Does Tourville 'get' to you too?"

"Oh, I love Tourville," Sandra protested. "Don't you?"

Tara put her head reflectively on one side. "I like it as a *place* well enough, but I never feel completely happy or at ease here. It's not as bad as it used to be—remember Claire always creeping around the house? You felt as though she were listening for ghosts."

Sandra laughed. "I don't think it was as bad as that." She smiled her thanks as the footman brought her fresh toast and a pot of steaming coffee which he started to pour for her.

"I wonder if you ever miss Tim?" Tara asked casually. She had long since finished her breakfast which only ever consisted of grapefruit juice and black coffee. She sat there smoking a cigarette, some of the coffee still in her cup.

"Not at all," Sandra said immediately. "Next question."

"I'm sorry, I didn't mean to upset you. Really, Sandra." Tara paused as if she were anxious to find the right words. "I do want us to be friends."

"We *are* friends," Sandra assured her, buttering her toast. Then she raised her head and looked across the table. "What gave you the idea we were not?"

"Somehow there's a lack of closeness, of trust. I guess it's Zac. You don't really like him at all, do you?"

Sandra didn't reply for a few moments as she tried to think of a diplomatic answer.

"I don't *dislike* Zac; but so much has happened between us."

"It's a question of trust, isn't it?"

"In a way."

"Zac's a very disappointed man," Tara said.

"I know that."

"He does want to like you, however, and he is desperately anxious for you to like him."

"Is he?"

"Oh, yes. Yes, he is. Since . . . since I came back from Italy he's been so different, as though he wants to make up for everything that happened before. He realizes his behavior to me was bad, and to you too, Sandra. You must try and accept Zac at face value. And, Sandra . . ."

"Yes?" Sandra, still puzzling this last remark, looked up.

"Zac would like me to become involved with Jean Marvoine again. Belle, well . . . she's had this business with the diplomat, not herself for months really. Whether or not things will change now that he's gone I don't know . . ."

"Yes, Jean Marvoine definitely needs looking into," Sandra agreed. "I'm glad you brought it up. I think you need a new designer and a new image. Maurice Raison has had his day if you ask me."

"Oh, but we *daren't* sack Maurice." Tara held her hands in front of her face as if the very idea scared her to death.

"Oh, can't we?" Sandra gazed at her and, in that instant, Tara knew why so many people respected Sandra and also feared her. "I can."

"Well . . ." Tara gulped down the rest of her coffee. "I'd rather *not* be there the day you give Maurice his marching orders."

Sandra gave her a reassuring smile. "That might not be for ages. I'd like to meet you there, go through the books, the program, and talk to the staff. Maybe we needn't push Raison out. Just demote him and put over him someone who has a real idea of style, who is up to date with trends and fashions. Raison is so *dull.*"

Tara made a mental note never to wear her black Raison dress again, certainly not in front of Sandra.

It was difficult that morning not to think her fears had been exaggerated; that her morbid fears for Louis and the cries of pain in the night had been her imagination.

Sandra was not a highly imaginative person. She had flair and an instinct for daring, yet the basis of her life was practical, even prosaic: to keep two feet on the ground. She seldom heard noises in the night; nor was she prey to imaginary fears. She was a realist.

But being a mother had exposed an area that was vulnerable to emotions she had hitherto despised: exaggerated fears for the welfare of her son, his health and, especially, his safety.

She had engaged an extra bodyguard for Louis, a man called Hector who remained unobtrusively in the servants' quarters when they were at Tourville, making himself useful cleaning the cars, or exercising the horses. She didn't want Louis to grow up in the knowledge that he was being guarded all the time. One had to take some risks.

After breakfast she went through some papers, then took Louis for a walk in the grounds with Mireille, Hector well in the background.

Tourville in early summer was at its best. She remembered when she first saw it, thinking it was like a pearl, a pearl in a perfect shell; and it still was, with its graceful towers and turrets in white stone, its colonnaded balconies, its famous gardens and elegant, elliptical lake, set against a background of forest, and with, on either side, the steep, vine-clad slopes of the Montagne de Reims.

When they returned, Belle was sitting in the gazebo in the garden and hailed them, telling them they were going to be late for lunch. This was taken informally in the garden room. Belle and Zac seemed completely to have forgotten their row of the night before—maybe they'd spent some time talking behind closed doors. The children, who did not dine with them at night, were the main focus of attention. Gaida, Roberto and their cousin Constantine were polite and well behaved, as children who see little of their parents often are. Parents whose approval they were anxious for, whose love they could not take for granted; gentle, handsome children, very kind to Louis, especially Tara's daughter, Gaida.

There was such bustle and activity, such toing and froing of family and staff, that Sandra knew she was going to find it hard to talk to Zac and even wondered if an opportunity would present itself.

After lunch Belle and Zac went to play tennis while Tara went riding with her children, accompanied by one of the grooms. Louis went for his nap and perhaps Constantine did too, or for a quiet period while his nursemaid read to him.

Sandra and Lady Elizabeth sat by the side of the tennis court drinking coffee.

"Don't you play tennis, Sandra?" Lady Elizabeth glanced at her. "Why don't you have a game with Zac?"

"He didn't ask me." Sandra smiled. "I guess he wants to make it up with his sister."

"Oh, those two," Lady Elizabeth sighed wearily. "They really seem to enjoy a scrap."

"Oh, they really enjoy it? I wondered."

"No doubt about it." She shook her head vigorously.

"Did they always argue, even when they were small?"

"Always. When they were children you could never stop them."

"What did they argue about?" Sandra was curious.

"Everything and nothing. It drove their father mad." Lady Elizabeth gazed at them for a moment as they vigorously hit the ball between them, and then turned her eyes to Sandra, smiling serenely.

"You know some couples like to fight and then make love? Well, Belle and Zac are like that. They like to fight and make it up, usually by riding or swimming or playing tennis or some vigorous sport where they can pit themselves against each other." She paused, watching them again. "You would never think it but they really are quite devoted. See now how happy they are?"

It was true that, as the ball bounced back and forth and each scurried after it, hitting it hard over to the other side, there was a lot of laughter and insulting but gentle chaffing going on.

Sandra put her head back and gave a deep sigh. Who would *ever* know the truth about the Desmonds?

Out of the corner of her eye Lady Elizabeth was watching Sandra, a young woman who had changed a great deal over the years she'd known her; who had become confident, strong, yet somehow even more beautiful—as if she used her natural femininity and charm to counteract her reputation as a tough, successful businesswoman. Maybe it was her love for Michel, and motherhood.

"It is nice how the children have taken to little Louis, isn't it, Sandra?"

"It is indeed." Sandra didn't move. She was in that somnolent state, half awake, half dozing.

"It is really as though we were one big happy family—such as Georges so wished. Gaida, Roberto and Constantine regard Louis as a little cousin."

"Do you really think so?" Sandra opened her eyes and stared at the woman who had given her as much heartache as any of them, and who was as much an enigma. Her implacable hostility had, at first, seemed greater than the others' because she, Sandra, had disinherited Lady Elizabeth's children. The mother wolf had a natural desire to protect her cubs.

And then there had been the court case in London where Lady Elizabeth had testified that Sandra was not the daughter of Hélène O'Neill, a secret she had hitherto kept to herself. Sandra now knew who her mother was, but she didn't know who had fathered her. Could it possibly have been Georges Desmond? Did Lady Elizabeth know that and, if she did, would she ever tell?

Sandra sighed inwardly, smiling to herself. The Desmonds liked to foster the idea of the family, yet it was not the sort of "family" that Sandra thought she, or anyone else, would recognize: an odd idea of family life, to be constantly riven by strife.

"I often think of Bob, you know, Sandra." Lady Elizabeth snipped a piece of silk from her embroidery which she worked so exquisitely that sometimes she exhibited it. "It must be a great worry to you."

"It is."

"I was very fond of Bob."

"I know." Sandra looked at her. "And he of you."

Lady Elizabeth gave an expressive shudder. "And to think of poor Bob in the hands of those terrible bandits." She paused. "Have you thought, are you trying . . . I mean about the ransom."

"The whole thing is in the hands of the police now," Sandra said.

Lady Elizabeth appeared surprised. "But isn't that a little dangerous?"

"Antoine Dericourt advised me to call them in. We had no success by ourselves. They cut off Bob's ear . . ." Sandra kept her eyes on Lady Elizabeth to see her reaction. In fact she turned so pale that Sandra wondered if she were going to faint.

"Oh, my dear . . ." Lady Elizabeth put a hand to her chest.

"Mama." Zac ran from the tennis court looking worried. "Are you all right?"

"It's just that . . . did *you* know about Bob?" She gazed distractedly up at Zac.

"What about Bob?"

"That the kidnappers cut off his ear . . ."

"Sandra told me they cut off his ear. I wanted to spare you the details, Mama." Zac grimaced with distaste. "I tried to do all I could through that wreck Falconetti, who is up to his eyeballs in drugs. I thought he might have some influence with the Mafia . . ."

"Or whoever," Sandra corrected him.

"Whoever," he agreed. "However, we have drawn a blank. I think Sandra will have to pay the ransom, and pay it soon, or I'm afraid she'll get the other ear."

"Sandra says she's called the police."

For a moment it was as though the air trembled.

"WHAT?" Zac demanded in a voice that shook.

"I had to call the police after the episode with the ear," Sandra explained. "I didn't know which way to turn. In fact they were very angry I hadn't called them before. They have promised complete secrecy. Not a word to the media or TV." She looked questioningly at him. "I can't think why it concerns you so much."

"It concerns me because I have put out my own feelers. If the police are in on it it may be up with me too. Believe me, they will find out." Zac flopped on the ground and began mopping his face with his towel. "And *that* will be the end of Bob."

"Oh, Zac, *please.*" Lady Elizabeth put down her embroidery and dabbed at her own forehead with a handkerchief. "I am beginning to feel quite unwell."

"We'll drop the subject, Mother," Zac said, "but I do think Sandra has made a mistake. Only time will tell."

"Maybe I *should* go and see Falconetti myself," Sandra said reflectively. "Maybe he can remember something."

"I hope you didn't bring Falconetti into your conversations with the police," Zac said sharply. "Really, Sandra, you might have consulted me. It would have been only polite."

"I'm sorry, Zac, perhaps I should." She tried hard to sound contrite.

"Of course you should! You asked my help. I did my best. You now bring my brother-in-law into it. The very *least* you could have done was to put me in the picture. It would only have been courteous, Sandra. I'm surprised at you. The more we try to help the more you seem to spurn this help."

"I am genuinely sorry, Zac," Sandra said again.

By now Belle had joined them and sat on a chair listening, swinging her tennis racket between her legs. Suddenly she stood up and tossed her racket above her head, catching it athletically.

"I'm going to have a bath," she announced.

"Finished? No more play?" Zac looked surprised.

"For today."

"Sandra?"

"I'm not fit enough, Zac," Sandra smiled.

"You look very fit."

"Maybe tomorrow, Zac." She glanced at Belle who, on her haunches, was saying something to her mother, and said in a low voice, "There *is* something I want to talk to you about."

"Oh!" His cross expression changed to one of concern. "Do you need my help?"

Belle put out a hand to assist Lady Elizabeth from her chair. She was not an old woman but troubled with rheumatism which sometimes made movement difficult. Once on her feet she straightened her skirt and smiled.

"I'm going to go indoors and have a rest. I feel very upset about Bob."

"I'm very sorry I told you, Lady Elizabeth," Sandra said contritely.

"I don't think you fully realize what a rapport Bob and I established," Lady Elizabeth said reprovingly. "We confided in each other, and I became very fond of him. I only *wish* there were something that I could do."

"Come on, Mother," Belle said, taking her arm. "Come and have a little rest while I have my bath and we can chat."

"That would be nice, dear." Affectionately Lady Elizabeth patted her hand. "How grateful I am, at a time like this, to have the love and support of my children."

And she gave Sandra a rather meaningful glance which suggested she excluded her. Sandra watched mother and daughter go into the house, then she turned to Zac who, having towelled himself vigorously, opened a can of squash which he took from an ice box by the side of the court.

"Care for one?" he asked Sandra.

"No, thanks." Sandra shook her head.

Zac sat in the seat his mother had left and put the can to his lips. He was still scowling; whether because his game had been interrupted or because the news about Bob still upset him, Sandra couldn't tell. He was a man who found it hard to conceal his emotions.

"Silly to go to the police," he murmured, thus showing that Bob was still on his mind. "It will be all over the papers."

"Well, it's not. They've known for a week."

"A *week!"* he gasped.

"It would only get out now if someone told them, Zac," Sandra said, looking at him.

"Who would tell them?"

"Well, if you're so upset, you might."

"And why should *I* do that?" He looked at her angrily.

"To annoy me."

"There you go *again,* Sandra." He finished the contents of the can and, squashing it between his fists, dashed it to the ground. "Of course I wouldn't dream of saying anything. Of course I don't want to annoy you. I'm just upset that Mother knows about the mutilation. She's *very* fond of Bob. Incidentally, is that what you wanted to talk to me about?"

"No. Something quite different."

She sat for a moment staring in front of her and then took a deep breath.

"You remember the bottle you designed for the *cuvée* for Louis?"

"Of course." Zac beamed with pleasure. "That was quite an inspiration."

"The only thing is . . . that it mightn't work."

"Mightn't *work!*" The pleasure turned to indignation. "What are you talking about, Sandra?"

"The neck of the bottle is too thin, too long."

"The glassmaker was very enthusiastic about this bottle." Angrily Zac threw his towel on the ground. "His technical staff did not discover any fault or inherent problems."

"Legrand said that, had his advice been asked, he would have said the bottle was the wrong shape, the neck too narrow. There is weeping from the bottles that might destroy the whole *cuvée.*"

"Rubbish!" Zac brusquely picked up his towel from the ground and flung it around his neck. "I never heard such nonsense in my life. That bottle was perfectly designed, perfectly calibrated—the maths were worked out by someone in my bank and checked by the glassmaker."

"Then may it not be the cork?"

"The temporary cork was cut to our specifications too, the best quality of cork from Catalonia. Really, Sandra, are you again trying to tell me my own business?"

"I'm only saying that the bottles are leaking."

"Weeping is quite normal with champagne," Zac said with an exaggerated air of patience. "We remove the bottles which show signs of seepage, and those which may have broken. Because of the rate at which the carbonic gas rises during the second fermentation such happenings are not uncommon. At one time, until a stronger bottle was invented, some *négociants* had their whole *cuvées* ruined by bursting bottles. I assure you the bottle I have designed is strong enough to withstand the required internal pressure of six atmospheres or more. René Latour and the glassmaker had full instructions."

"You mean to say René Latour was in charge of all this?"

"Of course." Zac looked surprised. "He is the *chef de cave.*"

"I thought *you* were in charge of it?"

"René and I are old colleagues who studied at the École

d'Oenologie de Beaune together. I have implicit faith in him."

Sandra, again thinking of the affair of the *tirage,* said nothing, but the whole question of loyalty and trust rose to the surface of her mind again.

"I can tell you're still not happy, Sandra." Zac was looking at her closely.

"No, I'm not."

"Would it make you happier if I came to the caves with you to inspect the bottles?"

"Would you do that?"

"Of course." Zac jumped up. "This very day."

"Oh, that's not necessary."

"I *insist,*" Zac said. "I shall summon Legrand and Latour and ask them to bring an aphrometer which will check the pressure of the bottles."

"But it's *Saturday.*"

"My dear, if it will reassure you I don't care if it's the middle of the night. Besides, with champagne one never stops working."

Zac hurriedly began to gather his sports gear together. "I shall tell them to meet us in the entrance to the caves as soon as possible."

The precious bottles of the Louis d'Or *tête de cuvée* lay *sur lattes* in one of the caves twenty meters beneath the chalky soil of Reims. After descending the steep steps they had walked for several minutes past hundreds of thousands of other bottles resting on their sides, past the slowly turning *pupitres,* to the special cave which had been reserved for the Louis d'Or. Scratched in chalk on the wall of the cave were the words: Cuvée Louis d'Or.

Latour and Legrand had stood outside the entrance to the caves waiting for them, Latour with the aphrometer, a device like a syringe which was inserted directly into the cork to check the pressure.

Sandra, hunched in a thick coat despite the warmth of the day outside, shivered a little as she looked at the bottles, each of which contained the carefully chosen blend.

Zac walked forward and began closely examining the bottles with the practiced air of the expert he was. Suddenly he extracted one very gently and examined it.

"Perfect," he said, showing it to Sandra and to the two men on either side of her. "The cork is dry and there is no sign of weeping."

Tenderly he laid it back, then took another and another. In each case the corks were in place and they were all in perfect order.

Peremptorily he held out a hand and Latour passed him the aphrometer. Gently he inserted it through the cork with the air of a surgeon engaged in a delicate operation. The gauge in the aphrometer rose and Zac showed it triumphantly to his colleagues and then to Sandra.

"What was all the fuss about, Legrand?"

"There *was* no fuss, Monsieur Zac." Legrand was strictly on his dignity. "I *merely* pointed out to Madame Harcourt that there *was* a sign of weeping and I disagreed with the design of the bottle. I had always made that quite clear."

"Proceed then." With an extravagant flourish of his hand Zac pointed to the many thousands of bottles lying in front of them. "Find me *more* samples of weeping."

Helplessly Legrand looked about him, obviously feeling deeply humiliated and unhappy. Then, without attempting to move, he shrugged his shoulders.

"Maybe it was a chance bottle."

"Of *course* it was a chance bottle! You cause all this fuss for nothing? There will doubtless be more, but to indicate to Madame that the whole *cuvée* was ruined, to throw doubt on the design of the bottle by Latour and myself was irresponsible. I suggest you return to your home now, Legrand, and reflect on the mischief you have caused."

"Very well, Monsieur Zac." Stiffly Legrand bowed toward him and then Sandra.

"Madame . . ."

"There is no need to say anything. I'll see you on Monday, Étienne." Sandra felt both as inadequate and as helpless as he was, and very sorry for the venerable director of the establishment.

"I'll be off with Monsieur Legrand," Latour mumbled and, without another word, the two men turned the way they had come, walking quickly along the interminable series of caves which led to the steps.

"Idiotic fool!" Zac said, vigorously shaking the bottle he had in his hand. "See?" He held it up to Sandra. "Perfect. I have given it a good shake and does it weep? No, it does not. When it comes to the *poignetage,* shaking it as I have just done to disperse the sediment, you can easily tell which wine is weeping and which is not."

He laid it carefully on its side to join its fellows and, the aphrometer still in his hand, he stepped back and gazed at the pile with satisfaction.

"I think you will be proud of your Louis d'Or, Sandra."

"I hope so," Sandra said fervently.

As they left the cave and walked back to the enterance, Zac paused from time to time to examine the marks on other bottles made by the *cavistes* during the *remuage.*

Sandra knew all this. She was nearly as well versed in oenology as Zac, but she listened patiently and politely as he explained it all over again, lingering lovingly on the procedures for the making of Champagne Desmond, explaining which was a vintage year and why, and how he could remember them all.

By the time they reached the top of the stairs Zac was in a sombre, almost melancholy mood, and Sandra even suspected there were traces of tears in his eyes.

At times like this she wished so fervently that the past had never happened or that, if it had, it had happened differently. That Zac and she could be united as partners at the head of the House of Desmond, a champagne he loved so much it could have been part of his lifeblood.

Zac had left his car in the courtyard when they arrived and

they were just entering it when he remembered the aphrometer in his hand which belonged to Latour.

"Maybe I should leave it in the lab?" he said.

"Everything is locked up." Sandra held out her hand. "I'll give it back to him on Monday."

Zac seemed to part with the instrument reluctantly and got behind the wheel of the Mercedes as Sandra slipped in beside him, belting herself in as he started the engine and the big car made its way smoothly through the gates and into the boulevard from which Zac eventually took the road to Tourville.

It seemed to Sandra that Zac was fighting a battle within himself, and she decided it was best that he should do it alone. Anything he, or she, said now might be too fraught with emotion. She knew he wanted to become increasingly involved in the champagne business and, in many ways, she would have valued it. He, as the afternoon's proceedings had shown, was authoritative, knowledgeable, his opinion widely respected. Only she knew it wouldn't work. She was happy in Champagne, happy in Reims, happy in her house, and to have Zac there continually interfering would, despite his almost priceless knowledge of the business, be a disaster.

"You should get rid of him," Zac said at last.

"Get rid of who?"

"Legrand. He is too old. He has lost his touch. You should pension him off and put Latour in his place. Then promote Marcel as *chef de cave.*"

"But Étienne loves his work and is very good at it. He is not too old. He's not yet sixty."

"Nevertheless he's had his day. Also"—Zac frowned—"I would have expected more loyalty from him toward *me.* What he did smacks of spite. He selects one or two bottles that have wept and starts to behave as though he has uncovered an entire bottling. *I* like a man with loyalty . . ."

"Loyalty to you," Sandra said swiftly.

"Of course. I am, after all, a Desmond. Legrand was working there when I was born. To come running up to *you,* accusing *me* of designing the bottle badly, is mischievous. I tell you if he can do that to me, Sandra, he could do it to you. This affair leaves a nasty taste in the mouth and you would do well to think on it and take my advice."

It was early evening when they drove through the gates of Tourville and Sandra felt she had never seen it so beautiful, even on the day she had first arrived and fallen in love with it.

Instead of stopping outside the front of the house Zac drove to the garages and put the car alongside Belle's Porsche. He helped Sandra out, locked the doors of the car and then they strolled out of the garage and locked that.

"Thank you for doing what you did," she said, looking at him. "It's a big weight off my mind."

"I want you to trust me, Sandra." Zac pocketed the key and took her arm in a fraternal way. "And go *on* trusting me. Whatever has happened between us, never forget that champagne is my birthright, my love."

They were walking toward the house, meaning to go in by a back entrance when a window on the first floor was flung up and Tara called out to them.

"Oh, thank God you are back . . . wait, I'll be with you in a moment."

They stopped in astonishment as she threw down the window and, even as they were looking with bewilderment at each other, the downstairs door opened and Tara, still dressed in her riding clothes, ran out and threw herself against Zac, burying her face in his chest.

"Thank *heaven* you are back. What a disaster has happened . . ."

Sandra's blood froze. Something had happened to Bob. Her premonitions of the night before were being realized: the tears, the phantom cries of pain. She put a hand on Tara's shoulder as Zac stroked her back soothingly and murmured into her ear: "What is it, my darling? What has so upset you?"

"Oh, *Zac!*" Tara flung back her head and, her face streaked with tears, stared wildly at him.

"It's Carl. He's been found dead. Murdered. Shot through the heart. It's too awful . . . you must go to poor Belle. Sometimes I feel this family is cursed," and she flung her face against him again and renewed her torrent of weeping.

15

The murder of Prince Carl von Burg-Farnbach on the Orient Express captured world headlines. It had all the ingredients of a thriller by Agatha Christie: luxury, wealth, aristocratic connections, an illicit affair and, finally, death by shooting. To make it even more sensational the prince's mistress, Lady Palmer, was immediately arrested by the Italian police and charged with his murder.

Once more the Desmond family found itself in the full glare of world media attention. Sandra's mysterious inheritance was dragged up and the libel trial in London and the curious details of her personal life were re-examined in minute detail. All the skeletons she wished to conceal were once again laid bare and picked over by the carrion crows.

Yet this time, with the exception of Lady Elizabeth who had the gates of Tourville securely barred, the family could not go to ground. Belle hastened to Milan to identify her husband's body which had been found in his sleeping compartment by Lady Palmer, who claimed she had stayed up playing cards. Belle was accompanied by Zac and together they faced the paparazzi who dogged their footsteps, gathered outside their hotels, followed them back to Burg-Farnbach once the police had released the body and, finally, to the gates of the château high up in the Bavarian mountains where several dozen stout Bavarian huntsmen with guns managed, at last, to keep off the media.

Sandra stood just behind the family as on a fir-covered hillside Carl's body was laid to rest among his ancestors. Claire had come from Italy but without Piero. Tim had sent apologies. Most of Lady Elizabeth's family, the Fitz-Caldwells, had come from England and almost half of the Almanack de Gotha seemed represented.

Afterwards there was a reception in the castle, but it was a very subdued affair because of the tragic circumstances. This was a case of a man dying cruelly and before his time; not one whose death, in the fullness of years, allowed for some celebration.

Sandra had liked Carl von Burg-Farnbach; he was a kind and rather gentle man, despite his bloodlust, who had made her feel welcome when the rest of the family had been hostile toward her. He and Belle were, of course, completely unsuited—unless as opposites—and it was no surprise to learn he had a mistress.

However, after the funeral Sandra felt that she had no place there. She was not family. She was not wanted. When the fences were down the true Desmonds preferred to be alone. She had arrived by helicopter, and she left in one to return from Munich airport to Paris and the host of business problems which awaited her attention.

As Sandra's helicopter rose in the air Belle stood by the window of her bedroom watching it heading in the direction of Munich until it was no more than a speck on the horizon.

Then she folded her arms and leaned against the windowsill for a few moments more, looking, as Sandra had, in the direction of Carl's grave.

Even to someone as hardened to life as Belle, Carl's death had still been a terrible shock: the death itself, and the manner of it. Of course she knew about Christine Palmer, but he had known about Radu; and the life they had had together had in many ways been a satisfactory one. Live and let live. Now he was no more.

She went and lay back on the bed which was covered by a quilted counterpane, and fell into gloomy contemplation about the prospects for her life as a widow. A *widow:* one not yet thirty-five. A *young* widow.

Would she be a merry widow or a sad widow, a foolish or a wise one?

Would she, in fact, be one for very long? She liked men and she wanted to be married again. A single woman had no status, at least not in Belle's eyes. A divorcee was an object of speculation; a widow one of pity.

Well . . . banish the pity!

The trouble was that, on a comparative scale, she was relatively poor. An impecunious widow, lacking an immediate and obvious attraction, would be compelled to work harder. The lawyers had been through Carl's will and the sad fact was that his assets, apart from the ancestral home, were negligible.

The von Burg-Farnbachs had followed the path of many of their aristocratic English and continental cousins and gone gently downward. Not in prestige or social acceptability—they were second to none in that—but financially. While many members of the impoverished nobility had set out to earn their living, Carl had not. He was like the ostrich who put its head deep in the sand, hoping that when it withdrew it times would be better.

There was no doubt that Carl had left his head in the sand for much too long. Apart from the castle and a few jewels, and some beautiful antique furniture, much of it belonging to Belle, there was barely enough to pay taxes and death duties. Nothing more.

Belle had even wondered if this had something to do with Carl's death, if it could possibly have been self-inflicted? But suicide had been ruled out.

Then there was the question of Christine, whom Belle knew and rather liked. Indeed, she had introduced her to Carl, as the Palmers were old friends of the Fitz-Caldwells. What possible motive could Christine have had for killing Carl? She was a very wealthy woman. Was he trying to blackmail her? Had he told her he would leave her? On their lawyer's advice she and Zac had not tried to visit Christine in jail in Milan. Any attempt to sympathize might make others point the finger of suspicion at them. If Christine, after all, were innocent, what about the guilty, faithless wife? Besides, Christine had already been charged, and all this would come out at the trial. Belle shuddered. What a horrible business *that* would be.

Wearily she closed her eyes and for a little while she slept, hoping that when she woke it would all turn out to have been a nasty dream.

In the great baronial hall Zac and Claire were bidding farewell to the guests on behalf of Belle. Most of them had gone and only close family remained. Lady Elizabeth's nephew, Bunny Fitz-Caldwell, and his wife were staying on and also one or two of the Burg-Farnbach cousins who had a long way to go. Claire and Zac circulated among the guests, speaking in lowered voices.

Fritz von Hausen came over to Zac, his hand extended. Fritz was a member of a family which had been close to the von Burg-Farnbachs for generations. In a revived post-war Germany his father had made a successful foray into machine tools, and the company was now both large and successful within the EC.

"You're not going now, are you, Fritz?" Zac asked, with concern in his voice. He was obviously tired and his face had a greyish tinge. Carl's death was the last thing he wanted: to throw the family into the limelight just when he was on the verge of big things, to which he did not want to draw too much attention.

"As a matter of fact we were," Fritz said, looking at his American wife, who was talking to family friends on the other side of the room.

Zac then tucked his arm in a confidential manner through Fritz's and pulled him to one side. When he spoke his voice was very low.

"Fritz, there is something I want to talk to you about, a matter of business. It won't take five minutes."

"Well . . ." Fritz looked doubtful. But then he shrugged, and followed Zac to the library.

It was a gracious room with old volumes bound in vellum rising from floor to ceiling. At one end in front of the fireplace were a leather sofa and two chairs. Zac guided Fritz to the sofa and sat down next to him. Then, leaning forward, he offered Fritz a cigar from a silver box on the table beside him. Fritz took one, sniffing the bark of the excellent Havana. There was some rather obvious foreplay to do with cutting the end and lighting it and, when the two men had their cigars going, Fritz puffed smoke in the air and said: "Now, what's on your mind? I can see it's important."

"Heurtey wants to take over Cassini Drinks." Zac came to the point at once. "Of course, Cassini is much bigger in Europe than Heurtey, so we want to increase Heurtey's share price to make the bid seem more reasonable. We'd like you to buy Heurtey shares."

"You want *me* to buy Heurtey shares?" Fritz looked flabbergasted.

"It would be an excellent step for your company, and you personally."

"How many would you say?" Fritz sat back and stared at the baronial ceiling.

"About fifty million marks' worth."

Fritz whistled.

"Of course, if you could do it on your own account you and Eunice could net a profit of about five million deutsch marks. Now, what do you think of that?"

Fritz looked at Zac, his expression doubtful. "Can you guarantee the deal will succeed? A share support scheme could be illegal under Community rules."

"I'm backing it to the hilt; the bank, I mean."

"Oh, the Banque Franco-Belges is behind it?" Fritz looked relieved.

"Completely."

"Is Heurtey behind it too?"

"Of course."

"I'll have a word with him when I get back to Berlin," Fritz said, beginning to rise. "I'd better be making a move."

"Oh, don't call Heurtey," Zac called after him. "It makes a fool of me, you know."

"I don't see why." Fritz looked surprised.

"It makes it look as though I can't run my own business, or manage my own affairs," Zac replied in an injured tone. "Either do or don't but, please, don't ask Heurtey. Frankly, so many people are keen I don't think we'll have the slightest trouble. Even Madame Harcourt is buying."

"Really?" Fritz looked impressed. "Then I think you can count me in."

Belle was wakened by the sound of the door slamming and she sat bolt upright on the bed, her eyes staring.

No, after all it was not a dream; it was a nightmare. A living nightmare. She passed a hand across her brow and, taking a sip of water, looked to see what had wakened her.

Zac was advancing into the room, his face black with rage.

"Now, what in God's name is the matter?" she demanded as he flung himself on the bed beside her.

"That fool Fritz von Hausen!"

"What's he done now?"

"He judges Sandra's business acumen superior to mine."

Belle said nothing. In many ways she agreed with Fritz. Loyal though she was to her brother—after all, were they not partners in crime?—he could, and did, make a lot of mistakes. He had an absolute genius for putting his foot in things, as his father had found out long ago, due to over-enthusiasm and lack of proper research into the market.

"You asked him to buy shares in Heurtey?"

"What a devil of a time I had." Zac wiped his brow with a large handkerchief taken from his breast pocket. "First, he was going to call that ass Heurtey; but I managed to dissuade him from that and then I said Sandra was going to buy some. He said then it must be a good proposition!"

Belle laughed and put a hand lightly on his arm.

"My dear, you have made too many mistakes and people like Fritz know it. He is a businessman first, despite his relationship with Carl, and a friend second. You should be more careful who you draw into these share support operations. Neither Sandra, von Hausen nor Heurtey are fools."

"It's not illegal to buy shares in a company."

"No, but it is to offer sweeteners, the bank's money as a bribe."

"I didn't offer him a sweetener."

"That's good," Belle said with relief.

"I only said he and Eunice *might* make a bit of money." Zac smiled. "It's not the same thing, is it?"

"It depends on how you look at it." Belle put some cushions behind her head and lay back on them.

"Zac, I think you'd better drop all this business of buying Cassini."

"But why on earth should I?"

"We're getting too deeply into trouble."

"But *what* trouble is involved?"

"It's not just this. You're skating on the edge of illegality. It's not a sin to buy shares but it is to offer bribes, artificially to inflate the price. It's called share-rigging and you know it. You could lose *millions* if it fails."

"It won't fail," Zac said, with a confidence he didn't quite feel. "You're not being very loyal, Belle."

"On the contrary I *am* being very loyal. I'm trying to help you stay out of prison. Remember what happened in England in the Guinness affair?"

"This happens not to be England."

"In America you were nearly caught by the SEC."

"This isn't America either," he snapped. "Have you *no* confidence in me? I'm spreading the risk throughout Europe, and in many currencies. Anyone trying to untangle it would have a real problem on their hands."

"Nevertheless, they would do it. The bureaucrats in Brussels and Paris would relish the task."

Zac leaned over and put his hand on hers. "My dear, in a month or two it will all be over. You're overwrought. Carl's death has, naturally, affected you. Trust me. I have everything under control and, once Cassini is ours, we will restructure the companies and get rid of the playboy Heurtey."

"The company here is independent of America?" Belle demanded suspiciously.

"Quite independent. The Americans would never want to get involved. When she sees how ingenious my scheme is, even the Irish woman should be impressed." Zac rubbed his hands together with glee. "It was she, after all, who had the temerity once to try and take over the huge American parent company. She got her fingers burnt there."

Belle's expression remained troubled.

"It's not only that, Zac; it's the whole business with Bob. There's too much attention on us. Carl's death, Bob's kidnapping. The police will start sniffing about, I'm afraid."

"But we had nothing to do with Carl's death!" Zac exclaimed indignantly. Then he seemed to change his mind and his expression turned to one of doubt. "I mean, have we?"

"Of course we haven't." Belle turned furious eyes on him. "What a horrible suggestion."

"Then why worry about the police? What have you to fear?"

"Look." Belle sat up and took a cigarette from the bedside table. "I'm as sure as I can be that Christine Palmer wasn't capable of killing Carl. Why should she? She had no need to; besides she was fond of him. It doesn't add up."

Zac scratched his head, looking worried too. "It's something I wondered myself. Frankly, Belle, knowing how crazy you were about the commie diplomat, I wondered if you and he might not have hatched a plot to get rid of Carl. If so . . ."

Belle got off the bed with an energetic bound and swung her

palm across his face with all her force. Zac toppled back, both hands to his mouth.

"You swine," he said. "You bitch."

"You swine," she cried, attempting to strike him again. "Suggesting *I'd* kill Carl. I *loved* Carl. Truly, in my way I loved him. He was Constantine's father . . ."

"Maybe the 'commie' did it then because he wanted you . . ."

"And stop calling him 'the commie'." She stamped her foot angrily. "His father was a Romanian count. You just try and goad me and provoke me, Zac. I tell you if I could kill anyone it would be you . . . not Carl; not poor, poor Carl . . ."

She flopped down again on her bed and began to sob, the tears making large tracks, like lava, through the thick makeup she'd applied to get herself through the funeral.

"Not Carl . . ." she sobbed. "He was a dull man, with no imagination, but . . ."

"I'm sorry." Zac tentatively put a hand on her shoulder. "I shouldn't have said what I said. Forgive me, Belle . . ."

"You don't trust me," she wailed, kneading her hands in her face, "and *I* don't trust you. It's the way we were brought up."

"Father never trusted me," Zac said viciously. "Father turned my stomach into a pit of bile, of hate so that I don't know any more what sort of person I am, eaten away by hatred and resentment."

"You can't blame Father for everything," Belle vigorously blew her nose and, rising, went to her dressing table where she tried to repair the ravages to her face. She stared at herself in the mirror for a moment and then turned to him. "But you can blame him for leaving almost everything he had to that American bitch. That wasn't only cruel, it was *wrong*. I only hope that Father burns in Purgatory until we are out of the mess his thoughtless action got us into."

"Hush, Belle." Zac, looking horrified, put a hand over her mouth. "That is a *terrible* thing to say . . ."

"But it's true."

"Nevertheless, you mustn't say it, even think it. Wouldn't you say we had enough bad luck as it is without cursing the ghost of our father and wishing him harm?"

Though he loved his sister Belle probably better than anyone in the world, Zac returned to Paris angry and distressed by what had happened between them. Much as he resented his father, he still feared him and his feelings toward him were almost superstitious as though out there, somewhere, Georges Desmond were watching him.

Zac had always been in awe of his father, an awe that had never left him. He was afraid of him even in his memory yet, as if he were still alive, he wanted to show him how well he could do if only his father trusted him.

But, above all, Zac had one overriding ambition, an ambition that was greater than family, conjugal or sibling love. He wanted to resume the position which he felt to be rightly his at the head of the Desmond Group, and now he felt that at last the goal was in sight.

Whatever else he lacked, Zac Desmond did not lack self-confidence. Many people including, perhaps, his father would have called it self-delusion, because his abilities did not live up to his self-esteem. He had the instinct for a good deal, but lacked judgment; he was impulsive, irrational and, in many ways, quite unfit to be the president of a merchant bank.

The irony of his position was that his true genius lay in the manufacture of champagne, a subject he not only knew a lot about, but had a true instinct for. He was a *champenois* to the core and it was there that he belonged.

Yet his father had given him peripheral jobs, keeping him away from the true center of power. Maybe it was jealousy, or maybe it was fear of competition or merely distrust, but he had never given his elder son full rein; he had held him back and, in the process, turned someone with a naturally devious streak into a criminal.

Maybe Zac's deviousness had developed in order to try and

outwit his father. However, now it was so much part of him that in hatching schemes he achieved his greatest satisfaction.

When he returned to his office after Carl's funeral he knew that the moment was near for putting two of his schemes into operation: the acquisition of a company bigger than continental Heurtey, and the final destruction of his enemy: Sandra.

He spent his first morning back at work making a series of telephone calls to various companies around the globe where there were people who, in one way or another, owed him a favor.

The Banque Franco-Belges in the Avenue de l'Opéra was not the sort of bank one walked into off the street to open an account, to deposit or withdraw cash. It was a private bank occupying the whole of the first floor of an imposing building, where there was a commissionaire permanently on duty. This had a marble hall with great moments in French history in bas-relief on the walls, and escalators which took clients smoothly from one floor to the next.

The Banque Franco-Belges had combined with the Banque Pons-Desmond, also a merchant bank, established by René-Zachariah, mostly to help the champagne merchants who were becoming rich and successful in the nineteenth century to invest their capital. But in this it misfired as few of his fellow *négociants* were keen for a rival to know how much of their money there was, or what they did with it.

It kept to the objectives of its founder but was available to any kind of speculator engaged in risk. Accordingly its interest rates were much higher than those of other kinds of banks, because its risk was greater.

Zac loved risks so, in many ways, he should have been an ideal person to head such a bank had he allowed a little caution to temper his enthusiasm. He took too many risks, insufficiently studied the propositions that were put to him, failed to ensure that foreign assets covered foreign loans and, in his time, he had had some spectacular failures. One or two had, however, succeeded brilliantly and this kept the bank liquid; but only just.

It was for this reason that David Heurtey had hired Joanne Pasarro to come with him on his European trips and take a look at the various enterprises for which his conglomerate was an umbrella and, in particular, the Banque Franco-Belges.

But Joanne was not allowed to get very far in her investigations. Zac was an expert in disguising the truth and employing accounting methods which, while perfectly acceptable to him, defied the most searching investigations of others. In their way they resembled a kind of secret code, understandable only to a few. Happily the firm of accountants who audited his accounts were familiar with the tortuous processes Zac and his underlings had invented, and managed by astute manipulations to appear to stay just within the law.

When Zac had been forced to get rid of Paul Strega as his personal assistant he had engaged a young man called Hubert Jeantet who proved a genius not only at cooking the books, but also at explaining the tortuous figures plausibly to the accountants and tax authorities.

The first thing Zac did after he had made his series of telephone calls was to summon Jeantet, with whom he then spent a profitable hour going over plans. It was thanks to Jeantet that he had pulled off the presidency of the bank when his predecessor had been forced to retire. Jeantet was now to him a very important man, a partner, corrupting and corruptible.

It was Jeantet who had established in Switzerland a number of letterbox companies through which Zac bought and sold shares. These were controlled by a Swiss broker with offices in Zurich.

Hubert was ambitious, a fact of which Zac was fully aware. He knew how loyalty could be bought and he paid him a handsome salary and also gave him a percentage of the deals that came off.

Jeantet had at first been cautious about the idea of bidding for Cassini, but had now managed to overcome his scruples.

"Did you get rid of that tiresome woman?" Zac asked him after they had exchanged reports.

"I think Mademoiselle Pasarro went away a little mystified." Jeantet's pale eyes gleamed behind his spectacles. "She didn't seem to find our methods quite tallied with the ones she was used to. I explained to her how different accounting practices are in France to those in America. She seemed unconvinced."

"Nosy parker," Zac said dismissively. "Now, Hubert, have you managed to perfect Mr. Heurtey's signature?"

"I *think* so, sir." Jeantet modestly laid on the desk several specimens that to Zac looked fair imitations of David Heurtey's rather sprawling hand.

"You can see, sir"—Jeantet eagerly pointed to the paper—"that the twirl on the 'y' is not easy to copy. I think I have done rather well."

"You have done *excellently,* Hubert," Zac said, his eyes alight with pleasure.

"I have even had it vetted by a graphologist," Jeantet said with a note of pride.

"Was that wise?" Zac looked at him sharply.

"A close friend, Monsieur Zac, who owes me one or two favors."

"Oh, one can never have enough of *those.*" Zac lifted the telephone and winked at Jeantet. "Just listen to this." He then asked for an outside line and dialed a number.

"Signor Fratelli," he said, when a faint voice could be heard at the other end. *"Buongiorno. Come sta?"*

He nodded impatiently, not very interested in the man's health, needless to say. Then he came to the point: "Tell me, Signor, have you managed to consider the little matter we discussed in Rome the other day?" He raised his eyes as a torrent of words issued from the other end of the receiver. These Italians! he seemed to say, and then he lowered his eyes to his desk.

"Of *course* Mr. Heurtey agrees with us, Signor Fratelli. Do you think *I* would act by myself in a matter like this?" He nodded again impatiently and winked once more at Jeantet. "I will see the letter of authorization is faxed to you *immediately* and followed by a confirmation. Yes, signed personally by Mr.

Heurtey, *of course.* Yes, a hundred million lire. Yes . . . in cash, to be delivered to you personally. What do we do here?" He listened for a few moments, showing increasing signs of impatience. "We put it down to expenses, Signor. I have a very ingenious accountant. No, thank *you,* Signor Fratelli, for your cooperation. Needless to say any favor I can do for you at any time . . ." He nodded again several times then, with a loud sigh, put down the phone.

"The trouble with these Italians is that they can never stop talking. I have the same trouble with my wife."

"Your Italian is very good, sir," Jeantet said obsequiously. "I wish *I* had the gift of languages."

Zac leaned over and squeezed the arm of his subordinate. "You have the gift of figures and forging signatures, Jeantet. Believe me, that is good enough to be going on with for the moment."

It was an industrious and, as far as he could tell, profitable morning in the sense that his global attempts to manipulate financial and business colleagues seemed to have a chance of succeeding. What it would cost him in bribes Zac didn't even think about, convinced that the prestige of owning Cassini, and subsequently a reverse takeover of Heurtey, would make them seem minimal in comparison.

He soon forgot all his worries about the death of his brother-in-law, his quarrel with Belle, as he ensured that the price of Heurtey shares rose steadily and unspectacularly on the market. As yet Heurtey had done nothing to justify such a rise though, if questioned, Zac could always say that it might have something to do with the impending deal with Japan. Insider trading? Certainly not! Everyone knew about it. Then why didn't Desmond's shares rise too, as they were in the venture jointly with Heurtey?

Ah! Zac could only shrug regretfully and put that down to bad management at the top. He spent all morning on the telephone answering questions, fending off awkward ones, and he was just about to go to lunch when his secretary buzzed him on the intercom.

"Commissioner Renard here to see you, sir."

"Blast!" Zac said to himself, conscious at the same time of a tremor of unease.

"Tell the Commissioner I'm just off to lunch, but can give him a few minutes."

Zac heard her repeating his message to the policeman and had only time to put some incriminating documents on his desk in a drawer before Renard came in, hand outstretched.

"Good morning, sir."

"Good morning, Commissioner." Zac looked at his watch. "Unfortunately a lunch engagement . . ."

"Then I won't detain you, Monsieur Desmond," the policeman said politely, looking round for a seat.

"Do sit down." Zac pointed to the chair on the other side of his desk. "And tell me how I can help you. Is it to do with the disappearance of Bob O'Neill? Madame Harcourt mentioned the matter to me. Alas, I . . ."

The Commissioner put his head on one side and gazed carefully for a few unnerving seconds at a man about whom he had heard such a lot, whose name or photograph was seldom out of the papers, a man dispossessed, torn by emotion. Yet he seemed to have taken it remarkably well. He was a tall, thickset, imposing man, his hair receding a little in front, with alert, brown eyes and something in his expression of the bully: attractive to women.

Renard then turned his attention to the office suite, noting the luxurious pile on the carpet, the expensive furniture, the couple of Impressionist paintings on the wall, not reproductions either.

Not only had Monsieur Desmond apparently taken his dispossession well, but he seemed to have made a new and successful career. He had every appearance of being a wealthy and distinguished man.

"It is not exactly about Mr. O'Neill, sir, though we have drawn a complete blank so far in our investigations. But another matter has come up that concerns your family and, as I was on this case, I was asked to come and see you."

"Oh?" Zac ran his finger nervously round his collar.

"It concerns the death of your brother-in-law, sir."

Zac lowered his head and sighed deeply. "What a tragedy. I have only just returned from the funeral."

"The point is, sir," Renard said deferentially, "that Princess von Burg-Farnbach, your sister, was not above reproach herself, in a manner of speaking."

"What are you suggesting, Commissioner?" Zac looked him straight in the eyes, a technique often successful enough to deflect people from their objectives.

"She had a lover, sir."

"I am perfectly well aware of that."

"A Romanian diplomat."

"Yes. But what has this to do with the death of the prince?"

"Well, Lady Palmer strenuously denies that she killed her lover, and the Italian police are impressed by her."

"It certainly *seems* that Lady Palmer had no motive." Zac tried to look eminently reasonable. "Far be it for my family to accuse the wrong person. She and my brother-in-law were on their way to Venice for a cruise. It is inexplicable. But my sister had certainly nothing to do with her husband's death. It may seem strange to some people but they had an arrangement to live separate lives, and had done for some time."

"You mean they *knew* about each other's affairs?" The policeman, who came from a respectable suburb of Paris where he, his wife and three children led blameless lives, looked shocked.

"Yes."

"And did the prince know about Monsieur Lupescu?"

"I expect so," Zac said offhandedly. "I didn't really ask. But my sister was hundreds of miles away in Tourville at the time of the tragedy. The family were all together."

"I'm not suggesting the princess *personally* had anything to do with this, sir." The Commissioner was anxious to impress.

"Only Monsieur Lupescu disappeared a couple of weeks before the killing. Don't you think that strange?"

"Not at all." Zac felt the icy finger on his spine again. "He told my sister that he was going to be recalled to Bucharest."

"Oh, she knew that he was going?"

"I think so. I don't really know if she knew precisely when." Zac looked at his watch again and picked up the phone.

"Sylvia, would you phone L'Ambroisie and say I will be a few minutes late for my lunch date? Thank you."

Politely he turned to the policeman again. "I think you had better wait until my sister returns to Paris," he said, getting up. "You will find her very willing and able to answer all your questions. I can assure you she was devoted to her husband and is devastated by his death. If you could have seen her as I saw her you would not have a moment's doubt about their affection."

Renard also stood up and fastened the buttons of his double-breasted jacket.

"I would be glad if you would ask her to contact us, Monsieur Desmond." He produced a card from his pocket and put it on Zac's desk. "We would like if possible to clear up the matter of Monsieur Lupescu's whereabouts."

"But why? What can it possibly have to do with Carl?"

"Well, as we can't find Monsieur Lupescu and the Romanians *claim* not to know where he is, we wondered if, by any chance, your sister might have any plans to join him?"

16

Louis was a very active baby, such a rapid crawler that his nurse had practically to run to catch up with him. Sandra loved to play with him on the lawn, seeing his delight as she too pretended to chase him, and when at last she caught him he screamed ecstatically while she smothered him with kisses.

David Heurtey sat under the tree in the garden in Reims watching them. He had a paper in his hands and was pretending to read but, over the rims of his half-moon spectacles, he was following their movements, unable to take his eyes off them. Mother and son. He loved one and was in love with the other, no doubt about that.

Sandra wore white which suited her. Maybe it was not the best color for playing on the lawn with the baby, but she wore washable cottons or seersucker, mixtures of cotton and polyester, in a variety of styles, some of them couture, some of them made up by a little dressmaker in Reims.

Breathless with her exertions, Sandra flopped onto the rug with Louis in her arms, kissing the top of his downy head. He had blond hair like hers; he was very obviously her child. She felt, in a way, that it was a pity Michel's child—all there was left of him in the world—should so little resemble him. She wished Louis did; but sons often resembled mothers and daughters their fathers. It was an odd thing, but it was a fact.

She looked up and saw David's eyes on her and Louis. At a sign from her he put down his paper and strolled eagerly across the lawn, also flopping down on the rug beside her, hands out for the baby.

"May I?"

"Of course."

Carefully, lovingly, she handed Louis to him and Louis grasped his hand, still gurgling, quite happy to be passed from his mother to . . .

Did Louis, perhaps, in his infantile mind, think David was his father? These days they were together such a lot.

David was a natural with children. He'd had four of his own, and obviously he loved them. She had seen few men as good with children as David was with Louis and it was clear that, as he got older, Louis would adore him more and more.

Was it fair?

Sandra turned away and gazed the length of the garden toward the small goldfish pond that was covered with netting as a precaution. It was warm in the garden, which was relatively small, and she wished they could be at Tourville with its acres and acres of space. But that was the last place she wanted to take David.

David, cuddling Louis, was watching Sandra gravely.

"What's the matter?" he asked quietly.

"Just thinking."

"Thinking of what?"

"You know." Sandra stood up and straightened her skirt, and he admired her slim, youthful form as she took a few steps away, then a few back as though she were undecided what to do.

"You worried about us?" he asked.

"I'm worried about Louis and you."

"And me?" David looked mystified.

"He thinks you're his father."

"I feel like I'm his father." David tightened his arms round the child and said in a low voice, "I love him like I was his father."

"Oh, please don't . . ." Sandra began, when Mireille appeared at the French windows and called.

"Is it all right if I take him for his lunch, Madame?"

"We'll all have it together," Sandra called back, "here, on the lawn."

"Then I'll just change him, Madame," Mireille said, walking along the path toward them. "He'll love a picnic, won't you, Louis?" And gently with a smile she dragged a reluctant Louis from the protective arms of David.

He remained on the rug on the lawn, his hands spread supportively behind him, gazing at Sandra, who was on her feet watching Mireille carry Louis up the path to the house. Louis, utterly content with whichever of these beloved people he was with, protected and secure, smiled winsomely at his mother over his nurse's back. Sandra waved until he was out of sight.

"You'd think he understood every word, wouldn't you?" Sandra turned laughingly toward David and sat down next to him.

"I think he does." David's arm lightly encircled her waist. "He's a very intelligent child."

"Oh, not *that* intelligent." Sandra smiled modestly, keenly aware of David's arm.

How long, she wondered, would it take before they became lovers?

"Of course he's intelligent." David's grasp tightened. "It was inevitable with parents like he had—a brilliant businesswoman and a father who was an internationally known medical researcher . . ." David stopped abruptly. "Sorry, Sandra."

"We never talk about Michel, do we?" Sandra said, turning to him. "It's not that I don't want to . . ."

"I know."

"In fact, I'd *like* to, but . . . it's painful."

"I guessed that."

"Painful," she hurried on, "not only because of his death, but because of our relationship before his death. That's what I feel so much guilt about. You see, David"—she turned to him, her expression anguished—"I was not a good wife."

He took his arm from her waist and sat up, clasping his knees between his arms. "What do you mean by the term 'good wife'?"

"Well . . . he wanted me to be with him. And I wanted him to be with *me.*"

"That seems quite natural," David replied good-humoredly.

"Natural, yes, but it was also a reversal of accepted roles and the consequence was war . . . a war of personalities. Michel wanted me to leave Desmond and, of course, I couldn't. We quarrelled a lot. He said I loved Desmond more than him."

"Sounds just like a Frenchman," David grimaced. "They're very chauvinistic. They want their women to stay at home, whereas in America we are more used to women working, although my wife didn't and never wanted to. Of course, she could also afford not to, not only because of me but because she had money of her own. Maybe if she had worked we'd have got on better. Who knows?" David gazed at some distant spot as though he were trying to see into the past.

"My pregnancy"—Sandra paused, aware that she was now revealing more of herself than perhaps she really wanted to—"was an accident. It does happen even between the best-regulated, scientifically minded couples. Michel didn't know I was pregnant, and I kept it from him."

"But why?" David looked puzzled.

"Because I thought he would use it to force me to give up Desmond. When I eventually told him—because I thought people were beginning to suspect and I would rather he heard it from me than someone else—he set off to come back to me. That led to his death."

"For which you, of course, feel unreasonably responsible."

"In a way." Sandra's chin trembled and David thought how vulnerable she really was, this apparently tough woman whose actions could unsettle markets. He felt then very close to her, privileged and very tender and he wished he could take her into his arms.

"Don't you believe," he said softly into her ear, "that everyone has his or her hour? That it was simply Michel's time?"

"No." Sandra set her mouth stubbornly. "I think if he'd stayed in Harare and I with him, he'd still be alive." They were interrupted by the return of Mireille with Louis, who were followed by Sandra's butler and a maid, the one with a table, the other with a tray of delicious cold food which she proceeded meticulously to set out on the table. It was amazing how quickly Sandra's well-trained staff could provide an al fresco picnic, or a five-course dinner for visiting businessmen. The butler returned with chairs and the maid was joined by the chef who pronounced himself delighted that Madame had decided to eat out of doors, and began carving the cold chicken.

The butler then reappeared with a bucket in which was a bottle of champagne and two glasses.

As Mireille settled Louis into his chair and tucked a bib around him, David nodded approvingly. "I see we have champagne at lunchtime too."

"We always offer champagne," Sandra said laughingly. "It is a Desmond practice I adhere to—sometimes I drink it, sometimes, if I have a lot to do in the afternoon, I don't. Today," she said, taking her glass and raising it to David's, "is an exception. Cheers, David!"

"A votre santé," he said, saluting her.

The food was excellent, quails' eggs en gelée, a coarse terrine, a game pie which was the chef's speciality and cold meats of various kinds. With this they had *pain de seigle,* freshly baked at the *boulangerie* around the corner and collected by the houseboy minutes before.

All the staff withdrew and Sandra and David sat up at the table. Mireille fed Louis in his chair on the rug. It was all so informal, indeed a lovely day for a picnic.

"Remember Manet: *Déjeûner sur l'herbe?"* Sandra murmured.

"Didn't that have a nude lady in?" David cocked an eye at her.

Their eyes met. She knew what he was thinking, and she felt the same. Only, wasn't it too soon? Michel had only been dead a year.

Louis by this time had finished his food and was eager to join his mother.

"Bedtime, my darling," she said, pulling him onto her knee. "This afternoon we can go for a walk."

"I thought we'd take a run?" David said, drinking the last of his champagne.

"You mean a drive in the country?"

"Yes."

"With Louis or without?"

"While Louis has his rest perhaps?"

And so it was decided.

With David at the wheel they drove swiftly across the Montagne de Reims, skirting Tourville, until, finally, they reached the Château de Marsanne, where the Pipers had lived, but now shuttered and looking deserted. It was set in a very beautiful part of the country amid vineyards, some of them perched steeply above the house on the hill, and for a long time Sandra and David sat in the car outside the gate, which was padlocked.

"Where are they now?" David inquired, and Sandra began to tell him about Henri Piper and the curious role he had played in her life.

"Did he love you?"

"Oh, I don't think it was *love,* though some people did. It caused enough talk for his wife to become very jealous."

David looked thoughtfully at the eighteenth-century house which had been modeled on the Château du Louvois twenty kilometers to the east, once the residence of the unmarried daughters of Louis XV.

"I can understand his wife becoming jealous."

"There was simply nothing between Henri and me," Sandra insisted. "I regarded him as a mentor, a guide." However, momentarily her expression was sad. "In the end Henri, too, turned against me."

"Why?" His long thin hands still on the wheel, David looked curiously at her.

"Because of Michel, I think."

"Ah, so he *did* love you?"

"I think his feelings were confused. He thought I should have told him Michel and I had married and, perhaps, I should. We don't always do what we should, do we, David? Don't always behave properly?"

"No, we don't," David said and, as if her words had encouraged him, he reached out for her and their mouths met in a long, lingering kiss.

When at last they drew apart they gazed at each other as if each was surprised by what had happened, despite its inevitability. Then, without saying another word, David put his arms around her, and she snuggled up to him. They kissed again, this time with more passion.

"When?" he asked as, finally, they drew apart.

"I don't know," she shook her head. "There are so many complications."

"It *must* happen, Sandra."

She nodded. "I know; but not just now, David." She fumbled for his hand. "But don't go away, don't leave me, as Henri did. I need you."

"And I need you. But please don't confuse me with Henri Piper, or compare me to him. I intend ours to be a very different relationship."

Letting her go, he engaged the gears and drove the car slowly around the walls of the château until, finally, from high up they could look down on its classical proportions in mellow sandstone, its twin gables rising from the surrounding trees which formed part of the Forest of Marsanne. In the foreground the Marne progressed on its stately journey until it joined the Seine.

"I wonder if Henri would sell it?" David said suddenly.

"To whom? To you?" Sandra looked startled.

"Who else? I like it, don't you?"

"I love it." Sandra's feelings were suddenly confused. "But I don't know if it's right for you."

He looked hurt. "But I'm a champagne baron too."

"Of course you are. It's simply that I always think of it as Henri and Sophie's and that one day they'll return there."

"But they live in California."

"They may come back."

"Do you want them to?"

She could see the disappointment slowly spreading over his face and was aware she'd hurt him. She groped for his hand.

"Of course I don't. You just took me by surprise."

Reluctantly he let go of her hand and started the car again. "Incidentally, our shares are showing quite a remarkable rise on the Bourse."

"I know. I've watched them rise steadily."

"But why should they?" He looked questioningly at her.

"Well, it's better than going down. The market must have confidence in you."

"But why start buying? Yours are remaining pretty steady, aren't they?"

"Given the economic climate, very. They don't vary by more than a franc or two from day to day."

"And yet ours rose twenty francs on the week. I don't feel I'm doing very much to justify such a rise."

"Maybe the market likes what it hears."

"I wondered if there might be rumors of a takeover," David said suddenly. "You don't know anything, do you?"

Sandra felt a shock of surprise. "My dear, if I did I would tell you immediately. Who would presume to take over Heurtey?"

"Maybe they think we're mismanaged, not well managed."

"I wonder if Zac's up to anything." Sandra's expression was thoughtful. "He suggested I bought Heurtey shares."

"Nothing wrong with that. Just being a good banker."

"True." Sandra frowned. "But there was a suggestion of a sweetener. I told him to forget it."

"Joanne can't find anything wrong," David said. "I have absolute faith in her."

"Who's buying?"

"People from all over the place, a strong concentration of Swiss. Incidentally, any news from the police about Bob?"

"Not a thing." Sandra shook her head, aware of a stab of guilt; she continually wondered if she was doing enough. "They are, for some reason, quite interested in the murder of Carl."

"What does it have to do with Bob? Isn't it a cut-and-dried case?"

"Apparently not at all. Lady Palmer is an extremely unlikely assassin and vigorously protests her innocence. She also has the best lawyers representing her. They wonder if the murder of Carl—in Italy—and the disappearance of Bob—also in Italy—are connected. It all goes back to the fame of the Desmonds—and me, I'm afraid."

"Sandra," David said, suddenly putting his hand on her arm.

"Yes?"

"Let's go away, just for a few days. You've had enough. I've got a very under-used house on a Greek island. Let's just go by ourselves and talk, see how things go." He watched her eagerly to see her response.

"When were you thinking of?" she asked quietly.

"Before it gets too hot."

"Well, I have to do a brief tour of Europe," she said, suddenly excited. "Why don't I meet you in Athens, say, in a couple of weeks' time and we take it from there?"

Zac gazed at the piece of paper in front of him and rubbed his hands like an excited schoolboy.

"Good," he said, "excellent, Jeantet. Madame is on her travels again and in exactly the places she went to before: Geneva, Milan, Rome, Barcelona, Athens last this time—I wonder why? Nevertheless, we can now put our plan into action. Tell Strega to come and see me immediately, will you?"

Jeantet, ever the dutiful assistant, was about to hurry from the room but Zac called him back.

"Hubert, get my secretary to call Strega. I want him here by this afternoon. I want *you* to brief me on what is happening on the Bourse."

"Oh, a rise, sir, a very definite rise in the price of Heurtey shares. Your strategies are working admirably, Monsieur Desmond."

"Of course they're working." Zac sat back and fingered his tie. "Now, tell me what Cassini is doing."

"They are still a *little* in front."

"How many days do you think before we pounce?"

"I should let it wait a while, Monsieur Desmond." Jeantet took a sheaf of papers from his briefcase.

"Why, is now not a good time?"

"Our own cash position is not very good, sir. We have barely enough to cover an initial bid."

"Then we must borrow."

"But we have borrowed a lot already."

"Borrow more," Zac commanded. "There's plenty of money around."

"Monsieur Desmond." The obedient servant began to look desperate. "I think soon your borrowing will exceed assets. It's not wise. As a banker you know that. Besides, the banks are unwilling to support you any more."

Zac's face darkened. "Fools, idiots," he cried. "What about the Turks?"

"Well, the Turks will lend, sir." Jeantet looked dubious. "But at exorbitant rates of interest."

"Never mind the rates. The Turks are the last people to ask questions. Get me Ankara."

"Yes, sir." Jeantet was only too glad on this occasion to leave the room in case he overheard a conversation that he might consider criminal.

He wondered if Zac knew how thin the ice was on which he was treading.

As it turned out it was not a very good day for Zac. Not surprisingly the Turks proved unwilling to lend except at rates which even Zac could see were folly, and the German banker he had hoped to browbeat at lunchtime proved stubborn too, even questioning the soundness of the Banque Franco-Belges, its ability to pay its debts and his willingness to do more business with it. Zac was so angry he left the man who had been his guest to pay the bill and, storming out of the restaurant, caught a taxi back to the office, arriving just at the same time as Strega, who had crept in through a back entrance.

"Am I glad to see you," Zac said, clapping his former assistant on the arm. "What a lot of wimps and idiots there are about. You're just the man I need to cheer me up."

"I hope I can do that, sir," Strega said, sidling into Zac's office in front of him.

"Bring us coffee," Zac called out to his secretary, "and see we are not disturbed."

Once ensconced in a chair with strong black coffee in front of him and an oversized Havana in his hand, Strega sat watching Zac, who appeared unable to keep still and was walking up and down the office. Strega recognized the signs of anxiety and indecision in Zac.

"I tell you, bankers are *idiots!* They have no imagination, no vision. All they think of is columns of figures, fractions, decimal points . . ." Zac imitated a shortsighted man peering at a ledger and Strega gave a sycophantic laugh. "Here I am," Zac continued with a flourish, "poised on the verge of an *enormous* coup and what do they do?"

Strega shook his head.

"They *shy* away. Right away, my dear Strega. However, this particular matter is not one that concerns you. What *does* concern you, however, is that I have discovered that the Irish bitch is about to take a trip resembling the last. I want you to get Romanetto and his woman to follow her and pick up the money. Now is the time. It is necessary for me anyway to release

O'Neill because Falconetti is getting nervous. The boy is not well and he feels he should move him to the country."

"Not *well?*" Strega looked apprehensive.

Zac shrugged. "He is tired probably of being cooped up. It's quite natural. He has a pain in his chest, a persistent cough. We can't call a doctor and I don't want the pest to die on my hands. Now, when can Romanetto start?"

"Well . . ." Strega coughed. "I'm not *sure,* Monsieur Zac."

"What do you mean, you're not *sure?*" Zac's tone was threatening.

"The fact is, sir, I don't know where he is."

"What do you mean, you don't know where he *is?*" Zac's tone was even nastier.

"He has gone to ground. He's missing, to tell you the truth. Anticipating your need of him I have done everything I can to find him, Monsieur Zac. I think he took the money and ran."

"The five million Swiss francs we agreed as a payoff?" Zac choked on his words.

"Yes." Strega gulped.

"You just 'gave' him all that and let him get away? Did you think he'd hang around after what we had done to him?" Zac's tone had now become sarcastic and Strega dreaded this more than his master's threats. He felt demeaned by sarcasm, whereas threats brought out his ability to fight.

"I told him there would be more and he should keep in touch. I said there would be a *lot* more as an inducement, Monsieur Desmond. He swore he wouldn't let me down."

"But this is absolutely the last straw." Zac sat down and started a rhythmic banging of his desk. "You mean I've set up this elaborate operation just to have Romanetto vanish into thin air? You've clearly misjudged him, you idiot. You were too afraid to tell me, I suppose?"

"There is always the *woman,* sir." Strega's mouth was dry as he realized that the moment was at hand to begin his own intricately complicated act of deceiving the man he feared most in the world. "I know where *she* is."

"They are not together?"

"Oh no, sir. He ran out on her."

"Took the money, I suppose, and disappeared?"

"That's about it, sir. But I don't think he'd talk. He'd be too frightened. He's probably gone somewhere—he likes the sun—and is lying quiet for the rest of his life."

Strega visualized the unmarked grave in the cemetery in Barcelona and thought there was an unintentional irony in his description.

"Well, if the woman's available"—Zac drummed his fingers on the table—"and *she* was the important one." He appeared to brighten.

"Except for Milan, when Romanetto bungled it, the whole thing went extremely smoothly, sir."

"And there were no inquiries about the accounts?"

"No, sir, deposited in the name of Sandra Wingate, signature and passport forged, of course."

"And all this is still correct and up to date?"

"Oh, indeed, sir," Strega said. "I anticipated that you would be wanting to get down to business soon. But, of course, Eva Raus will also expect a payoff . . . a substantial one, if *she* is to keep silent."

"I can tell you—and you may tell her—that if she's *not* silent"—Zac leaned across his desk and shook a finger at Strega—"she will be silenced, and remain so for a very long time."

"She's already *very* frightened, sir," Strega, enjoying the double meaning, said ingratiatingly. "I assure you I have her *well* under control."

Eva Raus gazed sulkily at Strega as they sat in a corner of the Left Bank café where they'd met before.

"So, what's in it for me?"

"Money for the rest of your life, you greedy whore," Strega said. "This is the payoff, the big one."

"And what do I have to do?" She blew the smoke from her cigarette in a steady stream straight out in front of her.

"It's a piece of cake. You go to the banks you went to before. Produce the passport and claim the money."

"Won't they be suspicious?"

"Why should they?"

"I was told banks were always on the lookout for dodgy transactions."

"There's nothing dodgy about this. You fit Sandra's description, you have Sandra's passport."

"Supposing they check with her?"

"They haven't and they won't. Now shut up asking questions and do as you're told. I'll get 'Madame's' clothes from her office as before. Make sure you're seen prominently because this time I shall be there taking pictures, and also keeping an eye on you," he said with a wink, "just to see you don't scarper with all the money."

Eva lit another cigarette with fingers that shook a little. Strega wondered if she sniffed cocaine. She was really a most unreliable operator. Undoubtedly it would be necessary to do to her what they did to Romanetto: a knife in a dark alley—say, Italy this time—and then he and Gomez would again split the money. He sighed. Life was cruel.

"I tell you something, Mr. Strega," Eva said, after taking a few puffs, as if she could read his thoughts, "frankly, I don't really trust you. Why should I, after what happened to poor Bernardo." She shuddered. "You didn't see his body. I did."

"Let's not talk about the past," Strega urged her. "Bernardo has gone and someone did him in. I don't want to go over all this again, for God's sake. You're being paid well and, after that, you can get out of my life for good. Frankly, I'll be pleased to see the back of you. You're too nervous for this kind of work, and we'd never ask you again, you can bet your life on that."

She sat broodingly as if she hadn't heard him. "I still think it was you," she said. "You did Bernardo in. You, Strega. If you didn't do it you had it done."

"Why should I do the bastard in, for Christ's sake?" He felt like screaming but had to keep his voice down.

"For the money. You would tell Monsieur Zac you'd paid out and hang on to the money."

"Well, I tell you I didn't. I wouldn't dare kill him, knowing that Monsieur Zac wanted to use him again, even if I wanted to, which I didn't. I had no interest in Bernardo or what happened to him. I wish I could convince you of that. I can tell you Monsieur Desmond fairly put *me* through the hoop yesterday when I told him Bernardo had vanished. I wouldn't like to go through *that* again. He's a man with a vile temper and vicious too."

"Then it was Gomez," she said stubbornly, "the one he met with the money. He took it."

Stregaa thumped the bar table in front of him and, as some people looked up curiously, he hissed: "Gomez is *my* man in *my* pay, acting under my orders. If I thought it was Gomez I'd slit his throat myself with pleasure; but I know it was not Gomez and I know it wasn't *me* because we lost all the fucking money. Someone stabbed Bernardo and made off with it. Maybe Bernardo boasted about what he was up to. Now get *that* into your thick skull, Eva, and shut up . . . else it will happen to you too."

There was enough menace in his voice for Eva to feel more frightened than she was already.

"I still don't trust *you,*" she grumbled.

"Look." He grasped her arm before the small but interested audience and whispered in her ear, "I will pay you the money in advance."

"In *advance?*" Her face brightened.

"In *cash.* You can put it in the bank, down your stockings, up your drawers, do with it what you like."

"How do you know you can trust me then?" she said, moistening her lips.

"Because, my sweetie"—his grip on her arm tightened—*"I* will be watching you, every day and every night, until we have collected all the money and returned it to Monsieur Desmond.

Out of the interest—believe me, he's a clever man—he will give me my cut, which will be handsome, you will have yours and you can clear out of my life for good."

But Eva remembered Bernardo's body, stiff in the morgue, and she felt it wouldn't be as simple as that.

Belle walked up and down the salon in Tourville while Zac, head thrown back, fingers tapping the arms of his chair, watched her.

"How do you *know* they suspect me?" she asked.

"They know about Radu. Everyone told you you were too open, too careless."

"But I was nowhere *near* Carl."

"But where was 'the Red'?"

Belle shrugged, too anxious even to take exception to Zac's customary pejorative description of her lover.

"The trouble with these bloody Romanians is you can't find out a thing."

"Did you go to the Embassy?"

"Of course I *didn't.*" Belle looked aghast at the idea. "What do you take me for? They'd tell me lies anyway."

"Then you'd better find him, *ma chère soeur,* and clear yourself. You think I want a wife *and* a sister arrested for murder? Too many people will remember Livio. The police do, I know."

"I suppose it wasn't you?" Belle looked thoughtfully at him.

"Me!" Zac screamed. "Don't you think I have enough troubles? What the hell should I want to kill that ass for? Carl never hurt a soul except about twelve million animals. Carl was about the *only* man in this family who has not given me trouble. I tell you the last person I'd kill or have killed would be Carl. Anyway the police want to see you, Belle, and you'd better telephone them and be *very* nice to them or they'll be after you. I've enough on my hands without *their* suspicions. I can't trust that brother of Tara's who has now sent Bob to the country. I should never have involved him. It was bad judgment on my part."

"You don't have *any* judgment, Zac, and never have had."

Belle gazed at him contemptuously. "What's wrong with Bob?"

"He can't breathe."

"Oh, my God." She raised her eyes to the ceiling.

"I mean," he corrected himself, "he can't breathe in that dungeon where Marco incarcerated him. It's very hot in Rome at this time of the year. He was getting nervous and weepy. I am just about to send Strega round with that girl and recover the money. I am almost ready to frame Sandra, but I can't do it yet. I can't be rushed. Not until I've got control of Cassini and am in a financial position to wrest Desmond from her."

"No wonder you're nervous." Belle's smile was unsympathetic. "You really *are* juggling with danger, Zac. You get yourself in some fine messes, don't you?"

"You're a nice one to talk," Zac snapped back. "Romanian diplomats who mysteriously disappear. You'd think *you'd* have better taste, Belle. Carl had no money. I tell you, you're dependent on me, win or lose, and, at this crucial moment in my affairs, you'd better be cooperative and not irritate me."

"And *you'd* better be cooperative and not irritate *me,*" Belle shouted. "Or I'll blow the whistle on you too. Believe me, Zac, you have far more to lose than I and, if you ask me, you're losing your nerve. Sometimes I wonder if you're fit to run anything; perhaps Father was right about you."

She saw that Zac's dark eyes were almost red with anger and as he got up from his chair and moved toward her she thought he was going to hit her.

"The sensible thing," she went on, backing away from him, "would have been for Father to have given us joint control if he needed a woman in charge. I could have stopped you from some of your worst excesses. I have more sense, better judgment. I . . ."

She was stopped by a loud knock on the door. Nervously they looked toward it.

"Who is it?" Zac called out.

"It's your mother." Lady Elizabeth's voice came from the other side of the door. "Please may I come in?"

Zac leapt toward the door and, unlocking it, flung it open. "Sorry, Mama, we were having a private talk. We did *not* mean to exclude you."

"You can be heard all over the house," Lady Elizabeth said angrily, coming into the room. "*Always* quarrelling, you two. What is it about *this* time?"

"Really, Mother, we're old enough to mind our own business," Zac said petulantly.

"You and Belle are always at each other." She lowered her voice. "You'd think you'd *cooperate* and concentrate on getting rid of Sandra. I heard you through the door just now say that Belle had no money. Well, as soon as you have control of what should have been your rightful inheritance you will have all the money in the world and Belle will be a rich woman again. I agree too with what Belle said. Joint control is an excellent thing. You are too impetuous, Zac. Your sister has a good head on her shoulders. You owe it to your sister, Zac, and your family to make this your prime objective."

"*Mamma mia*"—Zac flung back his head—"don't you think the objective is *always* before me, day and night; one I never lose sight of? But there are other fish to fry as well. I *want* to become even more powerful and to have Desmond as merely a part of a much larger worldwide group." He reached for his mother's hand and kissed it. "Just you wait and see. Now Mama, let us go into dinner and forget business. I assure you that soon we will again be very rich indeed. You can trust me absolutely."

Lady Elizabeth was not a foolish woman. She was, after all, a mother who loved her children. Each one was different and each one she loved differently. But she knew that, beneath this veneer of strength, Zac was weak. He juggled too much; he made too many misjudgements. Perhaps he had not been loved as he should have been loved when he was a child. Almost from birth Zac's personality had been difficult. He was a cryer as a baby, a faddy eater and then as he got older he became a difficult child: demanding, dissatisfied, above all sly. He had few friends and relied for companionship on his sister Belle. In a way each was the counterpart of the other: ambitious, ruthless, sensual but unloving.

Yet Georges Desmond had adored Belle and made no secret that he despised his elder son Zac, who, accordingly, had spent most of his adult life trying to regain the respect of a man who was now no longer alive to appreciate it.

Yet everything Zac did he did with one object in mind: to be worthy of being the son of Georges Desmond.

Tara came into dinner and, as usual, had little to say. She was quiet and sulky these days and Lady Elizabeth, who had never got on particularly well with her, was not sure what exactly was wrong. Tara was impulsive, impetuous, mistrustful, hard to understand. Zac had never confided in her about his wife, and one had to judge from appearances what was going on. These days it was harder than ever to tell.

"What's happening about Jean Marvoine?" Lady Elizabeth said conversationally when they were halfway through their meal.

"We're going to sell it," Zac said.

"Oh?" Tara looked at him sharply. "Who says so?"

"I say so. The account books say so. It's costing us money just to keep it open. That site in the Avenue Montaigne alone is worth a small fortune."

"But you don't own it. It belongs to Desmond."

"For the moment. Not for long." Zac smiled knowingly.

"Oh, does Sandra know that?" Tara's tone was sarcastic.

"Not yet," Zac chuckled. "I would love to see her face when she finds out that she no longer runs Desmond."

"I'd love to know what schemes you're hatching," his mother said anxiously. "You know Sandra is clever."

"And so am I, Mama." He took a sip of wine and glanced at her. "Although you may not always have thought so, and showed it in your lack of support."

"That's *not* true, Zac. I have always supported you, like a mother."

"But that is not enough, Mama. You have secrets. You never told us, your family, that Hélène O'Neill was not the mother of Sandra."

"There was a reason for that."

Zac shook his head. "Whether there was or not it *is* difficult to trust you, Mama, and I certainly couldn't reveal my business secrets to you, at this juncture. You were close to Bob, you even appeared to *like* the Irish woman."

"I do not dislike Sandra as a person," Lady Elizabeth said carefully. "And I was a *little* sorry for her and the situation in which she found herself . . ."

"As for Jean Marvoine," Tara, who had been listening, impatiently interrupted her mother-in-law, "Sandra is very anxious for it to continue and with me in charge. The *last* thing she wants to do is sell it."

"Ma chère femme"—Zac turned to her with an air of exaggerated patience—"please do *not* place any reliance on what that cow says or does not say. I . . ."

Zac stopped abruptly as Pierre hurried in without even knocking, and looked at him with an expression of irritation. "Yes, Pierre, what is it?"

"Sir, I think if you and your family would come at once to the television room . . ."

"But what . . ."

"Come at once, please. They have made the main announcements. A *most* interesting item. I *do* beg you to come quickly . . ."

With a frantic scraping of chairs the members of the family rose as one and hurried after Pierre to the television room where the voice of the newscaster could be heard coming to the end of an item about international events. When they reached the door they saw two pictures on the screen side by side. One was Carl von Burg-Farnbach and next to him was a man who closely resembled him. He had blond hair and a thick moustache like Carl.

The family stood transfixed, listening to the voice of the newscaster.

"Lady Christine Palmer, who was charged with the murder of Prince Carl von Burg-Farnbach, was immediately released on the news." The pictures faded from the screen and the newscaster looked straight to camera.

"The discovery that Herr Conrad Becksdorf, the head of the great German Becksdorf Bank, was also a passenger on the Orient Express has emerged as the result of a tip-off following exhaustive inquiries by Interpol. A hitherto unknown faction of the Baader-Meinhof group has confirmed that the intended victim was Herr Becksdorf and have apologized to the family of the victim. Last month the head of the Pragen Bank was killed in a similar outrage when his car exploded as the result of a booby-trapped bomb outside his home . . ."

The picture then changed to show a woman hurrying out of a doorway, a hand held in front of her face. "Lady Palmer was immediately released and though she declined to answer questions, is said to be on her way to England. She is said to be anxious to discuss with her legal advisers the question of possible action against the Italian police as she always protested her innocence.

"The Chancellor has condemned the outrage and expressed the sympathy of the German government to the family of the prince, whose funeral has already taken place."

FOUR

The Kiss of Judas

17

Eva passed the check over the counter at the Banco d'Italia and waited. The clerk looked at the check, then at her.

"Have you your passport, Signorina Wingate?"

With a smile, and an air of calm she was far from feeling, Eva slid the passport under the grille and watched as the clerk examined the pages, the photograph of her and, lastly and very carefully, her signature, comparing it with the one on the check.

"That seems very satisfactory," the clerk said smoothly. "I shan't keep you waiting a moment, Signorina."

Eva felt her pulse hammering in her neck as the clerk disappeared to the back of the bank and began talking to a man sitting in front of a VDT screen who glanced once or twice at Eva. They both turned to the screen and tapped some numbers into the keyboard. Then they studied the screen again for what seemed an interminable time, spoke together a while longer and the girl then went through a door behind the VDT and emerged a few minutes later with a man who accompanied her back to the counter.

"Signorina Wingate," the girl said with a friendly yet professional smile, "this is Signor Frattolini, the deputy manager. He would like a word with you."

"Is there something wrong?" Eva knew that, though her smile was assured, her legs were trembling.

Signor Frattolini had by this time come round the counter and appeared at Eva's side.

"This way, Signorina Wingate, please," he said in bad English, but with a polite gesture.

Eva, in one of Sandra's smartest outfits, a new creation by Thierry Mugler—surely Sandra would have missed *this* expensive item from the wardrobe? Yet she had left it behind—went ahead of the deputy manager into a small, impersonal room containing a desk and two chairs.

"Prego, Signorina." He gestured to the chair and Eva sat obediently facing him.

"It is simply, Signorina"—the man spread out his hands—"that you have deposited three hundred million lire and now you wish to withdraw it all."

"With interest," Eva said firmly.

"Naturally, with in rest."

"Is there anything wrong with that?" Eva's tone was cold. "It is, after all, my money."

"Nothing wrong at all," the man said, crossing his legs. "But, you see, we in banks have to be *very* careful. We are told to look out for any unusual transactions and this, if I may say so, *is* an unusual transaction."

"Is there any law that prevents me depositing my money in a bank and withdrawing it?"

"None at all." Signor Frattolini, clearly finding his task uncongenial, produced a handkerchief and mopped his brow which was covered by a thin film of sweat. "I assure you there is *no* hint of illegality. It is simply that we have to be sure."

"When I am traveling again in Europe"—Eva rose to her feet and drew on her gloves—"I shall be very sure *not* to leave any money with the Banco d'Italia. I am, you see, resident in the Far East and, as a buyer of antiques by profession, it suits me to have substantial deposits of money in certain locations so that, if needed, I can produce cash very quickly. Some people, for reasons of their own, will only accept cash, and many priceless items are lost if it is not available." She looked severely at him.

"As it is, a Bellini bust, still in private hands, in which I am interested, will probably have found another buyer by the time I get my money out of *your* bank." Her expression was so wrathful that the deputy manager quickly rose too.

"Oh, *please,* Signorina, don't say that. Antiques, you say. *Now* I understand. A million pardons, Signorina. The money will be ready for you in ten minutes maximum." Frattolini held up ten fingers for her inspection and then hastened to the door which he opened with a flourish. *"Dieci minuti,"* he said, turning to her, his fingers still displayed in what looked to her rather like an obscene gesture. As the door closed she found it hard to stifle a smile.

Yet Eva was clearly still nervous when she sat in the café opposite the bank with Strega, who had been waiting for her. He gave her a brandy and watched her anxiously.

"I am not being paid *nearly* enough for this," she said. "If I have to go through this ordeal every time, I shall be a nervous wreck."

"There will be a bonus, Eva," Strega promised. "A large one. You will be a wealthy woman for the rest of your life. Believe me, I, personally, will take care of it." Strega looked at the briefcase which, bulging with notes in large denominations, lay between them. "As long as Monsieur Zac gets his money we can also divide the interest between ourselves. I doubt if he would even have thought of it, Eva, his mind is on so many things." Strega smiled and drew a plastic toothpick from his inside pocket. "I think it could amount to a cool million dollars. What do you think of that?"

"Where next?" Eva said with a sigh.

Strega consulted a piece of paper. "From here Madame goes to Rome, Barcelona and Athens. Why Athens last, I wonder?"

The tiny Greek island of Lemonia, between Tinos and Naxos, was scarcely big enough to appear on any map. Had Sandra and David known about Phi Phi Don they might well have compared the two. It had the same isolation, the same rugged mountainside, although much of this was volcanic, the same tiny harbor and the whole surrounded by the same, but not quite the same, beautiful blue sea. In addition Lemonia was also covered with olive groves from which the oil used in Greek cooking was made. There was also an abundance of the lemon trees from which the island got its name.

Lemonia had been discovered by David's father after the War, in which he was a GI. He subsequently bought the island with its few ramshackle fishing huts and a house built by an eccentric English millionaire who had owned the island since the days of Byron, to whom he claimed to be distantly related.

Ebenezer Heurtey had built a house: not too grand, not too large or ornate, but with one of the best vistas on the island. On a clear day it was claimed that the coast of Turkey could be seen, though some suggested it was a mirage.

Over the years Ebenezer had let some of his closest friends build villas too, though they had to be kept out of sight of one another. The land was leased to the builders so that the whole island still belonged to him. If there were ever to be a dispute over the sale of a house it would probably have taken the wisdom of a Solomon to resolve it.

So far the houses had remained within the families that built them so that, in a way, Lemonia was a friendly place where everyone knew everyone else, and the Greek fishermen who kept their huts and their fishing rights were happy too.

Lemonia was reached from Naxos either by boat or helicopter. Sandra's helicopter had flown her in from Athens but would soon be sent back to the mainland so that she and David could have some isolation. They intended to walk, swim, eat, drink and picnic. To David's disgust Sandra had insisted on a fax machine because she had to have instant communication with her offices round the world.

By the standard of the other villas the Heurtey house was quite modest; but every room had a balcony, a view of sea or mountains, cool marble floors and all modern conveniences. The electricity came from a generator halfway up the hill. All the Heurtey children, cousins and friends had used it for so many years that in many ways it had an air of shabbiness, of being much used, which Sandra found attractive. There was a woman called Olga who looked after them. She cooked and cleaned, but otherwise she left them alone.

Sandra swiftly changed into a T-shirt and shorts. Her room, adjacent to David's, was large and cool, the blinds already drawn when she arrived. David had been there a week and he grumbled about the fax as soon as she stepped indoors. She had felt tired and tense from her long round-trip. Further negotiations about Bob in Rome had been fruitless. Joanne Pasarro, who had accompanied her, even made the suggestion he might be dead. There had been nothing but silence now for some weeks.

She and David lunched with Greg her pilot. He flew both her plane and helicopter and doubled up as a bodyguard when she went abroad, rather as Jacques did at home.

After they'd given him a lunch of fresh sardines, souvlakia and local wine, Sandra and David watched the helicopter fly off. Greg had seemed reluctant to leave her alone on Lemonia; but she gave him no option. He would go straight back to Athens where, as it happened, he had a sister who was married to a Greek, and wait for the call.

As if to guarantee her protection, David put his arm lightly around Sandra's waist and, as the helicopter flew out of sight, murmured, "Alone, at last."

He turned to kiss her but Sandra moved away, feeling still nervous and ill at ease. She now felt it had been set up in too obvious a manner and this fact made her unhappy. They were here to make love; there were no two ways about it. Greg had looked at her oddly as he said good-bye and there had been a suggestive smile on Olga's wrinkled face.

"What's the matter?" David asked.

"Just tired." She flopped in a wicker chair on the balcony and shielded her eyes.

"There's something else." He flopped down beside her. "Sorry about the fax. I should have tried to understand."

She noticed the word "tried."

Sandra looked round, cracking her knuckles. "It's just that the whole set-up is so obvious. It's lovely, but . . ."

"Setup?" He frowned at her. "How do you mean?"

"Us here, alone . . ."

"Setup for what?"

She shrugged her shoulders.

"If you think it's just set up for a fuck you've got another think coming." David got to his feet and angrily threw down the newspapers she'd brought him. "I'm spending all this afternoon playing golf with the Hendersons. They're old friends of the family who have a villa, and a private ten-hole course, a few miles away. I could go and *stay* with them if you'd prefer, Sandra. If it would make you feel safer."

"Don't be silly." Sandra studied her toes. "Maybe I'll feel better when I've had a sleep. You go and play golf. I bet you haven't played since this morning? It must seem like ages."

Her sarcasm annoyed him. Coming so soon after the slight altercation about the fax this seemed a bad omen. But David knew that Sandra was a woman who would only despise weakness in a man.

He went through the doors leading into the house without another word and, moments later, she heard the Jeep that she'd noticed at the back of the house start up. She listened to its noisy exhaust until he was out of earshot.

Well, now she'd made him angry. What a start. She went to her room, took off her clothes and lay down naked on the bed thinking about the situation that she'd got herself into. She considered it a bad sign they'd started with two rows, but it also served to emphasize the difference between them: that she had her mind on business, whereas David had his on pleasure. How could he run a multinational company and not have a fax, a means of instant communication with his offices round the world? He'd said something about no news being good news, but to Sandra that wasn't the point. It was irresponsible. One could enjoy oneself and keep an eye on business too.

Now it looked as though she wasn't even going to enjoy herself. Her remark to David about a "setup" had been crude. He'd been crude back. If they were going to go on opposing each other she'd soon summon the helicopter. That would make Greg smile.

For some time she lay worrying, thinking about David, about Bob, about Louis. She missed her baby and wished she'd brought him. Leaving him behind had undoubtedly cemented the notion that they were here for the purpose of fornication. Louis would have loved the golden sand, the clear sea where he might have begun to learn to swim. She was selfish and maybe the reason was that she'd had one thing in mind too.

Sandra drifted off to sleep and when she awoke she found Olga with her head round the door. Sandra reached for her gown and drew it over her body.

"Sorry, Madame," Olga said without blinking. "Mr. Heurtey said you liked the English afternoon tea."

"How kind of him." Sandra sat up, clutching her gown to hide her nudity. "I do, as a matter of fact."

"May I come in then, Madame?"

"Of course." Sandra quickly put on her gown and when the maid entered the room with a tray she was standing up tying the cord. "I must have fallen asleep."

"You looked very tired, Madame," Olga said sympathetically, setting the tea tray on a table near the bed. "Mr. Heurtey telephoned to say he would be back about seven."

"That's fine then." Sandra ran her hands through her hair and looked at the clock. Two hours' rest and already she felt better. She would make herself look nice for David and see what happened.

"May I say, Madame, how beautiful you are," Olga said, staring at her with frank admiration. "You are even prettier than I thought. I saw your pictures in the papers."

"Really?" Sandra looked surprised. "Here?"

"Mr. Heurtey brought them. He is very proud of you."

The maid had obviously catered for English visitors because she poured milk into the cup, then tea and asked Sandra whether or not she took sugar. Sandra shook her head and accepted the cup.

"I suppose you knew Mrs. Heurtey and the children?" she inquired, sipping her tea, which was well made. Olga, enjoying the chance to gossip—after all hers must have been a lonely life—nodded.

"Did you like them?"

"Mrs. Heurtey very nice." Olga, whose English was good, nodded approvingly. "The children . . ." She screwed up her nose and made an equivocating gesture with her hand. "The elder daughter I *like*. She very nice 'usband and two children. There is a very tall son." She pointed high above her head. "Taller than Mr. Heurtey. He *not* so nice, but he have very nice wife."

"In what way isn't he nice?" Sandra smiled over her cup.

"His father *very* charming man." Olga smiled fondly. "The son *not* like the father. Well, I go and prepare dinner, Madame. A special stew that I make with lamb and fresh spinach? Is all right?"

"It sounds absolutely wonderful," Sandra said. "I'm going to take a swim."

Olga went to the window and pointed to the side of the house.

"Is very small path which takes you to private beach, Madame. Very safe, like lagoon."

"How blissful," Sandra cried and it was already as though her cares were beginning to ebb away.

When David came back she was waiting for him on the balcony, sitting in a plain white caftan, a thick lock of hair, naturally waved, curling casually across her face. The swim had made her relax and she knew she looked good. David, running up the stairs, thought so too.

"Gosh," he said, staring at her, "you look marvelous."

She rose and went toward him, putting an arm round his neck and nuzzling her nose against his cheek. "I had a swim. Sorry."

"Sorry for what?" He looked down at her, unable to keep the yearning he felt for her out of his eyes. She was so very beautiful, and yet there was something about her that still remained out of reach.

"I was an absolute pig when I arrived."

"I shouldn't have complained about the fax." He let her go and slumped into a chair. He wore white shorts and a check shirt open at the neck. He was tanned, lean, fit and virile. She knew that she wanted him, and she'd almost blown the whole thing. Now she had to undo the harm, the hurt she had caused him earlier in the day.

"I guess you want your Scotch," she said, going to the table on the balcony which was stacked with bottles.

"There's a full case of champagne in the cellar. I think Olga has a bottle on ice."

"That's very thoughtful of you, David."

"I am a very thoughtful man," David said. "Truly." Then he jumped up and made for the door. "I'll go take a shower, change and be with you in twenty minutes. Does that suit you?"

"It suits me," Sandra said, and she knew the excitement she felt was only just beginning.

They ate by candlelight on a patio at the side of the house, also within sight of the sea. A few fishing boats were out in the bay, their lights reflected in the water. Olga had prepared delicious meze for them before the meal at which they nibbled, while David drank his whiskey and Sandra had a glass of chilled champagne. A breeze came up from the sea and the flames from the candles wavered in front of them. David reached for her hand and kissed it.

"Tell me what you found out about Bob."

"Joanne thinks Bob may be dead."

"Oh, my God." David jumped up and came round to her side. "Oh, my darling, no *wonder* you were in a mood."

"She only thinks. She has no proof; but all the leads are negative and we haven't heard from them for weeks."

"And the police?"

"I think they think Bob's dead too, or that he's pretending and is in hiding. They seem to suspect that the whole thing may be a hoax. They've even been making inquiries in California among his old friends as if they don't believe he's been kidnapped. That's a thing I hate about the police. They're so secretive, so distrustful. Anyway, they're *very* pleased with themselves over Carl."

"That is a hell of a relief for the family." David went back to his chair and broke off a piece of pita with which he mopped up the gravy from the lamb stew.

"It's a relief for us all, especially for Belle. They made inquiries about her and the diplomat. Apparently they never thought Christine Palmer had really done it. She's going to sue them. Can't say I blame her."

"She must be bitter," David grunted.

"But no one thought that Carl could have been killed by *mistake!*"

"Well, it's not the first time. These terrorists are always killing the wrong people. They kill without compunction and then they say 'sorry' as if *that* can bring anyone back."

Sandra, replete, sat back in her chair. She felt very tired but happy. The tension had to drain away before she could relax completely.

"I'm for an early night," she said at last. "Would you mind?"

"I think you need an early night, Sandra." David leaned toward her, looking at her intently. "I'll see you in the morning, my darling." She knew then that there would be no knock on her door at night.

When Sandra woke, the first thing she was aware of was the play of light through the slatted blinds onto the white ceiling.

There was a blueish tinge as though the iridescent rays bounced off the sea.

She got up and, pulling up the blinds, exclaimed with delight at the sight of the calm, blue sea dotted with small craft and, very far away on the horizon, the band of low, white mist that some people claimed was the coast of Turkey.

She had gone to bed at ten and now it was six. She felt well and thoroughly rested. The thought of the lagoon where she'd swum the evening before was so tempting that, instead of getting back into bed, she climbed into her bikini, put on her robe, took a towel and a beach bag and exited quietly from the house from which not a sound came, running lightly along the path to the beach. Completely surrounded by rock except for a tiny exit to the sea, there was not a soul to be seen.

Sandra felt a surge of exhilaration as, scarcely pausing, she tore off her robe, threw it down with her bag and towel and continued her run into the sea. Then when she was deep enough she struck out and swam strongly to the mouth of the lagoon, almost into the open sea. Even at this hour the sun was warm and she turned on her back and floated, eyes closed, conscious only of the sun, the sea and the sound of the birds wheeling around overhead in search of the catch cast back into the sea by the fishermen.

She gently propelled herself back toward the shore and when she opened her eyes she saw David, wearing trunks and with a towel in his hand, standing watching her.

"Hi!" She lifted an arm and waved. "We had the same idea."

"Guess we had," David called back. "Mind if I come in?"

"There's plenty of room," she called and she closed her eyes as she heard him splash and swim toward her.

When he reached her she turned and their mouths met. She sank down into the water, her body parallel with his, and she could just feel the sand between her toes. Still kissing her, he undid her bikini top and crushed her breasts to him, then put his hand down the front of her bikini pants and slipped them off.

She did the same to him and they joined together in the water like the primeval fluid that not only surrounded them but seemed to engulf them and draw them down.

With the buoyancy of weightlessness they floated together, borne along by the water, until they were beached on the golden sand, where they lay like two giant fish, irretrievably entwined.

From now on they were lovers.

As the boat drifted in the bay, Sandra lay back in the bows watching as he cast his line. He hardly ever caught anything but, toward noon, he would ship the oars, set up the sail and make for one of the smaller islands or the café on the beach of Lemonia, where they ate mullet grilled over wood and drank strong retsina that tasted like resin.

Then they went to bed for the afternoon; rose at about six, had a swim, and ate on the terrace a meal lovingly cooked by Olga, who knew that they now shared a bedroom. Sometimes they ate with the Hendersons, or the Paleys, who were ten miles away and, again, old friends of the Heurteys.

They regarded Sandra with a great deal of interest, even awe. They had of course all heard of her; but they had also known Edna Heurtey and obviously liked her. The situation, however, was not complicated or difficult. Edna and David were divorced. Sandra, who hadn't broken up anyone's marriage, was a widow herself.

They all seemed to think, however, that Sandra and David would eventually marry, and treated them already as a couple, even asking them their plans for the future. Sandra, satiated with warmth, food, sea, sand and, perhaps above all, love, took it all in good part; but when anyone went too far they got a sharp look from her, an indulgent smile from David. Maybe he thought their future was a foregone conclusion too.

Ten days of this kind of life were as welcome as they were strange for Sandra, who had taken few holidays in the past few years.

She had, however, her worries, of which the greatest was Bob.

She kept in touch with her office daily by fax and phone, annoying David, who only thought of business when someone rang him. Then he grumbled about it. For Sandra this attitude was very hard to understand, and was the chief cause of what minor disagreements they had.

But today, hat over her eyes, she was content to lie in the bows of the boat, one brown leg flung over the other, in shorts and a bikini top, arms loosely resting on the gunwales.

"Penny for them?" David asked her.

"Bliss," she replied, stirring his bare leg with one of her toes.

"Steady," David said, laughing, "you're distracting the attention of one of the world's great anglers."

"Did you ever go deep-sea fishing?"

"Yep." David, who had on a white, peaked cap, looked at the floater and began to haul in his line. "Beats this for excitement, but not otherwise."

He wound in his line, looked ruefully at the empty hook and stowed line and rod in the bottom of the boat. Then he uncurled his long body and stretched out by her side. He put an arm under her shoulders and she snuggled up to him.

"Guess this is one of the best holidays I ever had, David." She paused and looked searchingly into his eyes. "One of the best times in my life."

"Me too," he said and, removing his hat, he kissed her. Then, with the hand with which he was supporting her back, he unhooked her bikini bra, which fell away, exposing her breasts, also brown, as they frequently sunbathed nude in the private creek.

"I hope no one's looking," Sandra peeped over the gunwales.

"Not a soul in sight." David looked into her eyes but she shook her head and, sitting up, rehooked her bikini top.

"You're really a very sexy man, David Heurtey," she said reprovingly. "You seem to have little else on your mind."

"How could any sane man alone with a woman like you, half dressed most of the time, undressed some of the time, *have* anything else on his mind? It's enough to keep one in a permanent state of priapism."

Sandra smiled and reached for her shirt which she drew on over her bikini.

"I'd feel an awful fool if someone peered over the side of the ship and saw us at it. Later, darling."

She rested against his arm and shielded her eyes from the sun. Her wedding ring glowed on her finger. David resented it because he felt it was a barrier between them; but she refused to remove it and, perhaps symbolically, when he angered her she revolved it round and round on her finger. "I'm getting hungry," she said.

"I thought you were going to say you're getting very fond of me," he ribbed her, sitting up and putting on his cap.

"That too."

"I love you, Sandra."

She didn't answer because she didn't know what to say.

"I guess you don't feel quite the same about me," he said, after a few moments' silence.

"I don't know," she answered. "I like you enormously and, yes, I think I love you." She gazed at him for some time. "But I don't think I'm 'in love'. Not yet."

"Maybe because you won't let yourself?"

"Maybe."

"Is it Michel?" His eyes fastened on the ring.

"Mmm." She screwed up her face and shook her head. "It's not *true* to say it's Michel. I loved him passionately at one time, but we had too many disagreements. We were always at war. I think our love ebbed away. I didn't even tell him about the baby until I was nearly five months pregnant."

"Why not?"

"I knew that he'd say give up work . . ."

"Sandra . . . darling," David interrupted her.

"Yes?"

"It *is* a little unusual, you know, this feeling you have about work. You put it before everything."

"Not Louis," she said quickly. "In fact I feel guilty I didn't bring Louis with us. He would so have loved it here, on the beach, splashing in the cove. I feel I was selfish, thinking of me, and not of him."

"So there's Louis first." Half joking, David began to enumerate with the aid of a finger. "There's work and then, hopefully, there's me."

"About in that order," Sandra nodded. "And then . . . there's my uncertainty about who I am. Maybe, after all, that comes first and explains why I can't give myself completely to a man . . . really love passionately, totally and forever."

"What do you mean, my darling?" he asked tenderly.

"I don't know who my father was. You don't know what that means to a person. I have grown up without really identifying with either of my parents, and I think it's made me hard inside. That's why I love Bob so much because he's all I have, before Louis came along, that is."

"Even though Bob's no blood relation?"

"Yes. He's the past. He's very important. I cling to him." Suddenly her eyes filled with tears.

"If you would marry me you would cling to me," David whispered.

"But, David"—she struggled to an upright position—"that's just what I *don't* want. I don't want to cling to *anyone* in the sense you mean. I don't want to be dependent on a man or have him do things for me; but my link with my past is Bob."

"Not really."

"Yes, really. Hélène O'Neill looked after me from the time I was a baby and Bob was her child. I knew him from birth and I love him like a brother."

David dug in the pocket of his shorts and produced a cigar case from which he selected a long, thin cheroot. He lit it slowly, giving it his whole attention, and finally blew a thin stream of smoke in the air. The boat, oars shipped, drifted on; the sea was as smooth as oil. A few gulls lazily hovered above them, waiting, in vain, for titbits. Very far away, a minute speck in the distance, a steamer made its way to Naxos. In the haze they could see the outline of the tiny island of Lemonia, and Sandra imagined she could smell the fish already grilling on the wood.

"Darling," David said impulsively, lying down beside her again, "I guess we have to find your father. We have to get that sorted out. I realize now how much it means to you and, maybe, if you did get it sorted out, there'd be a chance for me."

She groped for his hand and held it in hers for a moment. Then she gently kissed it, letting her lips linger on his smooth skin.

"You *do* understand me after all," she said, her voice thick with emotion. "If I could find out who my father was, believe me, everything could change."

Half an hour later they reached the jetty and Petros, the proprietor of the café, ran down to help them tie up the boat. There were already a number of people eating under the awning and the air was full of the sound of laughter.

The Hendersons—mother, father, a grown-up son and daughter and her boyfriend—hailed them and Sandra and David joined them, David taking two glasses of Ouzo from the beachside bar with him as they went.

Sandra found her mind was suddenly more serene after her talk with David, and her newfound happiness, her confidence about the future, safe now in his hands, was reflected in her expression.

She looked like a woman who was very happy, very much in love, and as David sat down next to her on the bench that ran alongside the table their bare knees touched.

"Good fishing?" Irene Henderson asked.

"Not a thing." David shook his head, and the conversation turned to various subjects while, when they could, David and Sandra held hands out of sight below the bench.

Irene Henderson, who was a good deal older than Sandra, noticed them and smiled her approval. Not long now, her eyes seemed to say.

* * *

Lunch took a couple of hours. There was a lot of laughter, talk of plans for the next few days, the possibility of an excursion to Naxos and, after good-byes were said and as Sandra and David started walking up the hill to the villa, hand in hand, she said: "Something worries me."

"What's that, darling?" He let go of her hand and put an arm around her waist.

"We can't stay here forever."

"Why not?" His grip tightened.

"David . . . I said a week." She stopped and looked at him. "It's already nearly two. I shall really have to get back quite soon."

"Darling, every day you're in touch with your office." He stooped and kissed the nape of her neck as she bent her head reflectively toward the ground. "It's summer, a quiet season. Everyone's on vacation."

"It's Louis, too, as well as the office."

"Then let's have him flown out. He can be here tomorrow or the day after."

They had by now reached the steps of the villa and David held out his hand because she had trailed thoughtfully after him.

"Some people take vacations lasting many weeks."

"Some people," she snorted derisively. "You mean 'you'."

"Yes, I take lots of vacations. Why not? Nothing's falling apart without me."

"You hope."

"Nothing's falling apart without *you.*"

"I hope." But now her tone was jocular. They reached the villa which was cool and quiet, all the blinds drawn. Olga was either resting or across at the Hendersons, as the housekeeper there was her great friend. Olga was a widow and her grown-up family had scattered, though a son and daughter lived in Naxos.

Sandra and David walked quietly across the cool marble floor, their minds, perhaps, already on making love, the total surrender to each other which would come very soon, to be followed by sound, refreshing sleep.

In many ways it was a perfect existence. Sandra looked at her brown feet, still covered with sand as, in silence, they began to climb the stairs, the sexual tension between them mounting.

At the top of the stairs Sandra released David's hand and kissed his cheek lightly.

"I'll just pop in and look at the fax."

"Oh, *darling,* for heaven's sake." David let his impatience show. "Won't it do after?"

"How long is 'after'?" she replied with a smile and, putting the tips of her fingers to her lips, blew him a kiss. "See you in a second."

He stood at the door smiling, maybe just a little irritated. But then he went into the bedroom, and the sight of the large cool bed only covered with a sheet made him take off his shirt, shorts and underpants and, flinging them onto a chair, he went into the bathroom to make himself ready for her.

Sandra, her mind in that pleasant, anticipatory mood before sex, went into the room where the fax and telephone machines were, as well as the private scrambled line to her office. Technicians who, at great expense, had installed the equipment before her arrival, had thought that a senior member of some foreign government was due to arrive.

Several messages had arrived while they'd been fishing, most of them share price rises around the world, one or two queries from Antoinette that were largely routine. However, when she came to the final item it was marked *Very urgent, read immediately* and, rapidly, she continued to read:

The Heurtey Corporation of Europe in a surprise raid on Cassini Drinks.

This morning Heurtey Corporation of Europe staged a dawn raid on the Cassini Drinks conglomeration which immediately saw a startling rise in the share price.

Sandra rapidly read on, then she tore the paper from the machine and ran across the hall into the bedroom where David was already sprawled naked across the bed.

"David," she cried, sitting down beside him and thrusting the paper into his hands, "just read that."

David, who was already aroused, sat up looking annoyed. "Sandra, *can't* you leave business alone, just for once?"

"Read it, David, read it," she insisted.

David fumbled for his reading glasses which were on the bedside table and, feeling foolish as well as annoyed, drew the sheet across the lower part of his body. Then for some moments while Sandra watched him he absorbed the contents of the fax.

"Well, I'm darned," he said and, casting the paper on the bed beside him, removed his spectacles and lay down again while Sandra, astonished by his reaction, stared at him impatiently.

"What do you mean you're 'darned', David?"

"Well," he chuckled, "I'm darned, that's all."

"You knew nothing about this?"

"Of course I didn't." His expression became irritated again.

"And all you can say is that you're 'darned'?"

"Oh, for heaven's sake." He propped himself up on his arm. "What do you expect me to say, Sandra?"

"If you really *do* know nothing about it, and I don't suppose you do, I, in your place, would have leapt off the bed and gone straight to the telephone. I'd want to know what the hell was going on."

"I dare say you would," he said coldly. "Thank heaven I'm not so emotional."

"David, what *is* the matter with you?" Sandra stood up and went over to the window and pulled up the blinds. For a moment she stared moodily across the bay where, a few hours before, they'd been fishing with such tranquility. "Cassini is an *enormous* concern."

"I know."

"It's bigger than Heurtey."

"Yes. But Heurtey was bigger than you when you tried to take us over."

"And failed."

"Presumably this will fail too."

"I'm going to send immediately for more details," Sandra said. "If I were you I'd get up and get dressed. We may have to leave tonight."

"But, Sandra . . ." David heaved his legs over and, sitting on the bed, reached for his underpants and shorts which he hurriedly put on. "What *is* all this about? It isn't your company. Why are *you* so worried?"

"I'm worried, frankly, because you're not worried," she said sharply. "Your group, of which you are the head, is apparently acting without your knowledge or consent, and I consider that damned worrying, whereas all you can say is that you'll be 'darned'."

"Yes, but it's *my* worry, dear, not yours."

"But you are not worrying, David. I'm doing it for you."

"I'm not the worrying kind," he replied. "There'll be some explanation." He put on his shirt and tucked it into his shorts, then he got into his sandals.

"OK." He shrugged. "Let's fax for details. Let's find out what it's all about. Maybe Joanne has the answer."

"We will first of all fax my office," Sandra said. "God knows, there may have been a revolution in yours."

"What do you mean a 'revolution'?"

"David, someone has made a bid which must involve millions of francs. If it can't keep up the pace it could send Heurtey plummeting into liquidation. We have to see who is behind this and why, and I'm afraid a very nasty suspicion comes to my mind."

For a moment their eyes met.

"Zac," David said quietly, "who is the head of the Banque Franco-Belges."

An hour later they still sat in the makeshift office, trying to sort through all the information that they had been supplied with.

For the last few weeks there had been a strong rise in Heurtey shares which showed the company in a very favorable position.

It already owned two percent of Cassini but, since the morning raid, had been buying up all the Cassini shares, which stood about level with Heurtey. On the news of the bid the Cassini shares started to rise strongly and the head of Cassini, Max Boucheron, had said that the bid would be resisted. He claimed that Heurtey, through its bank, the Franco-Belges, would not be able to afford the increased share price and would lose.

Prompted by Sandra, David had faxed Zac who had not replied. When he tried to get Joanne on the phone he found that she was as bewildered by the bid as anyone else. However, the Tellier brothers were known to be heavily involved, and the object was to make an enormous combine, maybe eclipsing the parent company.

Joanne said that Zac had already appeared on the lunchtime news, claiming that victory would not be far off. When challenged, he denied that there were not sufficient resources to pay for the shares and said he had the support of several powerful European banks.

The staff at Heurtey headquarters knew nothing about it, or how to respond to the telephone calls by which they were besieged. The absence abroad of the chairman was thought incredible, possibly even sinister.

Sandra finally threw all the faxes and the sheaves of notes she had made on a table and ran her hands through her hair.

"I'll call the helicopter."

"You think it's really necessary?"

"David, I can't understand you."

"You've said that before," he replied, rising and turning his back on her. "I can't understand you, Sandra, as this isn't your company. Technically, it has nothing to do with you."

"Oh, yes, it has," she said, also standing up. "We own a small part of your bank and, besides, a big group with Cassini, Tellier and Heurtey merging would present a real threat to us."

"To you?" He looked astonished.

"To Desmond. It would be one of the biggest drinks groups in France and who knows where it would stop? But already the shares have advanced over Desmond's by ten francs. If you ask me, they will gain hourly. Apparently there was a bear raid on Cassini shares accompanied by innuendo that the company was in difficulties which initially caused its shares to fall. Also, it was not true. The management have issued a stout denial." She took the papers from the table and flourished one at him. "It all has the hallmark of a man whose complete lack of business acumen I know full well. This is just the sort of thing that Zac rushes into without the back up." She gazed searchingly at David. "You're sure he never spoke to you about it?"

"Never. I never heard the word 'Cassini' mentioned, although I know of them, naturally."

"You couldn't have forgotten?"

"Do me a favor," he said angrily. "You must think I'm a moron, Sandra, if I'd 'forget' a thing like that."

"But," she insisted, "there must be some authorization, some signature, for what has gone on. You're sure you weren't busy thinking of your next golf appointment, David, and absent-mindedly signed a document authorizing the takeover?"

"That *is* insulting, Sandra." David drew himself up.

"I'm sorry." She retracted her words immediately. "I am a bit fraught, actually."

"You're very fraught," he said with cool disdain, "for such a skilled businesswoman. I would have thought you'd react very calmly in a crisis like this."

"Like you, with golf on my mind?"

"If you use that insulting phrase again I really shall be glad if you summon your helicopter and get the hell out of here, Sandra."

"But without you?"

"I shall decide what to do for the best, and when I have decided, act on it. Not react with schoolgirl antics, like you."

"And when will that be, David?"

David stared fixedly at the fax machine which was now transmitting a stream of data. "Maybe in a day. Maybe more." He put a hand on her arm and, to his surprise, found she was trembling. *"Please* stay here with me, darling. Don't spoil this most wonderful idyll. Today you said it was the best time of your life."

"It is. It was."

Sandra suddenly leaned her head on his chest, but he did not take her in his arms, remaining still and impassive.

She felt that she had gone too far. It was the thing she dreaded: the Michel situation repeating itself all over again.

18

Zac seemed entirely confident and in command of himself and the bank of which he was president. He sat behind his large desk waving a gold pencil about as though to emphasize this point or that, to deny or confirm. Never for a moment did he appear to waver.

He had arrived at his office in the Avenue de l'Opéra to find that Sandra and David had reached Paris overnight and were already waiting to see him, looking very tanned and fit from their holiday. By contrast Zac's eyes were bloodshot as though he had had little sleep.

This in effect was true. He had spent half the night arguing with the Tellier brothers about how they were going to get him out of the jam they had got him into.

Not a trace of this showed on his face as he parried questions from his interlocutors.

They wanted to know why he had not consulted David Heurtey, the head of the organization. Zac managed to evade a straight answer, however many times it was repeated. Sandra left most of the talking to David, sitting behind him so that she could observe Zac. She was quite sure he was lying: trying to pull himself out of the biggest gaffe in his life.

"The essence of a venture like this is secrecy," Zac insisted at last in a partial answer to David's repeated question. "I judged that, as president of the Banque Franco-Belges, I had the power to back a takeover which was initiated by the Tellier brothers. Had it succeeded it would have been considered a brilliant coup."

"But it did not succeed," David said. "Nor will it."

For the first time Zac appeared to falter and carefully examined his nails.

"That is sheer bad luck," he said. "I didn't realize that Cassini shares would rally so strongly."

"Yours are now on the decline," Sandra intervened from the back of the room. "They face suspension on the Bourse and a full legal inquiry."

"I don't see what business this is of *yours,* Sandra," Zac said rudely, "or, even, why you are here."

"I'm here because I've every right to be here," she replied. "Desmond is an important shareholder in the bank."

"More likely to hold David Heurtey's hand," Zac sneered. "It is no secret what you two have been up to."

David's dark skin reddened, and he looked as though he were about to rise and take Zac by the throat. Sandra put out a restraining arm.

"David is new to the sort of ploys you get up to, Zac . . ."

"I object to that, Sandra."

"Nevertheless, it is true. At this moment Heurtey shares are in a decline because of a takeover that, from the outset, was opportunistic and unlikely to succeed. That is the least that you will get away with. If any actual criminal offences were committed they will be revealed as the result of a thorough inquiry into the whole affair."

"My conscience is clear." Zac sat back and put his hands on his chest. "I confess that, perhaps, I should have consulted David Heurtey . . ."

"Should!" David's tone was explosive. "Christ Almighty, I am the president, man."

"On whose authority did you launch the bid?" Sandra interjected.

"On my own. I judged we had sufficient resources to back it. My accountants had been very carefully into the whole position."

"To me it stinks to high heaven," Sandra said, "and you will be very fortunate if you don't lose your job." She stood up and pointed a finger at him. "If you do, Zac, you're finished. Completely and utterly finished. You will never be allowed to have any position in a company again."

"Joanne Pasarro will go over the books very carefully with accountants appointed by me." David Heurtey also stood up. "In the meantime I am suspending you as the president of Franco-Belges . . ."

Zac flew out of his chair. "But you can't do that."

"I can and I am. Frankly I don't care if you never work again. You have made my entire European organization look ridiculous. You have wiped hundreds of millions of francs off our shares. My brother might well summon the American Board and recall *me.* In the end, Zac, I am responsible. Not you."

Sandra listened approvingly. To her this was an eye-opener, and a welcome one. David was asserting his authority, taking charge. There was one thing, though, on which she disagreed, and hesitantly she voiced it.

"David, if I may say one thing . . . it is this." He turned to her and she could see the tension in his face.

She suffered for him now because she was involved with him: the two of them had become one. "I don't think Zac should be suspended."

"But he can't go on ruining my company."

"You, we, must present a united front to the world. It is the only way of saving face. There will be a press conference later today and what you say really *will* determine the future of Heurtey in Europe. I am afraid that you must say you backed Zac, that you knew about this deal. If you don't you may well lose the support of institutions and once they start selling your shares there will be a landslide. The financial authorities will step in and suspend your shares. That will be fatal and invite a full inquiry. It will be the end of Heurtey, of the bank, an explosive situation. I will intervene to support Heurtey and you must get your American company to do the same; but you must call off the deal. With any luck, between us we can save the situation. If you suspend Zac all the world will know that he went ahead on his own and the result will be a disaster."

Sandra sat in front of the television watching the confident way David and Zac, earlier in the day, had faced the cameras and the newsmen from the world's financial press. Despite his poor briefing David had proved himself a skilled operator. Zac said very little.

"Why was Mr. Heurtey out of the country at such an important time?"

"We had every confidence in Monsieur Desmond." David had turned to Zac with a smile. "As it is we made a miscalculation. This is what we shall have to look into: why it happened, and make sure it doesn't happen again. I assure you that we have sufficient funds to continue trading."

"Why did Heurtey shares rise so much in the weeks before the bid? Could there be a suspicion of insider dealing?"

"That's something we shall have to go into with the authorities," David had replied smoothly. "And you can be quite sure that we will cooperate with them completely."

He then rose and brought the conference to an end while the press scuttled to the telephones. The picture faded and another item of news took its place.

"Meanwhile in England, the Prime Minister . . ."

Sandra pressed the remote control button and switched off. Louis, delighted to see his mother, sat on her knee clapping his hands. Sandra rested her chin on his head. "Oh, my baby. How I've missed you."

Mireille came in to take Louis to his bath and Sandra went with her, enjoying for the next hour the pleasures of motherhood: bathing her baby, dressing him for bed, playing with him and then, lovingly and tenderly, cuddling him again until she put him gently in his bed and stayed with him until his eyes closed.

She looked at her watch. It was nearly seven. Time to change. David was bringing Joanne to dinner and that too would be a tough meeting.

Sandra had gone to her apartment on the Île Saint-Louis where Louis had already been waiting for her, Mireille having been summoned from Reims by telephone. After the interview with Zac she and David had spent the day discussing tactics, with the press, and with the financial authorities who were already making inquiries. All this David, as head of the organization, would have to endure, whereas only one man was responsible.

In many ways Sandra blamed herself. She should have wondered why Heurtey shares were rising so strongly, paid more attention to them. She knew the financial stock market in France much better than David. She should have warned him. Instead she was thinking of her own pleasure, her own gratification.

She tiptoed out of Louis's room and found that Marie had already run her bath and put out the dress she had selected to wear for the evening.

She lay for a long time in her bath, luxuriating in the comfort of home. After all, even in a well-appointed villa like the one in Greece, there was nothing like it.

She took her time getting dressed, making herself up, and she knew that she was no longer doing it for some unspecified reason, such as looking nice or conforming to her image as a wealthy and successful businesswoman, a well-known personality: she was doing it for David.

David and Joanne arrived promptly at eight. As the butler let them in, Sandra went to the door to greet them. Her first thought was that Joanne looked very pale; even beneath her thickly applied makeup the tension showed.

"Hi!" Joanne, who wore a trouser suit in black lamé, casual

but elegant, took her hand. David kissed her on the cheek, briefly squeezing her hand.

"I saw the conference." Sandra invited them to sit on the long sofa overlooking the river—the sun was just sinking below the twin towers of Notre Dame—as the butler arrived with champagne.

"This is very thoughtful of you, Sandra," David said. "Much better than a restaurant where everyone would stare."

"I thought you handled it awfully well. Thank heaven Zac kept his mouth shut."

"It's only the tip of the iceberg." David looked glum. "The authorities are convinced that there has been criminal activity. Joanne agrees."

"I'm afraid so." Joanne nodded, her smile rather forced, as she accepted champagne. "I've spent all day on the books. Zac, or someone in his office, undoubtedly used similar methods to those used by Guinness in England in their bid to take over Distillers' company. A number of people and organizations were promised 'sweeteners' to up the price of Heurtey shares. A clear case of share-rigging if ever there was one. There are receipts for 'services rendered' but no notion of what these services were. Heurtey will be very lucky not to escape prosecution. Maybe"—Joanne stared uncomfortably at the floor—"as he has accepted responsibility, even David himself."

"It's as bad as that?" Sandra clicked her tongue and, sitting by David's side, took his hand. "Then in that case Zac will have to be exposed. He *will* have to go. He and the Telliers are the ones to face prosecution."

"You really think that, Sandra?" David's grip on her hand tightened.

"I really do. He must have his comeuppance. Even a spell in jail. I'm sorry to say he deserves it. It is the one thing that will teach Zac a lesson."

"The thing is"—Joanne spoke hesitantly as if she herself were on the defensive—"there are letters signed by David authorizing the payment of 'sweeteners.' "

"Encouraging and therefore incriminating letters offering 'substantial thanks'—you can read the meaning into the word 'substantial'—in exchange for help. Letters I swear I never saw before."

"Forgeries?" Sandra said.

"Brilliant ones." David nodded gloomily. "I would be hard put to prove I didn't sign them. All I do know is that I never saw the letters concerned before, or knew the slightest thing about the business involved. That I can swear on oath. But who will believe me?"

"It's worse than I thought." Sandra kept her eyes on David as he went over to the champagne bucket to freshen their glasses. "David," she asked, nodding her thanks as he poured the wine into her glass, "why don't we go on with the bid? Complete the takeover of Cassini? Combined we'd possibly scrape together the funds, and it would give us the biggest drinks empire in Europe."

"I don't think you could do it now," Joanne spoke softly, "otherwise you might be involved in the illegality that will be exposed. After this publicity Cassini would be bound to demand an investigation. If you ask me the best way is to declare the bid unconditional, and have it rejected by the Cassini shareholders, as it will be. You will by then have a bigger stake in Cassini and, maybe, when the dust is cleared you might think about it again, using a new and more honest approach. In the meantime whether or not you cover up the dishonesty . . . it's up to you."

"What would you do?" Sandra asked.

"I would hope that your tactics work, otherwise find a scapegoat. Pin it all on Zac."

All three were suffering from lack of sleep and yet the next day would be busy. Joanne was out in the hall getting her coat as David leaned toward Sandra.

"When?"

"Tomorrow night? You can come here."

"Can't I stay tonight?"

"I don't think Joanne should know too much. Besides . . ." The expression on Sandra's face hardened. "Joanne let you down, didn't she? I find it pretty unforgivable."

"How do you mean?"

"You sent her in to inspect the books. She's supposed to be a corporate investigator. This plot wasn't hatched overnight. To a trained eye it should have been apparent *weeks* ago. I'd have it out with her if I were you, David. She's muffed it."

David looked across the coffee table in his hotel suite and Joanne tilted her chin defensively toward him as if she knew what was coming.

"I'm not at all happy about your role in this, Joanne. You should have spotted it earlier."

"I know." Joanne sighed and put the papers she had on her lap on the table. "I've thought of nothing else."

"You look as though you're not sleeping either."

"Can't sleep a wink. I should have spotted it."

"Why didn't you, Joanne?" David's voice was unthreatening.

"I guess, David, I wasn't familiar enough with French financial practice. It's a weak excuse, but it's all I can offer."

"You mean financial practices differ from country to country?" David's tone was gently sarcastic.

"No, not that."

"Then what *is* your excuse?"

"I don't really have one, David." She threw out her arms in a gesture of helplessness. "My knowledge of the language wasn't good enough, either. I was trying to be too clever, I guess. I failed you."

"I'm having to let you go, Joanne."

"I realize that, David."

"I would like you to do what you can to help clear things up but, effectively, you're fired."

"Yes. It's what I expected." She stood up, her coffee remaining untouched. "OK, I'll admit I was misled, maybe made a hash of my job, let you down. But I'm not gifted with second sight,

David. I'm only an accountant, a policewoman. But one thing I do know, Zac Desmond is *not* a fool. He's a real crook and a clever one. I didn't want to say it in front of Sandra, because there are too many issues involved which are obscured by her relationship with the Desmonds. Whether you wish to tell her yourself or not is up to you. But one thing I do know: Zac Desmond is clever and unscrupulous. He boosted the Heurtey share price by massive illegal support schemes. He disguised losses on the foreign exchange which he charged below the line to reserves and which therefore didn't show up against the profits he claimed. If you ask me the bank's debts and liabilities far and away exceed its assets. Technically it is bust. The drain on *your* funds, therefore, is enormous. OK"—she shrugged—"I missed the signs; but don't underestimate Zac Desmond. Ever."

David sat for a few moments after she'd finished, chin in hand.

"I sure do have a big problem," he muttered.

"You sure do." She sat down again, leaning toward him. "But you have a big asset. You do have the advice of Sandra. She has a first-rate business brain and, perhaps, more importantly, she loves you. She will help you."

"Will she go on loving me if she sees how I let things go? What a fool I made of myself. It matters a lot to her."

"By sacking me you can blame me. And David . . . I will do all I can to clear up this muddle but, if at any time in the future there is anything else I can do for you to help put things right, please tell me or I shall have this on my conscience for the rest of my life."

David's expression changed and grew more alert.

"Joanne, there may be something you can do for me, if you're serious."

"Anything. You're the nicest guy, David, you trusted me and I let you down."

"Sandra wants to know who her father is. You must have read about the libel case in London which showed that her real mother was the film star Virginia Wingate. However, her paternity remains a complete mystery. Virginia *claims,* privately of course, that she had so many lovers that she can't remember. But Sandra is tormented by it. She yearns above everything else to know who her father is. It's a long shot, Joanne, but when you return to the States . . ."

"I will get on to it straightaway." Joanne had a catch in her voice. "Anything I can do to help you and Sandra, David, I will."

Zac had assembled the Board of the Banque Franco-Belges and also invited Sandra to attend. The last few days had been ones of furious activity during which the bid for Cassini was formally called off and it was clear that the fraud department wondered whether or not to investigate.

Zac had been busier than most, operating mainly from Tourville where he felt he had more secrecy. There he telephoned his contacts round the world, assuring them the shares would not lose their price if they remained firm and the sweeteners *would* be paid. If it came to an investigation, with so many countries involved it would be hard to know where to begin.

He looked like a man very much the worse for wear, but still in command of himself. He was pale, his eyes were permanently bloodshot and he even seemed to have lost weight dramatically. Yet as he began the proceedings for the special Board meeting his voice remained firm and the hand holding a sheaf of papers was steady.

"Madame Harcourt, gentlemen," he began, "I have called this extraordinary Board meeting because of the circumstances with which we have been faced in the past two weeks. We attempted a takeover of the Cassini drinks group, believing it was in the best interest of the company and its shareholders . . ."

"*You* attempted—" David began, pointing a finger at Zac, who turned politely to him.

"If you would be so kind as to let me continue, Mr. Heurtey, I think that you will find everything is explained to your entire satisfaction. I have not rested in my pursuit of the truth and now I believe I have discovered it." He cleared his throat and in a sonorous voice continued: "We made this bid on the understanding that our assets supported the share price . . ."

"But *how* did the shares rise?" Sandra intervened coolly.

"I will come to that also, Madame." With a flourish Zac held up the papers in his right hand. "I have not slept day or night while I wrestled with this mystery, this problem and, at last, I have discovered a plot to discredit the whole group and myself in particular." He looked at his secretary who was diligently taking the minutes and nodded. Silently she rose while the whole room seemed to hold its breath.

When she returned she was accompanied by a tall, thin man somewhere in his thirties with large, round glasses behind which his eyes blinked rapidly. His demeanor was one of terror and as Zac indicated he should sit down the man sank with relief into the only chair which remained vacant.

"May I present to you, Messieurs and Madame Harcourt, the villain of the piece." Zac again gestured, with a flourish of his hand, toward his hapless victim. "Hubert Jeantet, hitherto a most trusted employee, even a friend. He has worked for me for five years in the capacity of personal adviser. Some of you know him well and doubtless, like me, trusted him." Hubert gazed at the floor, pressing his spectacles up the bridge of his nose with a forefinger, apparently oblivious of Zac's withering gaze.

"When this debacle was apparent I wondered who of my acquaintances could be guilty of such deception, such wickedness, impelled by a desire to ruin me. I could think of no one." His eyes roamed round the table like those of a malevolent toad until they rested on the person of Antoine de Lasalle, son of the previous president of the bank, who was doodling idly on a pad in front of him.

"Monsieur de Lasalle," Zac thundered, "I see you are not even paying attention, sir, and yet *you* have been exposed as the one behind this heinous crime . . ."

"Me . . . what . . ." Antoine de Lasalle spluttered. "What *are* you talking about, Zac?"

"I imagine you felt you were safe, didn't you, Antoine,

behind the shield of this poor man whom you have used for your own evil ends . . ."

"I haven't the slightest idea . . ." De Lasalle looked round with bewilderment at his fellow directors but saw only glimmers of suspicion in their eyes . . .

"No use denying it, de Lasalle." Zac, beating time on the table like a metronome, continued, "I *myself* have spent *hours* investigating the matter and when it occurred to me that the culprit *must* be Jeantet, my right hand, and I confronted him with the evidence he broke down. He confessed."

"Confessed what?" de Lasalle burst out.

"That you have never forgiven me for being responsible for having your father Philippe ousted as president of the bank and taking his place. That, for years, you, with him behind you, have worked to undermine my position and plotted, when the time was ripe, my downfall. This seemed an ideal opportunity."

"What did?" To those watching, de Lasalle was either a superb actor or a man in the grip of a genuine nightmare.

"Jeantet told you of our desire to take over Cassini . . ."

"He told me no such thing . . ."

"Please don't interrupt because I shall introduce evidence to corroborate this," Zac said sharply. "Jeantet, with your connivance, set about devising a set of completely false figures which disguised losses and boosted overseas assets. In fact we could not *afford* to commence a takeover bid, and I was as much misled as anyone." Zac once more emphasized his point with his fist and leaned menacingly toward Jeantet, who had never once raised his head all the time Zac was speaking.

"Now, Jeantet, am I speaking the truth or not?"

Slowly Jeantet raised his head and looked straight at Zac.

"Yes, Monsieur Desmond . . ."

"I absolutely deny . . ." de Lasalle rose to his feet.

"Sit down, please," Zac barked sharply. "You not only cooked the books, Jeantet, juggled the figures, but forged Monsieur Heurtey's signature, making us think he had agreed to the bid when he hadn't."

"Yes, Monsieur Zac . . ."

Zac threw a paper toward him which clearly was in the form of a letter.

"That letter, purporting to be from David Heurtey, was not in fact signed by him but by you. True or false?"

"True, Monsieur Desmond . . ."

"And, in return, you were told that you would be made a director when I was exposed and Antoine de Lasalle took my place."

"Yes, Monsieur Desmond."

"You would swear to that, Jeantet?"

"Yes, sir."

"There!" Like a prizefighter who had just knocked out his adversary in the ring, Zac looked triumphantly round. "I think that I am completely exonerated. I have unmasked the villains and saved the reputation of this company. I think I should be congratulated on my detective work where so many others"—he looked meaningfully at Sandra—"have failed. However," he said, after a pause during which he rapidly turned over several pages of documents, "I am proposing that, as happened with his father—like father like son"—he gave a hapless shrug—"and in order to keep the confidence of the public in the Heurtey Corporation but, particularly, in this bank which could lose millions of francs and make many small companies and people bankrupt, we should not prosecute if Antoine de Lasalle and Hubert Jeantet agree to sign a document of culpability which I have had drawn up. Obviously if the authorities persist, then we cannot save them. But, meanwhile, we should do our best. In exchange of course de Lasalle will resign immediately and Hubert Jeantet will be dismissed without any compensation or the slightest possibility—given the references *I* shall provide him with—of finding another responsible job."

David could tell her mind was not on making love. He wanted her so badly, but she was stiff and unresponsive. Her kisses lacked passion, her body didn't yield or open for him.

Finally, in frustration, he abandoned the attempt and flopped on his side.

"Sorry," Sandra said.

"Can't you take your mind off business?"

"No." Sandra lay for a moment gazing at the ceiling. Then she turned her eyes to David. "I'm sorry, darling, I can't. It's a thing men can do, but women don't seem to be able to do."

"I thought love was supposed to relax us both," David grumbled, taking a cigarette out of the packet by his bedside and lighting it. "Why are you so tense and angry?"

"Because I *know* Zac is guilty."

"But, darling, Jeantet confessed. The document is pages long."

"I recognize the mastery, the hand of Zac. I recognize *all* the signs: the forced anger, the production of the stooge, the recriminations. It was exactly like this with the *tirage* where he blamed his then personal assistant Strega and another hapless underling called Pagés. It was an exact rerun."

"But what about Jeantet's confession?"

"Pagés was hauled before the Board and confessed in exactly the same way. However, this time Zac just may have bitten off more than he can chew because de Lasalle is consulting his lawyers. I don't think he'll let it rest."

"Why did his father resign?"

"There was a suspicion of insider dealing in Desmond shares. De Lasalle knew about a prospective deal to sell our fighters. He denied complicity but, like an honest man, he immediately resigned. Zac then did a fast one and had himself made president of the bank. I was engaged in trying to take over Heurtey in the US at the time, and my attention was deflected."

"Did you think Philippe was guilty?"

"Of being foolish, yes, but I don't think his son is guilty at all. He looked absolutely amazed by every word that Zac uttered. I have never for a moment thought him dishonest. Ambitious, yes, but not dishonest."

"Then he will cause a terrible fuss. We shall have to see what happens." David ground out his cigarette. Like Sandra, his own sexual desire had diminished.

"He may not, after consulting with his father. He may think it better just to resign quietly unless, of course, there is an official investigation. Then the pot will come to the boil and the lid will blow off completely. We must just hope"—Sandra glanced at him and put her hand out for his—"and pray. Do you know any prayers, David, because if you do this is the time to say them. For Zac, a man dispossessed of his rightful inheritance, will do everything he possibly can, by fair means or foul, to regain it."

"Monsieur Desmond, sir," David's secretary announced and David returned to his chair.

"Show him in."

A week had passed since the Board meeting and Joanne, having completed her investigations, was even now on her way back to New York. The financial authorities were showing some interest of a perfunctory kind, but there was a hope that Heurtey and its bank might survive the crisis. Zac Desmond was not liked, but he had friends in high places, one or two who owed him favors. Zac always liked to have something in reserve, and had got one or two highly placed Treasury officials out of tight spots. In return they had promised, if they could, to return the favor one day.

Zac now strode confidently into David's suite in the Ritz, as if he owned the hotel, and did not attempt to shake hands.

"Yes, Heurtey?" he barked. "What is it? I'm a very busy man."

"Monsieur Desmond, please sit down." David gestured politely toward the chair opposite him. "Forgive my informal way of doing business."

"Very informal, if I may say so." Zac glanced disapprovingly round him. "Most inefficient. No wonder you didn't know what was going on."

"Monsieur Desmond." David, apparently unruffled, leaned back in his chair and lit a small cheroot at which he puffed away for some time as if he was thinking seriously. He was dressed casually and his golf bag was prominent in a corner by the door. "Monsieur Desmond, *I* didn't know what was going on; but I've gotten a pretty damned good idea now. Joanne Pasarro might have missed a few tricks when she first looked into your affairs, but she has made up for them." David slapped a thick volume on the table in front of him. "*This* is her report and I have been up almost all night reading it."

"And if we ask her to substantiate it I believe she is halfway across the Atlantic," Zac said smugly. "Dismissed, by all accounts."

"Your intelligence is, as usual, excellent." David smiled briefly. "How and when you get it all so quickly and so accurately we shall one day doubtless discover. But, in the meantime, let me tell you this." He took up the heavy volume, shook it at Zac and then flung it on the table again. "There is no doubt of your culpability, your guilt. It was *you* who acted with Jeantet, not de Lasalle."

"That you will find hard to prove," Zac said with a smirk.

"We might find it hard to prove but we know it."

"We?" Zac looked mildly amused. " 'We' includes your whore, I suppose."

David rose to his feet with alacrity and leaned menacingly over the man opposite him.

"Don't you dare refer to Madame Harcourt like that. I tell you, Desmond, if you can play dirty I can too and if Sandra's honor is impugned I wouldn't hesitate."

"Honor!" Zac said with a titter. "What a quaint expression in so far as it concerns *her.* All right, all right," he added quickly, as David reached out to shake him by his lapels. "I'm sorry. I apologize. But, frankly, whenever I come across *any* skulduggery, any double-dealing, there is Sandra somewhere in the background. She spends her time causing mischief as far as I'm concerned whenever she has the opportunity. She may bamboozle *you,* but she doesn't bamboozle me."

"She doesn't bamboozle *anybody,*" David said thickly. "She

is a highly intelligent, most honorable woman. She knows things intuitively that it takes others weeks to find out. She told me about the affair of the *tirage* and Paul Strega. She told me about the insider dealing scandal in Desmond shares at the time of the sale of the aircraft and how you framed Philippe de Lasalle. She recognizes your hand, Monsieur Desmond, and, what's more, I can tell you I believe *her.*" His hand landed on Joanne's document again. "Every word that Joanne Pasarro has written involves you. It is dynamite. An eminent graphologist confirms that the signature cannot be mine. You want I should call him in court? You want I summon Strega, Monsieur Pagés, Philippe de Lasalle, Hubert Jeantet and goodness knows how many others you've corrupted or involved in your attempts to unseat Sandra?"

"You wouldn't dare," Zac said. "Your own empire would collapse."

"If it is necessary I would." David sat down again and, crossing his legs, appeared far more relaxed than his adversary. "I am a wealthy man. I am not ambitious. I would rather play golf and sail round my Greek island. I could bring you to book, but I won't because, as you anticipated, the price would be too high. The scandal would be enormous and would damage not only our company, the bank and our lives, but the lives of thousands of small investors, as well as many employees."

Slowly, laconically, David rose to his feet and, hands in his pockets, confronted Zac.

"I serve warning to you, Desmond, that, from now on, you consult me about *every* move; do you hear, *every* move? You are a man with no real knowledge of business but who loves to make deals, the riskier the better. When we looked at the finances of the bank we found them in a parlous state. Probably, technically, it's bankrupt but Heurtey USA, with whom I am in close touch, will shore it up, and so will Desmond.

"We are doing what we can as honestly as possible so that we don't get smeared, tarred with your brush. But if there *is* an investigation we shan't hesitate to throw you to the wolves. Do you realize that, Desmond? Have I made myself clear?"

"Very clear," Zac said, without the slightest sign of repentance.

"In six months' time," David went on, "after the dust has cleared, I want you to resign, get the hell out of my organization and my life."

"And what am I supposed to do?"

"You can do what you like. I'm sure you're ingenious enough to think of something as long as it doesn't concern me, or people who are close to me."

"Like Sandra?"

"Like Sandra. However, I think she is firmly in control where the Desmond Group is concerned."

"I understand you, Monsieur Heurtey." Zac rose unhurriedly. In height he matched David and the two adversaries stood for a few moments glaring at each other.

"I don't think we like each other, Monsieur Heurtey," he said. "I don't think we ever did, and I hope our paths won't often cross. I accept your terms not because I admit guilt, but because I do have plans of my own, as it happens, and in six months' time"—Zac paused and a smile flitted over his taciturn features—"in six months' time they will just be about to ripen.

"Good day to you, sir. Good-bye."

Even before David's secretary had time to get to the door Zac had reached it, opened it and closed it firmly behind him.

19

Bob lay on his bed, arms, as usual, under his head, gazing at the white cracked ceiling with the solitary light bulb in the middle. It was a sight so familiar to him that it was like a map of some part of the world he traveled often. In fact the crack did resemble the path of the River Po as it made its way from the hills of Umbria to the sea.

Bob coughed and turned over in bed to reach the glass of water which, together with a spittoon, always stood by his bedside. Since he had been taken to the hills—he thought he was in Tuscany or Umbria—his health had improved but only marginally. He coughed incessantly and once or twice he had spat blood.

Soon after the first sign of blood he'd been removed from Rome in a closed van and driven for about eight hours, tossed around in the back, his feet and hands tied. His companions had once again been Niki and Luigi: Niki who said nothing and Luigi who smoked incessantly, which made him feel sick.

The destination had been a neglected villa in an olive grove halfway up a hill which could only be reached from the road by a rough uneven track.

There his guard had changed and there had been a couple of peasants who spoke a dialect he could not understand and who never communicated with him. Once they had brought a man who said he was a doctor, who sounded his chest and looked at his throat before he went away shaking his head, implying he could find nothing wrong. Bob had been quite sure he wasn't a doctor at all, and had been sent merely to pacify him.

But he continued to cough. He thought he had TB or cancer and he found it very hard to take his mind off his physical condition, which merely contributed to his emotional worries.

The hillside house was marginally better than the dungeon in the city. It had obviously once enjoyed the status of a country house, but its stone facade was cracked and crumbling; some of the shutters at the windows were broken beyond repair and the once elegant garden was derelict and overgrown with weeds.

An old couple lived in the house and cleaned, cooked and looked after him and his gaolers. He was never permitted to speak to them and would sometimes find them gazing curiously at him before scurrying out of sight. In the company of his guards, however, he was allowed to walk not only in the garden but also in the olive grove and he could see the blue sky and smell the fresh air.

One day he found a skinny cat washing itself outside the back door. He stooped and stroked it and, purring, it rubbed itself against his legs, walking back and forth, arching its back. The old woman who stood watching at the back door waved and pointed to the cat.

"Is it yours?" he asked in Italian, but she shrugged.

"What's its name?" he called.

"Tomas," she cried back.

"Tomas," Bob said, picking the cat up and cradling him to his chest. He took him up to his bedroom and played with him all day like a child with a new toy.

Tomas—whether he belonged to the old couple or not—had then become his companion. Bob would find him outside his door waiting to be let in, and then he'd lie on his bed or sit on Bob's table, watching him with his shrewd green eyes, and take pieces of food from his hand. It grew into a kind of love affair between the prisoner and the pet, who was cared for in a way he had probably never been cared for before: pampered, stroked and loved.

Bob saw now from his watch that it was six in the morning and, rising from his bed, he looked anxiously out of the window for a sign of Tomas. There he was as usual, sitting outside the back door in the sun washing himself until the old woman let him in.

Bob went downstairs and one of his guards, Alfredo, appeared immediately from his bedroom in his pajamas, his face pale and unshaved. His guards were so sloppy that Bob thought it would be quite easy to escape; only he had lost the willpower. Besides, he would miss Tomas and also, to be truthful, he doubted if he could find his way in his weakened state before they caught up with him.

Alfredo opened the door of the main room and Tomas came running in, rubbing himself up against Bob as he sat at the table having breakfast. Bob had the run of the house but was never allowed to go into the kitchen or converse directly with the couple. Both of his guards carried guns at their waists. Both drank a lot and spent most of their time playing cards. Benno, the other guard, liked practising his shooting out of doors, aiming at tin cans. The cooking was passable and Bob, who had lost a lot of weight in Rome, slowly began to regain it.

Bob gave Tomas some sardines left over from the antipasto they'd had the night before and then he took his coffee and the cat back to bed. He drank the coffee, thick and black without sugar, and he knew it did him no good at all; it made him nervous, gave him the shakes. But he needed it for the vital stimulation to keep alive.

He had no idea exactly which month it was except that it was summer, maybe August or September, and still very hot. He was sure that, had he stayed in Rome, he would have died.

Bob lay back on the bed and began studying the course of the River Po with Tomas on his chest, eyes half closed, purring deeply. Tomas was a tabby with a sleek coat and unusual markings. He could maybe have been a pedigree, an aristocratic cat, and he had been neutered. Bob wondered whether he really belonged to the couple or whether he was a stray who, before he came, they had given refuge to and looked after. Tomas talked quite a lot, muttering away as though he were telling Bob what he had got up to in the night, and Bob lay with his hand on the cat's back, stroking him, looking into his eyes.

"I love you, Tomas," he said, and Tomas half closed his eyes, a sure sign of understanding.

Sometimes Bob lay on the bed all morning, sometimes he stayed there all day. He knew it wasn't good for him but, despite Tomas, the loneliness and boredom were affecting his mind. He had an idea that he was dying and that he would probably never be released. Maybe he'd be buried in an unmarked grave on the hillside. Maybe Tomas would come and visit him. He clung to Tomas, believing that in his last days he had the affection of a living being, even if it was only a cat.

Today, however, Bob felt a little more lively. His view of the world was more positive and, instead of lying on the bed gazing at the ceiling, he rose at about noon, shaved and had a shower and put on a clean shirt and trousers. He knew Sandra never got his letters, or he was pretty sure she didn't, but he wrote them anyway in the form of a diary. Like her, he felt they were related, and he poured out his thoughts and feelings to her: his regret at his past life, the sense of hopelessness he had now because he was ill, his love for and dependence on Tomas, and his hopeless passion for Tara.

He was in the middle of one of these missives to Sandra when he heard a car coming up the narrow track through the olive trees from the road. He felt curious enough, as visitors were rare, to look out of the window. There he saw a very dusty Fiat saloon car bounding along at a great pace, causing even more dust to cover it so that it was almost impossible to tell what color it was: maybe gray, blue or black. It was driven with great purpose, so obviously knew its way and then, finally, it reached the courtyard in front of the villa and stopped. For a moment there was no movement, and then out of the doors on either side stepped Niki and Luigi, the latter with a freshly lit cigarette in his mouth.

Bob's first reaction was one of fear; of wanting to hide. He thought about the unmarked grave on the hill, of dying before his time. He had seen neither of them since he'd been brought there and how long ago that was he didn't know because he had no newspapers, no calendar. He was allowed to watch TV but never the news, as though it was the intention of his captors to cut him off from time. Why? Maybe so that he would be unable to account for it later.

Bob took the letter to Sandra and tucked it under his pillow. Tomas, in the middle of another wash, interrupted his ablutions to watch the proceedings with interest. Like all cats he was immensely curious.

A minute later Benno bawled up the stairs and moments later the door opened and Niki and Luigi appeared.

"Hi!" Luigi said, while, at the same time, Niki raised a hand and asked, in Italian, how his language study was progressing.

"Not bad," Bob said, also in Italian, and he introduced Tomas to them. Luigi ignored him, but Niki stroked him quite kindly as though he liked cats.

Even though it was a hot day Luigi had on an overcoat. He was a pale, sallow man who could have suffered from some form of ill health himself; his eyes were deeply sunk, his pallor unhealthy, his hair seemed lifeless. Maybe it was the incessant inhalation of smoke that seemed to kipper him, as a cigarette was never out of his mouth.

Luigi sat on the bed and jerked his head in the direction of the door.

"Get your things together, Bob," he said. "We're off."

"Off?" Bob's first reaction was of excitement and then the fear returned again. "Off where?"

"Just off," Luigi said. "Don't ask so many fucking questions."

"You mean I'm leaving here?" Bob looked at Niki but he was still stroking the cat.

"What about Tomas?" Bob said, going over to the table and enfolding the cat in his arms.

"You can't take the bloody cat," Luigi said unemotionally. "Don't be childish."

"But what will happen to him?"

Luigi looked amused at the thought of anyone being so concerned about an animal.

"I'll take the cat," Niki said.

"You'll do no such thing," Luigi replied. "Leave the fucking cat here and let's go."

"I don't want to leave Tomas," Bob said stubbornly, pressing the cat close to his chest, aware of a feeling of wanting to cry. "Don't you understand?"

Luigi put a finger to his temple and smiled insinuatingly at Niki as though to indicate that there was something wrong with Bob's head. "If you *don't* put that bloody animal down," he snarled, "I'll slit its throat and that's a promise. *Then* you can take him with you."

Luigi went impatiently toward the door.

"Look," Niki said sotto voce, "I like cats too. It will be all right; you can leave that to me."

Quickly he raised his head as Luigi turned and glared at him. "What are you talking about?"

"Nothing," Niki mumbled. "Coming right now."

Thankfully Bob put Tomas outside the door and he went back into the room, where he started to pack the few things he had. When he went downstairs the front door was already open and the four men stood in front of it talking in low tones. Of the woman and the man there was no sign. Tomas sat on the windowsill unconcernedly cleaning his face and ignored Bob as he stopped in front of him.

He gripped the handle of his suitcase and knew that he mustn't show emotion. He knew how much pleasure it would give Luigi to carry out his threat in front of him.

Nonchalantly he passed Tomas by and said to the men at the door: "I'm ready."

"About time," Luigi said. "Sure you haven't got that cat in your bag?"

"Sure," Bob said, gulping as Luigi looked around as if in half a mind to carry out his sadistic threat.

But Tomas was a cunning cat. Maybe sensing danger, he was suddenly nowhere to be seen.

The car set off down the dusty road, Niki and Luigi in front, Bob in the back. He didn't say good-bye to the old couple or his captors, who had shut the door as soon as the car started through the olive grove. Bob sat back, thinking of Tomas, what would happen to him, his heart racked by a sense of anguish and loss.

"Where are you taking me?" he asked.

"Shut up," Luigi commanded and lit a cigarette, the first of many he would smoke on the journey.

They drove all that afternoon and well into the night, stopping only once for a meal at a café on the edge of a town Bob thought might be Orvieto. He seemed to recognize it from its position on a hill but, otherwise, he was given no clue. They ate mostly in silence with Luigi and Niki concentrating on their food, or speaking rapidly in Italian, too fast for Bob to understand.

In his judgment he thought that, were he going to be killed, they would have done it by now. At about ten they were approaching the outskirts of a city which, by the way it lit up the sky, and from the distance they had traveled, could only be Rome.

Bob gazed about him with some astonishment as they entered the city, driving openly along the broad streets until they came to the Via Veneto with its brightly lit shops, restaurants and cafés. Abruptly Niki pulled into a side street and they stopped.

"Get out," Luigi said without looking round.

Niki then jumped out of the driving seat and opened the door. Now, Bob thought with a sense of despair, they would put the bullet in his head and leave him in this dark alley, the way Aldo Moro had been left in the back of a car.

But by the time he emerged clutching his suitcase Luigi had also got out and was standing lighting a cigarette.

"Give me five minutes," he said to Niki who got back into the car, then took Bob roughly by the arm. "Come," he said and led him back onto the brightly lit thoroughfare where Bob, as if wondering if he should make a run for it, started forward.

"Don't be a *fool,"* Luigi said, pulling him back. "I'm taking you to freedom. You're being released."

"You're not kidding?" Bob stopped.

"Not kidding." Luigi pushed him ahead, nodding to the doorman at the Hotel Excelsior, and let him go as they went into the lobby where he looked around.

After a moment or two a tall, thickset, familiar figure rose and, hand outstretched, came over to them.

"Bob," he said with a smile, "welcome to civilization."

Bob gasped, shaking his hand, and spluttered: "Can . . . how?"

"It will all be explained, Bob," Zac said jovially, pumping his hand. Yet, when Bob looked round for his companion, Luigi, like Tomas the cat, had wisely disappeared.

Sandra, sitting at the window of her lounge with its view of the floodlit cathedral of Notre Dame, the *bateaux mouches* plying up and down, was working late. Sometimes she stayed at the office, and sometimes she took work home. When she wasn't seeing David, entertaining or being entertained, she enjoyed an evening by herself watching a little television but, usually, including some work as well. In the course of the evening she would call Mireille to see how Louis was, at home in Reims where she preferred him to be.

David was in Spain playing golf. Sandra despaired a little about David. Even after the crisis with Zac he was still happy to leave things to underlings. She personally liked to have her hands on the reins of every aspect of her business. David liked to delegate; Sandra did not. David liked to play. Sandra found it difficult even to relax.

When they were together everything was perfect, but when

they were apart the things about David that irritated her seemed exaggerated.

It was true that the storm created by the abortive takeover bid for Cassini had quickly died down once Sandra emerged as a supporter of Heurtey shares. But the offer price of Heurtey never compared with the asset backing of Cassini. That, and the vigorous opposition of the directors of Cassini, was enough to scupper the deal.

Questions were asked, eyebrows raised. Maybe there would be a few insinuations about the legality of the bid, but it was nothing to the storm that would have followed had the bid been successful. The notorious Guinness affair in England would have looked quite tame in comparison.

David had had a narrow squeak and that he had survived it with his company and integrity intact was, in no small measure, due to Sandra.

Yet had he appreciated it? Had he really known what sort of danger she and he had been in? She doubted it. David was one of those people cushioned from birth by comfort, always having someone to take care of them, who never seemed to envisage that things could go seriously wrong.

He was one of life's optimists. She was one of life's fighters, who never took anything for granted.

It was a very big difference.

She heard the doorbell ring and, looking at her watch, saw that it was well after midnight. She didn't like nighttime calls unless they were from David, and he had only phoned her hours before from his hotel outside Madrid. There would be no surprises there.

After the affair of the ear her butler was warned to take care at night and to detain anyone who delivered parcels or packages of any kind. There was also a security guard downstairs. The fact that he had admitted someone must have meant that all was well. Still Sandra couldn't help remembering the incident with the ear and, as she went toward the door, involuntarily she suppressed a shudder.

She heard the front door open and her butler give an exclamation—an unusual reaction on the part of that perfectly trained man. But it was a cry of pleasure rather than fear. There were sounds of hushed voices and, unable to contain her impatience, she opened the door of the salon and looked into the face of Zac, which was wreathed in smiles.

Sandra's eyes, however, only rested for a moment on Zac until they became riveted on the person who stood behind him. Tired, ill-looking, disheveled, but, undoubtedly, Bob.

Now the dawn was brushing the Parisian sky and Sandra had never left Bob's side.

She sat with her arm around him on the sofa. Of course there had been the inevitable opening of a bottle of champagne. Zac had explained that the negotiations for Bob's release had been very complex. They had begun some weeks ago and he had not dared to speak of it to Sandra, because one of the conditions was that there should be no police.

"I knew you were already in contact with the police," Zac had said accusingly. "This put Bob's life in grave danger.

"It was all due to Falconetti," he went on to explain. "He got wind of Bob's whereabouts through a contact, and it seemed that the kidnappers were getting a little tired anyway of holding on to Bob. The ear was a senseless trick and they wanted money."

For a while, Zac continued dramatically, Bob's fate literally hung in the balance, and his captors didn't know whether to release him or kill him. Sandra at one time had buried her face in her hands while Bob had watched Zac in a kind of fascinated way as though mesmerized by him.

Finally Sandra said, "I don't know how to thank you, Zac." She took hold of Bob's hand and squeezed it. Bob, looking very tired, leaned his head against her shoulder.

Zac gazed at them for a few moments and then rose. He too felt very tired, having had his plane on standby to fly to Paris as soon as Bob appeared. The car had whisked them from the lobby of the Excelsior straight to the airport.

"You can thank me by trying to understand me, Sandra." His tone was demonstrably sad. "You've never trusted me or even attempted to like me. I know why and, maybe, I've responded harshly. You accused me time and time again of plotting, yet here I am restoring your brother to you."

Sandra, for once at a loss, gazed at the floor. "I don't know what to say, Zac."

Relishing her weakness, Zac hurried on.

"You and Heurtey have done nothing but vilify me and all the time, despite the insults and accusations, I was looking for your brother, stealthily playing the Camorra at their own game."

"Then Bob *was* held by the Camorra?"

"Oh yes." Zac seemed surprised. "Who else?"

"Joanne said he wasn't. She said none of the big gangs would have sent a false ear, but the real one. She thought it was the work of amateurs."

"That woman was too clever for her own good." Zac's tone was bitter. "She was also dishonest, falsifying the report against me in the Cassini fiasco. She failed *completely* to detect the culpability of Jeantet and de Lasalle. Moreover she told lies, time and time again. If *anyone* should be investigated it is that American bitch who wished me nothing but harm."

Sandra bit her lip.

"Again I don't know what to say," she murmured. "You've caught me with my defenses right down, Zac."

"Your conversation is always conducted in terms of war, Sandra." Sensing victory, Zac pressed home his point. "I wonder if you realize this? Maybe it's instinctive with you. You never gave *me* any credit for genuinely trying to enhance the image of Heurtey with the bid for Cassini."

"I supported the shares."

"But only after you shot me down. Only on condition the bid was dropped."

"Zac." Sandra removed her arm from around Bob's shoulders.

He was half asleep and she wondered if he had been drugged. She got slowly to her feet and faced Zac.

"Zac," she said, "*please* don't let's confuse two things: business and the issue of Bob's release. I can't tell you how grateful I am and what it means to me; but the Cassini deal and its wisdom has nothing to do with this. There you were in the wrong. Here you are not, and I shall always be grateful to you. Believe me, I will never forget it and I *will* do all I can to repair the damage to our personal relationship."

"You're always saying that, Sandra." Zac sounded petulant.

"This time I mean it. As long as *you* play straight too. Play straight, Zac, not on my emotions, my joy at seeing Bob again."

"You must come to Tourville this weekend." Zac's tone changed again. "Mother will be overjoyed to see Bob. It will be like a family reunion." He looked into Sandra's eyes and smiled. Then, almost in a whisper, he added, "The money we can deal with another time."

"Money?" Sandra's eyes opened wide.

"It was costly, I'm afraid." Zac shrugged regretfully. "Very costly, as you can imagine. Of course you get nothing from the Camorra cheaply. No favors, thank you. But I'm sure you will be relieved that it's not as much as you were first asked for."

"How much?" Sandra asked, aware of the accelerating pace of her heart.

"A mere five million pounds sterling." Zac let out a little hiss as he spoke. "In used notes. I have given the Camorra my word."

Then he went up to her and looked into her eyes with an apologetic little smile before bending down and kissing her lightly on the cheek.

It seemed like the kiss of Judas.

In the bar in which they habitually met, the proprietor was becoming used to these scenes. He was not an imaginative man, nor an especially curious one but, as he stood watching them argue, the woman sometimes seeming on the brink of tears, the man occasionally lifting a hand threateningly as if he were going to strike her, he would wonder casually exactly what the setup was.

He suspected, naturally, that they were illicit lovers; that both were married and they argued over who should tell whose spouse first, what the consequences would be of divorce. Maybe the man was reluctant and the woman persistent. Maybe she was unmarried and wanted to have a child before it was too late.

Maybe . . . yes, here they were at it again: the woman white-faced, her hands clenching and unclenching in her lap; the man, well, he was an aggressive, nasty-looking piece of work. But some women liked that. The barman turned and began stacking his glasses on the shelves.

It never occurred to him that they were criminals.

"You said *riches!*" Eva hissed over the table at Strega who lifted his beer to his mouth. After he'd drunk there was a thin film of foam on his upper lip like a white moustache which made him look even more evil than he was.

How she hated Strega. What a fool she'd been ever to trust him.

"It didn't quite come off as expected," Strega said, putting down his glass and, aware of Eva's contemptuous gaze, wiped the froth off his lips with the back of his hand. "You don't know what a mean-minded, vicious sod Monsieur Zac can be. Well, I did pay you *something* in advance."

"Fifty thousand francs!" Eva snapped. "That is peanuts for the job I did. The risks involved."

"But, it *was* in advance," Strega said slyly, "as I promised."

"*And* the rest later," she said. "You promised me a fortune. A cool million *dollars* you said, Mr. Strega, not francs, that we could divide between us."

Strega began to pick his teeth with the plastic toothpick he fished out of his trouser pocket, a characteristic gesture of his when he was agitated, one she knew well. He had jagged, uneven teeth, yet curiously white with a high polish. Every physical detail about him nauseated her.

"That *was* a bit of an exaggeration," he said with a deprecating smile. "I said I *thought* it might amount to a cool million dollars. Well, frankly, Eva, it didn't. Monsieur Zac is no fool, I can tell you that. He made sure the interest *and* the capital sum was paid in full straight over to him."

Eva agitatedly snatched her handbag from the table and, rising, leaned threateningly toward Strega.

The barman, polishing a new set of glasses, watched wryly. It was a familiar scene. There they went again. One day he wouldn't wonder if she really hit him.

"You've given me *fifty* thousand. You offer me fifty thousand more. One hundred thousand miserable francs after all that I've been through . . . all the anxiety, suffering and *horror.* You think I'm going to be satisfied with *that,* Mr. Strega?"

As she raised her bag to hit him Strega, quick on his feet, caught her arm in midair. Then conscious, not only of the interest of the barman, but of those who sat at the tables around them, he lowered her arm with a vice-like grip and pulled her down onto her chair.

"Now, look," he hissed, *"everyone* is looking at us. Sit down and shut up. I don't want to see you again, do you hear? And I don't want to *hear* from you either. As for Monsieur Zac, if you *dare* go near him he will deny knowledge of anything you're talking about. So if you're tempted by *that* idea, forget it. He'd probably have you thrown into prison for impersonating Madame Harcourt. He has got you, and he has got me, incidentally, in a very tight situation, Eva, and I've been fooled by him as much as you. Look." He put a hand into his pocket and pulled out a grubby envelope. "Here's the money. It's the best I can do. And that really *is* the payoff. You're lucky, incidentally, you didn't go to prison for embezzlement. Don't press your luck or you still may."

Eva snatched the envelope from him and, without inspecting the contents, shoved it into her handbag. Then she snapped it shut and rose, still aware of the pain he'd inflicted on her arm.

"Don't think you've heard the last of me, Mr. Strega. Don't think I'll take this betrayal and humiliation lying down. And as for Monsieur Zac . . . he need never imagine *he's* immune . . ."

"I tell you he is, you silly bitch." Strega leaned toward her and spoke so softly he hardly appeared to move his lips. "You'll never get the better of Monsieur Zac, and you'll never *ever* get the better of me. One more peep out of you and I'll slit your throat from ear to ear. I'd do it with pleasure, just as someone did to poor old Romanetto."

He sat back with an uneasy smile as Eva half walked, half ran out of the bar, watched, once again, by the bemused barman.

But this time Strega knew he'd never see her again.

Strega drove home from Paris that night in an unusually thoughtful mood. He couldn't entirely disregard the menace that Eva presented to his plans. An angry woman bent on revenge, with nothing to lose, could be dangerous. He had swindled her and he had blamed Zac. If Zac ever found out the truth there *would* be a knife in his back, that was for sure, and no questions asked. He knew how adept his master was at laying the blame on other people. Eva had only to go and see him and spill the beans for Zac to realize that Strega had not paid him back all that had been collected. He had not repaid the interest and, from that transaction alone, was himself now a wealthy man. His appropriation of Romanetto's money, and all his other criminal activities, combined to make him a remarkably wealthy one.

Time to quit, Strega decided, by the time he parked his car by the side of his shuttered house, tranquilly bathed in the light of the moon.

And all that night lights burned from Strega's house, unseen by the villagers who were fast asleep by then. When most of them got up around dawn they thought Monsieur Strega had also risen early, unusually for him.

At about seven Strega started loading his cases into the boot of his car. Then he made coffee, went carefully round the house again and, when he judged the travel agency would be open, made a call.

A one-way ticket to Puntarenas. It would be ready for him by noon.

Strega left some money for his housekeeper and a note saying he was going away for an unspecified period. Then he put on his hat and had a last look round. He locked the door, put the keys into his pocket and backed out of the side passage, making a smart turn in front of the house as he drove away.

He was not a sentimental man but it had been a nice place and, in a way, he had been happy there. But now it was time to move on.

20

To people of Joanne Pasarro's age—late thirties—Virginia Wingate was a star whose light had blazed gloriously, but briefly, on the firmament in the 1950s. Then, just as quickly as it had risen, it declined again like a vanishing comet. But the legend remained. She remained a name. She became famous for declining parts which other hitherto lesser-known actresses went on to make successful.

When she was nineteen she had married a millionaire, Chauncy Parkes, and subsequently got a substantial amount of money from him in the divorce settlement.

It was said that Virginia Wingate hadn't needed to work; that she was lazy and, anyway, not a very good actress, though for her best-known film, *Meteor,* she had been nominated for an Oscar.

Although she had not quite her fame, like Garbo, Virginia enjoyed mystery. She never granted interviews or appeared on chat shows. She preferred the more exalted company of various United States presidents—visits to the White House were frequent—and she was always seen at charity premieres and, naturally, the Oscar ceremonies.

She had the kind of aura that people have who are famous for being famous, rather than for what they have achieved. Occasionally her films were seen on television, but for the last twenty years she had not acted at all.

The sudden notoriety, therefore, that came to her when she was revealed as the mother of Sandra O'Neill during the famous libel trial in London must have been traumatic. It did not show her, the legend, in a good light. She was pestered by newspapermen, then the media from all parts of the world.

Her answer was simply to vanish. Her Beverly Hills house was shut and she disappeared. No more seen at premieres or Oscar ceremonies, no more available even for invitations to the White House.

Thus an interview with Virginia Wingate was a scoop. Maybe the anonymity had grown tiresome and, like all stars, she secretly yearned to make a come back.

However, for American *Vogue* at last she had agreed to be interviewed. The first one she had given to the press since her days of fame.

Joanne Pasarro was not a journalist, nor had she ever worked for *Vogue;* but she had connections. It was agreed that if she could find Virginia Wingate, in the unlikely event that she would agree to an interview, she could do it. The interview would then be professionally written up by a staff writer to adapt it to the high standards of *Vogue.*

To Joanne it was an assignment that mattered very much. She was a complex woman who, despite an apparent sangfroid, was not happy with her life. Except that she had not her looks, she had some of the ability of Sandra. She was a hard worker, a stickler. She was clever. But she was not clever enough. Her humiliation in France had demoralized her, stuck in her craw. It was something she badly wanted to overcome.

For Joanne was not only impressed, but some would say obsessed, by Sandra. She had fascinated Joanne from the first day she had seen her: a legend in her lifetime, far more famous even than her mother. She had wanted to please Sandra even more than David Heurtey, her employer, and her failure had thus been doubly felt. She had fluffed it; she had got the sack. She had no wish to return either to the police force, accountancy or corporate investigation until, in some way, she had atoned for her lapse.

For she should have seen what Zac was up to. She should have detected some inaccuracies in the books, some whiff of the impending fraud. Yet she had not. Why? Had she been so blinded by her success; her position as the confidante of an important man like Heurtey? Had the suave charm of Zac pulled the wool over her eyes? Made it seem unlikely that a man as important as he was could possibly be a swindler? To this day she didn't know and she returned to the States frustrated and humiliated, but also determined to try and make up and, in her book, she knew that doing something for Sandra was tantamount to doing something for David.

So she achieved the impossible. She found Virginia Wingate, got her to agree to an interview, and now she sat studying the legendary star who, dressed in a shantung afternoon dress reminiscent of the fifties, her era, sat in an easy chair with a clearly spoilt pet poodle on her lap.

Virginia Wingate had a beautiful woman's reticence about her age and, although she could have passed for forty-five to fifty, she must have been at least sixty. Thus she would have been thirty when Sandra was born in such mysterious circumstances and smuggled away to be brought up as another woman's child.

But it was some time before Joanne dared broach the subject of Sandra. She had had to woo her subject, flatter her, convince her of her bona fide intentions. She concentrated at the beginning on the success of her films, particularly the first, *Meteor,* in which she had starred with Geoffrey Chance, another famous film star of the fifties, who was to die in a plane crash.

Joanne discovered that, far from being reclusive, Miss Wingate enjoyed talking about her past. She spoke well and fascinatingly about the studios in the fifties, when the star system was still at work and contracts dominated everyone's life.

It was then that Joanne, fearing that she might be shown the door, drew a deep breath and mentioned the unmentionable:

"May I ask, Miss Wingate, was that why you felt you had to keep the birth of your famous daughter so secret?"

Like the dive of a blazing comet Miss Wingate's smile vanished. She pursed her lips and her beautiful eyes smouldered. It was then that Joanne could see a faint likeness to Sandra, one that had hitherto eluded her. Because whereas Sandra was fair with blue eyes, Virginia Wingate was a brunette—or, apparently, had been—and a natural one with dark skin and limpid brown eyes. She probably dyed her hair now, but pigment didn't change.

In appearance then mother and daughter were unalike. Maybe this was a clue to the father?

"I only think it does you credit, Miss Wingate," Joanne assured her, "that is, that you went through with the pregnancy. It would have been very *easy* to have had an abortion. How brave of you not to. Imagine if the world had been deprived of the fabulous Sandra O'Neill?"

This flattery seemed to throw the star, who appeared uncertain what to do.

"I *did* say no awkward questions, Ms. Pasarro," she said, looking meaningfully at the clock on her mantelpiece.

"Miss Wingate," Joanne said earnestly, "greatly as your fans, of whom I am one, admire you, I don't simply want to do a whitewash job. You are a great woman, a great star; you did a bold, brave thing and your daughter is a credit to you."

"So they say." Miss Wingate looked vague.

"It's a long time since you've seen her?"

"Several years." Miss Wingate began to stroke her pooch who, his chin on his paws, stared soulfully, even a little reproachfully, at Joanne. "I used to see her when she lived in LA. She did not, of course, know I was her mother . . ."

"Did you ever feel *bad* about this?" Joanne gently, persuasively, tactfully, tried to draw her out.

"Oh, *very* bad." Miss Wingate's beautiful eyes widened. "Of *course* I did! I would love to have acknowledged Sandra; but it was always so difficult, never quite the right time, don't you know?" Putting her head on one side she pouted like a small child deprived of a sweetie. "The older Sandra got the more difficult it became and then, when she, too, suddenly became so famous . . . it was out of the question." Miss Wingate planted a tiny kiss on her poodle's pampered head. "Besides I was never very maternal, I'll be frank with you. Small babies and their messes were not for me." She grimaced with distaste. "Or little children running about the place and screaming. I knew Sandra was well looked after but, of course, when 'that woman' I employed abandoned her to go and live in France as the mistress of 'that man' I was *very* annoyed indeed. She had reneged on a promise. However . . ." Miss Wingate sighed dramatically. "Love is love, I suppose. I should know. I have done many foolish things in its name."

"Miss Wingate." Joanne shifted in her chair and inspected her tape recorder to make sure the cassette was still turning. "May I ask you a very bold question: was Georges Desmond Sandra's father?"

"Most certainly not!" Miss Wingate's eyes narrowed dangerously. "Do you think I would have an affair with the kind of man who, subsequently, would stoop to sleeping with my *secretary?* Absolutely not. Hélène O'Neill *was* my secretary, you know—a nice but menial person who had ambitions above her station. I should have realized that that was the sort of thing she would be unable to keep to herself. She betrayed me, made a fool of me on the world's stage." Miss Wingate seized the scruff of the neck of her nervous pooch and a spasm of rage seemed to pass through her body to the dog, making it tremble. "*She* alienated me forever from my daughter who could not forgive what had happened either. Can one blame her?"

"Are you sure?" Joanne looked searchingly at her.

"How do you mean 'am I sure'?" Miss Wingate, by now getting fidgety, kept on looking at the clock. Joanne knew that, having made the star uncomfortable, her time was running out and she would soon be shown the door. If that happened before she had obtained what she wanted to obtain the mission could be counted as a failure.

"Maybe Sandra *would* like to see you again. Has she contacted you?"

"That is not the kind of thing I want to discuss, Ms. Pasarro. I think now . . ."

"Just one last question, please, Miss Wingate." Joanne leaned forward, her hands tightly clutching the arms of her chair. "Could you tell me, *please,* in confidence, just who *was* Sandra's father?"

"No, my dear, I could not." Miss Wingate wagged an admonitory finger at her. *"That* is what the whole world would like to know."

"But *why?* Why won't you?"

"Maybe I don't know myself." Miss Wingate smiled enigmatically as she rang for her maid to show Joanne to the door.

Maybe she did not know herself! The idea was absurd, impossible. Miss Wingate may have had lovers, but she was a woman of taste if not discretion. Geoffrey Chance had certainly been one, but he had been killed three years before Sandra was born.

Joanne duly filed her story, sent a note of thanks to Miss Wingate, arranged for a photographer to take her picture; but she did not leave LA. She had been a detective, considered a good one, and this was one mystery she was determined to solve.

She began by re-reading everything she could about the star: her birth, her marriage, her training as a starlet in one of the major studios, when some very indifferent B movies were made and, finally, her selection for *Meteor,* costarring Geoffrey Chance and produced by Russell Ryan. She had been over all this ground before, but she went over it again.

Then had come *Fallen Angel* which was a success but not such a success as *Meteor.* By then Geoffrey Chance was dead and everyone said that Miss Wingate felt she would never find another leading man like him. From then on she started to turn down scripts.

Joanne spent days in the newspaper library and research archives of the film studio which now belonged to a Japanese corporation. However, its archives were still intact and slowly it dawned on Joanne that the one name which kept on recurring was Russell Ryan. Wingate's early work had been produced by Russell Ryan. His first big film was *Meteor* which made his name at the same time as hers. He also produced *Fallen Angel* and then, like her, he retired from the scene, developing a name for eccentricity because he kept on turning down projects just as she did. In many ways, it seemed, they were alike.

Joanne shifted her attention from Virginia Wingate to Russell Ryan and found him even more of a mystery. His name had not even been mentioned for over twenty years. Was *he* still alive? Yet, in his day, he had not only been a world-class movie producer but, already blessed with inherited wealth, he had made a fortune in real estate, buying up large chunks of California and Mexico and developing them.

Finally one day Joanne made a find which was to change her fortunes. In an obscure film magazine, which had long since ceased publication, she found a photograph of Virginia Wingate and Russell Ryan on holiday together. Over it was the banner: "The first furtive photograph" and, underneath the copy ran:

There has been speculation for some time that Russell Ryan the movie producer and Virginia Wingate, whom he made the star of Meteor, *have been more than good friends. However they have always strenuously denied this. Miss Wingate was believed to have been very much in love with Geoffrey Chance who was killed in a horrendous plane crash in Arizona. Mr. Ryan has also been married for twenty years to Melanie Baker, once a starlet from the same studio that produced Miss Wingate, but who never achieved her fame.*

When asked if she knew Miss Wingate and Mr. Ryan were on holiday together Mrs. Ryan dismissed the story by saying that they were seeking locations for a new film and were "just good friends."

Eagerly studying the picture, Joanne was inclined to disagree. The picture of them on some rocks, with a seascape in the background, made them look more than "just good friends."

They were in swimming costumes and, standing behind her, he had both arms tightly around her waist. They looked as though they had just been kissing, or were about to. They looked like a couple in love.

Joanne made a photocopy of the picture and caption and then, before she got too excited, she spent a further week trying to find more evidence of their involvement. She could not. There was also very little in the newspapers about Russell Ryan. His wife and he had eventually divorced, but ten years ago she had died and he had retired to Mexico, where he still had extensive property, to write his autobiography. But this had never appeared. He was still supposed to be a very rich man, but had gradually grown more reclusive and eccentric and never appeared in public. He had an only daughter who had died in an accident.

Joanne thought this a very interesting fact.

How had she died?

She turned to the obituary sections in the major American newspapers, and drew a complete blank. Her name had been Grace Ryan and she was about nineteen when she died, tragically, whatever the cause.

Once again Joanne was about to give up and, once again, chance came to her rescue. A Canadian paper gave her the lead she was looking for. Grace Ryan had died in Canada in a boating accident off Vancouver Island.

There, staring out from the pages, was a young woman, daughter of the producer and property magnate Russell Ryan and his wife Melanie Baker. Grace had been caught in a freak squall while on a boating trip with friends. The name of the friends and the circumstances of the accident were given. But it was not that that interested Joanne so much as the photograph of the dead girl.

She could have been looking at Sandra's sister, who must have been three years old when Sandra was born.

Later that day she sent a personal fax to Sandra:

Suggest your presence in LA essential. May possibly have found your father. Repeat only possibly. If interested please fax for further details and let me know travel plans. Regards to David. Joanne.

Sandra gazed with mounting emotion at the photocopy of the picture and article in the Canadian newspaper dated many years before, recounting the death of Russell Ryan's only daughter Grace. Not only, apparently, had it led to the breakup of his marriage, but his subsequent retreat into total seclusion on the coast of Mexico in the Gulf of Campeche, about fifty miles south of Veracruz. He had not been seen in public for at least ten years.

"If it's true," Sandra said with an air of wonder, "she'd be my sister." Sandra eyed Joanne, who sat on the other side of the table in her suite in the hotel in Veracruz. "My sister Grace, three years older than me." She paused for a moment to scrutinize the picture once again. *"If* 's true that could well be why he wanted to keep my existence a secret."

"But why would Virginia cooperate with him?" Joanne sat back and crossed her arms. "You'd think she'd feel spiteful, want to get her own back."

Sandra shook her head. "Too proud. Remember I know the woman."

"The woman." Joanne wondered whether Sandra ever thought of the film star by the tender name of "Mother." She thought not.

"Anyway, you fixed the visit." Sandra seemed reluctant to put down the photograph, continuing to gaze as though she were mesmerized at the dead girl she so resembled: blonde hair; fine aristocratic features; great, great beauty. "Seeing that he's such a recluse was it hard?"

"I approached his secretary," Joanne said. "I simply asked if he would receive the celebrated Madame Harcourt, formerly Sandra O'Neill."

"And that's all?"

"That's all."

Sandra gave a low whistle. She rose from the table and went

over to the cabinet to pour herself a cool soft drink. It was November and she hadn't been prepared for the humidity of Veracruz. In her many travels it was a city she'd never visited before, and Russell Ryan lived about an hour's drive down the coast toward the town of Alvarado.

Joanne stood up and followed her.

"I guessed it would tell us a lot. For instance, whether your name was enough to make Ryan wish to see you. Undoubtedly he's heard of you."

"It doesn't mean necessarily I'm his daughter. He might be intrigued to see *Forbes*'s most successful businesswoman in the world."

"I don't think success means so much to him," Joanne said. "I think he wants to see *you.*"

Sandra took another sip from her glass and returned to her chair by the table where all the newspapers and cuttings were spread out.

"You did a really wonderful job, Joanne. A fine piece of detection. We must pay you for all this."

"I wouldn't *hear* of it," Joanne said firmly. "I'm just repaying a debt."

"How do you mean?"

"I feel I let you down." Joanne avoided that inquisitorial stare. "You and David. David was a really swell guy and I let him down."

"You're talking about Zac?"

Joanne nodded. "I should have spotted he was up to something. I missed all the signs. I don't think I'll ever live down the shame I feel about the whole thing."

Sandra put her glass firmly on the table and, rising, went over to Joanne, standing behind her, hand on her arm.

"My dear, we have *all* done things we regret. I have done my share, believe me. I have made some huge mistakes since I took over Desmond, and never sufficiently getting the measure of Zac was one of them."

She squeezed Joanne's shoulder and returned to her chair, gladly flopping down in it again because of the heat.

"I still can't decide about Zac. Would you believe that? He went to *terrific* efforts to find Bob . . ."

"Again, I failed there . . ."

"But you didn't have Falconetti as a brother-in-law, and Falconetti is *heavily* indebted to Zac and God knows how many criminal concerns which supply him with heroin. That gave him the lead."

"You still don't think Zac had anything to do with it?"

Sandra gazed reflectively out of the window toward the sea. It was night and lights twinkled right around the bay. "Why should he? What did he have to gain?"

"Five million pounds, the money you paid out. Supposing he split *that* with Falconetti. Not bad, eh?"

"Zac doesn't need that kind of money. He's still a very rich man, whatever he says, whatever mistakes he's made. Well . . ." She gazed at Joanne in rather a helpless way. "I can only believe what he says. It's impossible to prove otherwise. Bob was there and all I know is what he told me. The men who held him were, and behaved like, gangsters."

"But I was *told* the Camorra were not involved," Joanne said firmly.

"Then I think you were told wrong." Sandra's voice was soft, but her tone firm. "Now if we're to make an early start we should go to bed. I'm absolutely whacked."

"Not too early." Joanne, also fully weary, got up. "The car will be here at nine thirty. We should be there by eleven . . . and then you'll know."

"Tomorrow I'll know," Sandra murmured almost to herself. "Or will I?"

The drive along the coastal road around the Gulf of Campeche was spectacular and almost took Sandra's mind off her ordeal, but not quite. Because it *was* an ordeal. She might or might not be meeting that mysterious man so vital in her life, whose identity she had sought for so long. She gazed out of the car window, trying to distract her mind with the beauty of the scenery, but it was difficult. There were so many things she wanted to know from Joanne.

"How did you find Virginia?" She made her tone sound as casual as she could.

"I found her very well. She's still an amazing-looking woman. She could pass for forty-five."

"Oh, any day," Sandra said casually. "She's looked like that ever since I've known her. I think she has her face stuck in a certain surgical mold which never changes."

Joanne threw back her head and laughed aloud. "Oh gee, you don't like her, do you?"

"I *hate* her." As Sandra turned her face toward her, Joanne saw an expression she had never seen before. It was primitive: violent, and curiously disturbing.

"I didn't know you could feel such passion," Joanne murmured.

"How would *you* feel about someone who pretended she was just a good friend of your mother when she *was* your mother?" Sandra demanded.

"I wouldn't like it. I'll confess."

"For all those years until I was a grown woman I always looked upon Virginia Wingate as my mother's employer, a kind of Lady Bountiful who kept an eye on us; on me and Bob. She rather treated us like that too: as though we were the kids of a servant. I never liked her then. I *hated* her when I found out who she really was." Sandra paused, aware of the emotions warring inside her. She tried to sound casual. "Did she . . . did she *ask* about me?"

"Truthfully, no." Instinctively Joanne put a hand on Sandra's, and was surprised that she didn't remove it. She knew then that what she felt for this woman was a kind of love, not just warm and innocent, but also compounded with desire. She knew this was why she'd done all the things she had for Sandra, and why she felt so humiliated that she'd failed her. She wanted Sandra's warmth and approval, if not her love. Having seen her with David she knew she couldn't have this.

She wondered what Sandra Harcourt would say if she knew a woman was in love with her. Maybe she already guessed. Such was her extraordinary allure to both men and women, perhaps she was used to it.

"Thanks for being so truthful," Sandra said, and gently withdrew her hand from under that of Joanne, who couldn't decide whether she was referring to her mother, or something more subtle about Joanne's particular feeling for her.

The driver was gesticulating toward the hills and then, on the cliff, they saw a house of spectacular proportions surrounded by a high wall from which there was a sheer drop into the waters of the gulf. Sandra exclaimed: "How do we get into *that?*"

"There's a route," the driver, who spoke English, replied, clearly excited himself and pointing to a map on the seat beside him.

"The secretary sent everything," Joanne added. "We have a gate number, password, the lot."

"We have a password?" Sandra looked impressed.

"Desmond," Joanne answered, with a smile. "The password is 'Desmond'."

But first they had to negotiate the narrow road into the hills, through which they arrived at a wall which proved to be an outer wall secured by a heavy, metal-studded wooden gate. Beside it there was a grille. It looked quite medieval, and Sandra imagined that Russell Ryan was influenced by his past on the fantasy sets of the Hollywood film studios.

When the car stopped Joanne got out, and from a notebook in her hand punched in some numbers by the side of the grille. A voice then asked her for the password.

"Desmond," she replied gravely and even before she had climbed back into the limousine the heavy gate swung slowly open to reveal what seemed like a tropical paradise. On either side of the drive there were exquisite blooms and exotic flowers all backed by the high wall. Ahead of them was another open gate, delicate trellis work made of wrought iron, through which it was at last possible to see the mansion that Ryan had turned into a fortress to protect him from the world.

The house owed something to the influence of Spanish architecture. It was built of white adobe; in some places it was turreted, in others gabled while, at one end, there was a curious edifice like a square Norman tower as though to repel invaders from the sea. The overall impression was of a folly built by an eccentric millionaire who would sit in it protected from the wind, from the gales that blew with occasional ferocity, maybe writing his autobiography, or perhaps ruminating with who knew what regret?

The drive ended in front of the house which appeared even larger than Tourville. At the side of the house a man stood watching them, but he made no attempt to move as the large main doors swung open and two other men came running down the steps, one carrying a mobile phone which he held to his ear.

By this time Sandra's chauffeur had got out of the car and was holding the door open for Sandra, who stepped out first. One of the men came toward her while the other hung back, looking toward his colleague who still stood impassively at the corner. It seemed that, at some signal from him, maybe from an electronic gadget held in his hand, the great wrought-iron gate swung shut.

"Madame Harcourt," the first man said to Sandra, "I am Olivier Dunkel, Mr. Ryan's secretary."

"How do you do, Mr. Dunkel." Sandra turned as Joanne stepped out behind her. "This is Joanne Pasarro who has arranged the meeting."

Dunkel, a vaguely cosmopolitan character who spoke perfect English with an American accent, shook hands and, with a flick of his wrist, beckoned them to follow him. An eerie silence seemed to pervade the house and grounds, broken only now and then by the cry of some exotic bird or creature who lived deep in the forest at the back of the house.

Inside, the Moorish theme continued: a large hall with

a marble floor, a curious window on the side of one wall barred with intricately worked wrought iron. Did someone sit behind it, Sandra wondered, to keep an eye on what was happening in the hall?

Unlike outside it was very cool indoors, but they did not linger long, being led into a grassy courtyard, the walls covered with bougainvillea and clematis, a fountain playing in the middle. This was not unlike the cloister of a Spanish monastery, with columned alcoves; yet, instead of the plaster busts of saints, a couple of peacocks seemed to keep sentinel, their sharp beaks raised, while doves flew about on the terracotta tiled roof.

Mr. Dunkel, leading the way, saw her glance and nodded.

"Yes, it was once a Benedictine monastery whose monks led lives of seclusion and prayer. There is a school in the village which they ran until they closed the order about twenty years ago."

"And why was that?"

Mr. Dunkel shrugged his expressive shoulders. He was a small, neat man, with rather melancholy eyes, jet-black hair combed straight back from his head. He wore a white suit, a pink shirt and a discreetly patterned tie.

"Lack of vocation doubtless, Madame," he replied. "Sadly, young men do not easily give themselves up to the religious life in these secular times. In the end I think there were only five or six monks left."

"And what happened to them?" Joanne asked curiously.

Dunkel looked bored. "I *imagine* they were absorbed by another house." Clearly uninterested in the fate of the former inhabitants, he swung open a door and ushered the women into a sparsely furnished room, a sort of parlor with a parquet floor and, from a long window, a spectacular view of the gulf.

"Do sit down, Madame Pasarro," he said to Joanne, gesticulating toward the table on which there were scattered magazines as in a doctor's or a dentist's waiting room. "We shall not keep you long."

"Oh, I'm to remain here, am I?" Joanne said. "Very well."

She sat down on one of the easy chairs and waved at Sandra. "Good luck."

"Thanks." Sandra felt, for once, decidedly ill at ease, even apprehensive.

She waited in the cloister while Dunkel shut the door but then, to her surprise, he ushered her into the room next to it, furnished in a similar way.

Carefully closing the door, he looked conspiratorially toward her and said: "*Do* sit down, Madame Harcourt."

"Am I to wait here?" she asked, doing as she was told.

"Ah!" Standing in front of her Dunkel's sad eyes seemed to grow even more despondent. "Madame, I am extremely sorry that you have come all this way, but Mr. Ryan is unable to see you."

"That's impossible!" Sandra abruptly stood up and the Mexican nervously took a step back.

"No one regrets it more than Mr. Ryan, I assure you, Madame. He became unexpectedly and extremely ill last night. After the doctor left an hour ago it was decided that he is too ill to see you, Madame, a fact we very much regret."

Sandra gazed at him with an expression of such disbelief on her face that the secretary, rather than meet those accusatory eyes, stared at the floor, his hand on his chest, sighing deeply. "It is Mr. Ryan's heart. He is on oxygen, Madame. You see it is quite, quite impossible . . ."

Sandra knew then that she was faced with an immovable object. She would get no further in finding out if Ryan could possibly have fathered her, and the eyes of his secretary, now again raised toward her, confirmed this.

"Does Mr. Ryan *know* why I have come to see him?" she asked.

Mr. Dunkel gave one of his expressive shrugs but his eyes remained inscrutable.

"He, of course, was interested . . ."

"I could arrange to spend a few days more in Mexico if . . ."

"Out of the question I regret, Madame. When Mr. Ryan has these attacks they last several weeks. One day, of course, he will not recover . . ." He closed his eyes piously. "I can't tell you how much Mr. Ryan would regret what has happened but"—he opened the door and ushered her into the cool stone cloister once again—"let us hope that you will be hearing something from him very soon."

The interview had only lasted five minutes. The whole visit took less than half an hour and, as Sandra, a bewildered Joanne by her side, saw the great wooden outer door swing open, she wondered if, indeed, she would ever return; or had the chance to unlock the mystery of her past gone forever?

21

Antoine Dericourt seldom had occasion to meet up with Zac. The men had never liked each other and, but for the advent of Sandra, Antoine felt he would surely have lost his job in the Desmond organization had Zac succeeded his father. But that had not happened, and the whole of his life changed.

When he was in Paris, Antoine stayed at the Ritz or the Plaza Athénée in the Avenue Montaigne, a haunt frequented by Zac because of its proximity to the fashion house of Jean Marvoine to which Tara, in her boredom, was giving more of her attention.

Zac, cultivating the impression of the loving husband, occasionally picked her up and took her for a drink, but, as he hardly ever did anything without a reason, on the particular day that he called at her office at five thirty she wondered why.

"Just to see how things are, put myself in the picture." Zac looked round her office, cluttered with fabrics and swatches of different-colored cloth. "Is Caroline Reboux here?"

"She and Maurice have gone to a modelling session," Tara replied. "They want to take advantage of the autumn leaves in the forest at Fontainebleau for our Christmas campaign."

Zac sat down, crossed his legs and joined his hands. "And how *are* things, my dear? In general, I mean."

"In general, they are not as good as they should be," Tara said, sitting on the desk, swinging her hips as she did and revealing a sight of her thighs beneath her short skirt, a sight Zac found exciting and erotic. "If Belle would only take more interest . . ." Tara began.

"Belle has enough problems of her own with the Burg-Farnbach estate. She is either going to have to sell that huge house or do something with it. Carl left nothing but debts. God, what a fool that man was." Zac shook his head. "If she sells it she will get practically nothing."

"Can't you buy it?" Tara looked at him. "You've always had designs to turn the Palazzo Falconetti into a hotel. Imagine what a ski resort Burg-Farnbach would make!"

"I *have* designs, but a shortage of funds too, my dear." Zac smiled blandly. "I burnt my fingers badly over the Cassini affair. I was very fortunate to escape investigation by the police. In fact I'm not sure I have escaped it. However"—he held up a pair of crossed fingers—"I think I have deflected their attention for the moment. When I have put my further plans into action they will be too busy concentrating on Madame Harcourt to think of me. Beside hers', my activities will pale into insignificance."

"What are you up to now?" Tara gazed at him suspiciously.

"Just you wait and see, my darling." He blew her a kiss before glancing at his watch. Then he stood up. "Let's go and have a drink at the Plaza. We have time before dinner."

Tara shook her head. "I'm not in the mood, Zac. Besides I have a few other things to do."

"Do them tomorrow, my little bird." Zac bent to kiss her. As he did he slid his hand under her flimsy panties.

"You are *disgusting,* Zac." Tara indignantly jumped down from the table. "You have the habits of a lecherous schoolboy."

"Have I really?" Zac said. "If I let you go, my angel, you would soon find that a schoolboy's pocket money would not be enough to keep you in sweeties for half an hour." He then slapped her bottom quite hard and gave her a pinch. "Go and get your coat on."

As Tara ran from the room Zac took the opportunity to look

round: at her desk, her untidy cupboards, the drawers half shut and full to overflowing.

He supposed that many rooms of couturiers looked like this. It was the sort of mess that such people indulged in. However, the point was that Tara's did not appear to him to be a creative mess. It just looked a mess without the creativity: the sort of untidy dereliction of failure. Zac gave a sigh of despair and went over to the window to watch the rush-hour traffic, the brightly lit buses plying up and down that fashionable street known for its chic, the heartland of the French fashion industry.

A Jaguar car drew up outside the Plaza Athénée, which was almost opposite the fashion house, and someone got out whom, even in the dusk, Zac immediately recognized. His heart lifted. Antoine Dericourt, who was saying something to his chauffeur before disappearing into the Plaza Athénée, seemed just the sign he was waiting for before he could start his massive operation against Sandra. Here was his quarry.

"This place is a mess," Zac said irritably, as Tara re-emerged, buttoning up her coat. "I feel you're floundering, you don't know what you're doing, Tara. The business is going downhill."

"You can sell it for all I care." Tara tried unsuccessfully to shut the drawer of her desk but it was stuffed too full of papers.

"Do you really mean that?" Zac watched her with growing irritation. He was a tidy, meticulous man which went with his passion for secrecy: locked drawers, closed cupboards, combination safes. Everything must be put away, out of sight, secure from the prying eyes of others.

She looked up at him. "Frankly, you can do what you like with it."

"But it belongs to Desmond. You said so yourself."

"Then *Sandra* can do what she likes with it," Tara said as, triumphantly, she succeeded in closing the drawer and locking it. Together they made their way downstairs to the pillared hall, which had a fountain playing; the concierge, smartly saluting, stood at the plate-glass door, holding it open.

"Sandra will soon have other things on her mind," Zac said

with a mysterious smile. "Soon Jean Marvoine will be the least of her worries."

"I wish you'd tell me what you're up to with Sandra," Tara said peevishly. "Whenever you try and get the better of her you are always the one to get hurt."

"Not this time, *ma belle,*" he said, taking her arm as they darted through the traffic. "This time I have her well and truly on the hook." On the other side of the pavement he stopped and glanced at her, his expression quite cold. "And if you so much as breathe a *word* to her, something will happen to you that will be less than pleasant. That I do promise you."

Tara roughly withdrew her arm from his.

"There you go again—always threats. I never know what you mean."

"I have good reason to doubt your loyalty to me. For instance"—he tapped her under the chin and gazed into her eyes—"seriously, my dear, what would you do all day if you did not go to Jean Marvoine?"

"There's plenty to do," Tara said nonchalantly, brushing his finger away.

"Find another man in a garage, if I know you."

"I could find a man in a garage *and* work at Jean Marvoine," Tara said spitefully, "if that's really what I wanted to do."

"Only it *isn't,* is it, my darling?" Zac said with a lascivious sneer. "I keep you much too busy."

Tara tried not to smile, if only because she did not want Zac to know how much she despised him. He was an inexpert lover and always had been. He was beginning to enjoy violence. He lacked finesse, the delicate touch. But for the moment she tolerated him, only hoping one day that she would be free.

Once they were inside the hotel Zac went straight up to the reception desk and, leaning confidentially toward the clerk, asked, "Is Monsieur Dericourt in?"

"I don't believe . . ." The clerk turned and studied the room keys behind him. "Yes, he is, sir."

"Would you ask him if he would like a drink in the bar with Monsieur and Madame Desmond?"

"Certainly, sir."

The clerk lifted the house phone and, after speaking quietly into it for a few seconds, said: "Monsieur Dericourt has an evening engagement and is having a shower and changing. But he will be pleased to join you for a drink in about ten minutes."

"Fine." Zac put his arm through Tara's. "That is just fine."

Once inside the bar he ordered champagne.

"Desmond, sir?" the waiter asked.

"Tellier," Zac replied. "The '82 Brut Reserve."

The waiter made no comment but Tara looked at Zac with some amusement.

"Sticking the knife in, are you?"

"Not yet, my dear, not yet but nearly." Zac smiled. "And by the way when Dericourt comes down I want you to make yourself scarce, if you would. There's something I want to talk confidentially to him about."

"So what *are* you up to now?" She looked at the unfamiliar bottle of champagne the waiter had put before them. It was the first time she could ever recall Zac asking for a champagne other than Desmond.

Zac put a practised hand round the neck of the bottle to see if it was cold enough; then he nodded to the waiter who began to pour it.

"Just you wait," Zac murmured, taking his glass and sipping it. Then he grimaced. "I'm afraid there's no doubt about it. Tellier can't touch Desmond for quality."

"Why did you choose it then?"

"I have recently made a vow that as long as Madame is in power, in a position she does not deserve and to which she has no right, I will not contribute one franc toward the company she is running down so badly."

"But I thought it was doing *well?* Sandra recently got you out of a nasty spot. You'd think you'd be grateful; that even *you* would agree Sandra had flair."

"I agree?" Zac looked appalled. "My dear, she certainly has no flair, but she does possess a certain, shall we say, facile quality, that is doubtless the gift of the devil himself. However, *that* is about to run out. Ah." He pointed toward the door where Antoine Dericourt stood hovering uncomfortably on the threshold. "There is my quarry." He stood up and waved to attract Dericourt's attention and, straightening his tie, sleeking back his hair, Dericourt came nervously over to them.

"Don't forget, my angel," Zac murmured without moving his lips, "leave us alone for ten minutes as soon as you can."

Hand outstretched, he crossed the room to greet the head of Desmond Aeronautics, clasping him on the arm as they met and vigorously pumping his hand up and down.

"My dear Antoine, what a *pleasure* to see you."

Antoine shook hands politely with Tara and then, sitting beside her, said, "But how did you know I was here, Zac?"

"Tara and I often have a drink here if I pick her up at Jean Marvoine. I saw you leaving your car and going into the hotel. Really it's ages since we met. How are things?"

The waiter picked up the bottle of champagne from the ice bucket and began to fill their glasses. Dericourt studied the label on the bottle, a gesture which did not escape Zac who, however, said nothing.

"Thanks." Obviously still a man ill at ease, Dericourt took the glass with a smile. "Seriously, things are fine, and with you?"

"Fine, fine," Zac said. "I could do without Heurtey sticking his nose in but, then, I suppose you could too."

Dericourt felt like a fly who, having just alighted on a sticky web, was trying rapidly to extricate itself before the spider appeared from its hole.

"I hardly *see* Heurtey," he said, determined to make this a brief drink and be off.

Seeing that he was clearly a man in a hurry—besides which there had never been any love lost between them—Zac winked at Tara who rose at once, saying, "Excuse me for a few moments. I can see a friend in the corner by the bar."

Both men stood up perfunctorily as she left.

"So, things are going well?"

"Very well." Dericourt sat on the edge of his seat, quickly sipping his drink in nervous gulps. "No, Heurtey doesn't bother us much, as a matter of fact." He chuckled self-consciously into his glass. "I believe he's over-fond of golf. Sandra isn't too pleased about that."

"Is that so?" Zac smiled. "And talking of Heurtey, how are things between you and that attractive assistant of his?"

Dericourt knew that the more he struggled the more his legs were becoming enmeshed in the web.

"I beg your pardon?" he said, looking straight at Zac.

Zac put his head on one side. "Not pretty, but sexy. Yes, a very *sexual* woman I would say."

"I haven't the least idea what you mean." Dericourt rapidly drained his glass and looked at his watch.

"Don't rush off, Dericourt," Zac said, a certain menace by now quite obvious in his voice. "I am talking about the affair that you are having with Joanne Pasarro."

"I am not having an affair with Joanne Pasarro. The idea is absolute rubbish and I don't know where you ever got it from."

Zac turned an innocent face to Dericourt, pointing with a finger at his own eye.

"I saw you in Paris, my dear fellow, an intimate tête-a-tête in a restaurant on the Rive Gauche, I think. Kissing her hand, kissing more for all I know."

"That was business," Dericourt said sharply. "Strictly business."

"It sure looked like it," Zac chuckled. "I wonder if Fleur Dericourt, that charming lady, would feel the same?"

"Look, Zac, what is this?" Dericourt, finding a crumb of courage, folded his arms and stared at his accuser. "I know you, Zac. You never do or say anything without a reason, usually a mischievous one. I'll tell you something. Frankly, when I heard you were here I wanted to avoid you."

"I bet you did," Zac said, chuckling again. "But I should think this affair would sink you with your wife."

"There is *no* affair." Dericourt raised his voice, but not too loud. "There never was and there never will be. Joanne Pasarro has, anyway, returned to the States."

"I bet she'll be back," Zac said with a wink. "I bet she was a good lay, eh, Dericourt? I always thought she looked slightly butch, but maybe after Fleur you like that kind of thing."

Dericourt swallowed what was left in his glass and stood up.

"Look, Zac, I don't have to take this. I was *not* having an affair with Joanne. I love my wife and I would never contemplate relations with another woman. Fleur trusts me. Besides I hardly knew her and you have not the slightest evidence of anything else."

"Don't worry, I can make it," Zac said, with a suggestive smile. *"That's* no problem."

"Zac, why are you doing this?" Dericourt abruptly sat down again, his hands on his knees, in an attitude of desperation. It was rather unwise of him to give such obvious signs of his capitulation to Zac.

"Antoine," Zac said meaningfully, fingering the stem of his glass, "I may need your help. I have evidence that Sandra O'Neill has been involved in very risky business with the company that is rightfully mine."

"I find that hard to believe," Dericourt said stiffly. "She is a woman of the greatest integrity."

"So you think, and so you are *meant* to. However, I have evidence to the contrary and I propose to use it. If you cooperate with me I can assure you that when I assume control your position will be secure. I promise not to touch Desmond Aeronautics or your position on the Board. You have my word on that. And I assure you the secret of your love affair will be quite safe with me. I can just *imagine* how let down poor Fleur would feel. But, apart from all these personal considerations, surely you wouldn't *want* to defend an embezzler, would you, Dericourt?"

"An *embezzler?*" Dericourt's voice was almost hoarse. "You're saying this about Sandra?"

Zac leaned conspiratorially toward his victim, his voice scarcely more than a whisper. "You remember Romanetto?"

"Yes, I do remember Romanetto." Dericourt stroked his cleanly shaven chin.

"I have evidence that the Irish whore and Romanetto were in league."

"But frankly I would find *that* impossible to believe. She didn't know him."

"Oh, but she did. She had dealings with him through her bank in America. Before she got into waters too deep for her she was an investment analyst and had dealings with financiers all over the world. I have evidence that she helped him swindle that money and has now been cleaning up. It is part of a plan to enrich herself, hatched a long time ago."

Dericourt was silent, but at the back of his mind was a clear recollection of Sandra's apparently curious obsession with the whereabouts of Romanetto. Even at the time he had considered it odd, that's why it had stuck in his mind. Why should she suddenly become so interested in the whereabouts of a man she had apparently never met, even known, if she were to be believed?

However, he knew Sandra and he knew Zac, and if he were going to give anyone the benefit of the doubt it would not be him.

"I can't believe that of Sandra," Dericourt said finally, standing up and putting out his hand. "Thanks for the drink, Zac."

Zac also rose and took his hand but, instead of letting it go, he held on to it, drawing Dericourt toward him as if to impress on him the sheer malevolence of his presence. Dericourt had a powerful whiff of his aftershave, felt the forceful grip of his hand, and started to sweat.

"I might need *you* to give evidence, Dericourt," Zac said in a voice so quiet that Antoine could scarcely hear him. "It's *your* word against mine. You may deny an affair with Pasarro but

I will bring conclusive proof. I can, believe me. I would hate you to discover that you had no job, no position, no money and . . . no wife."

As Dericourt stumbled across the room, his self-confidence in tatters, he passed Tara without seeing her. She stared after him, then she looked at Zac, who was bending calmly toward the table pouring out more champagne.

"Well, were you successful?" she asked as she joined him with a backward glance toward the door.

For answer Zac lifted the glass in her direction and winked. "Have you *ever* known me otherwise, my dear?"

The finished artwork covered all of Sandra's desk, and a table also had been brought into service so that a full display of the designs could be studied comparatively. Claude Maison, flushed with triumph, had his head designer Martin de Poivre with him, a man who commanded such high fees that he earned more than the director himself.

His concept for the Louis d'Or launch was, indeed, simple but brilliant. A stylized silhouette of a beautiful woman behind the photographed bottle: "Louis d'Or . . . *tête de cuvée:* Desmond quality at its best."

Simplicity and style were the keynotes: subtle colors, imaginative typography, luxury, a hint even of sumptuousness.

"Perfect!" Sandra said, pleased that so much effort and hard work had produced the right result. To either side of her René Latour and Étienne Legrand beamed with satisfaction. "You are to be congratulated, Monsieur de Poivre."

De Poivre gave a complacent smile. He looked tired, but he knew he was a genius and took these compliments in his stride. He began to sweep up the artwork for the labels and the advertising campaign into his portfolio.

"If Madame would be so kind as to send the print order as soon as possible?" he said.

"And the timing?" Sandra consulted a schedule.

"To begin just as soon as possible, Madame." Maison bent his head to consult the schedule with her.

"You realize that the cost will be many, many thousands of francs . . . Madame?" He put his head on one side as though to be sure she approved.

"It is as much a public relations exercise as anything else," Sandra replied diplomatically, well aware of how much it cost. "Not only for my son, but for the company as well."

"Will you and the little boy be available for personal interviews, Madame?" Claude Maison asked, scribbling in his book, but Sandra vigorously shook her head.

"No, not at all. I want Louis to be shielded from all publicity. He must lead a normal life for as long as he can."

Maison looked crestfallen. "Not just *one* shot?"

"Please, Madame," Étienne begged. "It could be so *tastefully* done."

"I have Mike Zamburger in mind." Maison mentioned the name of a celebrated American photographer well known for his portrayal of female beauty.

"Zamburger!" Sandra sounded interested. *"He's* very expensive too, I bet."

"You said expense was no object, Madame," Maison slyly reminded her. "I could just visualize an absolutely *beautiful* picture of you and Louis by the window of your home . . ."

"Just a *profile,* Madame," de Poivre added persuasively.

"Oh, all right, set it up." Sandra gave in with good grace. After all there was nothing to lose.

By the following week all the material was printed, and Sandra had approved the proofs in her Paris office.

The effect was to be sensational, coinciding with the advent of the festive season. All the top-class French magazines would carry full-page ads in color and so would those with the biggest circulations in America, England and the rest of Europe.

Sitting by the window overlooking the Seine, Bob apathetically picked up the proofs and then helped himself to a drink.

He was having a hard time coming to terms with his freedom; every day he was seeing an analyst to help him through his trauma, his nightmares, his depression.

But the person he knew would help him best refused to see him, even to talk to him on the telephone, to answer his letters sent to her office in Avenue Montaigne.

Bob watched the lunchtime news and was just about to go for a blustery walk in the rain along the banks of the river when he heard the doorbell.

He suffered from anxiety and every unscheduled call made him jump, shake with apprehension, until he knew who it was. Sandra, who had engaged a bodyguard for him who accompanied him everywhere, was worried to death about his condition. The analyst had told her that time alone would heal. Patience was the keyword.

There was a discreet tap on the door which Bob always kept locked and he called out: *"Oui?"*

"It is a lady to see you, Monsieur," the butler replied from the other side of the door.

A lady. Bob jumped to his feet and, going up to the door, put his mouth to it.

"Who is it?"

"Bob, it is I," Tara whispered back and, with a racing heart, Bob hastily unlocked the door, throwing it open, unable to believe his eyes; but, yes, there she was, her fur coat pulled tightly around her, her beautiful, dark eyes a little frightened too.

Behind her stood the butler and behind him Christophe the bodyguard, with a question in his eyes.

"It's OK," Bob reassured them, reaching out to draw her in. Then he shut the door behind them and leaned against it while Tara walked hesitantly into the center of the room and stopped.

"Bob . . ." she began.

"Oh, *Tara . . ."*

She knew that grown men could cry like women, and Bob had been through a terrible ordeal; but she hadn't expected quite this reaction nor, for a while, could she stem his tears. She made him sit beside her on the sofa, to rest his head in her lap.

"Bob . . . Bob." She gently stroked his face, knowing that she was like his mother rather than his mistress. What he wanted was comfort and love, understanding, a sense of closeness, security—not sex. She had been tormented by doubt, but now she was glad she'd come.

But the guilt remained that she was responsible for his ordeal and that, through fear of her husband, she had done nothing to help him.

For how long could she live with that? But Tara Desmond, beautiful woman, was a selfish woman too. Nor was she brave enough to suffer for a man she knew she had wronged but didn't love.

Finally the flow of Bob's tears stopped. He dried his eyes, apologized for being a baby, explained that his nerves were in a bad way.

"Understandably," she said, "understandably, *mon petit* Bob."

"You think once you're free you'll be OK." Bob stood up and tucked his shirt back into his jeans. "But it's not like that. I have a bodyguard. I feel frightened everywhere I go, even if there's a ring on the doorbell . . ."

"I should have *told* you I was coming . . . but I didn't know." She looked apprehensively toward the door as though she too were afraid. "You know Zac is so possessive, so *suspicious.* I have to be very, very careful. There was Livio, there was you . . ."

"I know, I know." Bob nodded vigorously. "And I have to thank Zac for freeing me. *I* don't want to offend or upset him either."

"You have to thank my *brother* for getting you out," Tara said indignantly. She threw off her fur coat and nervously lit a cigarette. She wore a leather skirt and a very tight jersey that emphasized her prominent breasts. But Bob found that he was no longer excited by them, nor did he feel any desire for her, a fact that amazed him. He wanted instead to feel her arms around him.

He knew he wanted to be possessed rather than to possess, to be protected rather than to hunt. He knew he had become a child again and Dr. Baker, his American analyst, had explained that, until these childish fears and insecurities had been released, he would not function as a normal male. Bob hugged her again and then dropped his arms, his head bent in thought.

"I feel bad about Marco. Do you know I never said 'thank you'. Never wrote to him?"

"Why don't you go and *see* him?" Tara suggested. "Say 'thank you' then I know it would mean a lot to him."

"You think it would?" Bob got up and wandered over to the window.

"People *like* to be thanked," Tara went on. "I imagine Marco put himself in considerable danger, exposed himself to all sorts of unpleasant influences. I think when you're well enough and strong enough to go to Rome again and thank Marco personally he would be very grateful."

"I will," Bob said suddenly. "I'm going to Italy for Christmas, skiing with some friends from Berkeley. Then I'm going into a private clinic Dr. Baker recommends high up in the Dolomites which combines psychotherapy with relaxation techniques. After that I'll be well again. I promise I'll go and see your brother."

Tara looked at him for a while, wondering what had happened to the virile young man whose passion had briefly transformed her life. Sad . . . so sad to be destroyed by Zac . . . and how much was Marco responsible? Maybe better *not* to say "thank you"?

"Perhaps you should forget Marco," she said suddenly. "Put the whole thing out of your mind."

"No—no," Bob said. "I'll do it, but not yet." Perhaps never. Why concern oneself with things that might never happen?

Tara rose and drew on her coat again. Downstairs her car waited and she had told her chauffeur she would not be long. "I must go, dearest Bob," she said. "I have an errand to do, but

I wanted to see that *you* were all right and to tell you that . . ."

"That?" he asked with a rueful smile that reflected an unspoken question.

"That I'll never forget you." She didn't go near him but put her hand to her mouth and blew a kiss.

"Ciao, darling."

"Ciao," he said. *"Arrivederci."*

Then he went to the window and waited until he saw her run onto the pavement, jump into her car and drive off. She never looked up.

FIVE

A Woman Scorned

Heaven has no rage like love to hatred turned,
Nor Hell a fury like a woman scorned.
William Congreve

22

"Happy Christmas."

"Happy Christmas, darling."

David raised his glass as they drank to each other's health and then he took from his pocket a small, velvet-covered box. Sandra, opposite him on the other side of the fire that roared up the great chimney in the main salon of the Château de Tourville, raised her head as he stooped to kiss her. At the same time he placed the box in her hand and, as she gazed at it, he said: "Open it, Sandra."

It was a very small box, just large enough for a ring and, for a moment, she hesitated. Was the die cast? Was David asking her to marry him and, if so, how would she reply?

Too late. As she raised the lid the relief must have shown on her face which immediately broke into a smile of pleasure. "David, it's beautiful!"

It was a brooch in the shape of an "L", her son's initial, entirely fashioned from diamonds and with a surround of the purest gold.

She raised her arms to thank him and, as he again stooped to receive her kiss, their mouths met and lingered.

"David," Sandra said as they drew apart, "it's the most beautiful, most *thoughtful* present I could ever have imagined."

"But you expected it to be something else, didn't you?" He continued to smile at her. "I saw it in your eyes."

"Perhaps." She nodded as she took the brooch from its bed of silk and pinned it to her evening dress. They were dining *à deux* on Christmas Eve, drinking a bottle of the 1947 special reserve champagne that had been created to celebrate the wedding of the then Princess Elizabeth of England to Philip, Duke of Edinburgh; one of the last bottles remaining.

"There," she said, rising and studying in the ornate gilt mirror over the marble fireplace the effect of the brooch on her dress. "Exquisite." She turned to David, who was also in evening dress. "Thank you very much, darling. I will treasure it forever."

Upstairs, Louis slept in his bed, watched over by the devoted Mireille. Apart from them, his mother, David Heurtey and the household servants, the house was empty of Desmonds. Lady Elizabeth had gone to spend Christmas with her family in England, Zac and Tara had taken a party which included Belle and their children to the Desmond chalet in Gstaad, and Bob was skiing in Cortina in Italy with a group of friends with whom he had been at university in America.

Sandra put a hand on the brooch which she had pinned over her heart and David placed an arm around her, leaning his cheek against hers so that they formed a cameo in the mirror. By any standards they were a very handsome couple and yet there was nothing narcissistic in the way that they gazed at themselves.

"You were thinking," David said to her through the mirror, "that it was a ring."

"Maybe." In the mirror she smiled at him.

"And that I was going to ask you to marry me."

Solemnly she addressed him again through the mirror.

"Not yet, please, David."

"But *why* not, darling?"

"Because I don't know . . . I'm not ready."

"You don't love me."

"I do love you." She turned to look at him, feeling secure in his arms. "But marriage . . . not yet."

"Michel has been dead over eighteen months."

"It's not Michel. I can't tell you what it is. I don't know myself. If I did I'd tell you."

She touched the smooth, shiny cloth of his evening jacket. "It's just . . . it will change everything."

"It's a very good time. Everything is calm. The businesses are going well. Even *Zac* has shut up and is not causing problems . . ."

"But, darling," Sandra said quietly, "it isn't a business arrangement, it's a marriage."

"I don't mean it like that, Sandra, and you know it." He removed his hands from her and she could see that she had angered him. "All I mean is that you are so devoted to your business, in a way that I am not, that if everything is going so well you may even be persuaded to take a few days off for a honeymoon!"

She left his side and walked back to the chair in which she had been sitting. She took up her champagne glass and studied the golden bubbles still winking inside.

A beautiful vintage. Over forty years old and still drinkable. More golden, more mellow. A vintage made for a marriage; might the next one, after Louis, be for her?

They dined together in the great Italian dining room that was usually used for occasions when all the family were together, maybe entertaining some important guest. The long mahogany dining table had belonged to the princely House of Savoy, and the light from the candles in the heavy silver candelabra was reflected in the brightly polished wood.

Pierre stood by the sideboard supervising the serving of the meal, himself pouring the wines. David and Sandra sat opposite each other but at the sides rather than at either end. Even then it was slightly formidable to be sitting *à deux* at a table that could seat up to thirty people in comfort.

As the liveried servants were present they spoke in generalities, and after dinner they returned to the salon where Pierre brought coffee on a huge silver tray that had been part of the dowry of Lady Elizabeth nearly forty years before.

"Will there be anything else, Madame?" he asked, after he had handed her and David their coffee.

"No, thank you, Pierre. Mr. Heurtey is staying the night, as you know, and tomorrow I think he will be out riding early. Won't you, David?" She looked at him.

"I hope you will be joining me, Sandra."

"What a splendid idea," she said immediately. "We'll ride before breakfast, Pierre. Breakfast at about nine, nine thirty, David?"

"To suit *you,* my dear," he said gallantly and, after settling on nine thirty so as to give the servants time to sleep in on Christmas Day, they said goodnight.

David remained in front of the fire, filling his pipe, and, as Pierre shut the door behind him, he said: "Strange that he is so loyal to you when he has been employed by the Desmonds for years. He must be aware of the tensions."

"He is, but he is also the perfect servant, loyal to whoever pays his wages."

"Do they talk . . . about *us,* do you think?"

"I'm sure they do. But as you have a separate bedroom there's not much they can actually talk *about."* She seemed to find the conversation amusing.

"But this is a marvellous place." David lit his pipe and, as it began to draw, he gripped it between his teeth and looked around. "Do you ever regret that it isn't yours completely?"

Sandra met his eyes. "It *is* mine completely."

David looked surprised. "I didn't realize that."

"It *was* very strange that Georges left it to me but he did. But he meant me to share it and I have always said that as it *is* the Desmond family home I would never bar anyone from it." She bowed her head. "I have, however, twice barred Tim Desmond from it, and that I do regret."

David studied the ceiling toward which the smoke gently spiraled from his pipe. "How involved were you with Tim?"

"I fancied I was in love with him. We were lovers. He didn't behave very well; but neither did I . . . and then, of course, there was the possibility that he might be my brother, which was awful."

"And you're sure he's not?" David removed his pipe and looked at her with concern.

"I'm not sure. Not *quite* sure. No."

"What about Russell Ryan?"

"That mysterious episode has not yet resolved itself. As a matter of fact"—she delved into her evening pouch and produced a letter which she held up to David—"I wanted to show you this. It came with the Christmas mail."

David reached over and took it from her. It was a sheet of paper with a typewritten message which read:

Mr. Russell Ryan sends Madame Sandra Harcourt the compliments of the season. He regrets he is not sending cards this year.

"How *very* strange." David frowned as he passed it back to her. "Why take the trouble to do that?"

"Why indeed? But now you know there *is* still a mystery about my father."

That night when the house was dark and all the servants were asleep, David Heurtey crept along the corridor and into Sandra's room.

She was waiting for him lying on the bed completely nude, like the Rokeby Venus.

He sat on the bed and touched her, letting his finger delicately caress the contours of her exquisitely proportioned body. He could not believe that such a prize could really be his and, as she drew him into her arms, into her bed and then into her body he thought that there was no more fortunate man alive in the world.

Louis was still too young to be excited by Christmas, but there were toys and presents exchanged round the Christmas tree in the main salon after breakfast. David and Sandra had been up early riding, despite their hours in bed together which had given them little sleep. David had bought Louis a rocking horse and, for an hour, he played with the child, holding him on the horse and scrambling over the floor giving him piggybacks.

The rapport that David and Louis obviously shared worried Sandra, but she tried not to show it as she sat and watched them while, upstairs, Mireille got the nursery tidy for the day, sorting through Louis's clothes.

The whole ambience of the huge house had somehow been turned into one incorporating an intimate family atmosphere in a way she had never experienced with the Desmonds. Sandra, David, Louis: a family group. The reflection made her a little sad. It was one she rapidly tried to banish from her mind.

But there was the same intimacy later at lunch, not a big Christmas dinner, but a light meal eaten with Louis and Mireille. David and Sandra would dine more formally later, as they had the night before.

Afterwards Louis was taken for his nap and David, walking along the hall with Sandra, put his arm round her waist and said: "I want to show you something. Can you get your coat on? It's a ten-minute drive."

"Another surprise?" Sandra said. "I thought we were going for a walk?"

"We are, but not here," he said taking her arm. "Come."

Outside it was a cloudy but not very cold Christmas day. A slight breeze rustled the stillness of the lake, disturbing the reflection of the skeletal trees whose bare branches seemed to hang rather sadly over the water.

David's Bentley was already parked in the drive, having been brought round by one of the footmen during lunch.

"You're being very *mysterious,"* Sandra mused as he opened the door for her.

"Do you like mysteries? I do."

"Sometimes," she said and, as he got in next to her and switched on the ignition, he replied:

"I hope you'll like this one."

The great car leapt toward the gates, which were electronically controlled from the house, and thus swung to behind them as David drove swiftly down the road that led to the river and then pointed the car in a westerly direction toward Verneuil.

Sandra sat back and gazed in front of her as they swept past the tall trees lining the Marne. She was aware of a sense of utter contentment such as she thought she had never known in her life, even in Greece. So far the Christmas holiday had been perfect: the three of them together in the beautiful château, mollycoddled by the servants, surrounded by beauty, cherished by the strong, primeval ties of love.

As David took a turn off the main road she guessed where they were going and, almost before the thought occurred to her they had stopped in front of the Château de Marsanne and, for a moment, they sat where they were, staring at it.

"I guessed this was our destination." Sandra opened the door and swung her legs out of the car. "It fascinates you, doesn't it?"

"Sure does," David said, putting a hand on her arm, "but don't get out, Sandra. I have a key."

Wonderingly she watched him as he left the driving seat and opened the main gates to the château which were only secured by an old-fashioned lock and chain. He then returned to the car, drove up the straight drive and stopped by the steps leading to the front door.

"Don't tell me you've got a key for the *house* as well?"

David put a finger to his lips, nodded his head and, taking her by the hand, led her up the steps where he put a key in another old-fashioned lock and the door silently swung open.

Sandra paused and took a deep breath. How many times had she been in this house in the company of Henri and Sophie Piper? It was not as grand as the Château de Tourville, but it was a home of great charm, intimacy and distinction.

Yet now it felt curiously dead, and she immediately realized why. The house was empty; all the furniture had been removed and the rooms were bare. Only the curtains remained at the windows and some of the floors were still carpeted. She wandered from the salon into Henri's study, into the dining room, where there had been a magnificent oval dining table and a perfect set of Louis XV chairs, through the door to the vast, empty kitchens. Then she came back to the salon again with its view of the Piper vineyards stretching in straight, graduated lines up the hill.

"I've bought it," David said quietly.

"You've *bought* it . . ."

"I officially became the owner only yesterday." He held up the key. "I should have lifted you over the threshold, my darling, because I hope that one day you and I will live here together. I want it to be our country home."

"Oh, *David!*" Sandra gasped as, suddenly, he took her in his arms, crushing her against him.

"I don't want you to say a *thing,* Sandra. I know how you feel and I'm not forcing you. I want you to marry me when you're ready, when *you* want to; but don't leave it too long, my darling, because I want us to have children. I want to think of us and our family living here together, growing up and old in this lovely place." Finally he let her go and, feeling dumbfounded, she watched him as he began to pace restlessly up and down round the room.

"I've been negotiating with the Pipers' lawyers for *months.* He wanted to keep it, but his wife wanted to sell. I remained an anonymous buyer because I thought it was best that way."

"But you don't know Henri Piper."

"But he knows who I am. He may know what Zac feels about me, and he may not have *wanted* to sell to me. I thought it better that way."

"Perhaps you're right."

"You're not angry, are you?" He looked anxiously at her and she hurriedly shook her head.

"No, no. Not at all. It just feels kinda *strange,* that's all."

"For me too," he assured her. "I told them that the deal had to be completed, the furniture out before Christmas because I wanted it to be mine. I'm going to take my time doing it up and furnishing it. Since the Pipers decided to settle in California it's been neglected and there are quite a few structural defects. However . . . I'm also going to take over his vineyards, not as part of the Heurtey group but as belonging to me personally."

"They're fine grapes," Sandra said with a smile. "They make fine champagne. But David . . . I feel so peculiar." She put her hands to her face and leaned her back against the wall. "It's just so odd to think of the Pipers not being here any more and that *you* own it."

Suddenly she felt a strange sense of desolation and began to move around the vast, empty room as though it were full of ghosts. She thought the reason for her sensation was that the place didn't seem right for David. He no more belonged here than she did at Tourville.

They were the archetypal rich people from the new world thinking they could possess the old. Try as she might there was no way she could see a place for David here, for herself . . . but she couldn't tell him yet.

Watching her a little warily, he said: "Sophie Piper much prefers California if that's what's worrying you. Her health is not good anyway."

"I know." Sandra nodded and then she reached out for him and grasped his hand. He took hers and pressed it to his lips. It was warm and vibrant but, despite that, her attitude had chilled his heart. He thought she would be as excited as he was—a place of their own where the Desmonds had no rights. He had thought hard about it and when he acted he was convinced he had the key to Sandra's heart. Now he wondered.

"Let's take a walk," he said, adopting a deliberately casual tone, "and then we should get back before dark."

They arrived at Tourville just as the lights were going on in the house and the evening mist rising from the lake cloaked the trees in a mysterious, evanescent haze.

In front of the door stood a Deux Chevaux and David said: "Looks like we have a guest."

"I wonder who?"

David left the Bentley in front of the house and stood looking at the Citroën; then, as he and Sandra hurried up the steps, they were met at the top by Pierre, who had a worried look on his face.

"Ah, Madame, I'm glad you're back," he said, pointing toward the interior of the house. "Marcel Dupois is here to see you urgently."

"Marcel . . ." David looked questioningly at Sandra.

"He's the head cellarman at Desmond." A sense of foreboding suddenly clutched at Sandra's heart and, as she saw the face of Marcel who stood in the hall, still with his coat on, waiting for her, she knew that her apprehension was justified.

"Madame." He came quickly toward her. "I came immediately. Christmas or no Christmas, I felt you had to know . . ."

"It's the special *cuvée,* isn't it?" she said at once.

Dupois gazed disconsolately at her, nodding his head. "I'm afraid most of it is ruined. There has been weeping on a colossal scale. I only discovered it this afternoon as I was on my rounds."

Hundreds of feet underground, in the very depths of the Desmond caves, a group of people stood with their eyes transfixed by the steady trickle of liquid running along the troughs leading to a central point in the cave. These had been constructed a hundred years or more before, when weeping and the breaking of bottles due to the colossal pressure of carbonization were quite common. But since the design of new bottles and the adoption of more modern methods they were regarded as quaint relics of the past. The smell of spilt wine was overpowering and it was evident that the spillage was on a large scale.

Sandra, David and Marcel had been joined by René Latour and Étienne Legrand, who had insisted on rising from his bed to which he had been confined with the influenza. He stood there coughing and blowing his nose and, whether the tears in his eyes were from his illness or the disaster that confronted him, it was difficult to tell.

Two other *cavistes* had arrived to help and were carefully shifting the bottles at the front which seemed largely to have been spared the disaster.

These men had been working ever since Marcel had spotted the extent of the weeping during his daily inspection, in order to try and save as many bottles as possible.

"How *much* of it is ruined?" Sandra asked the dreaded question at last.

Marcel, who now seemed to have taken charge of the operation, shrugged. Legrand, and especially Latour, perhaps realizing that their jobs were on the block, remained silent.

"Maybe half. Maybe more. In fact"—he took a bottle from the front and inspected the cork—"you can just see it is starting here, and these are the bottles that remain, on the whole, unaffected."

"It was the neck," Legrand said at last, with an enormous splutter accompanied by a sneeze. "I said it was too thin, Madame, too long. I *said* it all the time."

"Is this true?" David turned to Sandra, who nodded.

"Then *why* was he not heeded?"

"He was not here." Sandra found it hard to keep the emotion out of her voice. She turned to search the face of the man standing in the deep shadow behind her: René Latour.

"Above all it was Monsieur Zac's suggestion, his specification." René Latour was quick to pass on the blame.

"But, Monsieur Latour, I don't recall that you tried to dissuade me."

"I would never *question* Monsieur Desmond's judgment, Madame," Latour replied. "He is the expert. It is in his blood."

"So is deceit," David murmured in Sandra's ear so that only she could hear. "What a pity you didn't think of that."

Sandra peered at the huge pile of bottles lying *sur lattes,* piled up on one another, in the caves. "Isn't this inspected every day?"

"We inspect the bottles every day, but only those which are ready for the *remuage* have a careful inspection. The *remuage* for these was not due until the beginning of the month so . . ."

"But it was our own prestige *cuvée.*" Sandra found her temper mounting as her sense of shock receded. "I would have thought *special* attention should have been given to them. I was assured it would be."

"It was, Madame." Marcel turned to René who seemed to have retreated even further back in the shadows. "That was the specific concern of Monsieur Latour. He insisted . . ."

"I inspected them. I saw nothing," René said stiffly. "One or two bottles did show signs of weeping, which is normal, and were removed . . ."

"What happens, as a matter of fact, to bottles which weep?" David asked. "You realize I'm a novice."

"Normally, Monsieur, these bottles are arranged in a circle, that is we pour the remaining wine into a special vat. At the time of the next *vendange,* this wine will be mixed with that year's wine. It will contribute to raise the quality of that *cuvée:* good aging is the secret of the quality of wine from Champagne! Some houses use the *'rebuts'*—that is what we call them—in the liquor. It is not the style of the House of Desmond! Here, we avoid making petty savings."

Legrand held up a bottle and it was indeed possible to see how extensive the weeping had been. Positively a flood. He sighed deeply.

There was total silence while the significance of what had happened sank in and, finally, Sandra broke it.

"Then what are we to do?"

"We will immediately begin an examination of *all* the two hundred thousand bottles, Madame," Dupois said, "and see if there is anything worth saving, enough to put on the market and justify your extensive advertising campaign. It will be a great loss of prestige for us all if the *cuvée* cannot be marketed. But"—he gave a huge Gallic shrug of his shoulders—"I doubt if very much can be saved."

"There will have to be a *full* investigation into this," Sandra said in a tense voice. "It will begin tomorrow in the offices here and continue until we have got to the bottom of it. In the meantime"—she turned to Latour—"I would like a *special* word with you upstairs and perhaps you too, Étienne." She turned to Legrand whose eyes were streaming. "If you're up to it."

"Madame, I would *insist* on being there," Legrand said, "but first of all I want to ensure that enough men are summoned to work through the rest of the day and tonight so that by tomorrow you will be completely au fait with the extent of the disaster."

On the way up to ground level Sandra said to David: "I think I should handle this alone."

"Sure," he said. "I'll go back and wait for you."

"Maybe you'll play with Louis and tell the staff dinner will be late?"

"Will do," he replied, and when they had reached the top he went straight to his car and, with a wave to Sandra, set off. She was grateful for the support of someone who understood without fuss.

The door to the main office was already unlocked and, in complete silence, René and Sandra got into the lift that took them to the chairman's private suite.

By now it was completely dark outside and Sandra went through the office rapidly switching on the lamps. It was also cold because the central heating was at a minimum and she sat down at her desk in her coat, rubbing her hands and blowing into them.

"Golly, it *was* cold down there," she said to Latour who, instead of taking the seat she had offered him, remained standing, his expression difficult to fathom.

"I see you're going to blame me for this disaster, Madame," he went immediately onto the attack, "as you did with the *tirage*. It was quite apparent to me from the beginning. You have had it in for me ever since that time . . ."

Sandra held up a hand to stop a flood of words that threatened to turn into hysteria.

"Hey, wait a minute! Before you go on, Monsieur Latour, I have *not* said a word of blame against you."

"I see it in your eyes, in your manner," he replied truculently. "It was the same with the *tirage*. I have a *very* long memory, Madame."

"So it seems," she said laconically, leaning back and tucking her hands under her arms. "I am *not* blaming you, René, until the full facts are known. However, as *chef de cave* you are officially in charge. Moreover, Marcel Dupois said you especially made it your responsibility. These bottles should have been inspected regularly for signs of weeping, particularly as we had evidence of it quite early on. In that case does it not stand to reason that more care should have been taken?"

"I gave instructions that *every* care should be taken, Madame. I was fully aware of my responsibility, I assure you. I cannot personally inspect forty million bottles such as we have in these caves. I have to delegate to my *chefs d'équipe,* most of whom have many years of experience. However, as soon as I heard of the damage I expected this onslaught on me. I knew *I* would be blamed. I have been a victim from your lack of confidence in me from the beginning. I hereby tender my resignation as *chef de cave,* Madame, and will take no further part in this inquiry in which I am only made a scapegoat . . ."

"But you can't do that." Sandra rose hurriedly to her feet just as the door opened and Legrand came in.

"Do excuse me, Madame," he said, burying his nose in his copious handkerchief. "I am at a complete loss . . ."

"Monsieur Latour has just told me he is resigning."

"Eh!" Legrand gave a shrug.

"I have told him he can't do it. If he does it is tantamount to admitting his responsibility, and I may feel I have to take legal action."

"Oh, Madame Harcourt!" Legrand seemed shocked. "Such disputes are better settled internally."

"What else can I do? Here I have a *very* serious loss, the reason for which I am trying to unearth, and my *chef de cave* resigns. What would *you* do in the circumstances?

Legrand looked pleadingly at his subordinate. "I am quite sure René *will* cooperate."

"I will *not* cooperate," Latour said. "I will not be a victim. I *also* shall consult my lawyer and refuse cooperation. I have been misjudged. I will prove it. I . . ."

Étienne put out his hand.

"There, there, my good man. You are upset. It is understandable. It is Christmas Day. It should be a *happy* occasion and it has turned into a disastrous one. I feel very sorry for Madame, but I also feel sorry for you. I understand your reaction but I must tell you"—he put a hand on the younger man's arm and smiled at him—"I deplore it. I am sure that when you get home and discuss it with Madame Latour you will see that cooperation is your best course. *No one* is going to blame you, my friend, until the full facts are available. It is known how just and thoughtful Madame Harcourt is." Gently Étienne pushed him toward the door. "Go now and see that you and your wife have a glass of champagne when you get home. It is sure to restore your balance."

He then carefully shut the door on René and, with another lengthy blow into his handkerchief, came back into the room and sat down, wearily shaking his head.

"I am more sorry, Madame, about this than I can say. I do hope you don't catch it."

"Oh, don't mind about the cold." Sandra sat in a chair opposite him. "I'm afraid the lack of heat in this office will do you no good either. But, tell me, Étienne, now that we are alone, *how could it happen?* I certainly do not want to make a scapegoat of Latour but, in the end, is he not responsible?"

Étienne rocked on his seat for a few moments as if it aided his thoughts, and when he spoke it was almost as though he were musing to himself.

"Everyone is responsible for the disaster. There was a gross lack of coordination and cooperation between all those involved in this venture, from the glassmaker to Monsieur Zac who initiated it. You and I were also part of it, Madame, so where can we lay the blame?

"Every day an experienced *caviste* was deputed to inspect the bottles. You must understand that weeping *used* to be a problem a long time ago, but is not so now. Bottles used to break frequently, which is the reason for the channels you saw in the ground. Sometimes a complete *cuvée* was ruined in that way, as unfortunately seems to have happened now. But those days had, we thought, passed. With the new strong bottles, the hard corks, we have not had a problem on this scale in all my years here, from the age of fifteen, Madame. So . . ." He leaned forward, pressing his hands to his stomach as if he had a pain. "I can only surmise that in some way this disaster was not accidental. Therefore, you ask, who exactly *is* to blame?"

He raised his eyes and looked at her. "Alas, I can't say. We will have to discover who has been inspecting bottles, on whose orders, how much weeping has been found since the summer . . . why it is that only the bottles at the back are affected and not the front which, you see, prevented anyone knowing what was going on. If this is a deliberate act of sabotage, Madame, it is extremely serious. But would it not be coincidental if there were *two* people in an organization who, within the space of a few years, were responsible for acts of sabotage like this? Last time we blamed Monsieur Pagés and Monsieur Strega. Maybe we should look again to see what Monsieur Strega has been up to. Maybe . . . who knows?" Étienne raised his eyes thoughtfully to the ceiling. "He lives not far from here. Maybe, in a way we do not know, he is trying to get revenge for his dismissal? But if *that* seems too farfetched, Madame, and I must tell you I personally think it is—perhaps one is influenced too much by detective films on the television—I think a more logical and rational explanation is the singular design of the bottle.

"The neck was too long, too fragile to support the cork, and the pressure of carbonization during the second fermentation. We would certainly have had a serious problem with the corkage, and we shall have to look closely into the whole affair. As you know, had I been consulted, I personally would strongly have advised against it."

By the first week of January the extent of the damage had been assessed. The two hundred thousand bottles had been inspected and three-quarters were found either in a bad state of weeping or on the point of it. Fifty thousand bottles would make it a very select *cuvée* indeed, but it could hardly justify a massive advertising campaign, part of which had already begun in the glossy magazines which had appeared on the bookstalls at the beginning of January.

Zac returned from his skiing holiday on 2 January, but a fax had already been sent to him in Gstaad with news of the disaster and he had spoken several times on the telephone to Sandra, to whom he promised his full cooperation.

Leaving his family still enjoying themselves in Switzerland, he flew back to Paris and Sandra sent the helicopter to bring him to Reims. Once he had landed on the lawn and briefly greeted Sandra, he was taken immediately to the caves where he could inspect the disaster for himself. The particular cave where the bottles had been racked still emitted a heavy, almost overpowering smell of spilt wine.

Zac, looking very grave, kept on picking one bottle up after another of the ones which remained, examining the corks closely.

"Fifty thousand bottles you say," he murmured as they walked slowly back to the top, accompanied by a cohort of grave-faced executives: Legrand, Marcel Dupois, Alain Lecouvrier who was in charge of marketing, and Claude Maison whose Christmas had also been virtually ruined by the news. Whatever the reason for the failure of a campaign it always reflected on the agency which thought of it. A sudden cessation could be disastrous.

They all gathered in Sandra's office where they were joined by Alain Fournier, who had manufactured the bottles, and a representative of the firm which had supplied the corks. Of the people sitting round the boardroom table there was one significant exception: René Latour, reserving his rights, had still refused point blank to attend.

In front of each person was a clean sheet of paper and a pen. They all looked uniformly very grave, their elbows on the table, the expressions on their faces deeply thoughtful.

"Well . . ." Sandra nevertheless managed to greet them with a welcoming smile. "Thank you all for coming, some of you for giving up most of your Christmas holiday to this problem. René Latour has indicated that he will not attend and has sent formal notice of his resignation. I consider this a *very* serious step and if we do not resolve the matter satisfactorily internally I may feel obliged to prosecute for serious professional fault and, maybe, even voluntary sabotage."

"But René would never sabotage this firm." Zac, appearing horrified, leaned toward Sandra. "I have known René all my life. He is devoted to this company. He is as incapable as I am of such an act of treachery. He would *never* do it. Besides"—Zac held up his hands and looked round the table—"why should he?"

"Madame thinks that René never got over the business of the *tirage.*" Étienne, who had recovered from the worst of his influenza, still looked pale. "She thinks it may well have been an act of revenge for that."

Zac continued to look about him with an air of incredulity. "But René was *so* enthusiastic, was he not, Sandra?"

"He seemed very keen." Sandra didn't miss a move of Zac's. "Especially about *your* design for the bottle."

"Exactly. He said he thought it was exquisite and it was. It *is.*"

"Some people seem to think that *that* is the real reason for the disaster," Sandra murmured, but loud enough for Zac to hear.

"I agree." Étienne nodded his head affirmatively and folded his arms.

"I do *not* agree." Alain Fournier, who seemed to have a

temper, thumped the table. "*I* made that glass. I supervised it myself. It was *exactly* to the specifications, to the millimeter." He thrust a piece of paper, of which he had made several photocopies, in front of Sandra, and distributed the rest around the table.

Once again she had the feeling of *déjà vu.* It had all happened before. There were the instructions neatly typed, the specifications listed underneath and there, at the bottom, was her signature: Sandra Harcourt. There was no doubt about that at all.

"The specifications were given to me by Monsieur Desmond," Sandra said, in a slightly distracted tone.

"Nevertheless, *you* signed the paper, Madame," Fournier insisted. "If it comes to court you are responsible."

"Court? It will not come to court." Zac sounded horrified. "This is an internal matter that will be settled internally. However . . ." He cleared his throat. "Madame signed the order and it *is* her responsibility. Nevertheless, the specifications are mine, the calibration worked out mathematically, and I stand by them. I will support Madame."

"Thank you, Zac." Sandra gave him a grateful smile.

"Then maybe it was unwise," the cork supplier, whose name was Jérôme Bordeu, spoke for the first time, "to use an agglomerated cork for the *bouchon de tirage.* Did no one think of that? I would certainly have suggested a laminated cork to give it further strength, despite the added expense." He turned courteously to Sandra. "You see, Madame, in my opinion in this case it was unwise to use cork at all for the *bouchon de tirage.* A stopper made of aluminum would have been more suited to the ring of the bottle, as well as being cheaper than cork."

He threw out his arms in a gesture of irritation and sat back. "*Voilà!* Had *I* been consulted that is what I would have suggested."

"But you *knew* the thickness of the bottle," Zac said accusingly. "Surely you could have used your common sense?"

"But I was not instructed, Monsieur Desmond," Bordeu said with the hauteur of one whose business has been in the family for generations. "See, Madame, here is the order"—he passed a single piece of paper to Sandra—"signed by Monsieur Latour. It is perfectly clear; pure Catalan cork is specified, size and thickness indicated."

Sandra looked at the paper which was meaningless to her. For once, however, she saw that it did *not* have her signature on the bottom, for which she silently thanked God. Then without comment she passed it to Zac who stared at it.

"Well, that foolish man, Latour, *deserves* to be sacked," he said, pushing the paper away as though he found the very sight of it offensive. "However, one thing we can be sure of is that the matter is solved. It was *not* conspiracy, only a simple case of misjudgement on the part of Latour. Well," he sighed, and threw up his arms, "he has paid the price. He does not deserve to be *chef de cave,* and, as it is, he has resigned—with good reason as we now know."

Sandra still did not appear to be happy. "But I don't see why he should resign if he did not consider himself responsible?"

"My dear Sandra." Zac gave her a patronizing look. "*I* can think of a reason, but I will not say it in front of these good people." He pushed back his chair and stood up.

"But *please* do say it." Sandra also stood up. "In front of witnesses. I want no secrets, Zac, nothing underhand as we had with the *tirage.*"

"Then, if you ask *me,* my dear"—Zac's eyes narrowed—"René made an error of judgment for which he knew you would not forgive him or try to understand. He felt, quite justifiably, that you had always blamed him for the error of the *tirage,* when he was head cellarman, and that you would blame him now. He lost the will to fight, poor man. He felt, Sandra, in short"—Zac paused to draw a deep breath—"that he was a victim of your prejudice and I am sorry to say it in front of your colleagues—but remember you did ask me—I think he was right." Zac shot out his arm and looked ostentatiously at his watch. "Now I'm afraid I must go. I have many other more important matters to attend to than the careless loss of a few thousand bottles of wine."

He was about to go to the door but Sandra went quickly ahead of him and stood with her back against it.

"No, I will *not* let you go," she said. "I refuse to let you leave in this fashion—casually casting suspicion on *me,* exonerating Latour. This was your idea and *he* carried it out. *You* designed the bottle." Sandra made an imaginary sketch in the air. " 'Oh, a beautiful bottle, Madame, so elegant.' " Growing increasingly heated she now raised her voice. "Why did you not specify the *bouchon de tirage* too, Zac? You must have known the risk. *That's* what I would very much like to know."

"Oh, really, Sandra." Zac made as if to brush past her. "If you had capable people running this place, such accidents would not happen. If you ask me, there are too many of them. Please don't attempt to pass the buck to me. Now may I pass?" He gazed at her coolly and, lowering his voice, said, "And take my advice. Try, please, *not* to make such an exhibition of yourself, attempting to blame others for your own gross failures in management."

Aware, at last, of an overwhelming sense of defeat, a premonition of disaster, Sandra allowed herself to step aside and averted her eyes as Zac swept past her, leaving a room full of stunned, silent people behind him.

Zac sat in his car in one of the small side streets of the town, not far from the busy Pont de Vesle and the autoroute. He had taken a blue Peugeot belonging to a member of his staff and had left his Ferrari Testarossa at Tourville. For someone like Zac who had been born in the city and whose face was familiar to almost everyone who lived in it, it was difficult to arrange a rendezvous where he was absolutely sure of not being recognized. Tourville had been out of the question, so were any of the hotels or bars. He seldom walked in the streets of Reims, but when he did so he was invariably stopped by half a dozen people, mostly former employees of Desmond Champagne who had known his father or his grandfather.

Yet the venue still made him feel nervous and he anxiously tapped his fingers on the steering wheel while listening to the car radio and waiting for the headlights to flash, which was the agreed signal. There was a tap on his side window and Zac jumped nearly a foot in the air. Then he saw a familiar face pressed against the glass, and, leaning over, he unlocked the door of the passenger seat.

"You fool! You scared me to death. I thought you were supposed to *signal* with your headlights?"

"I'm sorry, Monsieur Zac," René Latour said humbly, slipping into the seat beside Zac. "I left my car round the corner. In view of your anxiety about secrecy I thought it would be safer."

"Of *course* I'm anxious about secrecy," Zac snapped. "If any word of this collusion got to the imbecile Irish woman we'd have had it." He felt inside his breast pocket and withdrew an envelope which he handed to René. "As agreed," he said.

"Thank *you,* Monsieur Zac." Latour slipped the bulky envelope into his own breast pocket. "I can't tell you how grateful I am."

"You're grateful!" Zac managed a laugh, albeit a strained one. "Without you I could never have pulled this thing off and, believe me, the humiliation of losing her precious *cuvée* is only the beginning of what I have in store for that lady. However"—he turned to René and placed a hand on his arm—"you have sacrificed yourself, my friend, for the greater good. The least I can do to thank you is to pay you handsomely. I think this little sum will tide you over until I have disposed of Madame and can employ you again."

"You really think you *will* regain control of Établissements Desmond?" René's eyes gleamed in the dark.

"Think? I know. It is a matter of days, weeks. However, I should not be able to re-employ you immediately, but when I do it will be as director general of établissements de Champagne Desmond, and that traitor, that sniveling wretch, Legrand, will get the elbow. *Not,* I may say, before time."

"Oh, *thank* you, Monsieur Zac."

"No, you did a very good job, René. It must have been a Herculean task moving the good bottles to the front, the bad to the back."

"Oh, I had assistance, Monsieur. Don't worry."

"You had *what?"* Zac hissed. "You don't mean to tell me you *employed* somebody to help you?"

"Someone I can trust implicitly, sir," René said smugly. "My seventeen-year-old son, Robert. He did exactly what he was told without question, besides which his lips are sealed."

"You are certain Robert will not talk?"

"Robert will not say a *word* to a soul, Monsieur. I can stake my life on that."

"Then there will be work for him too," Zac said with satisfaction. "How I *wish* I could have seen Madame's face when she first saw all the piss that little Louis was making in the cave. Oh dear, how I *wish* I could have seen it!" And then he started to laugh so much and in such a bizarre fashion that, eventually, the tears ran down his face.

On the way home René, who had been startled by that insane laugh, wondered to himself if Monsieur Zac were really in control of all his faculties, or whether the intense hatred he felt for Madame Harcourt had eaten half his brain away.

23

Sandra, with her marketing director Alain Lecouvrier, and Claude Maison sat in a huddle in the Paris office over the papers on the boardroom table. Before her she had the costs of the campaign and the possible revenue from the sale of the bottles that had been saved; not the fifty thousand that had been hoped but a mere thirty thousand.

"For God's sake, this is a disaster." Sandra frowned angrily at the people who sat round the table.

Sandra knew she was rattled. She hated the feeling she was losing control. She was convinced that, once again, she had been the victim of a conspiracy and she was sure the instigator was Zac but, yet again, he had covered his tracks so astutely that no one could prove it. The corkmaker, the glassmaker, and nearly everyone involved had come to the conclusion that it was a tragic accident that could have been prevented with a little foresight.

She made an attempt to recover herself and said briskly: "We have spent a fortune on the advertising and we are left with only thirty thousand bottles. The *remuage* has been proceeded with immediately, so all is well. Do we sell them, or do we call the whole thing off?"

"A very special champagne, Madame," Alain suggested. "Say you sell each bottle for six hundred francs. They will become collectors' pieces."

"And maybe drink fifty of them on a very special occasion"—Claude felt that for the first time in this whole disastrous affair he could see a chink of light—"held for charity and attended by the Prime Minister and his wife."

"What an *excellent* idea," Sandra said, getting to her feet. "And it will be in aid of the Harcourt Medical Foundation. Better still"—she spun round—"we will give the proceeds of the *entire cuvée* to charity."

"You mean we will not recoup *anything,* Madame?" Alain, a careful man where money was concerned, said with a gulp.

"Not a sou. It will be to the glory of champagne and, of course, the benefit of medical research in which my late husband was interested."

"Excellent, excellent." Alain threw down his pencil and sat back, running his hands through his hair. "And now, I think, we have finally solved that problem."

The telephone rang and Antoinette rose to answer it.

She spoke in a low voice and Sandra caught "No, no, no," repeated several times, accompanied by anxious glances in Sandra's direction.

Finally she replaced the receiver and, going over to Sandra, murmured in her ear.

Sandra looked a bit startled but then shrugged and, rising, said to the men at the table: "Please excuse me for a few moments. Something needs my personal attention. I'm sure it won't take long."

She then followed Antoinette to the door.

Commissioner Renard got to his feet when Sandra entered the small office into which the receptionist had shown him.

It was a back room with a view of the fire escape of the neighboring house, also now turned into offices. In retrospect Sandra thought she would remember that particular room, its sparseness and air of melancholy, for the rest of her life. On the other hand maybe, with hindsight, she imagined it all rather as one does when in a certain place on a sad occasion. It was furnished sparsely with a desk, a table, a few chairs and was only occasionally used for meetings when both the boardroom and her own office were occupied.

"Monsieur Renard," she said, putting out her hand, "how nice to see you again."

"And you, Madame." Renard bowed politely as he shook her hand and then gestured toward the figure who stood just behind him. "May I introduce Monsieur Bloc from the Ministry of Finance who is here on behalf of the Customs."

"Really?" Sandra found it hard to conceal her surprise, but politely shook hands with the impassive Frenchman who stepped into the background where he appeared clearly more at home.

"Is it something to do with Mr. O'Neill?" Sandra turned toward Renard. "I'm afraid he's still skiing in Italy. The ordeal of his imprisonment took a great deal out of him . . ."

"I'm sure, Madame." Renard managed to introduce the right note of sympathy in his voice. Yet there was also another note, a certain timbre, that made Sandra look at him sharply.

"Your visit then is *not* connected with Mr. O'Neill, Commissioner? Please sit down." She indicated a chair by the desk for him and one slightly behind for Monsieur Bloc, and then turned to Antoinette. "Please tell my colleagues to proceed without me, and then rejoin us."

"Madame," Commissioner Renard intervened, "I think you might like to hear what I have to say in private. Of course, it's entirely up to you."

"Well . . ." Sandra thought for a moment and then said to Antoinette, "I'll call you if I need you."

"Yes, Madame." Antoinette darted a worried look at the policeman and went quickly out of the room.

"Now, Commissioner." Sandra sat opposite him and, crossing her legs, folded her hands in her lap, noting as she did that Bloc had produced a notepad and a pen which was poised over the page. The sight unnerved her even more. "What *is* this mystery?" she asked uncomfortably.

Renard was in the process of producing some documents

from his briefcase which he laid in orderly fashion on the desk between them. He studied them for a moment, like a judge in a court of law, and then he too joined his hands together and gazed at her.

"Madame, I have reason to believe you have *not* been entirely honest with us in the matter of the release of Mr. O'Neill."

"Oh? How is that?"

"You paid a ransom."

"I told you I'd paid a ransom after Monsieur Desmond secured Bob's release. I paid it to him for transmission to the abductors."

"You told *us* five million pounds."

"That is correct."

"You paid it in cash?"

"In used notes."

"What I do not dispute, Madame"—Renard quickly glanced again at his papers—"is that you paid a ransom, but *how* much you paid. I have information now that it was ten million pounds."

"Who told you this?"

He looked at her and smiled.

"That, I'm afraid, I am not at liberty to say."

"Did *Monsieur Desmond,* for instance, tell you this?"

"I'm afraid I cannot say."

"Well, wherever or whoever you got it from, your information is wrong. It was *five* million."

"And how did you come by this money, Madame Harcourt?" The Commissioner's tone was growing more and more unfriendly as if he were attempting to distance himself from her.

"Some of it I had and I borrowed the rest. It is not such a great sum, after all. I was initially asked for much more."

Bloc temporarily stopped his writing before quickly resuming, while Renard, to whom ten or even five million pounds sterling was also a considerable sum of money, went on impassively: "From whom did you borrow the rest?"

"From the bank . . ."

"You didn't, for instance, embezzle it, Madame?"

For a moment there was complete silence in the room and the traffic that plied up and down the Champs Élysées, round the Étoile, seemed like a distant hum of bees.

"Did you say 'embezzle'?" Sandra said after a while. "I don't believe I heard you correctly."

"I'm afraid it *is* a case of embezzlement we are investigating, Madame. Acting on information received I have reason to believe that you conspired with a Bernardo Romanetto to steal this money from the Desmond Group. You planted it over a period of time in certain European banks, and then when you needed the money to ransom Mr. O'Neill you collected it in cash."

"I have *never* heard such nonsense in my life," Sandra cried, pushing back her chair and lifting the telephone. "I am going to telephone my lawyer immediately."

"Please let me finish, Madame Harcourt," Renard said so quietly and politely that Sandra immediately replaced the receiver. "I think you should hear me out. I wanted to give you this information privately because you are a woman of some position in society. I wanted to spare you, at least initially, the painful process of interrogation in front of witnesses. I must confess that I myself found it *very* hard to believe; but I'm sorry to say the evidence against you at the moment appears overwhelming. Do hear me out, Madame."

"Very well, proceed." Sandra sat back, trying hard to conceal her consternation. This time it was difficult, even for her. "I should tell you," she said, "that the embezzlement happened *well* before my time as group president and I have never met Mr. Romanetto in my life."

"Nor do you know where he is now?"

"No."

"I see." Renard tapped his fingers on the table. "Why, then, Madame, were you so interested in the whereabouts of Mr. Romanetto, let me see, about eighteen months ago?"

"Because I had time before and after the birth of my son to look carefully into all aspects of the organization I had been managing for four years. I found out many unknown aspects of the business which fully explained why Monsieur Zac Desmond might not have been considered by his father fit to run it. But the embezzlement of *twenty-five* million US dollars frankly took my breath away! Nothing had been done about it, no attempt made to find Romanetto. That is when I became interested."

"That is all?"

"That is all."

"It has been suggested that in your capacity as an investment analyst with the Hammerson Trust in California you had previous contact with Mr. Romanetto's office in Geneva."

"That is *completely* untrue. I had not. The whole idea is *bizarre* in the extreme." Now no longer quite so frightened at the scale of these absurd accusations, she was beginning to show her annoyance. "*Who* on earth suggested that?"

The Commissioner, apparently unimpressed, evaded an answer by pressing forward his attack.

"Then *why,* Madame, did you go and see Madame Romanetto in Geneva and suggest her husband might be dead?"

"I did not *suggest* it. I asked her if she had ever suspected it."

"You then, apparently, set out on a trail, Madame, of depositing large sums of money in various banks under the name Sandra Wingate."

"Oh, that *is* ridiculous." Sandra threw back her head and laughed for the first time in this tense interview. "*That's* the name of my natural mother."

"So I understand. Not a very *subtle* way of concealing your identity, Madame."

"Exactly. Then one I would not choose."

Renard leaned forward, a glint of excitement in his eyes. "But as you *are* such a clever woman, Madame Harcourt, that is just the way you might have expected us to think. 'I would *never* choose that name because I hate my mother. Therefore I *will* choose it.'"

"My mind would never work like that, I assure you," she

replied. "Anyway it's quite beside the point because I didn't do it."

"I see." Renard looked at his notes again. "Monsieur Dericourt has told us he was surprised by your interest at the time in Romanetto."

"He told *you* that?"

"He did."

"But he is my loyal lieutenant, my second-in-command."

"Well, he spoke most reluctantly; but he *did* confirm that you showed a great interest in Romanetto and his whereabouts, and he thought it odd, even suspicious, at the time."

"Indeed!" Sandra pursed her lips. "I must remember that."

Renard opened a sealed envelope and, from this, he produced a set of photographs which he carefully placed before Sandra. Bloc, clearly familiar with the photographs, sat back, his pad resting on his knee, and stared thoughtfully at the ceiling.

"Would you *deny* these pictures are of you, Madame Harcourt?" Renard inquired, carefully watching Sandra as she picked them up and studied them. He observed how her mobile features underwent subtle changes as she gazed at the photographs. He saw interest, bewilderment there . . . could he also detect any sign of guilt?

"I would certainly say it *looks* like me," Sandra said at last, "and it certainly *is* one of my suits. It is a couture model by Thierry Mugler and thus made only for me. But"—she smiled at him as she put the photographs back on the desk—"it is not me. It is a long time since I entered an ordinary commercial bank." She pointed to the name BANCO D'ITALIA in the background. "I conduct my personal affairs privately, usually by fax or telephone."

"We have had these photographs tested by specialists and they are all inclined to think they are genuine photographs of you, Madame Harcourt."

"But the face is rather blurred."

"Taken from a distance . . ."

"Why then," she demanded, her courage fully restored as she

tapped the table in front of her, *"why* then should *anyone* take a picture of me going into or coming out of a bank? Please answer that, Monsieur Renard."

Renard inclined his head. "That *is* the question, Madame. Why? But we have gone into the details very carefully. You were in those places at the times the money was deposited and later withdrawn. We have seen the documentation with your signatures. Naturally we believed them to be disguised. It is also *your* suit, it seems to be *you,* Madame Harcourt." He stood up and looked at her rather sadly while Sandra, seemingly still composed and thoughtful, remained in her chair. Finally she looked up at him and he saw a light of grim determination in her eyes. He had always, from the first meeting, been a little in awe of her and now he was again.

"Could you tell me, Commissioner Renard," she said slowly, "why on earth you suppose I would need to go through such an *elaborate* deception for a few million bucks I could easily have got by lawful means?"

Renard stroked his face. "It is a question I have asked myself frequently since this matter arose, Madame Harcourt. In fact I have no answer except the evidence I've been presented with.

"For instance, where *is* Romanetto? He has not been seen for years. Maybe he was blackmailing you and you felt you had to get rid of him. Maybe you found raising five million pounds quite easy, but not ten. That would explain the difference between *your* version and an informant's. Frankly, Madame Harcourt, I have come across worse cases of villainy than this whose perpetrators you would imagine above suspicion. Just like you." He shrugged again. "Alas, the evidence against you *does* appear at the moment to be overwhelming. I hoped you would be able to refute it in detail, but you can't. I'm afraid I have therefore to ask you to accompany me to police headquarters."

"Now?" Sandra rose as if in a daze.

"Now, Madame, if you would. You may, of course, now call your lawyer."

"Someone is trying to *frame* me, Commissioner," Sandra said.

"Don't you understand that? And," she added thoughtfully, "I have a pretty damn good idea I know who that someone is."

Eva Raus hurried into the small fourth-floor room she rented in the Trocadéro district and, with an air of profound relief, kicked off her shoes and spread herself on the sofa with the evening paper.

She worked from nine to five thirty in the Galeries Lafayette and, at the end of the day, her feet were killing her. But this evening the pain was forgotten in the excitement of what she had read on the billboards selling the evening paper:

ARREST OF MILLIONAIRE BUSINESS WOMAN ON EMBEZZLEMENT CHARGES.

And here, under a picture of Sandra, were the facts in black type to indicate the gravity of the charge.

There was a shock arrest today at her sumptuous office in the Place de l'Étoile of Madame Sandra Harcourt, the widow of the celebrated medical pioneer, and millionaire directrice of the Desmond Group.

Today's arrest must come as a double shock to a woman who has dazzled the whole world by her spectacular career yet who has had her share of misfortune and is no stranger to litigation. Three years ago she successfully sued a London newspaper for defamation . . .

There followed an account of Sandra's career, the damaging revelations at the trial about her parenthood, the violent death of her husband, and there was even mention of David Heurtey, now "a constant companion". The article also contained the information that what were tactfully referred to as "technical problems" had caused her to suspend the production of a special *cuvée* in honor of her son Louis.

On the inside pages there was a double spread of text and more pictures which included the one due to be released of Sandra and Louis by Max Zamburger; the pair of them were looking enchanting, standing in the morning sunlight by an open window. There was more text outlining yet again her relationship with the Desmonds who had also had more than their fair share of gossip.

There were pictures of Belle, Zac, Carl von Burg-Farnbach and his mistress; on other pages there was even more to titillate the tastes of a jaded public in the absence of more substantial news events.

Eventually Eva put down the paper and went to the sideboard where she poured herself a generous measure of pastis, going into her tiny kitchen to add water. She then returned to the sofa and, lighting a cigarette, sank back to mull over the paper.

Finally she put it on the floor and, leaning her head on the arm of the sofa, wearily closed her eyes. She was certainly a member of that jaded public, her senses dulled by repetitive, routine work, who had once enjoyed the easy life with Romanetto and had expected to again. But it was not to be. She had been cheated, stolen from, denied her rights. And she had just been waiting for the opportunity, the right moment to arrive when she could take her revenge.

Dreams, dreams of revenge . . . oh, how *sweet* were the dreams of revenge that she nurtured both waking and sleeping. And now it seemed she might at last turn dream into reality.

There was no one in the world Eva hated more than Zac Desmond, unless it were Strega, although he had always claimed he was only a cypher, a servant of the great man who had so much of a hold over him, knew so much about him, that he was forced to do his will.

She hated them both in equal measure and maybe now she could strike.

She opened her eyes and stared at the ceiling, which was yellow with age.

And she had been promised half a million! She had thought she would live out her days in a villa overlooking the Lake of Lucerne, or Geneva. If ever a woman felt used and bruised, if ever a woman nursed a grudge, that woman was Eva Raus. Yet it appeared now that it was not only people like her and Bernardo whom Desmond destroyed, mere ants on the pavement probably, as far as he was concerned; but he went after the big fish too: even the great Madame Harcourt was not immune, and she, Eva Raus, had helped to bring about the downfall of a woman she didn't know, a widow, the mother of a young child.

Eva swung her legs off the sofa, massaged for a moment her aching feet, and went and poured herself another drink, her excitement growing moment by moment. Then she looked at her face in the mirror and felt it was not bad; some makeup from the cosmetics department of the Galeries, a new dress or two, maybe smuggled out by the staff entrance . . . and Monsieur Zac would get his just deserts.

Not, it seemed, before time.

The next few weeks were a nightmare from which Sandra felt she would never wake up; worse, much worse than the ordeal of the libel trial in London where, again, her name had never been out of the papers.

There would be no special *cuvée* now because there was nothing to celebrate. Louis d'Or would only have brought further unwelcome publicity and the whole matter was quietly dropped.

This time the entire world's press seemed to have congregated in Paris or Reims, ferreting out the minutest detail they could discover about her. In the States Virginia Wingate had, yet again, to close her house and go into hiding. Even the Pipers took refuge in the anonymity of a large hotel on the West Coast. Anyone who had at any time known Sandra Harcourt was not spared, and those who had not even known her very well made the most of it. Sandra thought that once the case was over the rest of her life would be spent bringing actions against those who daily defamed her in the columns of the newspapers.

For, knowing she was innocent of the grotesque charges, she was quite sure she would win. David had suggested that Joanne Pasarro should be called back to go to the places allegedly visited by Sandra, which she gladly did; but all she received was corroboration.

Sandra had indeed visited the places on the appointed dates, had been identified personally by the banks as the person who had deposited the money and drawn it out again.

A team of police officers experienced in fraud got a warrant to take Sandra's office apart, inspecting all the books and records.

They drew a blank, apart from ascertaining that Madame Harcourt did keep spare traveling clothes in the office, including the suit in which she had allegedly been photographed, and an official seal was put on the cupboard containing them until they were produced as evidence in court.

Zac, meanwhile, kept a low profile and appeared with reluctance to cooperate with the police. Although the documents accusing Sandra had been sent anonymously by him, the police instinctively turned to him for corroboration.

When Commissioner Renard came to see him again he was alone, as if to impress Zac with the secrecy of his mission, one which he was keen to keep off the record, as it were.

Zac hurried to the door of his office as soon as the policeman was announced and, dismissing his secretary at the threshold, ushered him in.

"Do sit down, Commissioner," he said immediately, showing him a chair and offering him the humidor of cigars. Grim-faced, Renard shook his head.

"I do not, thank you, Monsieur. I am here, in fact, on a mission of the utmost confidentiality."

"Naturally you can trust me implicitly, Commissioner." Zac replaced the cigar container on the table, suppressing at the same time an almost overwhelming desire to smoke one. Better to be seen to have the same high ascetic standards as his guest.

"Now, Commissioner . . ." Casually unfastening the button of his jacket he pulled up a seat so that he was near—but not too near—and facing him, his expression one of attentive concern. "Please proceed."

"It does, of course, concern Madame Harcourt, Monsieur

Desmond." The steel-gray eyes peered bleakly into those of the man she had supplanted.

"Ah . . ." Zac threw up his hands in a gesture of despair. "What a tragedy. Who would have thought . . ."

"You, of course, had no idea . . ."

"Of course one had no idea!" he exclaimed with a further gesture of horror. "However . . ." He paused and examined the polished surfaces of his fingernails.

"A *suspicion* perhaps, Monsieur Desmond," Renard suggested, "that all was not exactly *comme il faut?"*

"A suspicion perhaps," Zac admitted, with a regretful expression. "She was, you know, unsuited for such an exalted position. Implicit is the suggestion that my poor father bordered on premature senility when he made her his heir, though of course we had no idea of this."

"Madame was not in fact up to the task?"

"Not *really."* Zac's expression was one of infinite sadness.

"And of course she effectively removed you from your birthright."

The Commissioner's tone seemed sympathetic rather than suggestive.

"Well, I had to accept that my father, in his apparent wisdom . . ." Zac smiled, again a little sadly. "Now, Commissioner, is that all you wish to say?"

Renard shifted in his seat. "Monsieur Desmond, what I have come to ask you is *extremely* confidential. It is, in fact, based on Madame's past and you should know more of that than most. As she *strenuously* denies any embezzlement of Desmond funds I wondered if, as has been suggested, she really *would* have had occasion to meet Romanetto before she became the head of the group?"

Zac thoughtfully put a forefinger to his chin.

"Meet? Oh no. Not *meet,* Commissioner. I am quite sure they would not have met. But of course it is perfectly possible they had *contact* with each other. She was an analyst for Hammerson

Trust, an organization with which our holding company certainly had dealings."

"She would then, perhaps, have had dealings personally with Romanetto?"

"Almost surely, I would have thought . . ." Zac's voice trailed off as if the importance of what he was saying had only just occurred to him.

"You see, all the relevant documentation about Monsieur Romanetto is missing from the Geneva office," Renard added.

"That could explain a lot then, could it not?" Zac's tone of voice appeared to corroborate the suspicions in the detective's mind yet, as he rose to take his farewell, there was a bad taste in his mouth. The interview had shaken him. Zac's charm was so obviously false, his undoubted emotion one of revenge.

Renard had no doubt that Sandra's downfall pleased Zac very much; but in his eyes, although the nicer and more appealing person, Sandra was the criminal, not Zac.

Sandra could find no peace. The examining magistrate was a courteous man and she thought he was half inclined to believe her; but, maybe, like Renard, he believed in her guilt but was impressed by her charm.

She was released on bail of five million francs, her passport was confiscated and she had to cooperate with the police. She knew they would find, as they did, everything in order at the Desmond headquarters both in Paris and Reims.

She also knew that, had they not been deflected by her apparent guilt, but had taken the trouble to take the Banque Franco-Belges apart, they would probably have discovered the real source of the mystery.

Could it be that, finally, Zac had won?

When she wasn't with the police or the magistrate Sandra took refuge in Reims. The press knew where she lived and everything about her. They knew about David and his visits, and they followed him about too. There was only one place they didn't know about: the Château de Marsanne.

It was nearly ready for occupation. During the weeks since he'd bought it David had found it the refuge he needed almost as much as Sandra.

David was as protective toward Sandra in her ordeal as it was possible to be; but nothing could really help Sandra except proof of her innocence and, although he believed in her, this proof was proving hard to find.

Late one night Sandra was working quietly in the office at Reims, having got into the main building through a little-known entrance to the caves. There was always a posse of the press outside the gate but, at night, it thinned, leaving only one or two persistent hacks. Sandra's office wasn't visible from the gates so she believed that, here at least, she could get some peace, and if the Desmond empire was to be saved it was only here that she could do it.

But could it be saved? The shares had slumped on the Bourse and were going even lower. Suspension loomed. Heurtey was helping to keep up the share price, but the shipment of the automatic assembly plant, already on the docks in Japan, had to be postponed. Some wondered if there would be a Desmond empire left.

Zac and the family had kept their distance, except for one or two perfunctory phone calls pledging a support which it was hard to take seriously. When the storm broke they had attended an emergency board meeting and promised her their full cooperation. But there was a false ring about it. There were no invitations to Tourville or the Paris house. One felt that the Desmonds were distancing themselves, and with reason: it was logical that they wouldn't want the family to be too closely associated with a woman who had betrayed them all and who one day might find herself in prison.

Faithful Antoinette was in the building with her, working next door, which was a comfort to Sandra who felt almost childlike in her fear of the night.

Antoinette came in with coffee and said anxiously: "Madame, it is very late. Shouldn't you go home?"

"My dear, there is so much to do." Sandra took the coffee with a grateful smile. "If I am to go down I must do all I can to prevent the company going down too."

"You will *not* go down, Madame," Antoinette said firmly, sitting uninvited in the chair opposite Sandra. "It is inconceivable that you are guilty. I was with you and I know."

"And yet they will subpoena you for the prosecution." Sandra reached over and took the hand of the woman she regarded as a companion and friend. "You accompanied me to the various cities where the money was deposited. You can swear what I wore . . ."

"But not on the specific days, Madame. No one could remember those."

Sandra's brow furrowed as she took a sip of the reviving liquid. "You know, Antoinette, I have always thought there must have been a spy in the office. Maybe more than one. All my movements were known. My clothes were worn. I have been framed and set up but by whom, and why?"

Antoinette glanced at her nails.

"*You* know who set you up, Madame. All you need is the proof."

"But what, if we are right, has he to gain from it?"

"He will gain control of the company again, Madame. *That* is his object. That is why he avoids you as well. He is like a spider, Madame, biding its time to catch a fly."

Sandra finished her coffee and put down her cup.

"You remember Agnès who spied on behalf of Zac? We caught *her* in time. Maybe there was another Agnès." She smiled ruefully and shook her head. "I must tell you that, at one time, I thought it might be you."

"Oh, Madame." The loyal Antoinette looked crestfallen.

"You were with me, you knew my routine, you knew my clothes." She reached over and, again, lightly touched the older woman's arm. "But I knew it *couldn't* be you. Yet I am sure there has been a spy in the office. Someone, somewhere, an insignificant clerk perhaps . . ."

"There *was* Marie-Claire Laurent." Antoinette shrugged. "But no . . . she would know nothing at all."

"Marie-Claire? I don't know her."

"She worked in the typing pool, Madame. I only say it because she left not long after you were arrested, but I'm sure there is no significance in that."

Sandra scribbled down the name. "Try and find out where she lives and why she left . . . you never know. Little things . . ."

The telephone shrilled sharply and Sandra picked it up at once. Only a few people had her private number, and as soon as she heard the static on the line she knew it was long distance.

"Sandra?"

"Bob!"

"How *are* you?" His voice sounded very far away.

"Bearing up. How are you?"

"I'm fed up at having to be here in this clinic. I'd rather be with you."

"But Dr. Baker says you're a lot better."

"Sandra, I'm returning to Paris in a few days."

"Oh, Bob . . . there's nothing you can do. The stress for you will be awful."

"Nonetheless it's where I want to be. You've been *framed* and I want to see if I can help you."

"Bob, there's nothing. Everything that can be done is being done. I've an excellent team of lawyers. There's no chance they will convict . . . it's just the waiting that's the darnedest thing."

"Still, I want to be there. I love you . . ."

"And I love you too, Bob."

"Anyway I'm checking out of the clinic this weekend and going to Rome to take the plane. I want to see Falconetti before I go."

"Bob, is that *wise?* He's lied about the money. I think he's implicated."

"*Zac* lied about the money. All Marco did was to help free me and I feel I haven't thanked him enough. Anyway maybe I can find something out."

"Well, maybe you can. Take care though."

"I'll take care, and you . . . and Sandra . . ."

"Yes?"

"I'll find my own way to you. I know what those news hounds are like, but, so far, they have not got on to me. God bless."

"God bless, Bob," Sandra said and as she put down the telephone there were tears in her eyes.

Already while she had been on the phone there was a knocking at the door and Antoinette went quickly over to open it. The night porter stood outside looking apologetic.

"This letter was delivered a few moments ago, Madame," he said, handing a large white envelope to Antoinette. "It is for Madame Harcourt."

He bowed to Sandra and withdrew while Antoinette, scrutinizing the name on the envelope, began to open it.

"Be careful," Sandra said anxiously. "It might be a bomb."

Antoinette stiffened and felt it.

"It's just a sheet of paper," she said and, carefully, she slit open the envelope and withdrew the letter inside it. She read its contents, giving nothing away, and then, without a word, handed it to Sandra.

It went:

Dear Madame Harcourt,

You will recall that, according to the will of the late Georges Desmond, a council was constituted which had the power to remove you from control of the Desmond Group if you showed yourself unworthy of the office.

I am sorry to tell you that, after very grave deliberation, the members of the council have decided to hold a meeting on [a date was given] to consider the matter.

They deem it only a courtesy to invite you, or your legal representative, or both, to attend.

With every good wish, Madame, I am,

Yours sincerely,
Auguste Laban.

Sandra let the letter flutter to the desk and gazed up at Antoinette with resignation in her eyes.

"At last," she said. "I was expecting this. This leaves me in no doubt as to who was responsible and, above all, why."

24

Zac sat in the bar of the Plaza Athénée Hotel reading the evening paper. As usual Tara was late. He sat in a corner away from the crowd which gathered toward the end of the day because he was tired of being stared at, accosted or jostled in the street. It was a high price to pay for getting rid of Sandra, but it was worth it. However, he wore dark glasses, even sometimes a hat, and kept a very low profile. For several reasons it was, in any case, advisable to do this. He had played for the highest stakes and now he couldn't afford to lose.

Everything was going well for Zac, tremendously well. So well he couldn't believe it. Yet, still he felt that he was skating on thin ice; at any place, at any moment, it might crack. He knew it was vital to play it cool, and he was not a cool person by nature. He was impetuous, mercurial, prone to misjudgement and to make mistakes. Thank God for someone with a level head on her shoulders like his sister, Belle, who had most capably taken charge of the campaign. Belle had almost stage-managed affairs from the moment it was obvious that their strategy might succeed.

Keep cool, calm, distant, was her advice; but let us all *pretend* to be sympathetic toward Sandra. Poor Sandra. Above all let us keep out of sight and say as little as possible.

With difficulty Zac did as he was told. He kept quiet, he kept cool, he tried to keep out of sight. But what to do about Jean Marvoine was a problem. It was a third owned by Desmond, a third each by Tara and Belle. In theory, therefore, Tara and Belle could take control but they would have to buy out Desmond. Once, however, he had ousted Sandra there would be no problem. Then they would probably sell the fashion house to the highest bidder. As it was being so badly run it might not actually fetch much. Belle was a good businesswoman but had no interest in fashion; her sights were set on something much higher. Tara, though loving fashion, knew nothing about business.

Zac looked toward the door, but there was no sign of his wife. He turned over the pages of the evening paper and then signaled to the waiter to order another whiskey. Thank heaven, the drama about Sandra was at last beginning to die down. Less of Sandra, less of the Desmonds. There was only a small paragraph about it, and he thankfully put the paper on the seat beside him, as a mature but extremely elegant woman slipped into the seat on his left and began to try and catch the eye of the waiter as well.

She was about thirty-five with blonde, streaked hair, a good profile and firm skin, sexy rather than beautiful. He thought for a moment that he knew her and then decided it was because she very faintly resembled Sandra; they had the same coloring.

She looked toward him and, as their eyes met, she gave him an aloof smile. She wore a wedding ring and some good jewelery, a suit that didn't look quite couture—a bit too loose on the shoulders—but her accessories were acceptable. She could be the wife of a prosperous man; or perhaps in business herself. She was quite heavily made up, which he considered a mistake. Otherwise he found her attractive.

The waiter approached her after indicating that he was aware of Zac.

"Madame?"

"I'm waiting for someone," she said in a voice that had a slight accent, maybe Swiss or German. "But in the meantime I'll have a Perrier." He bowed to her and then to Zac.

"Monsieur?"

"Same again," Zac said, indicating his glass.

As the waiter went off Zac found that he and the woman were again looking at each other. Simultaneously they both smiled.

"You must forgive me," the woman said, leaning slightly toward him, "but I can't help recognizing you, Monsieur Desmond. You're a celebrity. Your picture is in the papers almost every day, and the TV news."

"Do you know it's funny because I thought *I* recognized you at first," Zac said conversationally, "and then I realized it was someone else." He held out a hand. "Since you know who I am, may I say how do you do, Madame . . .?

"Rouet," she said. "Justine Rouet."

"But not French, I think, Madame?"

"Swiss," she replied, "but my husband is or, rather, was French."

"Ah!" Zac looked sympathetic but thought it rude to inquire whether Monsieur Rouet was deceased or whether they were merely divorced. Anyway it didn't matter. Madame Rouet was trying to tell him that she was available. He felt his pulse quicken with excitement. Maybe she was a whore, but she was a good-looking one, with a style that he liked.

"Are you here on business, Madame?" He edged a little closer to her.

"I'm here for the spring fashions."

"Ah, a journalist or a buyer?"

"You could say both," she said mysteriously.

"Just 'buying' then, Madame, eh?"

"Maybe."

The waiter appeared with her Perrier and Zac's whiskey, and he insisted on paying for both.

"My wife is a director of the fashion house, Jean Marvoine," he said, after tasting his drink. "Perhaps you've heard of it."

"Of course."

"Then shortly you'll be meeting my wife. You'll know her picture from the paper too."

"It must be very tiresome for you," the woman murmured sympathetically. "But even in Switzerland we read about it every day."

"It was in Switzerland it began," Zac said. "The embezzler with whom Madame Harcourt was involved was Swiss."

"Oh, then you *do* think she's guilty?"

Suddenly Zac recalled Belle's warning. For all he knew this woman, whom he thought was simply on the game, or at best trying to pick him up, might be an investigative journalist.

"I can say nothing about it," he said, putting a finger to his lips. "They're sealed."

"Of *course.*" Madame Rouet looked around and then glanced at her diamanté-studded watch. "My date is late." She tapped the face as though to check that it was right and then put it to her ear.

"Are you staying here, Madame?"

"Yes." She gave him a remote but suggestive smile. "It's my favorite hotel in Paris."

At that moment Zac was distracted by a movement at the door as Tara, looking for him, stood on tiptoe and waved.

"My wife." Zac rose abruptly from his seat and, bowing toward his companion, said: "We shall be late for an engagement. I hope I see you again, Madame."

"I hope so too," she said and turned her face away just as Tara arrived, a question mark in her eyes as she looked first at Madame Rouet and then at Zac.

"Madame Rouet recognized me from the papers, my dear," Zac said, taking Tara's arm. "Madame, may I present my wife?"

"How do you do, Madame?" Madame Rouet put out her hand and the expression in her eyes as she looked at Tara was so odd that, involuntarily, Tara shivered, as though someone had walked on her grave.

On their way to their engagement Tara said: "Who on *earth* was that woman?"

"I haven't a clue," Zac said, his eyes on the back of the chauffeur.

"Did you get speaking to her, or did she speak first to you?"

"She said she knew my face from the papers."

"I didn't like her," Tara said.

"My dear, you're jealous, as usual."

"It's not that. She looked evil." In the light of the street lamps she looked thoughtfully at Zac's profile. "The sort of person who could do you harm."

"My, how you do exaggerate, you Italians," Zac said cheerfully, taking her hand in his.

Bob got out of the taxi in front of the Palazzo Falconetti and paid the driver, giving him a handsome tip.

"Grazie, buongiorno."

"Prego," Bob said, and turned into the vast stone building which occupied a whole side of the narrow street near the Pantheon. Two great bronze gates, allegedly by Ghiberti, enclosed a courtyard within which stood the palace, one of the great glories of the Renaissance. One half of the gate was open and through this Bob stepped, to be greeted by the concierge, who amiably asked his business.

"I would like to see the marchese," Bob said, producing his passport as proof of identity. "I was passing through Rome and I wanted to thank him. He helped save my life."

Bob's Italian was by now fluent; the concierge understood immediately and, with a smile, disappeared inside her room, and Bob could hear her on the house telephone.

"Signor O'Neill, Monsignore . . . si . . . si . . ."

As if Marco had not fully understood she then went on to tell him what Bob had told her.

"Tell him only if it's convenient," Bob said, popping his head through the door. It occurred to him that the marchese did not seem very keen to see him . . . perhaps it had something to do with his relationship with Tara.

The concierge emerged, nodding her head and smiling toothlessly. She then led him across the courtyard and through an imposing pair of double doors while Bob gazed about him with interest but also, curiously, with a feeling that there was something familiar about the place, as though he had been there before.

Although it was a cold but sunny day, once inside the palace everything changed. It was very dark and the huge hall, hung with faded tapestries, was lit by a solitary chandelier with only one or two bulbs. The myriad pieces of glass were dull with age and, jostling against one another, seemed to echo disconsolately in the foetid air.

From the huge hall, a staircase lined with portraits of ancient Falconettis led to the first floor: statesmen, cardinals, poets, doctors, artists, writers, scientists, many by famous artists and in various poses, seemed to peer out of the canvases upon the passers-by. At the top waiting to greet him in corduroy trousers and an old cardigan was the present head of the distinguished family: Marco, Marchese di Falconetti, the latest of an ancient and noble line.

However, the smile on the face of the marchese as he took Bob's hand was as chilly as the interior, his clasp was limp, and Bob immediately felt unwelcome and wished he hadn't come. A formal letter of thanks, such as he had sent, should have been enough.

"I wanted to thank you," Bob stuttered as Marco let go of his hand, "in person . . . I was passing through Rome on my way to see my sister."

"Ah, yes," Marco said in a distracted manner. "Come in. Come in. Please don't think me inhospitable, but I was about to go out."

"I shall only stay a moment," Bob said as he was ushered into an enormous salon which was so cold that he looked round to see if there were any windows open. The marchese immediately made for the tiny fire in the huge grate and stood with his back to it, rubbing his hands and looking suspiciously at Bob.

"Back to Paris, do you say; to see your sister?"

"She's in great trouble. She's been arrested for something she didn't do. It's all linked up to me."

"I wish to God I'd never got involved with it and could wash my hands of the whole thing," the marchese said truculently.

"We were most grateful for your help."

"I should hope so. Police sniffing round, reporters . . ." Marco shivered with distaste. "I've a good mind to go into hiding myself. I went to a lot of trouble, you know." The marchese seemed rather relieved to be able to have a moan and pointed to a chair. "Do sit down. I put my life in danger. There was nothing in it for me at all. I . . ." He stopped, realizing that Bob was paying no attention to him, but, before he sat down, was looking intently at the chair. He seemed so fascinated by it that Falconetti said querulously: "Something the matter? It needs upholstering, that's all. Everything in this place is due for repair."

Bob sat gingerly on the chair, his heart pounding, almost unaware of what was going on in the room. Falconetti continued to bleat about the state of the palace, his need of money, the meanness of his sister's relations, their ingratitude, but Bob scarcely heard a word.

"This chair is a genuine antique, would you say?" he blurted out at last. "A genuine antique?"

"Of course it's antique," Marco looked at him indignantly. *"Everything* in this palace is antique. Were it all to be restored I would be able to sell it and become a very wealthy man. No, that chair"—he scratched his head—"is one of a pair. I dare say I could find the other. Are you interested in buying them? I could give you a good price."

"I *might* be," Bob said cautiously. "How much would you want?"

"Well, I'd have to ask my advisers," Falconetti said guardedly. "Let me have a note of your telephone number and I'll let you know."

"Thank you." Bob rose, trembling with fright, hoping it wouldn't show. He knew now the reason for the familiarity, the sense of *déjà vu.* He recognized the smell which had filtered from the windows or through the floorboards to his cell below. He recognized the sound of the chimes from the nearby church of San Ignazio.

He had been imprisoned for many months in the cellars of this ancient palazzo and he now knew, without any doubt, who his gaoler was.

Falconetti, obviously glad to see him go, and still prattling inconsequentially, ushered him toward the door, along the corridor and down the stairs to the hall.

There on the mat in front of the door a skinny tabby cat sat washing itself. As Bob stopped, it looked up at him with obvious recognition and, momentarily ceasing its ablutions, came up to him and rubbed itself against his legs.

"Nice kitty . . . good kitty," Bob said, stooping to pat its head. A sudden lump in his throat prevented him from saying more.

Like a jigsaw everything had fallen into place and the last piece was his recognition by Tomas, dear cat, treasured companion during so many solitary hours in the country, and now returned by his kidnappers to Rome. What a strange, unfortunate coincidence for them that Niki had kept his word.

Of course, the Council had tried to unseat her before. Zac had threatened to have her removed over the affair of the *tirage* but Sandra had prevented him.

This time it was a fact.

It took place in the boardroom of the office in Reims and was conducted by Maître Laban, in accordance with his interpretation of the wishes of the late Georges Desmond, with efficiency and some solemnity. Sandra, attending with Le Bâtonnier Doublet, a very senior and experienced lawyer, was only allowed to enter the boardroom when everyone else was seated, rather like a prisoner being brought to the bar.

And, like a jury, they were all there, sitting round the table as they had been on that important occasion before: Lady Elizabeth, Belle, Claire, and even Tim and Henri Piper, who had come over from America. Both men took great care all through the meeting to avoid eye contact with a woman to whom each of them had once been close.

A notable absentee was Paul Vincent, the confidant of Georges Desmond whom Sandra had sacked for his duplicity. Unknown to her it was his niece, Marie-Claire, who, carrying on a family tradition, had helped to provide the incriminating evidence against Sandra.

On this occasion as she took her seat she observed that few of those present met her eyes. She looked at them each in turn but only Lady Elizabeth was brave enough to admit recognition and, with a slight smile, acknowledge her. Henri turned his face away, Tim's eyes remained staring at the table. Their duplicity disgusted her and she too turned her eyes away.

Zac had needed to brave instinct as he watched his adversary advance from the door to the table where she had presided over so many meetings. His eyes never left her, as though he could not wait to wrest the power from her that his father had denied him. He sat, hands together on the table in front of him, bull-like neck thrust forward: a deadly, dangerous adversary who had the scent of the kill in his nostrils.

Maître Laban immediately opened the proceedings, his intonation rather solemn like a judge delivering a verdict, or a priest officiating at a sacrificial Mass.

"Members of the Council, we are meeting here today according to the will of Monsieur Georges Desmond, which stipulated that a Council would be formed of members of his family and other persons specified, including myself." He glanced at a piece of paper beside him. "We are all here except Paul Vincent, who has sent his apologies. The purpose of the Council was to help and guide Madame Harcourt—at that stage Mademoiselle O'Neill—who had been appointed president of the Desmond Group." He paused for a moment as if to collect his thoughts. "If, in the opinion of the Council, the president's conduct of affairs was unsatisfactory or to the detriment of the group, it had the powers to dismiss her." He turned pointedly to Sandra. "You, Madame Harcourt, have been summoned here today so that the Council may consider the proposition put to it by one of its members that you are indeed unfit."

"May one ask who that member is?" Sandra, her tone solemn in keeping with the proceedings, looked straight at Laban.

"I do not think it necessary to answer that question, Madame," Laban replied.

Le Bâtonnier Doublet, who was leading the team of lawyers preparing Sandra's defense on the embezzlement charge, cleared his throat.

"Speaking, Maître, as Madame Harcourt's legal adviser, I think it is a relevant inquiry and she has every right to know the answer."

"I think . . ." Maître Laban began, at which point Zac, as if unable to contain himself, leaned over the table, glaring at Sandra.

"I too think Madame has every right. I have no hesitation in saying that *I* am her chief accuser who, over many years, have observed her attempts to undermine this company, her bungling mismanagement, her absurd schemes at self-glorification like the ridiculous idea to have a special blend of champagne in honor of her *son!* To cap it all, Madame now stands accused of the gravest charge of the embezzlement of company funds. She has thus proved herself unfit to continue as its president."

"Have you anything to say in your defense, Madame?" Maître Laban appeared angered by Zac's outburst.

Sandra, unbuttoning the jacket of her suit, looked round for supporters, but there were none. Not a single person present spoke up in her defense—not Tim who had loved her, or Claire whom she had befriended, or Henri Piper to whom she had been so close, or Lady Elizabeth who had pretended to welcome her as a daughter. From these few she might have expected a few words of support, but none came. Perhaps her true adversaries, Zac and Belle, were more honest in their now openly declared hostility.

"I am not guilty as charged," she said, "and all of you know it. I shall even state in a public court of law that I am innocent, and I shall emerge without a stain on my character . . ."

"Once more!" Zac exploded. "But this scandal is never out of the newspapers! You have already disgraced this company! Already our shares have halved . . ."

"That I agree and I am more than sorry about," Sandra said firmly. "But none of it is my fault." She raised her hand and pointed a finger straight at Zac. "The fault, as you very well know, Monsieur Desmond, is *yours.* For years you have plotted against me, always managing to conceal your crimes by blaming others. This time you have overreached yourself and you can be sure that one day I will make you pay. I here accuse you, Zac Desmond, before these witnesses, of kidnap, embezzlement, extortion, fraud, robbery and, almost certainly, murder."

She paused, then continued in the same solemn tone: "I have evidence which I do not propose to produce here because I wish it to be heard in a public place. But you can be sure that when I do produce it the corpse of your poor father will turn in his grave and you, Zachariah Desmond, will rue the day you were born."

Everyone watched her, openmouthed. Le Bâtonnier Doublet sat back in his chair and mopped his brow. Maître Laban signaled to the secretary to stop taking the minutes. But it was too late. The words were said, the deed done.

Sandra casually took up her bag and document case from the floor, briskly straightened her skirt and, without so much as a nod, turned quietly on her heels and walked toward the door which somehow mysteriously opened for her, as though pushed by an unseen hand.

Once outside she waited, heart thumping, but pervaded by a feeling, overall, that she had triumphed. She did have all the cards and, once she had conclusive evidence, she would play them.

Meanwhile Zac would feel like a top spinning on ice, not quite certain which way he would topple.

There was a silence in the room next door and then she could hear names being called out as, no doubt regardless of her words, the vote was being taken. Of course the family would stick together. They were almost uniformly frightened of Zac.

Then, after a few minutes, Maître Laban, accompanied by Le Bâtonnier Doublet, walked solemnly out and paused in front of her.

"I am sorry to tell you, Madame Harcourt," Maître Laban said, without the slightest emotion in his voice, "but today the vote went against you by a majority of those present, only one person abstaining. Therefore, according to the terms of the will of Monsieur Georges Desmond, you are from this moment effectively no longer chief executive of the Desmond Group. All powers are withdrawn from you. Your functions have been taken from you absolutely and irrevocably and passed by right to Monsieur Zachariah Desmond, eldest son and now the heir of his deceased father. The Council for the Administration of the Desmond Group will meet tomorrow and automatically confirm our decision. Good afternoon, Madame."

Then he inclined only slightly and returned to the boardroom, leaving Sandra standing stiffly to attention, with tears in her eyes.

It was over—irrevocable. Whatever happened, there would be no going back.

25

The furniture vans were at the gate of the château and David already had some of his staff installed. His newly engaged butler was supervising the operations and, after a while, he left the château to join Sandra who was sitting in the gazebo, her hands in her pockets, the collar of her coat turned up against the cold. On the hillsides around them the vines were being pruned in order to produce the grapes from which the new wines would be made the following year. What sort of vintage would it be? Whatever, it no longer mattered to her. She was aware of David beside her, putting a comforting arm around her shoulders.

"Penny for them?" he said.

"You can guess. I was thinking about the vintage for next year, and how it would no longer matter to me."

"Marry me," he said, "then all your problems are solved."

Sandra rose from her seat and, hands deep in her pockets, started slowly walking across the lawn, David following her.

"It's the sensible thing to do," he said. "I can support you. I can give you everything you need. I will give it to you, anyway, but if you marry me it will be easier."

"You'd marry a gaolbird?" she said with a half-smile.

"It will never come to that, you know it."

"I have to prove that Zac, and not Falconetti, *is* responsible for what happened to Bob. It's not nearly as easy as I thought it would be when Bob told me the story of his discoveries in Rome, when I made that brave speech at the Council.

"Le Bâtonnier Doublet told me I was foolish. Maybe I was. But *I* know Zac is guilty although the extent of his deception staggers even me. I never gave him enough credit for his ability to be so wickedly clever. He is behind everything. Yet no one will accuse him.

"We have *always* underestimated him. Always. He has bribed, corrupted, falsified, stolen . . . no one would ever believe all the things he has done or is capable of doing."

She looked at David for a moment. "I don't think even you can believe the depths of the iniquity of that man."

David was silent. Sometimes it seemed to him that, rather than a war with participants, a deadly duel was being fought solely between Zac and Sandra. Each, in a way, was as headstrong and as irrational as the other.

"You don't really *believe* me, do you, David?" she asked, as though she could read his thoughts.

"Of course I believe you, darling. But I hate to see you so unhappy. You are destroying yourself, and I know that I . . ."

"You want me to forget all about this. Act as though it had never happened, and marry you, isn't that it, David? I have lost my job, my home, my prestige, my livelihood, if you like, because of one man."

"But, Sandra, *I* can give you . . ."

"Oh, please don't tell me what you can give me . . ." She turned upon him eyes in which there was such torment that he felt deeply shocked. "I know what you can give me, David, and I thank you for it. You want to take me out of the hurly-burly of life, settle me quietly in the country with a few ducks and some vines, a baby or two to keep me quiet . . ."

"Sandra, you know I want to do no such thing!"

"You *do,* David. You don't realize it, that's all. You think of me as a woman. You want me to be a *womanly* woman. You always said I took too much interest in business . . ."

"I said you should *relax* more, that's all . . ."

"You didn't really like me as head of Desmond and now that I'm not you think 'fine, we'll settle down' . . . but it's not for me, my dear." Suddenly her stormy expression seemed to evaporate and her tone softened.

"Dear David . . . forgive me. I didn't mean to hurt you, but what I am going to say will, I'm afraid, hurt you more. I love you, really, but I can't marry you, not now, not ever. This house is not for me and, honestly, I don't think it is for you . . ."

"But, Sandra . . ." He backed away as though suddenly she'd produced a whip and stung him.

"It's a French château, David," she went on. "Henri Piper's house. French men and women belong here, as they belonged to the Desmond Group. I see that now, and that's really why I lost. Georges Desmond was wrong. I had no *business* there and what happened was bound to happen." She turned away, kicking restlessly at the grass under her feet.

"Do you know what, David? I would *never* go back to Desmond whatever happened, even if they begged me. Irrevocable they said, and irrevocable it is. No." She raised her head. "After the trial, which I shall win, I'm going to sell all my possessions and start again. If you do love me, if you don't hate me for what I said, you can, if you like, do one thing for me: lend me the money to buy Jean Marvoine. It is for sale. I will build it up and make it the greatest fashion house in the world. Just you see."

David turned quickly away before she could see the expression in his eyes.

He knew he'd lost her.

Eva straddled the man, her long breasts brushing his chest, her hips keeping time with his rhythm: up and down, up and down like a jockey.

She stared fixedly at his face, contorted with passion in the throes of his orgasm, and she hated him. She wished he were feeling pain not pleasure, not such intense pleasure; but the pain would come.

Zac Desmond had not many moments of life left, and she hoped that the final pain, coming so soon after intense pleasure, would be of unsurpassable agony.

As he reached his climax he clutched at her breasts so hard that pain began to seem a relative matter. He let go and his whole body became limp as over his face spread a smile of beatitude. Her breasts were already raw red, her nipples swollen, and there were streaks of blood all over her body where he had scratched her. He was a violent man, a pervert, and a killer. How she pitied his wife. She recalled once again vividly, as she so often did, Bernardo's face in the morgue, his vacant eyes, and the thought that soon Zac would join him was a source of the greatest satisfaction.

Eva gradually eased herself from him and, as she attempted to get off the bed, an arm encircled her waist like the tentacle of an octopus. But, escaping just in time, she rushed to the bathroom to wash everything she could out of herself. She sat on the bidet for ten minutes, her head sunk on her chest.

When she returned to the bedroom Zac lay with his head on the pillow, a sheet covering his body, his eyes wide open.

Not much longer now, Zac Desmond, she thought. And if she feared anyone it certainly wasn't him. It was Strega. Strega, she was sure, would kill her as slowly as he could, deriving every ounce of pleasure from her final agony, just as she would from Zac's. Stealthily she got the long, evilly sharp knife from the drawer of the dressing table and put it carefully in the pocket of her gown. Then she sat on the bed and bent down to kiss him. Hungrily his greedy lips gripped her mouth and drank from it.

He threw back her gown and examined her breasts, bruised and swelling.

"Sorry I hurt you," he murmured.

"You like it, don't you, Zac?" she asked without smiling.

"A bit."

"It excites you, doesn't it, to hurt?"

"A bit," he said again, his expression sly like a boy caught with his pants down.

"Does your wife like being hurt too?"

"Oh, leave my wife out of it!"

"I thought she might enjoy, you know . . . *three.*"

Zac's beady eyes grew as round as saucers.

"You mean that?"

"Why not? Do you think she would?"

"Would you?"

"Sure."

"I bet you've done it before, haven't you? I bet you've done everything."

As if inflamed by the idea of a threesome he reached for her shoulders and flung her onto the bed, tearing at the cord of her gown, and then he launched himself upon her, his weight quite hard to bear.

"I feel breathless," she groaned, feeling in the pocket for the knife. Zac put his hands around her face and looked into her eyes in such a peculiar fashion that she wondered if he could read them.

"You're an odd woman, Justine Rouet. I don't understand you. Are you on the game? What are you? Who are you?"

She had the bone handle now in her fist and she stretched out her arms, praying he would not move.

"I am Eva Raus. Remember me? Remember Romanetto? May the Devil take you, Zac Desmond," she cried, hoping he would see the hate in her eyes. Then she plunged the dagger with enormous force right into the small of his back.

The agony was intense, but it didn't last long enough. He gave a cry of anguish, his body jerked as if in a coital spasm. Then it went limp, and his eyes closed very gently.

He seemed like someone sleeping.

But the Devil didn't want his own, and a lot of people worked hard and long to save the life of Zac Desmond.

The cluster of green-robed professionals, doctors and nurses, performed their allotted tasks round the operating table on which the supine figure lay. The eyes of the surgeon, normally calm, showed a trace of anxiety as he peered through his pince-nez at those around him. He muttered something to his assistant as he probed the delicate tissue of the open wound.

At the head of the patient the anesthetist carefully watched his monitors, the ECG, the blood pressure and the pulse oximeter.

They discovered that the long, thin knife had penetrated the spine, pierced the liver, just grazing the heart. The emergency that had begun two hours ago when Zac had been found on the blood-soaked bed was in full swing.

The anesthetist said tersely: "Blood pressure is falling."

The surgeon glanced at him but continued with his work.

The atmosphere was one of controlled panic, because of who they had on the table and the seriousness of his wounds. Zac's life, literally, hung by a thread.

"Heart stopped," the anesthetist announced suddenly and immediately turned off the anaesthetic gases, just leaving the oxygen on. The ECG registered a single line.

The surgeon, handing his instruments to his assistant, began rapidly to administer external cardiac massage, his eye on the ECG. Nothing happened. The anesthetist, watching the gauges while he continued to ventilate his patient, and also undertaking the emergency procedures for cardiac arrest, shook his head.

"Scalpel," the surgeon commanded and, taking the thin-bladed knife, made a surgical incision into the chest, exposing the patient's heart, and began manual massage, his eyes alternately on his patient and on the ECG. Great beads of sweat began to burst out on his brow. He knew what publicity the Desmonds attracted and he had never yet lost a patient on the table. Nor would he do so now. He redoubled his efforts.

Suddenly a wave appeared on the ECG which grew stronger and, beneath his hands, the surgeon felt the heart begin, slowly at first, its rhythmical pumping. A nurse wiped the sweat from his brow. The anesthetist smiled. There seemed to come from everyone in the theater a collective sigh of relief.

The emergency, for the time being, was over.

Belle sat in the waiting room of the private clinic with her mother. Claire and Tim had been summoned but had not yet arrived. Tara had been told of the incident but had not appeared either.

The operation had already been going on for three hours and the two women had run out of conversation. Belle drummed her fingers while her mother turned over the pages of the glossy magazines without seeing what she was reading.

"I knew one day it would come to this," she murmured. "It was inevitable."

"But *why* would a prostitute he didn't know try and kill him? It doesn't make sense, Mother."

"There are mad women as well as mad men," Lady Elizabeth said. "Maybe that's how she got her satisfaction; you read about that kind of thing. But Zac . . . he has always played with danger, Belle. If it was not one thing it was something else. His plots against Sandra . . ."

"This has *nothing* to do with Sandra," Belle snapped. "How could Zac's sexual peccadilloes have anything to do with her, Mother?"

"It's happened all at once," Lady Elizabeth said sadly as if to herself. "I dreaded it. One day I knew there would be serious trouble. There was always the danger of violence. What is going to happen now to the great organization your father left?"

"We don't *know,* Mother." Belle tapped her heels impatiently. "We don't know how sick Zac is, how long it will take him to recover."

"And *then* what will happen in the meantime, with Sandra gone?"

Belle walked to the window, her arms akimbo. In the distance she could see the tops of the trees in the Bois de Boulogne.

"Do you think *I* am incapable of running Desmond,

Mother?" Belle swung round. "Surely not *just* because I am a woman?"

"Of course I don't think that, Belle." Her mother gazed at her with astonishment. "It just never occurred to me . . . but, at least until Zac is better, I suppose it is perfectly possible."

"Sandra ran Desmond and, although we liked to pretend to the contrary, she ran it well. What she can do, Mother, *I* can do even better because, although—let's admit it—she had a great business head, she could never in a lifetime have acquired the knowledge of champagne that Zac and I were born with. I already have that advantage over her. And I have ideas, Mother . . ." Belle crossed the room rapidly and sat next to her mother, gripping her hand. "Don't think I have not wished to run it on a par with Zac. Yet I was passed over. The Council appointed him automatically without a glance in my direction . . ."

"But we never thought . . . my dear . . ." Her mother looked at her doubtfully. "You showed very little interest in Jean Marvoine . . ."

"Mother, I had very little interest in *fashion.* And imagine what it was like working with that featherbrained Tara. Besides, I had Carl then . . . now I have time on my hands, energy *and* the ability to succeed, Mother. I *know* I have it in me. The Council acted too hastily in its desire to get rid of Sandra. In fact Zac, as we know, *has* made many errors of judgment. His bank has been close to ruin several times and only his innate luck and the support of others allowed him to survive. Now, if you ask me, Mother, his luck has finally run out and for the foreseeable future, if not forever, I shall take control of the company." Belle removed her hand and stood up again. "I shall demand a recall of the Council to ratify my appointment as soon as possible. The ship cannot be left without a rudder."

As Belle turned sharply toward the door, as if to make an immediate telephone call, it opened and the surgeon, still in his green operating gown, came in.

"Lady Elizabeth, Princess." He bowed solemnly, first to one and then the other. His unsmiling face did not look as though his report would be encouraging. "I have good news, as well as bad. Monsieur Desmond *is* alive; the operation, which was a complex one, has been successful. However, his heart stopped on the table and we had to restart it. He should make a reasonable recovery but the nature of his wounds makes it unlikely that he will be able to lead a completely normal life again . . ."

Lady Elizabeth also stood up, her expression trance-like as she walked toward the surgeon.

"What are you trying to tell us? That his brain has been affected?"

"No, Madame," the surgeon addressed her directly. "I do not think that. However, the blade of the knife caused serious internal damage. It is, unfortunately, sometimes the case with a wound of that nature that the induction of the anaesthetic causes heart failure. However, this time we were able almost immediately to restart the heart. The gravity of Monsieur Desmond's wounds are another matter. We had to remove part of his lung; his spine is affected. In short it is not impossible he will be confined to a wheelchair, and live the life of a semi-invalid for the rest of his life."

"My name is Eva Raus."

"And why did you do such a terrible thing?"

"Because I hated him."

"What did Monsieur Zac Desmond do to you that made you hate him so much?"

"He destroyed my life, and the life of the man I loved."

"Come off it. You were a tart who picked him up in the bar of the Plaza Athénée . . ."

"No, no, you're wrong. I knew him long before that."

"You mean you had an *affair* with him?"

"No, I knew him. Or, rather, I knew *of* him. I'm afraid you won't begin to understand until you've heard the whole story. Could I have a cigarette?"

The policeman investigating the murder looked startled. He whispered something in the ear of the sergeant next to him who was handing Eva a cigarette, watching her as he lit it: those haunted eyes, the tight, grim lines of the mouth.

"You had better begin at the beginning," the detective said, reaching for a fresh sheet of paper and turning on the tape recorder.

"I'm going to tell you everything," Eva said. "Absolutely everything. I *want* to begin at the beginning, and go right through to the end."

Sensation.

The Marchese Falconetti was arrested. Monsieur Zac Desmond, already incarcerated in intensive care, had a policeman by his side to guard him day and night, and the hunt was out for Paul Strega.

The confession of Eva Raus occupied inches of column space in the international press for days. The body of Bernardo Romanetto was disinterred from its lonely grave in Barcelona and brought to Paris for forensic examination.

The Banque Franco-Belges was sealed off and a team of detectives from the fraud department took it to pieces.

The scandal was so big that the dropping of the case against Sandra almost went unnoticed. She was glad that, for once, the spotlight was turned from her.

If she knew Zac he would wriggle out of this affair eventually, if only because Strega's disappearance had put him in the worst possible light and thus made him a potential fall guy for Zac. However, he was still too sick to think of anything but his own recovery, possibly survival.

Eva Raus declined to be bailed and preferred to remain in prison. There was only one person left in the world whom she was really frightened of, and she hoped that the police found him before he found her.

Paul Strega, cast as the villain of the piece, would never be able to return to the anonymity of his house in Champagne again.

* * *

Belle would rather have sold the Jean Marvoine fashion house to anyone but Sandra; but the offer was good and they needed the money. The Desmond shares had been slow to recover on the stock market and the company was borrowing heavily. Zac, with extreme difficulty, began to make his way back to health, and when he was fit to travel he was sent by private plane to the Mayo Clinic in America for further treatment.

It was autumn, the time of the harvest, when Sandra finally signed the papers that made her the new owner of Jean Marvoine, and she at once got down to business.

She ordered a complete reorganization, but in carefully thought-out, structured lines. She retained the directrice and all the staff except Maurice Raison. Against fierce competition she bought the services of Lorenzo Malaguti, the darling of Italian ladies' fashion, and his first collection for the house would be shown the following spring. Finally, when she had begun to settle down and the coast was clear, she made a personal phone call and invited an old friend to come and see her.

Tara Desmond had been hard to track down. She had publicly left Zac and was filing for divorce, but Sandra eventually found her in Switzerland and asked her to come back to Paris.

As Tara entered Sandra's office she rose to welcome her. They embraced affectionately and then Tara, looking round, said: "I see everything is the same. I expected it would change."

"All that needed to change here was the style," Sandra remarked. "We needed a little streamlining, a bit more organization."

"I can't understand how Belle thinks she can run Desmond when she couldn't run this," Tara said derisively.

"Ah, but she loves champagne." Sandra smiled. "Champagne is in her blood. It was never in mine."

"What *is* in your blood?" Tara asked curiously, still a little nervous, as she sat down, looking at the woman who had made such a comeback.

"Business," Sandra said, spreading her hands on the papers in front of her. "Balance sheets, profits and loss." She returned to her seat, swinging her long legs as she turned excitedly round in her swivel chair. "I feel the same excitement here that I felt when I first entered the Étoile office at Desmond."

"But why not start your own house, why buy this?"

"It is much *easier* to buy an established house than begin a new one. It had once a very good name . . . it will again."

"Well, you got Malaguti and that was a coup." Tara didn't attempt to hide her admiration.

"Incidentally he's *dying* to meet you."

"Me?" Tara flushed, but looked flattered. "Why me?"

"He remembers your great days as a model. He knows about your flair, Tara . . ." Sandra paused and ran her tongue round her lips. "How would you like to return as fashion director? You were very good. You were held back, by Zac, by Belle . . . do you think we could work together?"

An expression of uncertainty came into Tara's eyes. "But why should you need me?"

"You're the best. I want the best people. Malaguti likes you already, and he hasn't even met you. He's so warm and charming. All the staff here remember you and like you."

"Really?" Tara looked pleased. "You're sure you're not just being kind, Sandra?"

" 'Kind?' " Sandra looked astonished. "How do you mean, 'kind'?"

"Just because I've . . . had a bad time."

"My dear." Sandra rose and, going over to Tara, put an arm round her shoulders. "Believe me, I am not doing this to get my own back on Zac, or Belle. That is all past. The person I need is you."

"And I need you," Tara said a little tearfully, taking her hand. "People used to say a lot of hard things about you, Sandra. But I think your gesture now is just about the nicest thing anyone ever did. Zac . . . it will take a long time to get over Zac. He's a shit. I know he's a shit. I always knew he was a shit . . . but . . . the way he did it."

"Zac was a victim too," Sandra said gently, "don't forget that." Then, Tara's hand still in hers, she looked toward the window in the direction of the hotel where Nemesis had finally caught up with Zac. "He certainly paid a high price."

EPILOGUE

"SANDRA HAS DONE IT AGAIN!" screamed the newspapers, which gave precedence to the Jean Marvoine spring show over all the other fashion houses competing for front-page news.

The irresistible combination of the inspiration of designer Malaguti and the genius of Madame Sandra Harcourt have combined to produce a show which is the best in any house this season [enthused the fashion editor of The Times *in London]. The catwalk at the house of Jean Marvoine was crammed with international journalists, buyers from all over the world, and some of its richest women as the first collection by Lorenzo Malaguti was shown.*

It is less than a year since the former head of the Desmond empire bought the fashion house and transformed its fortunes, just as she did the now-ailing Desmond organization. Princess Arabelle von Burg-Farnbach is not thought to have quite the touch of her predecessor, who invariably brings her own special flair to everything she does.

Pictured here . . .

Pictured there was a beaming Sandra, a proud David, who had provided the capital, a smiling Malaguti and a much more relaxed and happy Tara Desmond. Toasting one another, they were, of course, drinking champagne.

Sandra drank her tea and put down the papers. One after the

other, as they fell to the floor, all sang the praise of a woman who a year before had seemed on the ropes.

Much water had flown under the bridges of the Seine since then. Sandra lay back in bed, aware of Mireille prattling away to Louis in the room next door. Soon he would come in and bounce on her bed and kiss her.

The door opened but it was not Louis, but Marie with the mail.

"A beautiful day, Madame," she said approvingly, looking first at the sky and then at the papers scattered on Sandra's bed and the floor. "You must feel very pleased. I always knew you would do it again."

"And you were right, Marie." Sandra held out her hand. "As usual. But only with my trusted and true friends around me can I succeed."

"There is a message from Mr. Heurtey," Marie said. "Also a *huge* bunch of flowers." But Sandra, leafing through the mail, was more intrigued by a fax from Alvarado, Mexico, which her office had just sent round.

Dear Madame Harcourt,

This is just to tell you how excited I am personally by news of your great success in the spring fashion shows. I have now made a good recovery from my illness and hope that, one day, we shall have the chance to see each other and talk.

Best wishes,
Russell Ryan

Sandra read the message several times while Marie gazed at her excited face with curiosity, noticing the unopened envelope from David Heurtey, along with the many others that had been consigned to a heap on the floor.

"Is it *very* good news, Madame?" Marie found it hard to contain her curiosity.

Sandra returned as if her mind had been in another world and gazed at her.

"I hope so, Marie. I think it may be very good; but who knows? Time alone will tell."

She then sprang out of bed and to the window, thrusting it open and leaning her head out as far as it could go.

From where she stood, with the sun breaking over the rooftops, over the twin turrets of Notre Dame, and all Paris aglow, the world did, indeed, look very, very good; the outlook, perhaps, even sensational.

Nicola Thorne was born in South Africa but grew up and was educated in England. She has a degree in sociology from the London School of Economics, and worked as an editor before deciding to write full-time. She lives in Dorset, England.